$\mathcal{A}$ kiss. He'd

What could it possibly

do it again? And did she want him to?

Maybe, she thought. Maybe yes.

Will You?

Resounding praise for
JUDITH IVORY

ONE OF TODAY'S MOST TALENTED
HISTORICAL ROMANCE WRITERS."
Knight-Ridder News Service

IVORY ENCHANTS HER READERS."
Publishers Weekly (*Starred Review*)

IVORY'S WRITING IS EXCEPTIONAL,
OFTEN EXQUISITELY PRECISE, AND SHE
IS A MASTER AT PORTRAYING
EMOTIONAL INTENSITY."
Minneapolis Star-Tribune

"SPLENDID, ELEGANT...POLISHED
WRITING...LUSH, ARTISTIC ROMANCE."
Romantic Times

"JUDITH IVORY IS IRRESISTIBLE."
Susan Elizabeth Phillips

Other Avon Books by
Judith Ivory

Beast
Sleeping Beauty

JUDITH IVORY

THE Proposition

AVON BOOKS ◆ NEW YORK

AVON BOOKS, INC.
1350 Avenue of the Americas
New York, New York 10019

Copyright © 1999 by Judith Ivory, Inc.
Excerpt from *Someday My Prince* copyright © 1999 by Christina Dodd
Excerpt from *Married in Haste* copyright © 1999 by Catherine Maxwell
Ecxerpt from *His Wicked Ways* copyright © 1999 by Sandra Kleinschmit
Excerpt from *The Perfect Gift* copyright © 1999 by Roberta Helmer
Excxerpt from *Once and Forever* copyright © 1999 by Constance O'Day-Flannery
Excerpt from *The Proposition* copyright © 1999 by Judith Ivory, Inc.
Inside cover author photo by Tony Nelson
Published by arrangement with the author
Library of Congress Catalog Card Number: 99-94816
ISBN: 0-380-80260-0
www.avonbooks.com/romance

First Avon Books Printing: December 1999
First Avon Books Special Printing: June 1999

AVON TRADEMARK REG. U.S. PAT. OFF. AND IN OTHER COUNTRIES, MARCA REGISTRADA, HECHO EN U.S.A.

Printed in the U.S.A.

WCD 10 9 8 7 6 5 4 3 2 1

Part I

Mick

My luve is like a red, red rose. . . .

Robert Burns, stanza 1 of "A Red, Red Rose"
JOHNSON'S MUSICAL MUSEUM, 1796

Chapter I

🌿

The most highborn lady Mick had ever been with—the wife of a sitting member of the House of Lords, as it turned out—told him that the French had a name for what she felt for him, a name that put words to her wanting his "lionhearted virility"—he liked the phrase and remembered it.

" 'A yearning for the mud,' " she told him. "That's what the French call it."

Mud. He hadn't much liked the comparison. Still, from the moment he heard it, he hadn't doubted the phrase's clear sight or wisdom. Posh ladies who took a fancy to him had to make some sort of excuse to themselves, and this was as good as any. He was a novelty at best. At worst, a bit of mud to play in for ladies whose lives'd been scrubbed clean of good, earthy fun.

He lay now on the floor, dirtier than usual, truth be told, his palms and belly flat to the floorboards of a dress shop in Kensington. Three silky ladies stood over him—they stood very far over him, one on a chair seat, one on a countertop, and one on the last inch or so left of a shelf taken up mostly by bolts of fabric. These three watched him, breathless, while Mick, his ear turned to the floor, listened.

He was a big man—he took up a long length of floor. He had wide shoulders, a hard, muscular chest,

long, weighty limbs. Handsomely made, he didn't
doubt it. Vigorous. Five minutes ago, he'd been out
back, using this very fact to flirt with the seamstress's
assistant. He'd made her laugh, his first triumph, and
had just stepped a little closer, when the seamstress
and her customer inside the shop had begun screaming,
"Mouse! Mouse!" The only man nearby, he'd been
pressed into service.

Now, when scared, mice had a nasty habit. They'd
run up anything, including a person's leg. The nightmare for a lady was that a mouse'd scamper into the
understructure of her dress—her petticoats, dress-
improvers, and half-hoops—where it could run around
indefinitely in a maze of horsehair and steel wires.

Hoping to avoid a mouse circus inside their dresses,
the seamstress, a patron, and now her assistant had
climbed as high as they could in the room, pressing
their dresses to themselves, frightened out of their wits.
Mick could've told them it wouldn't do them no good.
Mice could get onto tables and chairs easy. But he
didn't mention it. He didn't want to frighten them
more.

He lay quiet, scanning the floorboards, palms flat,
elbows up, toes curled to support some of his weight,
ready to spring up if a mouse came into sight. Then
he spied it, and it was sort of a letdown. A little thing,
it was more scared than the ladies, shaking over in a
corner at the base of a sewing machine in the shadow
of a press-iron. Barely more than a baby. He could
catch it in his hand. There were no others, no noise
under the floor, no activity.

"Is there a nest?" whispered the seamstress, her
voice hushed with worry. "Are there more?"

Now, right here, Mick should've said no and stood
up. But he didn't. He got distracted.

He turned his head to use the other ear, to listen
again and make sure. And there, through a doorway
into a back room, under a painted screen, in a mirror
he saw a pair of legs, a second customer. There were

four women, not three. This one'd been trying on dresses, he guessed, when the commotion broke out. She was trapped in the dressing room. In the mirror he could see she'd leaped on top of something, maybe a trunk. Anyway, with his position, her having moved up and out of the protection of the screen, and what with the angle of the mirror, he was looking right at a pair of devilish long legs. Bloody gorgeous, they were.

He lay there, caught in his own admiration. She was on her toes, dancing a little, nervous, the long muscles of her legs flexing beneath pink stockings with a hole at the knee. Long. Hell, *long* wasn't the word for these legs. They went for yards and yards—she had to be a tall one, this one. And shapely—her legs were poetry. Balance, muscle, motion. They gave new meaning to *fine*.

Now, normally, Mick was a polite man. He would've protected a woman caught off guard by turning his head. Or at least he thought maybe he would've. But these were the damnedest legs. "Sh-h-h," he said in answer to the seamstress's fears.

In unison, the ladies above him drew in their breaths, trying to calm themselves, to allow him to hear any skittering or chewing or other nasty mouse sounds. One of them murmured, "This is so heroic of you, Mr.—" She was asking for a name.

"Tremore. Sh-h-h."

Oh, yes, heroic. The hero lay on his belly, getting his eyes as low as he could so as to stare across the floor into a mirror at the prettiest legs he'd yet seen in thirty years of living. If he'd been standing up, he'd've seen to maybe just above the ankles—the screen in front of her came within a foot of the ground. That alone would've been an eyeful, since her ankles were narrow, her foot pretty with a high arch and instep, the anklebone showing against the soft leather of her shoe.

But when he got his head just right, he could see in the mirror: from the toes of high-buttoned shoes up long, neat shins, plenty of curvy calf, past the knee-ribbons of silk knickers to halfway up willowy thighs that went forever. Dream legs.

In his dreams, Mick *did* see legs like these. He loved long legs on a woman. In his sleep he got to put his mouth on them. It took a dream-eternity to get his tongue from the back of the knee, up the thigh, to the indentation under the buttocks. Strong legs. In his dreams they gripped him with athletic urgency. They could squeeze him till he was nearly unconscious with lust.

"Mr. Tremore, Mr. Tremore!" one of the ladies behind him called. "Over here! It's here."

No, it wasn't. The ladies were jumpy, imagining mice everywhere. They began to make noise, thinking the mouse active again. Little shrieks, ladylike huffs, nervous giggles as they shifted around on their perches.

Mick held up his finger. "Sh-h-h," he said again.

He hated to get up and take care of a mouse, when there were legs like these to look at. Legs and knickers, a blessed sight if ever there was one. Above him on the counter, though, the seamstress was gulping air so hard that, if he didn't do something, she was going to lose her tea biscuits.

Softly, Mick said, "Wait. I see him. Don't move."

Mouse time. He shoved against the floor, pushing up, getting a knee and toe under him, and sprang, quick and quiet. He went after the mouse from the side of the pressing iron, so when he scooted the iron a fraction, the mouse fled forward. With a sideways lunge, Mick snapped him up by the tail, then, straightening, dangled a mouse in front of him, out for inspection.

The seamstress shrieked. He thought she was going to faint. "Easy," he said.

The customer, nearest him, climbed down bravely from her chair. "O-o-oh," she breathed.

As they all clambered down, he stood a head or more taller than any of them. He looked down on three women who tittered and made a fuss now that the danger was past. Mick was "so brave." He was "so agile." "Lionhearted," one of them said, and he laughed. Then: "With such a deep, rich laugh."

He turned. Now, even when covered in floor grit, Mick was fairly used to sending a stir through the ladies. The younger ones were generally at a loss, but the older ones he had to watch out for.

The customer who liked his laugh came right up to him, looking at the mouse. She was decked out in a lot of velvet and beads, her thin face sort of lost under a big hat decorated with a large feather and a stuffed bird.

She stretched her arm out toward him, her gloved hand dropped at the wrist. "Lady Whitting," she said. "The Baroness of Whitting."

He stared at her hand. She expected him to kiss it, he guessed, but he didn't do that sort of thing, even when he wasn't holding a mouse. "Nice to meet you." He turned around. "Nell?" He looked for the seamstress's assistant. "You got something to put this fellow into?"

The baroness walked around him to put herself in his way again. Lowering her hand, folding it into her other, she eyed him then smiled. "That was quite a feat, sir. The way you leaped and captured that mouse. Quite impressive."

Mick glanced at her, knowing she wasn't impressed with mice or heroism or anything very noble.

She said, "You should have a prize. A hero's prize."

He stopped. He was a workingman with a lot of family back home who counted on him, so a prize interested him, especially a monetary one.

The way her smile sort of softened when she got his attention, though, told him they weren't talking about money.

"I don't need nothing, duck," he said. "My pleasure to help you."

The other ladies were watching, keeping their distance. Mick turned away from the baroness, remembering his coat on the floor. As he bent to get it, he happened to glance into the back room. He caught a glimpse of a dress floating into the air. Purple. The most beautiful shade of purple. The dark color of lavender in August. Behind the screen, narrow sleeves raised overhead, long fingers wiggling their way out, up and into the open. The dress shushed loud enough that he heard its rustle as it dropped down, ending all hope of ever seeing again the finest legs he could imagine.

He straightened up, gently dusting his coat, then pushed back his hair—his hand came away with soot. He frowned down at his dirty palm. Oh, lovely, he thought, just lovely. This must have happened when he looked up the flue for the mouse.

The baroness continued, "So what is the payment due a hero?"

"A jar for the mouse would be nice." He looked past her to the seamstress.

As if she wasn't listening, as if it had been her plan all along, the seamstress quickly reached under the counter and handed him a button tin, empty. He unscrewed the lid.

"How about these?" the baroness said. Beside him, she tapped her gloved finger on top of a glass case. A soft, dull click.

Mick dropped the mouse into the tin as he glanced over at what she pointed to. The case held a lot of intimate feminine things. Knickers and stockings and garters. He paused, staring at what was inside the case more from curiosity than anything else. There were some pretty things on the glass shelves. Amazing things. Lacy, thin, feminine. Not a speck of it practical.

The baroness didn't ask so much as she commanded, "Miss?" She spoke to the seamstress, a woman at least ten years older than her. "Can we please see these?"

The seamstress brought out a pair of dark pink garters ruffled with lace, heaped with bows, and weighted down with a lot of pearls the size of tomato pips. "These would make a nice prize for a hero," said the baroness, turning to dangle one off her finger.

The garter was one of gaudiest things he'd ever set

eyes on. She thought they'd appeal to him though, which said what she thought of his taste.

When he didn't immediately light up at the sight, she explained, "They're expensive."

So maybe it was her taste that was on the flashy side, he thought. He shrugged. He pointed to garters still in the case that sat next to where the others had been. "These be nicer." It was more a matter of trying to straighten her out than anything else. He pointed to white ones, the color of cream. Narrower. Satin, with one creamy-pink flower on each, two tiny leaves the color of moss. Nothing more. Simple. Elegant.

She raised one eyebrow. At first he thought it was his taste that struck her. But no, it was his accent. She said, "What an amusing way you have of pronouncing things."

His sound came from a country dialect. He could actually speak a little Cornish, a lost language.

The baroness smiled at the tall, handsome mud she was keen to welter in. "These then," she said. She indicated the garters he'd chosen. The seamstress handed them to her.

On the end of her crooked, gloved finger, the baroness offered Mick a prettier garter. "Here," she said. "You take this one. I'll take the other. Then we'll meet somewhere"—her eyes lit—"and unite them."

He laughed. The rich got up to the damnedest games.

Games he'd played more than once. He thought about this new offer. The baroness here was on the pretty side. Making a rich lady happy had its moments. He couldn't complain that it'd ever been terrible.

Mick stroked his mustache a moment. It was soft and sleek, his mustache. Thick, dark, his pride. His "lionhearted virility" on display. His thumb to his cheekbone, arms across his chest, he dragged his finger down the mustache till the inside of his knuckle rested in the indentation of lips. There, he thought. The gesture did something to his head. It made his mind clear.

Against his finger, he murmured, "A yearning for mud."

"What?" The baroness in the bird hat got a puzzled look.

He took his finger away, straightening. "It be from French," he said.

Now he'd really confused her. A country man like him wasn't supposed to know beggar-all about French. He shrugged, trying to make little of it. "What it means is, I guess not, love."

He stepped away, slipping his arms into his coat, thinking that was the end of it. He smoothed his hand down the front of him and absently weighed his pocket, checking its contents. Good, still there.

"Ah," the baroness said. She added in a cynical tone, "How unusual. A faithful man."

Faithful to himself.

She continued, "So there's a lucky lady elsewhere?"

He let her think so.

She lightly hit his shoulder, a rap with her folded fan, then laughed. "Add them to my bill, will you, miss? A pair of garters for our hero here to give to his lady fair."

He looked over his shoulder, thinking to tell her not to bother, but she was out the door, just like that, with him the proud owner of a pair of fine lady's garters— and way too many lady-fairs to start trying to pick which one.

Well, hell. What was he going to do with those? he wondered. But then he thought, Well, of course. He went into the back.

The only person there was Nell, the seamstress's assistant. She sat with her blonde head bent close to the sewing machine. She was trying to thread its needle, but stopped when he entered, smiling up at him.

"Where be the lady who was trying on clothes back here?" he asked.

"She left." Nell tipped her head in the direction of a back door. When he dropped the garters onto her sewing table, her smile got bigger. "Coo, these are plush, aren't they?" She laughed, picking them up. "And about ten times nicer than those horrid things Lady Whitting wanted."

"The other lady," he said. "The tall one what was trying on dresses. She buy anything?"

"We altered some dresses for her."

"She take 'em?"

"We're sending them."

"Then put those in her package, will you?"

She held up the garters looped round her hand. They were fine. Not scratchy like the lace ones. Soft. Simple. Right diabolical in their appeal. Like the long legs he imagined wearing them.

Nell said, "I don't think she'd accept garters from you, Mr. Tremore. She's a proper lady, Miss—"

He bent, putting his finger against the girl's lips, leaning his weight, his palm down, on her sewing table. He didn't want to know a name. He didn't want to know nothing about the lady behind the screen. He already knew enough. "Tell her they're from you then."

"From me?"

"From the shop. For being a good customer, you see. No need for her to know where they come from."

There now. Perfect. Tomorrow, somewhere in London a long-legged lady would be walking around in a sweet pair of garters that were just right for her pretty legs. The idea was a little on the indecent side, but Mick felt heroic anyway for making it happen.

Then Nell blindsided him. She stood up from her chair, her face coming right up to his, and whispered, "No one would know if, well—" She murmured in a rush, "My father's asleep upstairs. He works the night shift. So does my brother. My uncle and cousins are out, and Aunt Milly is busy in front. No one would know if, say—" She paused, like she wasn't sure where to go from here. "If, say, I fixed your shirt for you."

"My shirt?" Mick looked down. "What's wrong with my shirt?"

She reached out, casually resting her hand on his chest. "It has a hole."

"No, it—"

Yes, it did: He looked down and watched her put her fingernail through a smooth place where the linen was worn. His shirt had a fingernail-sized hole before he had the presence of mind to grab her hand and hold it.

She let out a soft sound, more satisfaction than distress. He watched her lower her eyelids as a little smile spread on her face.

Oh, fine. He laughed, a single burst. Well. Nellie girl here was surely unexpected. He'd been wooing her all week with little success—till he'd caught a mouse then been propositioned by a baroness.

And at least *she* knew the difference between pretty garters and gewgawed ones that were only costly. But . . . what was wrong? She was . . . too short, he decided. He wanted longer legs all of a sudden.

He was shaking his head no, pushing her back, when Nell got hold of his trouser button. She was going to pull the damn thing off, if he wasn't careful. He took hold of her hands again. She resisted, and damn if she didn't like resisting. She wanted to fight him, but in that way women sometimes wanted to. She wanted to lose.

So how did he win without winning? This wasn't going well.

Then it complicated. "Nellie?" Her aunt wasn't nearly as busy as Nell had thought. "Nell? What are you doing—"

Old Nellie here was making fast work of what buttons were left on his shirt, was what she was doing—she'd popped two off, the clumsy girl.

And, from here, the whole situation went to bloody effing hell.

Chapter 2

$\mathcal{E}$dwina Henrietta Bollash was sitting in Abernathy and Freigh's main tearoom, quietly eating the best scones and cream in London, when a very undignified racket rose up outside in the street—like the cater-wauling of a dozen cats and dogs fighting over butcher scrap. Inside the room, a little chorus of teacups clinked on saucers. Heads lifted, faces turning, as the noise grew louder, closer. Then quite suddenly—chairs scraping back in alarm—the ruckus burst through the tearoom doors.

A tall, half-naked man—his frock coat open, his shirt partly out and mostly undone, his trousers unbuttoned at the top—careened into the room. "Blimey!" he shouted as a furled umbrella behind him whooshed through the air, narrowly missing his head.

The weapon was wielded by a woman who chased in after him. She yelled, "You blighter! You—you—you ratcatcher!" as she attempted to thrash him with her umbrella.

Another man, then two more charged in behind the woman, a parade of ranting people all of whom seemed intent on catching the fellow for reasons that did not sound for a minute friendly.

"When I get me 'ands on you . . . !"

"We'll be makin' meat pies out a' ya!"

"Yer dirty ferrets can pick yer bones when we're through . . ."

Edwina laughed at first, at the surprise, the unlikely spectacle that had claimed the crowded, dignified tea parlor.

A young woman charged in behind the others. She wept and called to the rest—something about nothing having happened like they thought. Ah, Edwina concluded, young lovers caught *en flagrante delicto*.

More people entered. Another man raced in behind the crying girl. After him, two well-dressed gentlemen trotted in, though once inside they immediately stepped back against the wall as if to watch—the wild goings-on apparently bringing in the curious from the street.

Edwina herself came to her feet. Other patrons of the teahouse rose, tried to move back, yet it was hard to tell which way to turn in order to stay out of the fray. She was stranded in the midst of clamor that grew around her. Over the sound of ladies' shrieking and men's "Now see here!" carried the righteous exclamations and bitter complaint of the fleeing fellow. His pursuers shouted after him, promising mayhem, while he narrowly avoided it, cursing them and dashing round one table then the next. He left behind him a trail of quickly vacated chairs and tables and clanking, shimmying china.

His adversaries, less spry and more worked up, whipped against people and objects he avoided, rather like the tail of a cyclone. They knocked chairs sideways, overturned a table, then sent one man sprawling. When they grabbed for the frisky fellow over another table, they ended up pulling off the table linen. They sloshed over countless teapots and tossed clotted cream onto the floor by the bowlful.

At this point, an apron-fronted waiter joined in, then another waiter. Mr. Abernathy himself materialized from the back offices, his glasses on his forehead. The stout little owner frowned, then waved, trying to organize his staff; he gave chase, too.

Thus pursuers multiplied. Then divided—Mr. Abernathy and the waiters split up, darting round a table from two directions in an effort to corner a fellow who couldn't be cornered: His frock coat and shirt flapping open on his bare chest, the man vaulted the dessert trolley (with nary a cream puff disturbed). Everyone in pursuit, from both sides and behind, collided at the cart—catching their prey only insofar as to spatter the backs of his leaping boots and trousers with crème anglaise. Every last pursuer went down, their limbs floundering like spatulas in a concoction of mixed pastries. As they rose, they were covered in berries, cake, cream-puff cream, and biscuit bits.

Edwina laughed outright. Even though it wasn't funny, of course. No, no. It was awful that Abernathy and Freigh's famous Saturday afternoon cream tea should become a free-for-all. She put her hand to her mouth, stifling the laughter that wanted to break out.

The leader of the parade headed for the front door in the lull, and would have made his exit, but a bobby came in just as the fellow was about to run out. "Dia-bol-ical!" he said emphatically as the bobby spread his arms, blocking the doorway.

The fellow swerved back into the room. The umbrella-flourishing woman—who now looked familiar somehow, as if Edwina would know her in a different context—landed a good swipe as he sailed past. "Ai! That 'urts, loov," he said.

The vaguely familiar woman led the pack again and, for a brief moment, was close enough to deliver several more thwacks on the man's forearm as he protected his head.

"Stop! This be blewdy insane, ye silly old cow."

Edwina tilted her head, her interest shifting. The man had the oddest speech pattern. Beneath a strong dose of East Side London lay a country idiom that rarely left the southwest tip of England. A mishmash of Cornish and Cockney. Remarkable.

"Beggar me," he protested. "Nothin' 'appened!"

After which his feet hit some of the cream that had

spilled on the floor. His arms flew out as he slipped in it, his reflexes agile enough to keep him upright—though not sufficient to keep him from pure, blind swearing. "Aw-w, blewdy 'ell fokin' mawther a' Gawd. . . ."

His words gave Edwina only momentary pause. She quickly ducked down under her table to dig a notebook and pen from her drawstring purse. What luck. Why, she could have traveled miles and never heard the Queen's English so marvelously slaughtered.

"What's he saying?" someone asked behind her as she took a step back.

She interrupted her rapid scribbles, thinking the question addressed to her. But no, she realized it was one of the two curiosity-seekers who had followed the commotion in; they were talking together.

"Who cares?" answered the second. "I'll give you five-to-one odds they brain him here."

"Here in the tearoom?" asked the other. Both men were well-dressed: dark frock coats, striped trousers, gray gloves, gray top hats, as if they had come from a garden party or wedding. Then she blinked and looked again: The men were twins, all but identical. One was perhaps ever so slightly taller and thinner.

"No, no," the taller one said, "they'll get hold of him by the scruff here, drag him into the street, and brain him outside. My fifty against your ten pound note."

"You're on. He's bigger than any of them. And faster—they aren't even going to catch him; they've been trying for more than a city block. . . ."

She dismissed their silly conversation; neither the syntax nor inflection was interesting. Both born near Brighton. Upper-class. The taller one had been to Eton; neither had seen university.

Inflections and syntax, yes. She made notes: The crying girl was from the London district of Whitechapel; so were her relatives—the pursuers were all related, same household, though the girl and the woman with the umbrella had veneers of refined diction, the sort learned if trained in a nice London shop.

It occurred to Edwina: the seamstress and her assistant from the dress shop off Queen's Gate. That's who the two women were. Not that it mattered. Any interesting facts buried in their speech were tidbits, mere crumbs of richness, when compared to the treasure trove of linguistic atrocities coming from the mouth of the elusive, bare-chested man.

As an extra bonus, his voice rang, distinctive, deep; it carried with an athletic vocal clarity. Which made for a nice, clean study of the aberrations he put into English speech. His attack of initial H's, some dropped, some added where they didn't belong, was unequivocal. His short vowels were prolonged so clearly they almost made for an extra syllable.

Rarely had she heard anyone who could so completely distinguish himself, by simply opening his mouth, as coming from the bottommost rung of the lowest order of society.

His speech put him from the mining districts of Cornwall, come to London now no doubt to make his fortune as a—well, he could have been anything from a dustman to a pickpocket. Or a ratcatcher, wasn't that what someone had called him? Perfect.

His resounding voice all at once let out a roar. "Na-a-w! Bugger me!"

Edwina looked up from her notebook just in time to see her study-subject dive after something, something that seemed to have come from his coat pocket. A *live* something. A brown bit of fur scampered into the debris on the floor.

With more guttural sounds of exasperation, the fellow rose onto his hands and knees. Several of his assailants tripped over him as he scooted toward the thing, making small smacking sounds with his lips. " 'Ere, loov. Now, now. Come to yer Mick, loovey."

His importuning made the thing halt. It looked to be no more than a wiggly tail of an animal, a tail come alive on tiny paws. With it momentarily stopped, the man snatched it up and dropped it back into his pocket.

Before he could get to his feet, though, a waiter had hold of his coattail. The seamstress and her umbrella got another clear shot. She landed a blow on the kneeling fellow's back. He flinched, raising an arm in defense, and grabbed, knocking the umbrella flying. But the two older men got hold of his arm, and he was down—protecting whatever was in his coat by putting his cheek to the floor, tenting himself over his swinging pockets.

At this point, confusion broke out in earnest as everyone converged on him.

Those who had chased him in wanted his hide.

Mr. Abernathy pounded his fist on his palm, demanding recompense for untold damages.

Patrons spoke loudly in umbrage at the mess of their clothes.

The bobby called for order, but didn't get it.

Everyone talked at once, while the poor fellow on his knees and cheek, one arm pinned back, cursed the air blue as he absorbed blows from any enemy who could reach him.

The police officer yelled louder. Edwina stopped writing when, over her spectacles, she saw the man on his knees take—she blinked, her chest tightening in spasm—a blow from the policeman's billy truncheon.

No. Perhaps he deserved trouble. Yet he had stayed so swashbucklingly ahead of it until he'd decided to save the tail-thing that had leaped from his pocket: He didn't deserve to be on his knees taking a clubbing— or at least he didn't deserve it more than anyone else who'd participated in the chase. No, no—

"Excuse me," she said. She began to push her way into the little pack of arguing people. "Excuse me, please," she repeated, this time louder in her no-nonsense tone. She felt less confident than she sounded, but the crowd opened up for her anyway. She marched forth, a tall woman with a businesslike walk.

At the front of the group, the bobby was saying to the captured man, "I'm asking you again, Do you live here in London?"

"Ace, ye bug-brine," said the man below him, his slander, happily, skewed by the fact that his mouth was pressed to the floorboards. "Ace, ace, ace."

The policeman raised his billy again. "If you answer 'Ace' one more time—"

"*Yes*," Edwina interrupted. "He means *yes*. If you'll let him up, you'll be able to understand him better."

"Do you know this man, miss?"

"No."

"Why are you speaking up for him then?"

"I'm not—"

"Then mind your own business. He's bein' smart—"

"With regard to that particular word, he's being Cornish—in a way one hardly hears in London. He was raised somewhere near St. Just, I'd say." The man below them made a sound of satisfactory startlement, an indication that she was on the mark. More confidently, she added, "Though heaven knows his accent has more than Cornwall in it. Let him up, would you please."

One thing she could say for herself: Her own accent—through little or no effort of her own—was as genteel as ever came from a lady's lips. The diction of the Queen herself did not imply more quiet authority. It always struck her as a marvelous contradiction that she could sound so sure of herself for no more reason than the openness of her vowels and the briefness of her final R's.

The little group straightened themselves, looking from one to the other as they stepped back and let the bobby and a waiter bring the fellow up by his arms.

The man they brought to his feet was huge, much taller than she'd thought, wild-looking, and utterly furious. If his good nature were put upon by being chased, it did not survive at all being pinned to the ground and beaten. He stared narrowly down at her.

A novel experience. A man had to be over six feet to look down at Edwina Bollash. This man was easily. Long-limbed, wide-shouldered, he stood at least six and a quarter feet tall. He was also more robust than she had imagined. Not heavy so much as well-built, filled-out—with his arms held back, his frock coat and shirt gaped open onto chest muscles that looked akin to the tanned, tooled breastplate of an old Roman cuirass, if such armor had had—

Edwina blinked, widened her eyes, then glanced down. (While her mind continued on its own: *Hair. If such armor had hair that flowed into a wedge of black that narrowed downward into a neat line.* She had never seen a man's naked chest, except of course on statues, which never had hair. She felt a pinch of betrayal—what else, she wondered, was inaccurate on the stone men she had so carefully and curiously studied?)

"Could someone get him a proper shirt?" she asked. She might have requested instead that he button his own or his coat, except his shirt had exactly two buttons on it, both at the bottom, and was ripped down the front as if it had caught on something. His coat had no buttons at all, not a one down its long placket.

After a small to-do, a tablecloth was draped over the fellow's shoulders. As it fell over the front of him, he spoke to her. "Ye'll be excusin' me, duck," he said. "Idden me choice to stand 'ere without me shirt done up."

"I'm sure," she said. She let herself take in the more modest sight of him, tilting her head till the flowers on her hat shifted, taking her head sideways another degree.

The hair on his head was long, wild, and dark. He wore a positively feral mustache—walrus-like and jet black. It went with the dense stubble on his cheeks. Beyond this, he had a faintly alarming face: a broad, square jaw, its sharp right angles below his ears made more severe by knots of muscle that flexed, an angry man trying regain control of himself. Dark coloring. A deep, jutting brow. It was a dramatic face, strong. The word *villainous* immediately leaped to mind, though, in fairness, it was a handsome face—handsome enough at least for a seamstress's assistant to risk her reputation.

Edwina couldn't help but ask, "So you were born in St. Just, but how long have you lived in Whitechapel?"

He frowned at her. "Do I know ye?"

"No. I'm a philologist. I study people's speech. And yours is most interesting."

The bobby interrupted. "Excuse me, miss, but we have things to settle: I'll be arresting this fellow now."

"Arresting me? What'd I do 'cept keep meself from bein' kilt? In fact, I be reporting these bug-brines here fer . . ."

Bug-brains. Diabolical a few minutes ago. He was verbal in the way some Cockneys were: a love of words and colorful talk. Neither won him any ground here, however.

Mr. Abernathy drowned him out, calling for everyone's arrest. Others joined in, the chaos rising again in waves of defense and accusation. The apparent father of the weepy shop assistant said something that made her begin to cry again. The seamstress, the girl's aunt apparently, stiff-armed the father with the heel of her hand, telling him to button his lip. And so it would have begun all over.

Except, surprisingly, one of the gentlemen twins who had followed the fracas in stepped from behind Edwina and held up his hand. "Stop! Stop!" he called.

The group quieted reluctantly—as they watched him remove a notecase from his coat pocket.

"Most of this is just mess," he said, then added cavalierly, "that the waiters can clean up. Other than mess, I see one broken chair, which I am happy to pay for." He slid a ten-pound note from the notecase's billfold, enough to buy half a dozen chairs, offering it to Mr. Abernathy. "Call it the cost of a morning's good sport." He beamed at the fellow wearing the tablecloth. "You led one jolly good chase, old chap. And earned me fifty quid for it."

The mustachioed fellow laughed as if they were sud-

denly mates. "Which we'd be 'appy to take 'alf of."
Tike 'arf of. Edwina was mesmerized by the muddled
syntax and thickness of his self-invented dialect.

The other brother, standing beside her, concurred.
"Amazing," he said, "I can barely understand a word
he says. It's English though, isn't it?" He shook his
head, a condescending smirk on his lips. "Honestly,
don't prolong his agony by helping him, Jeremy. If you
had any mercy, you'd just shoot him for being so poor
and stupid."

The Cornish-Cockney turned around sharply. "I
ain't *stupid*," he said. *Styoo-pid.* He mimicked the
other man's pronunciation quite well. "And I ain't a
blewdy poncey-arsed nob whot thinks his buttocks
don't smell when he shites."

Happily, the smug twin didn't understand what the
man had said. He turned his back as his brother with
the open notecase withdrew another bill. When Mr.
Abernathy still didn't take the money, the mediating
twin swung his arm like a boom around toward the
whimpering girl and her family. "She's your daughter,
yes? It seems you could do the lady the honor of believing her. When a lady says nothing happened, then
nothing happened."

The idea of the girl's being a lady made her whole
family scratch their heads—and stare at the money. As
encouragement, he added, "The truth is, I'd pay a good
bit to beat my brother here in a bet. Take this money
for the young lady's trousseau or dowry, then let her
be." He nodded, a small bow toward her as he offered
the money to her father. "To your future, made-
moiselle."

The father snatched it up.

To Abernathy, the gentleman opened his billfold,
showing a wad of bills inside. "How much? What is
the price of a new chair, a good mopping, of asking
your baker to come in early and turn out some more
of those delicious scones? Why, sir, by tomorrow, you
could be as good as new. In fact, better than before.
Everyone will want to come see the scene of today's

adventure. You will be the talk of London.''

It took three more bills to appease Mr. Abernathy, along with the assurance from first one brother then the other that they were very willing to take tea presently at a small side table while the mess was being cleared away.

And that was that. As if by magic, the angry group dispersed. Mr. Abernathy ordered his waiters to get mops. The bobby followed the family out. Edwina was left at the side of a demolished tearoom standing with a tall ratcatcher wearing a tablecloth.

''I thank ye kindly,'' he said, ''fer speakin' up fer me.'' He ran his hand down the front of his threadbare frock coat, as if straightening an elegant garment. Then he bent forward slightly, adjusting himself into his trousers before his grimy fingers rather indiscreetly fastened the top button.

His trousers had faded to a shade so colorless it was impossible to say if they'd been brown, black, or gray. These were tucked into a pair of hobnail jackboots, the waxy pitch on them cracking from age.

He was in scruffy shape. His thick, dark hair looked to be cut in hanks by an axe. It dangled onto his collar, touched his shoulders here and there; it stayed back from his face in a gravity-defying way that suggested pomade, though, if so, the predominant ingredient in his pomade seemed to be soot. He had a high forehead, or possibly a slightly receding hairline. In either event, the feature lent him an air of intelligence: cunning. His mouth, up against the mustache, was wide, with plump, rather perfectly shaped lips for a man. Chiseled. A pretty mouth on a shrewd piece of riffraff.

This mouth pulled up on one side in what was half a smile, a crooked sense of humor. ''And I bain't Coornish, loov. Though Feyther and Mawther was.'' He wiggled his eyebrows. He was making a joke. Then he smiled more crookedly still—one side of his mouth simply and naturally went up higher than the other, cutting a deep dimple into one cheek. ''I be a Londoner now,'' he explained. ''The best ratcatcher from Hyde

Park to the borough of Bethnal Green. If ye got rats, I'd do ye fer free.''

"Um, no, thank you. So this *is* your profession, catching rats?''

"Indeed. I be the pride of me family, a great success at it, ye see.'' He laughed softly, perhaps even ironically, then tipped his head, a man blatantly trying to see into the shadows under the brim of her hat.

She bowed her head enough to be a hindrance. In the face of a directness she rarely saw: He showed no fear in revealing himself. As if he had not a thing in the world to hide.

A little foolish of him, she thought, but useful in speech studies. He wouldn't be self-conscious about his pronunciation. On impulse, she said, "I'll give you five bob if you'll come by my house in Knightsbridge tomorrow afternoon and do some speaking exercises for me.''

"Yer 'ouse?'' he said. His lopsided grin broke slyly back onto his face. He cocked his head to the side. "Alone?''

Boldly, he glanced down the length of her. Edwina cranked her head back. The look he passed over her was purely obnoxious—almost too trite to be insulting. Honest to goodness, what could he possibly think?

Then she felt her cheeks infuse with heat.

She knew what he thought: Gangly. Over-tall. Over-educated. A myopic spinster for whom there was no brim in the world wide enough to hide all that was wrong with her. Edwina was accustomed to people thinking her unfeminine, unattractive. She was, however, unaccustomed to anyone leaping from that judgment to the notion that she was so desperate for the company of a man that she would hire one off the street.

She drew herself up, showing the scallywag her most righteous demeanor. There was a flicker of something, a teasing in his lopsided smile—though, if so, it was the wrong subject on which to tease her.

She scowled. "My house is not empty. I do not live alone, Mr.—" She paused for a name.

He supplied, "Mick."

"You have a family name?"

"Yes, love"—*Ace, loov*—"Tremore. But everyone calls me Mick."

"Well, Mr. Tremore, I'm not your love. My name is Bollash, Miss Edwina Bollash. And I merely want to study your speech, do a palatographic, perhaps make a gramophone recording. So if you are interested in—"

"Excuse me," said a voice to the side. "I have to ask: Are you *the* Miss Edwina Bollash?"

She turned to find that the two gentleman brothers had not dispersed with the rest. The slightly shorter one, the one who was generous with his billfold, was addressing her.

"I know of no other," she answered.

He shot his near-duplicate a smug look, then held out his hand by way of introduction. "My brother, Emile Lamont. I am Jeremy Lamont of Sir Leopold Lamont's family, of Brighton and lately of London." He offered his card as he nodded toward Mr. Tremore. "So you speak this chap's language?"

She nodded.

The thinner, and somehow more snide, brother asked, "You are the same Miss Edwina Bollash who is renowned for her skill in teaching"—he left a pause—"shall we say, less than graceful young ladies how to enter gracefully into society? The one who did the Earl of Darnworth's daughter?"

"*Did* her?"

"Turned her from that—that *thing* she used to be into the elegant creature who married the Duke of Wychwood last month."

Edwina was rather proud of this particular feat, but she never, never took public credit for her work. It demeaned the accomplishments of the young ladies themselves. "I can't imagine where you heard such a thing, though it is true that I tutor private students in elocution and deportment, if that is what you are asking." She opened her reticule, offering her own card in exchange. *Miss Edwina Bollash. Instructor of Elocution and Deportment. Philologist, Phonetician, Linguist. Expert in Social Graces and Polite Behavior.*

"You groom the ugly ducklings of society into swans of the upper class. All the rich mamas were whispering about it in Brighton this summer," said Jeremy as he shot a look of significance, a raised brow, at his thinner, more skeptical version.

Emile Lamont laughed. "Come now. You can't be serious," he said to him.

His brother protested, "I am. And you are absolutely wrong. Why, she could take this very fellow here and make him into a gentleman in a fortnight. I would bet it." Turning to her, "Couldn't you?"

"Make him into a gentleman?" The idea startled a laugh out of her.

"Yes. Change the way he speaks—being a gentleman is hardly more than talking properly, wearing decent clothes, and few polite manners."

"It's a good deal more than that, I'd say—" She glanced at the beggarly-looking fellow, who now watched her with the same interest he might have given to a houseful of rats.

"Yes, but you could do whatever it took," Jeremy insisted. "I know. I've spoken with Lady Wychwood. She confided that you helped her, that you picked her clothes, had someone come in for her hair, taught her how to move, even how to intone her voice."

Emile Lamont let out a derisive snort. "Lady Wychwood *was* a lady," he said. "That was no trick. I still say there is no science that can make—well, a silk purse out of a sow's ear. And I still say"—he poked the air in front of his brother's face for emphasis— "that anyone who can't speak the Queen's English properly may as well be shot, for there is no hope for their ever living a decent life. They are nothing but a drain on society."

"You see? You see?" his brother exclaimed. His

face reddened. "I have to live with this arrogant fellow! Have you ever heard such a thing?"

In Jeremy's defense, she said to his brother, "You're quite wrong. You can change the way a person speaks. Heavens, you can teach a parrot to talk."

"But not well."

"Well enough."

"She could do it well enough," Jeremy said. "You see? It can be done."

There was a pregnant moment, in which his brother seemed to contemplate their discussion—after which he raised one eyebrow and smiled. "Let me buy you each a cup of tea." He smirked then added, "You, too, Mr. Tremore. For I have an idea. I can see a way here for me to win back my money from my brother and then some."

Edwina allowed herself to be sat at a table to the side of the cleanup, facing the strangest trio of men she could remember in a while. Two rich, idle young gentlemen who had little to do beyond bicker. And a robust-looking ratcatcher wearing a tablecloth.

As a waiter walked away with their orders, Jeremy said, "Emile, I know what you were thinking—"

"You like to think you do—"

"You were thinking that this man was born poor and will die poor, that his poverty is in his blood. But I say it's in his speech. And I'm willing to back my opinion with a wager you will be hard-pressed to refuse." He took a breath, then leaned intently toward his brother. "I'll bet you a hundred pounds that she"—he pointed at Edwina—"can turn him"—he jabbed a finger in Mr. Tremore's direction—"into a gentleman by simply fixing the way he talks and teaching him some manners."

Oh, my. She had to interrupt. "No, no. I appreciate your faith, but I can hardly take on such a large project—"

"How long would it take?"

She blinked. "I don't know. More than a fortnight, certainly. And it would be expensive—"

"What if we covered your fees and costs?" Throwing a nasty grin at his brother, he added, "The loser, of course, would have to reimburse the winner."

She blinked again. "I don't know." She glanced at Mr. Tremore. He was listening carefully, wary but curious.

He was certainly an interesting case. Perfect in any number of ways. The clear pronunciation, or mispronunciation actually. He loved words. He could mimic accents. Moreover, a man who simply said what he had to say would make faster progress than one who hesitated or hedged.

Emile Lamont tapped his long, thin fingers, then after a moment lifted an eyebrow speculatively. "We'd have to find a way to determine who had won the bet," he said.

His brother pulled his mouth tight, till his lips whitened. "I win if he becomes a gentleman."

"Yes, but who will decide if he is a gentleman or not? You? Her? No, no. You'd simply clean him up, dress him up, then *call* him a gentleman."

"Well, we're not going to let *you* be the judge, if that's what you're suggesting."

Emile Lamont shrugged, as if he had won the bet already because his brother could not find a way to validate the end result.

"We will find an arbitrary judge, an objective third party," Jeremy protested.

"Who? One of your friends?"

"Well, not one of yours."

"Mine would be more impartial, but never mind. It can't be done, and you'd cheat anyway." Emile shrugged again, losing interest.

The bet was off.

Then on again: "Wait—" He sat back, smiling as he tented his fingers. "I have an idea." It was a wicked idea, she could tell by the way he narrowed his eyes. "The Duke of Arles's annual ball," he announced. "It's in six weeks. If you can pass him off there as— oh, say, a viscount." He laughed. "Yes, a viscount. If you can bring him, have him stay the entire evening with everyone thinking he is a titled English lord, if no one catches on, then you have won.'' He laughed heartily.

Edwina almost laughed herself. She felt light-headed all at once. The Duke of Arles was her distant cousin—though there was no love lost between them. Arles had inherited her father's estates twelve years ago, leaving her with whatever she could eke out on her own.

Passing an imposter off at his annual ball would infuriate her cousin.

She stared down into her teacup. Yes, it most certainly would. Why, it would make the old goat apoplectic.

The notion took on a strange, unexpected appeal. Arles's annual ball was a hurdle she always enjoyed surmounting, though in the past she had always done so legitimately: seen girls made comfortable there who deserved to be comfortable in the presence of the duke and his friends. But passing off an imposter. Well, it was absurd, of course. And if people found out, it could be damaging. She was allowed her little life on the fringe of society partly because she had been born to society, but partly too because she didn't challenge it.

But, oh, to fool the duke and know she had fooled him for the rest of her days. Yes—

No. No, no, it was a dangerous idea. But in imagination, it was amusing to consider. In fantasy, the idea made something inside her give a joyous jump. A small, vindictive lurch in her chest that was surprising for its liveliness. What a thought: Old Milford Xavier Bollash, the fifth Duke of Arles, mocked by his plain cousin for whom he had no use.

She looked at the mustachioed man in front of her. He swilled tea like a pint of lager, grasping the teacup whole in the palm of his hand. He drained his cup, then raised his hand, clicking his tongue and snapping his fingers to get the waiter's attention. When the waiter looked over in alarm, Mr. Tremore pointed, a downward poking gesture with his finger, and called, "We'd 'ave s'more, Cap'n."

Dear Lord. His manners were a nightmare. He was unwashed, threadbare, and coming apart at his buttons.

Yet there was something about him. His posture was straight. His teeth were good. Excellent, actually. A shave, a haircut, some good, clean clothes. And a trim, at the very least, of that feral-looking mustache. Why, there was no telling. He would probably clean up rather well, which, with the girls at least, was always half the battle.

When the second cup of tea came, he wouldn't let the waiter take the old cup. Then Mr. Tremore reached under the table and withdrew a surprise—the animal from his pocket, the one he'd saved at his own expense.

It was a small, weasly-looking thing. A ferret. It had to be, though Edwina had never seen one. But that was what ratcatchers used, wasn't it? Ferrets and terriers? What a vocation.

It had a shiny brown coat and a long, supple body, which it folded in half to "kiss" Mr. Tremore on his dark-stubbled cheek. The animal's shape was strange but good, she supposed, for wiggling through rat mazes and rabbit burrows. One of nature's better adaptions.

When Mr. Tremore lowered it out of sight, he also took the teacup. A moment later, the cup returned to the table, missing tea—or rather tea was in different places, in little sprinkles all around the inside of it.

She frowned. While the two brothers continued to argue, she argued with herself, staring at a ferret's teacup. A ratcatcher. Don't be preposterous, Edwina. An illiterate, crude ratcatcher—

Yet Mr. Tremore's eyes, as they remained intent upon his animal, his livelihood, were alert. Astute. He was a sharp one, there was little doubt. Not well-educated, but not unintelligent.

He glanced up suddenly, from re-pocketing the ferret, then caught her staring. He winked at her.

She jerked, blinked, then picked up her own teacup,

pouring her attention into it. Goodness. Certainly, if he were willing to tone down his swagger to mere arrogance, he would have enough of it to fit in with Arles and his lot. A little help with his diction, a few rules and manners. . . .

Besides, he only had to get through one evening, not a lifetime. And he seemed able to wind his impromptu way through any number of scrapes.

A ratcatcher. Oh, yes. It was delicious. To pass a London ratcatcher off on the duke as a . . . a viscount.

Not so dangerous, she told herself. She could do it. No one would know. Just herself, a thirsty Cockney-fied Cornishman, and two quarrelsome brothers—none of whom would want the truth to come out.

Meanwhile, what a gift that knowledge would be: I outdid him, outfoxed him. Made a mockery of what deserves to be mocked. It would be her triumph, her little joke for the sake of her own amusement. At the expense of her old cousin, the Duke of Arles, also known as the Marquess of Sissingley—once her own father's title—and other lesser titles, who, by any and all his names and titles, deserved to be made fun of. Most surely he did.

The brothers must have sensed her willingness, for Emile Lamont suddenly began to discuss expenses, how much she would need to begin. As if the bet were laid, her part agreed.

It was only at the end that Mr. Tremore folded his thick-muscled arms over his broad, tableclothed chest and leaned back in a lordly manner. He said, "Well, I be a very important bloke here, seems to me. But I ask ye: Whot's in it for ol' Mick?"

All three of them went quiet. Edwina herself had assumed the man understood. "A better way of speaking, for one," she said. "Without question, I can give that to you, provided you cooperate."

He eyed her suspiciously. "Ye'd be in charge?"

"Yes, in matters related to your learning how to speak and conduct yourself."

"Yer a woman," he observed.

Well, yes. She thought about shoving away from the table then, withdrawing from the whole farce. Here she sat, thinking to tutor a big oaf, who, though theoretically clever, was apparently not smart enough to appreciate that a woman—heavens, anyone—in matters of speech and genteel behavior might know more than he did. She stared at him, her gaze dropping to the brutish, thick mustache that took up most of his upper lip—

His chest has hair on it. The idea popped into her mind, just like that.

She jolted, scowled, and looked down into her teacup. What a strange leap of thought. Chest hair. No, no, don't think about such things, she told herself.

A good trick, though, how not to think about something.

Any glimpse of his mustache seemed now to proclaim the fact to her: Beneath that tablecloth was the strangest sight. A naked chest with dark, smooth-patterned hair—black, shiny hair, a thick line of it down the center of his chest between heavy pectoral muscles. Why, who would have thought—

No, *don't* think—dear, oh, dear. The mustache. Oh, she wished she didn't have to look at that wicked thing—wait, that was it! The mustache should go. He should shave it off. It was wiry, rough, like a broom on his lip. Not gentlemanly in the least.

Yes, oh, yes! Edwina thought as she stared at Mr. Tremore's mustache. The knowledge that she could tell him to clean himself up, smooth himself out, starting with his upper lip, made her feel jubilant all at once, eager for the whole business.

Meanwhile, Emile Lamont sneered at Mr. Tremore across the table. "You brawling, ungrateful swine," he said, "what you get out of this is you won't be hauled to the gaol for all the damage you wreaked today. I have a good mind to go demand our money back and call the constable again."

"No, no, no," his brother broke in quickly. "Mr. Tremore. Think of it this way: You'll have a cushy place to live for a few weeks. You'll get a regular gentleman's wardrobe, which you can take with you when you go. And"—he raised his finger dramatically—"you will be given a new manner of speech that will be yours forever, taught by an expert. Why, there is no telling what a man with your resources can do with such an advantage."

Mr. Tremore eyed them, a man suspicious of so much good fortune.

Then he drained his own teacup again, wiped the wet from his mustache with his arm, and smiled across the table at the three of them. He said, "I need twenty pounds today. It be fer me family who won't be getting anything from me while I do this. Then I want fifty pounds when I be through—"

"Why, you—" Emile Lamont came up out of his chair.

"Be quiet," Jeremy said. "Of course, Mr. Tremore. You'll want to have something to start yourself out in whatever new direction you take. It's only fair." He withdrew his ever-open notecase again, took out a bill, then with a flourish of his wrist he offered a twenty-pound note between two fingers.

His brother, however, quickly cupped his hand over the money, holding it back. "All right," he said. "But fifty at the end only if you manage it." He smiled condescendingly. "Not a ha'penny if you're too stupid to carry it off."

Mr. Tremore contemplated him stonily for several seconds. Then he said, "A hundred if I do it."

Emile laughed, a dry burst of reluctant amusement: disbelief. "You have some gall," he said, then shrugged, giving in. "Done." Taking his hand off the money, he glanced at his brother. "The loser pays."

The twenty-pound note sat there now between Jeremy's fingers, available, while Mr. Tremore stared at it for an uncomfortably long minute, as though it had turned to dung in the meantime. In the end though, he reached across and took it. "Yes," he said—*Ace*— "done." He stood, scraping back his chair as he pocketed the bill. "Now, where be the loo? I gotta shake 'ands with an ol' friend, if ye know what I mean. Blimey, but tea runs through a bloke. I don't know 'ow ye nobs do it."

Chapter 3

🌿🌹

*T*he Lamonts took Mick to a tailor's on a street called Savile Row. Bloody hell, it was a dandy place. And so long as Mick held out his arms or let them measure him up his leg, everyone let him crank his head and have a good look. The carpets on the floor were so thick and soft, the tailor kept having to haul him up by the arms—he wanted to touch them. The wood floor was polished up so shiny it looked wet. Old velvety chairs reflected like they stood on a lake. Tea tables floated on the floor's shine. The place had mirrors, gold vases with armloads of flowers that took up half a wall, and show-offy glass boxes as tall as a man's waist, with things inside he could buy, like buckles and buttons to sew onto the clothes they made him or neckties out of silk as colorful as peacock feathers. Who would've thought a place for blokes could get so fancy? He liked to think he'd seen some of the world, but he was impressed, he couldn't help it.

In the end, though, the Lamonts only wanted Mick to have dull things. Pah. Some brown trousers, some gray ones, a couple shirts, all white, a coat and waistcoat—Mick was allowed to pick the lining when he made surly over the whole ordeal. He picked a fine purple with gold cloverish things on it, like some draperies he remembered from a first-rate bordello he'd ratted.

35

When the bell over the tailor's door rang and Edwina Bollash stepped through the doorway, he was delighted to see her. His new partner, come to fetch him, in what was turning out to be a choice adventure.

He wanted to tell her all the good done them today. "We ordered some right fine clothes, then had some fixed up they be sending later."

She only froze in the doorway, though. Like he was bald and naked. "I thought they were going to see to a bath," she said.

"Naw. I don't need one."

He looked at the Lamonts who, in turn, looked at the tailor. They'd all had a little to-do over the bath idea.

He said right away, "You should feel some of the stuff we got, like God's own miracle under your fingers. And *hoo*, the rare, sweet smell what come off a bolt of new fabric." He laughed just remembering. "The whole shop smells new, don't you think? Like beeswax and varnish. No"—it was so true that it made him grin for having thought of it—"like fresh-printed money, etched and watermarked." It was a smell he knew from helping his friend Rezzo print near-perfect fivers in the cellar of the Bull and Tun. Not that he spent any of the false money himself, but Rezzo had fifteen children, and there was no other way for a dustman to feed them all.

Miss Bollash's voice, though, was a little unsteady when she repeated, "Etched and watermarked?" She let out a fainthearted laugh before asking, "What do you know about fresh-printed money?"

Didn't take him a second to know he wasn't answering that. He turned and said good-bye to the tailor and thank-you-very-kindly to the Lamonts.

He and Miss Bollash stepped out into the street, with her eyeing him and him ignoring her. Begger me, he thought. There they were, starting out off-kilter. Magic, his terrier, picked up and followed them as they walked shoulder to shoulder. He kept thinking, If he could see her face, he'd know better where he stood. But he could only see the lower half of it—the brim of her hat was that big.

She was sure a puzzle, Edwina Bollash. He thought she could be pretty. It was possible. She dressed nice. Quality. Her clothes sounded pretty, like reedy grass rubbing together in the wind—a noise that always sent him into heaven, silk on silk. He loved, too, the way she smelt like sunshine or clover or something. Not all flowery and perfumey, but a little cloud of smell around her. He wanted to get closer to it, sniff it in, but even he knew it wasn't polite. Anyway, she could be pretty under that hat. Or not.

She was a long girl, that was certain. In her shoes here, she must've pushed six feet. Almost as tall as him. A lot of woman, lengthwise speaking. Width-wise, though, the top of her was on the skinny side. Long bones, small bristols—sweet though, little dump-lings on her chest. The bottom of her wasn't so skimpy maybe. Her backside looked pretty full, though it was hard to tell what with the way fancy ladies padded out their bums these days.

She didn't have a pretty woman's way about her. He couldn't say why he thought so, except maybe how her hat tilted down when she walked. Like she was looking at the pavement, keeping track of it to make sure it didn't leap away from her. Smart steps, no doubts or dithers, but there was something nervy in her quick movement. Like a jill who been down the rat hole once too often, he thought: knew the job, knew her part in it, but knew, too, what it was like to be bit and just couldn't get over it. He wondered what bit her.

At the carriage, Mick could tell he surprised her when he held out his hand. He'd seen gents do it, so he tried it out.

He helped her into a carriage that had all its win-dows open, then got a bonus as he followed her in: a chance to look close up at her bum, no one to tell him not to. And yessir, it was all her own, he was pretty sure. A bottom as round as a pear. It made him smile. Her jacket fanned out into a little ruffle over her backside. It pinched in at her waist. Pretty. My, oh, my, he thought, weren't the gentry's clothes full of details plain folk didn't dream of—gold buttons, velvet ribbon sewed around the edges, skirts the color of lavender—

Wait one minute.

Tall.

A purple skirt. And Miss Bollash's legs here'd be long.

Did they go forever?

Would there have been time for his leggy lady to put on her dress, walk over, and order tea? As he reasoned this out, though, another woman walked past them—in a skirt with a lot of dark purple in it—and Mick laughed at himself. After what he saw in that mirror this morning, he must have legs on his brain, hoping they were walking under every skirt he glanced.

Still, as he sat down opposite Miss Bollash, he couldn't help but stare at where her knees made her skirt bend. Yessir, her legs'd be right long. Slender, too. There was no telling, though, how pretty a woman's legs were till you actually got her undressed. He folded his arms, sat back, and stared, smiling. He wondered if the woman under that hat fancied mud in any form.

Besides a lot of hat, she was a lot of skirts. Her legs were buried under folds and folds of that thin sort of stuff a man could almost see through, except there was enough of it he couldn't see through nothing. Edwina Bollash was like that herself. Lots of her, none of it coming to much. Hard to see through.

Being a long, thin thing lost in a pile of skirts didn't keep her from complaining though—as hardy as the Queen with her toes on fire—when Magic jumped into the carriage.

"May as well let him ride," Mick said. "He be the damnedest dog. He'll only run alongside till he drops, then find us a day later from the smell of the wheels or something."

She didn't like *damnedest* any more than she liked the dog in the coach, but she settled back and let both ride. Magic, Mick could tell, was grateful. It'd been a hell of a day.

As the coach pulled away, he realized it was finer than fine. All leather and soft cushions and springs in the ride. Funny thing, it wasn't near as strange as he might've thought to trot off in such a handsome bit of conveyance. Felt good. Felt right. All-bloody-right. Well, Mick thought, who would've predicted? A nice coach. Him sitting in it across from a long piece of fluff who was willing to squawk over a man getting his head bashed in. He liked Edwina Bollash. Good girl, this one.

The two blokes he did not like at all. He didn't know their game, but he knew their kind a mile off. Not that he could say—a ratcatcher didn't call gentlemen humbugs. Especially, Mick smiled to himself, if the humbugs were going to pay for him having gentleman lessons from a sweet little teacher in a fancy dress that made sliding *jsh-jsh* sounds just sitting there fidgeting.

He made her nervous. He should've tried to put her at ease, said something, but he sort of liked that she was nervous.

He decided to mention, "They be puppies, you know."

"Puppies?"

"Confidence men," he explained.

"Who?"

"Them two Mr. Lamonts."

"Don't be ridiculous. They're rich gentlemen."

He shook his head. "They be setting us up for something."

She clicked her tongue in a sort of high-minded way. "Granted, they aren't too nice to each other, but they were perfectly nice to us. Besides, they have money. They don't need to set up anyone."

He shrugged. It was all one to him, nothing he had to prove. It would prove itself.

After a while, though, in a very quiet voice, she asked, "Why don't you like them?"

He shrugged again. "They be arseholes." While

you, me darling, be a lovely long bit. He really liked the look of her. Though he wished for goodness sake she'd take off the blooming hat.

At *arseholes*, the only part of her face that he could see under the hat squinched up like she had a drawstring in her lips, a drawstring she pulled tight. Ha, he could've predicted. She made another one of those little clicks, teeth and tongue, that he was sort of coming to like. Then said, "*Are*."

She was correcting him.

It made him blink, frown. Well, hell. He knew fixing how he talked was what they were both going to do, but here it was, and he didn't like it. "Right. They *are* arseholes," he said.

The hat tilted. Her mouth pinched tighter.

He laughed and leaned back, stretching his arms out along the top of a leather seat, stretching his legs in front of him across fancy wood floorboards. Yes indeed, a fine day. A pretty ride.

When Miss Bollash's front door swung open, a fellow was standing behind it like he been waiting on the other side of it the whole time she was gone: ready to open it the moment he spied her come up the walk. He held it wide so Mick and her could enter, then closed it silent-like behind them—it made Mick turn around there in the entry hall just to see what happened.

Her house wasn't what Mick expected. Not like her clothes. It was plain. Better than anything he could claim, but not as big or fancy as he would've guessed.

She owned lots of books. *Hoo*, if the woman read all the books she had, she never did nothing but read. He'd been in lots of fancy houses for his job. Some had flowers for decoration. Some had carpets and fancy drapes or pictures all over the wall. Miss Bollash's house had books. Lines of them. Rows of them. Stacks of them. All neat. No mess or nothing. Just everywhere. They lined walls and filled tables.

"Thank you, Milton," said the lady as she pulled at the fingers of her glove. "Is Mrs. Reed still here? I'd like her to make up the east bed-sitter. This is Mr. Tremore. He's going to be our houseguest for a few weeks."

A few weeks. Mick frowned to hear the length of time. It seemed long all at once. He had regulars. He hadn't thought about that till now. Some might wait, but some for sure would take their problem to someone else when they couldn't find him.

As he walked down a hallway—with small marble statues in the niches of walls covered in faded green silk—a crawly feeling tickled up his spine. The way it did sometimes when he started to smell more under the planks of a job than he'd counted on.

Milton, the bloke who opened the door and looked old as Eden, was saying to Miss Bollash, "Mrs. Reed just left, your ladyship, but I can make up the rooms. And Lady Katherine is in the solarium. She's arrived early for her lesson."

"Thank you. I'll get to her in a few minutes." Miss Bollash slid her glove off as she said to Mick, "Milton will take your, um . . . tablecloth. Then, if you'll follow me, I'll show you upstairs."

Rooms. She meant it. Two of 'em. In Cornwall, Mick'd shared one room, smaller than the bedroom here, with his five brothers. His bed in London was in a cellar. In this house though, if he understood right, he got a big room with a four-poster in it to himself— he asked if he shared it with Milton, but the answer was no—*and* a room connected to the bedroom that had a desk, paper, pens, ink, lots of stuff. And of course more books.

It made him stop and think. Looking at an actual bed, rooms, thinking of the clothes, all so different than what he knew . . . well, the crazy, fool bet, what it really meant, all at once seemed to matter in a different way. No one else had the same investment as him. A bit of money. Some pride. And Miss Bollash was keen for bookish reasons, too. But him . . . why, they were all talking about changing how he was.

What kind of man, he wondered, slept on a bed that had curtains on it and a skirt around its legs?

A man, he figured, who better get by to feed the other dogs and ferrets, then see if Rezzo would watch over them till . . . till whatever it was he was doing here came to whatever end it did. A man with a case of nerves, he guessed, and a few arrangements to make.

Sometimes Mick dreamed of a fancy life. (Money and legs. He would have been embarrassed to tell anyone how common-minded his ambitions were.) He always felt guilty doing it. Disloyal or something. He was a workingman. A good, solid man of the working class. He didn't think fancy fellows were happier than him. Didn't think they were nicer to their families or that God gave them a easier time of it. They still got sick or lame or died, just like everyone else. So why was he here?

Aside from a hundred and twenty pounds, twenty of which he already had in his pocket—the total being more than he made in a year?

He laughed at himself. That was why. Hell, he sure didn't have dreams that turning himself into a gentleman for a few weeks was going to make him a better man somehow. No, sir, it wouldn't.

But the life nobs led seemed easier, he admitted. It smelled better maybe. They had time to think about things. Is that what he wanted? Was that the reason he dreamed of a rich life some nights? Time to think?

Meanwhile, all he seemed to have here was time to be surprised. Another door, one that he thought opened into the hall, opened into a loo, and not just a hole in the floor neither. There was a flush-toilet with a chain to pull on. And bloody hell, there was another pull overhead that made light come on. Electricity. He'd seen that once in a building he ratted over near Parliament. Miss Bollash's whole house had it, not a candle or gas lamp anywhere to be found.

She showed him all this in the time it took for her

to pull off her other glove as she walked her quick walk and pointed at rooms. Then, in his new sitting room, she said, "Do you need anything I haven't thought of? Will it do then?" She was in the doorway, about to leave him here.

He tried to sound chipper. "Not a thing, love. Cozy as a mouse in a churn." But he wasn't chipper.

"Love," she said.

He smiled, looking at a tall, thin woman in a big hat. Right friendly of her. About time.

But then she ruined it. She explained, "You said *loov*. It's *love*."

He frowned, feeling addled by a lot of correcting without much understanding doled out.

She stood there. She wasn't being nasty, he didn't think. Hard to tell. More like she was sizing him up. It was a nervy feeling, being sized up by a hat that looked right at him, being spoke to by a mouth with no eyes. What was wrong with her? he wondered. Were her eyes crossed? Was she bug-eyed?

She was ugly, he decided. Had to be a fright to wear her hat all the time.

"We'll work on it, though," she said. "We'll start in the morning. I have students this evening." Then she turned again and called over her shoulder, "Milton? Mr. Tremore will have a bath now. Will you please draw it. And see to a shave for him. Take off the mustache."

Mick blinked, then snorted. He went as far as the doorway, looking at the back of her. She was at the stairs in a second, on her way down. Hell, what was this? Even he knew gents wore mustaches. And he wasn't having no bath. He might've said, but she was going at her fast clip, a woman with the devil on her tail, not looking back. Her hat disappeared into the stairwell. Hell. All right then, he'd settle with old Milton.

As it turned out, though, the fellow was as stubborn as Magic.

"If Miss Bollash says you're to take a bath," old

Milton said with a poke, poke—Mick took hold of his finger to stop it—"then you'll have a bath, sir." With a big, stirred-up show of disgust, he added, "Just look at yourself!"

Now, Mick wouldn't mind cleaning up. He'd sort of had that in mind. It'd been a hard day. But he wasn't doing his private toilette the way Milton wanted him to, and not how Miss Fancy-Skirts wanted neither, for that matter. Too personal. Being a reasonable fellow, though, and just to be nice, he let Milton pull him into the room to show him the tub—the bloke was so bloody proud of it. A big, white, claw-foot thing that was just for bathing a body. The damnedest waste. Mick could've washed a month's laundry in it.

"Right nice," he told Milton with real wonder in his voice.

Things degenerated from here, though. *No, sir* didn't slow the old fellow down. *Not on your life, Cap'n* didn't give him the hint. *Not me. Not Mick.* And still that Milton ran a lot of hot water in the tub, talking like Mick was going to hop in any moment. When he started pulling on Mick's clothes, though, well—Mick was not the sort to let another bloke undress him for any reason. It pretty much sent him over the top.

"Since you like bathing so much," he said, "you try it." He picked the fellow up—he was light enough Mick could've done it by a fistful of coat, but he gathered the old bloke up real polite—and dumped him into the water. Clothes and all, a big swooshing *ka-plosh.*

Mick was gentle with him. Didn't want to hurt him, just sort of showed him he wasn't getting in any tub of hot water, which was fine for carrots but not the likes of Mick Tremore.

No sooner did the water slop to a standstill than he heard Miss Bollash, feet pounding up the staircase, all those skirts churning. When she burst through the doorway, though, he was struck dumb, nothing to say for himself.

Well, well, well. His new teacher certainly wasn't

ugly. No, sir. She wasn't pretty neither exactly, but with her hat off, God bless her, she was something to look at.

Her hair was red-gold, thick and shining. It lit her face—the way light coming through a window could make a ordinary room glow like a church. Her skin, white as milk, was dusted with pale freckles, like she been powdered with gold dust. Freckles so close and so many of 'em, he couldn't see between some. She had big, round eyes—or, no, maybe they were just startled. They blinked behind eyeglasses. But the best thing about her face was her nose. It was long and thin and curved like a blade, a strong nose—and a good-sized one, too, for such a thin woman. If she'd held her head up a bit and showed it off, he'd've said it give her real character.

Though, given the caution in the eyes behind Miss Bollash's eyeglasses, he was bound to say she didn't cherish her looks.

Still, with her hat off she was a sight. Bright-colored, funny-looking in a pretty way: like coming upon a fairy in the woods.

A tetchy fairy. She said, "Oh—Oh—Milton! Are you all right? What have you done, Mr. Tremore! I could hear your swearing downstairs!"

Milton and Mick talked at once.

"All I done was protect meself from his slimy fingers—"

"Yes, I'm wet, but fine—"

"I ain't swimming in no bloody tub. No one mentioned no tub of water today—"

"If I may say so, your ladyship, the man belongs in a zoo, not a bathtub—"

"Not for no hundred quid do I let some ol' sod—"

"Enough!" she said. "Enough of your oaths and fulminations, Mr. Tremore."

Ungrateful woman. Mick sucked himself up, squared his shoulders, and, trying to hold back from yelling, told her, "I'll have you know, duck, if it wasn't for me 'fulminations,' as you call 'em''—he mimicked the word, tone for tone, though he could only guess what it meant—"I'd be standing here in the rude with me widge hanging out."

That caught her back. Her big eyes grew. They got as wide and round as blue saucers.

Good. While he had her quiet, he drove home his point. "You can't tell me no gent soaks in water like a plucked chicken, like he was dinner—"

"Mr. Tremore, gentlemen most certainly do take a bath—"

"And how do you know? You ever seen one take a bath?"

She blinked, scrunched up her freckled brow, then swung her eyes onto the dripping fellow who was climbing over the edge of the tub. She asked, "You—you take a bath, don't you, Milton?"

"Indeed, madam. Though usually I remove my clothes first."

"Which explains," Mick pointed out, "why he's so wrinkled and stiff-looking. Too much water—"

The over-washed servant continued to mutter complaints, but she ignored him. She only shook her head at Mick with her lips pressed together. "You must take a bath." She didn't know how to make him do it, he thought, and it mattered to her. His refusal made her right upset. So upset that for a minute he wanted to do it. Almost. Just for her. For the sake of her worried expression and shy sort of pluck.

For his own sake, though, he had to tell her the truth. "I don't have to do nothing. And I gotta tell you, too, that the mustache stays where it be: on the lip."

She wrinkled her brow again, deeper, puckered her mouth, which in turn puckered her long chin. It was pathetic, her look. She stared at his mustache like it wanted to bite her, focusing on it. She was fighting looking lower, he realized—at his chest. He folded his arms over it, not to cover it but because he knew it flexed chest muscle. It made it look better, stronger. The hell with her. "The mustache stays," he repeated.

She squinched up her mouth some more, then said,

"Well, a trim then. We'll trim your mustache for now. But you have to wash in the tub."

"I won't."

Oh, she wanted him in that tub. Her mouth pressed into a strained, fretful line—while her eyes shifted nervously to stay above his neck. She told him, "I can't make you into a gentleman, sir, if you insist on the toilette habits of a beggar."

He let out an insulted snort. "Listen, duck. There be an important understanding to get to here. I know them blokes asked you to change me, but, thing is, I'll take charge of me, all right? You say. I'll listen. But I'll decide what be right for Mick Tremore. And a swim in soup water ain't right."

She put her fists on her waist, her long, thin elbows poking out into the doorway. Her face was getting pink. She was really working herself up. "Then it's over, because you're filthy. Which reminds me"—she pointed a finger at his pocket—"you have to get rid of that as well."

She meant Freddie. And she meant the bet was off, if Mick didn't get in the bathtub. He straightened, gently brushed his coat down the front, and tried to gather some dignity. Bad enough he stood here missing buttons and pieces of his shirt, bad enough he had to hold his manliness together against some fellow who wanted his clothes. Now some bossy woman expected him to put Freddie out.

Then she pointed at Magic. "And your dog has to have a bath, too."

Ha. Mick began reasonably, "Well, if you can get Maj in your tub, feel free to wash him. But Miss Bollash, if this cockeyed bet goes sour, Freddie here be me livelihood. Freddie be the best damn ferret what ever was. I gotta have her with me."

"I can't have some rodent—"

"Ain't a rodent. The opposite. She hates rodents. She hunts them."

"He can't hunt them in my house."

"She. Freddie be a jill, and she's gotta be with me. A good ferret is like gold, you see."

She waffled. He thought he was going to win for a second, when she asked, "How do you keep her where you live?"

"She has a cage she sleeps in sometimes."

"Can we get it?"

"I'd guess."

"All right. Can we put the cage out back in the carriage house?"

"No, gotta have her with me, I'm saying."

"Not in the house."

He thought about it. He wanted the bet to go, he guessed. It was going to be harder, more than he first thought, but he wasn't ready to give it up. He didn't lose a hundred pounds easy. Besides, the idea of talking posh and living nice, more for fun than anything, had grown on him. "Well, if the carriage house is close. And has light and lots of air, and I can go see her plenty. But no bath, all right? I'll wash up in a sink."

"And a bath, Mr. Tremore. For you. A bath and a haircut and a shave." She frowned at his upper lip again. "A shave every day," she continued. "And clean clothes. This is not going to be a lark, sir." She took a breath, pink-faced. For a skittish thing she sure could get her knickers in a knot. "You will be struggling with a lot of new ideas, a bath being your first, I suppose. You will have more than mere difficult sounds and constructions of the English language to learn. If you intend to be a gentleman in six weeks, you'd best begin by listening to me."

"I ain't the one who ain't listening," he said. "I'll learn all what makes sense to me, but nothing else. How can I? Things got to make sense or I'll just be mimicking what I don't see, what I gotta see from the inside, you know? And a bath I don't see at all. It be unhealthy for one. I'll catch me death. I could drown—I can't swim. I'll wash up in a basin. I always do. I'm a clean bloke—"

"Not clean enough—"

"Bloody clean enough for some." Damn her anyway. He told her, "You ain't the first fine lady, you know, to take me upstairs, Miss Bollash—"

He watched her face turn white. Oh, hell, he thought. He ran his hand into his hair—and got a palmful of soot. He'd forgotten. Bloody hell, he didn't doubt he looked like a cat caught all night in a coal bin. He'd been up a flue, crawled around on a floor, then been chased partway through London only to end up beat on by a dozen people.

All right, he was dirty. All right, he wished he could call that last back. The fact that ratting rich ladies' houses had occasionally landed him upstairs in rich ladies' beds—ladies a lot less particular than this one— was most surely something *not* to discuss with Miss Edwina Bollash.

As brittle as ice, she told him, "You'll have a bath or leave immediately." She wasn't joking. Once she had a bite-hold of something, there was no getting it away from her.

But he meant what he said, too, and would damn well see she give him respect for his part in what they were planning to do. "Not unless you and Milton here be strong enough to put me in it."

Her bottom lip came up, covering a piece of her top lip as she pressed her mouth tight. She looked pained for a moment. Then she said softly, "Leave."

"Pardon?"

Louder, "Leave."

He scowled, staring at her. Relentless, she was. "Fine then," he said. "Suit yourself."

He pushed past the two of 'em: the prudey Miss Know-It-All, wasting her time trying to wash life clean, and her manservant, soaking wet from trying to help her do it.

Didn't need this. Stupid idea. No, made no sense whanking around with a bloody-arse bet that wasn't good for nothing but entertaining a bunch a' rich folks.

Sod them. Sod them all to Hades and back. Let them play with their money, not him.

Halfway down the block, though, he was already regretting his decision. Dream or not, what if she *could* show him how to be a proper gentleman? What if he could change himself into a . . . a bloody valet or . . . whatever that fellow Milton was now, a butler, wasn't it? Then, Mick, ol' chum, you could live in a fine, clean house all the time, too. And send a lot more money to Cornwall and the brood. Everyone could live better. Even Freddie here might just appreciate a carriage house, if it was dry and clean and got sunlight into it. And you like the way she talks, you know. Not to mention the way she smells.

Besides, a gentleman almost certain got to get a lot closer than any ratcatcher to the tall, timid-fierce girl who'd thrown him out over bathwater.

Chapter 4

$\mathcal{M}$r. Tremore's foot treads diminished without a pause, his and the soft-click trot of his dog's. Down the stairs they went, through the front hallway, then the front door opened and slammed. Edwina stood there in her modern bathroom, listening to silence. It was a funny moment, the house achingly quiet where only a moment ago it had rung with the most colorful talk, and lots of it.

She listened, waiting to hear his knock downstairs on her front door. He'd return, because he was smart and because it was in his best interest to reconsider. And because he was wrong.

When hushed stillness, however, only attested to his intention to remain wrong, she was surprised by the steep descent of her disappointment.

"My lady?"

She startled. It was Milton. "Yes?"

"Shall I clean up the bathroom then? Do you wish anything further?"

She had to think a moment to make sense of his questions. "Oh. No." She shook her head. "I mean, yes. Please clean up. But I won't need anything further from you. Not till tea at ten." She always had a cup of chamomile before bed.

She left the room, thinking, So. That was that.

A shame, she consoled herself. Mr. Tremore was

perfect in any number of ways. She didn't very often hear a linguistic pattern as distinctive as his. And she would have guessed by his alert attention, not to mention the way he mimicked sounds, that he would have made a good student. An excellent study. Ah, well.

What a plummet though. She felt utterly depressed as she came down the stairs.

She went about her business. The house was calm and orderly. She spent the afternoon tutoring: first a lawyer's daughter with a lisp, then a Hungarian countess who wanted to pronounce English better, then the daughter of country gentry who had "picked up an accent" in her native Devon. The last girl left. Edwina went to dinner, which was punctual, elegant, and delicious, thanks to a French–schooled cook.

Very late that night, however—with her in her flannel nightgown, padding around in the dark, looking for the key so she could wind her father's old clock—she heard a faint knock at the door below stairs, then voices at the kitchen entrance.

She went to the top of the stairwell to be sure, then smiled: There was no doubt. The sound of Mick Tremore's unmistakable, deep voice filled her with a kind of joy. It was so delightful to hear his dropped H's, his *wadden*'s for *wasn't*'s, his ruined diphthongs and flat vowels.

"I come to a decision," he said. "And it wasn't"—*wadden*—"that chronic to get to."

"Chronic, sir?"

"Long and painful. Was easy, once't I saw it."

Edwina's smile widened as she heard Mr. Tremore ask quite clearly, "So would you help me"—*'elp me*—"what's your name again?" *Whot's yer nime?*

Clearly or not, Milton didn't understand him. They grappled with Mr. Tremore's pronunciation for a few moments, until Milton finally said, "Oh, you want my name?"

"Yes." *Ace.*

"Milton, sir."

"Milton, I be wantin' a bath and shave, since the lady says I got to."

Edwina felt her senses come alive. Elation. As she heard Milton admit Mr. Tremore into the house, she did a little dance in her slippers there on the landing. But she stopped still as a lamppost to hear, "She be a smart woman, ain't she?"

"Yes, sir."

"I shouldn't't've made such a fuss. I can get in some water."

Just like that, he admitted he was wrong. What an amazing conversation.

He continued graciously, "See, I be pigheaded sometimes." He laughed, a deep, rich vibration that made something move in her chest, *thudda-thud*, the way a bass drum did in a parade. "It come from bein' mostly right, 'course. But she knows a thing or two about the gentry, I guess."

"Yes, sir." She could tell Milton had little or no idea what the first part had been about. He responded graciously to the last though, saying, "She's gentry, sir."

"That's what I thought. Will you help me then?" *'Elp me thun?*

"Yes, sir. My pleasure, sir."

Edwina turned and all but floated up the main staircase to her bedroom. Why, she wouldn't be surprised if he shaved the mustache as well. He was being so reasonable.

In the morning, she would pretend nothing had happened, that Mr. Tremore had done just as he should have in due course, no argument, no embarrassment. She envisioned saying good morning to him at breakfast (his face clean-shaven), inviting him nonchalantly into her lab—*When you're finished with your meal, you can find me down the hall, last door on the right.*

Once in bed, though, she didn't go to sleep. She wasn't sleepy, she decided, so she picked up a book instead. She opened it, then never read a word. Instead, she listened to the water cut off, the pipes clanking as the flow stopped. She jolted slightly against her pillow as she heard a *ka-plosh*, then, "Ai, that be hot!"—Mr. Tremore entering a tubful of water. She lay there listening to the substantial splashes and sloshes of his large body moving through the business of a bath.

She thought about his naked chest again. Her memory of it both fascinated and repelled her. Hair. It had been there again as they had argued in the bathroom. She shuddered. Who would have thought? Yet she had studied it with surreptitious care: a pattern of dark hair, two perfect swirls over muscles that bunched when he folded his arms, swirls that converged to become a dense pattern in the crevice between chest muscles, then (when he pulled his arms away to push back his hair) ran in a dark, ever-narrowing line, like an arrow pointing downward. Mick Tremore in the rude, as it were. This way to the widge.

Edwina started. Heavens! Up till now, she realized, she had carefully avoided forming in her mind any word for that part of a man. Even the scientific word made her vaguely uneasy; her sensibilities veered away from it. Still, she'd known immediately what Mr. Tremore referred to when he'd said *that*. His word seemed friendlier. A fond name. Were men fond of that part of themselves? It was certainly not the best part of statues; she made a point not to look there. And it changed, it grew. She'd read that astounding piece of information in a book. That was the worst part, the horror—or it had been the worst until this very moment, when it occurred to her that, goodness, a man might have hair there, too. She did. Oh, something that grew larger, up and out of a tangle of hair. How disgusting.

No, no, she mustn't think of it anymore. Enough. She must think of something else.

The mustache. From down the hallway came *ka-plosh, ka-plosh*. Mr. Tremore getting clean. Truly clean—taking off all the thick, wiry hair that grew on his lip. Good. With that satisfying thought, punctuated by the pleasant, occasional lap of bathwater down the hall, she fell into a doze. There was no telling for how long, but she came to herself with a start, her reading light still on, the house quiet.

Then no: she rose up onto her arms, for a different sound reached her. The noise of movement, someone walking in the dead of night. Edwina sat all the way up, thinking, What the blazes. It seemed to come from the direction of her father's study.

She hopped off her bed, putting her arms through the sleeves of her faded blue dressing gown. She walked quickly out into the hall, lifting her heavy braid from where it was caught with one hand as she pushed her spectacles up from where they'd slid down her nose with the other.

At the far end, the door to her father's study indeed stood partly open. The light was on. She walked toward it, continuing to hear the soft shuffle of someone moving about. She thought irritably, It must be Mr. Tremore prowling around. But when she pushed the door open further, she could only step back.

It was a stranger, standing in quarter profile and holding her father's crystal decanter of cognac up to the light.

The room's wall lamp made the brandy, as it tipped gently back and forth in the decanter, cast amber prisms across the side of his face, his shirt. Gold light. It made him look like an apparition. She might have said the intruder was a handsome, genteel burglar, for he was elegantly proportioned and certainly well-dressed, but he was in no rush—too much at his ease to be robbing the house. His shirttail was out, his shirt cuffs turned back. He wore a vest, but it hung unbuttoned. Less like a burglar, more like a ghost, one of her father's old friends come as a houseguest.

Mr. Tremore, she thought again, trying out the idea. Who else? It had to be him. Yet the man standing before her seemed so unlike her new student. Yet similar: He had the same dark hair, dark as night, but it was slicked close to his head and combed away from his face. Was Mr. Tremore this tall, so square-shouldered, so straightly built? This man looked leaner, neater. Handsomer. His clothes were simple, but nice. His white shirt was neatly pressed, open at the neck; it was missing its collar. The vest—

She frowned. His vest was oddly familiar. As were the trousers somehow, or what she could see of them. He stood behind the edge of her father's desk.

He turned toward her, lowering the decanter in front of him, as if suddenly aware of her. Their eyes met. His face changed, drawing up into a crooked smile, showing a deep dimple to one side of a thick, well-trimmed mustache that rose up on a lot of even, white teeth. A remarkable contrast. Edwina was halted for an instant in the warmth of his smile, the way a small animal is stopped foolishly in the road sometimes when the beam of a carriage lamp swings, too bright, suddenly onto it. Lord, the man was good-looking. A sharp good looks, the sort that absorbed a woman's good sense and turned it to mush in her head. Refined, cultured somehow, with a subtle air of competence.

Not Mr. Tremore, who certainly was vigorous-looking and masculine, but—

He held out his arms, the bottle in one hand, the other palm up, and said, "Well, whaddaya think?"

Edwina quite nearly fell over as he offered himself for inspection, turning slowly. It was, of course, none other. "Mis-Mister Tremore," she said, though almost as a question, looking for confirmation. "I—um—ah—you—" she stammered.

Even staring right at him, she couldn't quite believe it was the same man. To say he cleaned up well was so much an understatement, it stood reality on its head.

"How do I look?" he asked.

"Unbelievable." His mustache. Someone had trimmed it, made an attempt—not all that successful a one—to tame it.

"Diabolical," he suggested, wiggling his eyebrows, then laughed. He loved the word; he must, he used it enough. "I look like a bloody lord, don't I?"

Edwina cleared her throat. Well, yes. And here stood another unwelcome bit of truth: The handsomest "bloody lord" she had ever seen was a ratcatcher wearing her father's outdated trousers, shirt, and vest—and wandering her house in the middle of the night so as to steal brandy or whatever else he could find, no doubt.

She drew herself up, then demanded, "Put that down."

He looked at the decanter, seemingly surprised to find his fingers around its neck. "Ah," he said, as if now understanding. He made a knowing cluck with his tongue, then grinned gleefully, a man smiling at a good joke. "Wasn't pinchin' none, if that was what you be thinkin'. It just shook me, see, a little—"

"Put it down."

He put it on the desk, though he frowned, doing a very good imitation of a man unfairly called to account. He repeated, "Wasn't pinchin' none. See, I have this dream sometimes—"

"I'm not interested in your dreams of easy liquor, Mr. Tremore. You may not enter this room, unless you do so in my company."

He grinned again. "Well," he said. "Then come in, Miss Bollash."

When she only stood there scowling at him from the hallway, he came toward her.

Lord, with his mouth shut, he even moved right. Lithe, graceful, a male who was physically confident of himself, in the full flush of bold health—and probably used to smiling at women who stood in a dim hall in the middle of the night.

"You be a right fine sight in that, Miss Bollash."

She looked down. Her dressing gown was un-sashed on her night-shift. She quickly pulled the gown around her. Not because there was anything here to make a man misbehave, but for pride's sake, so neither one of them had to admit there wasn't.

He stopped at the doorway, her in the hall, him in

the room. "Do your mates call you Edwina?" he asked. "Ain't you got a sweet name?"

She stiffened, frightened somehow. "I don't have any 'mates,' Mr. Tremore, and *Miss Bollash* sounds respectful—sweet enough to my ears."

He screwed up his mouth, making his mustache slant sideways—it looked more fashionable for its coiffing but no less rough, bristly.

"Winnie," he said suddenly.

She jumped.

He put his hands on either side of the doorjamb, arms spread, elbows bent, and contemplated her for a few moments. Then he repeated, "Winnie. That be it. That be what you call an Edwina, right?" He smiled because she admitted, either by her frown or her jump the moment before, that she identified with the name, a name she hadn't heard in ages. "Ah." He nodded. "Much nicer. Soft. Dear-like, you know?"

The way he said it . . . His tone gave rise to a kind of confusion. Embarrassment somehow. Fright again. His expression invited her to smile back at him, but she couldn't have if she'd wanted to. And she didn't; she certainly didn't want to, she thought. He was playing her for a fool, trying to distract her from the fact that he'd been stealing liquor, which, of course, she had to put a stop to.

She said, "No, *Winnie* is not nice. When I was little, my cousins used to neigh like a horse when they said it. They used to call me Wi-i-i-n-n-ie." She whinnied for him as she said her name. Then she wished she hadn't.

Because he winced, reacting to the pain of it. His concern made her look away. She heard him say, "Well, you bloody well fooled 'em, Miss Bollash. 'Cause you be a beaut, if ever I seen one."

She glanced at him—as harsh a glare as she could muster—then contradicted his malarkey. "Mr. Tremore, I am a gangly, plain woman with speckled skin, who wears glasses on a nose that looks like an eagle's. I'm taller than any man I know." In a moment of confusion, she had to rethink that statement. "Except you." She went on with forced patience, "But I'm an honest woman, a smart woman. And I don't hold truck with a lot of lying falderal from some Cockney-Cornish womanizer who thinks he can talk his way out of being caught red-handed in the liquor shelf. If you wish to drink, you may go to the public house on the corner of the next block. Sit in the pub, drink till your heart's content, then come back when you are sober."

Goodness, she couldn't remember telling anyone off like that. Of course, she couldn't remember anyone trying to flatter her so dishonestly. The injustice of it made her angry. Surely there was something else she did right, something he could praise, without dragging her odd looks into the matter.

His face remained focused on her, furrowed with curiosity and consternation. He shook his head. "I didn't take a drop," he said. He smiled his crooked smile that, despite herself, was somehow appealing. A charming villain, this one. "Want to smell me breath?" he offered.

God, no. She took a step back.

He took a step closer, letting go of the doorjamb, coming through the doorway into the dim hall. He smelled of soap and something else, barber's talcum perhaps. Milton had taken some scissors to his hair. It was shorter, neater. Up close, with her standing there in her bare feet, he was tall enough that she had to bend her neck back to look up at him. She wanted to laugh: She felt short next to him. "I'm not pretty," she murmured.

His shadow, a silhouette with the room's light behind him, shook its head. As if speaking to a dim child with whom he was having difficulty communicating, he said, "Miss Bollash, we already know you be better with words than me. So all what I can tell you be this—"

His head bent toward her. No, he wouldn't, she thought, almost giddy now from the absurdities that ran through her head. He certainly wouldn't . . . well, no— Men had to know women well to do that, didn't they? So, no—

But, yes. Much to her dismay, her new student's moustache brushed her lip, then his mouth pressed to hers. The feel of his lips, the warmth that radiated off his face were such a surprise—a disarming surprise—it didn't leave her with the presence of mind to do anything. She just stood there befuddled. Being kissed.

Strange, what her first kiss, at the ripe old age of twenty-nine, brought to mind. Her first reaction was to cry. To just plain weep and wail. Damn you, she thought. Damn you. Don't play like this.

Her second thought, though, was to simply blank out the first thought. She said nothing, did nothing—half-waiting for him to laugh, to announce his funny joke on her, half-praying he would be kind about it: while one of the most elegant-looking men she had ever seen pressed his mustache, warm and dry, against her mouth.

It wasn't prickly at all. Not bristly. Not broom-like. It was soft. Cushiony. It moved gently with his mouth.

She backed away a little; he followed. She drew in a breath, though it sounded more like a hiccup of air than breathing. He caught her arm, pulling her toward him a little, his hand strong, warm, sure. The skin of her lips was more sensitive than she would have dreamed. His mouth was smooth against hers, and so soft—she would never have thought a man's mouth was so soft to touch, when the rest of him looked so hard and rough. As his mouth skimmed hers, she knew a tiny place on the curve of his lip where it was chapped. She could feel so much with her own mouth. Who could have imagined it was so . . . alive with feeling like this?

His thumb touched her cheek. She made a small jerk to realize his hand was at her face. Jumpy. Nervous. While pleasure materialized in the pit of her belly like smoke, wisps of it that became soft billows. The feeling was so keen and foreign, she didn't know what to do with it. His mouth stayed on hers till the clock

downstairs suddenly began to chime. *One, two, three*
... It awakened good sense. She jumped at *four*,
shoved away at *five*. It continued chiming, counting off
the moments till midnight, while her palm lay flat
against the chest she'd seen. Its predominant feeling
was hardness, as solid as a cliffside under the shirt.
And warm. His chest was several degrees warmer
where it provided resistance against her hand.

His face was close. "Ah," he said. "Yes." *Ace*, his
ridiculous *ace*. He nodded, as if he were agreeing with
something. "I was fair enough sure I'd like kissin'
you, and I do. You, Miss Winnie Bollash, are better
than pretty—"

Oh, the insult of his game. The hurt of it. Tears rose
up. She wanted to knock him down, to laugh, to cry.
Outwardly, though, she moderated herself, only pushing him back more firmly. She was, after all, the so-
phisticated one here, the one who was supposed to
teach him rules he didn't know to play by.

Her throat tightened around the words even as she
said them. "I want you to know"—she paused, gathering herself—"that I am not angry with you." Just
the bare bones, Edwina. Just make him stop. "Um, you
caught me off guard, Mr. Tremore. You can't do,
well—do what you just did. Don't ever do that again."
There. Hold to the rules, she thought, and all will be
fine. "It's not right. You can't do what you normally
do." Something made her add, "I'm not a shop girl
who can be flattered into believing nonsense, just because it suits your cheeky sense of fun."

He laughed. "Fun," he repeated, saying that particular word exactly right. "Miss Bollash, life be rich.
Why don't you bite yourself off a piece?"

She had no answer. Speaking to him in the middle
of the night in a dim hallway—about whether or not
he could kiss her—was like walking into an unfamiliar,
pitch-dark room. She wasn't sure which way to turn
without running into something, without hurting herself. Every direction was potentially unsafe.

His head bent. He was looking at her nightclothes.

As if her simply standing there in them was somehow provocative. Now *that* was an unusual feeling. It made her spine shiver. It made her heart beat in a panicky rhythm. The shadows of his shirt rose and fell, his chest making it move, a deep rising, falling. The sight sent such a shot of apprehension through her, her knees turned liquid.

She'd already told him once, and he wasn't stepping back. She burst out with, "I wouldn't be standing here in my nightclothes, Mr. Tremore, if you weren't prowling my house in the wee hours like a piece of Bow Bells riffraff, taking stock of what he can steal."

He cranked his head back. Light from the study cut across his shoulder, revealing a plane of his face: the look of insult. She regretted having said those precise words, yet couldn't think of different ones, better ones.

He tilted his head to look at her, then said quietly, "You can rest easy, lovey." *Loovey*, he said. "I ain't no thief. I work hard, and I be good at what I do."

She continued to be up in arms. "Not so good that you can keep yourself clean and in decent clothes."

His insulted expression softened into a kind of disappointment. He folded his arms over his chest, letting his weight fall against the edge of the door frame. "You be a snooty thing, ain't ya? Think you know everything there be to know about a bloke, because he don't talk like you, because he catches rats for a livin'—"

"I know a man too lazy to sew the buttons onto his coat. And who ends up being chased—"

He let out a single snort of laughter, loud enough to silence her. "First," he said, "who I be chasin' or who be chasin' me ain't none of your business." His face took on the shadows of his crooked smile before he added, "At least not yet. Second, the coats what I can afford don't right off have many buttons, and what buttons they do, I sell. See, I got ten younger brothers and sisters in Cornwall what depend on me to support them. I send most of me money home. And third— you will notice, I can count, by the way, all the way to *third*, and I can read, too, Public Education Act, you see. And third, loov, you ain't so funny to look at as you think. You be right nice to look at. True, you ain't pretty exactly, but you be—'' He struggled for the right word, frowned, looked down, then said, ''I can't explain it. I like lookin' at you.'' The dim light seemed to show him grinning again; it was hard to be sure. But there was wryness in his voice when he offered, ''Different. A long pretty thing with the face of a moppet. You be loovly, Miss Bollash.'' He repeated softly with satisfaction, ''Loovly.''

Lovely, he meant, of course, but the softness and rhythm in the way he said it struck her.

''Loovly,'' she repeated, saying it his way. Then laughed. She meant her laughter to be ironic, a hollow humor full of disdain. Her usual kind of laugh when confronted with her own looks. But despite herself, she felt genuine amusement. ''More on the long side though than the loovly side,'' she added.

''Well, long *and* loovly, yes.'' He laughed, too, possibly at her attempt at his word, at her saying it less naturally than he did.

He stood there, his chest reverberating with that low, base-drum sound again. While Edwina released herself into her own laughter, letting it out softly, letting it go till it ended of its own accord. The two of them slowly calmed till they were just looking at each other.

And there it was: For an instant, reality permutated. For an instant villainous black mustache and all—a handsome gentleman smiled on her. It seemed suddenly plausible that a man could find her appealing. In a loovly sort of way. Mind-boggling, but plausible.

Then a moment later she truly *did* want to burst out laughing. For here in the half-lit corridor, of course, was only mousy, lanky Winnie Bollash—being flattered by a ratcatcher who didn't know any better.

She sighed, both her smile and the nice feeling dissipating into that sure piece of truth. She stepped back, pulling her dressing gown up tight, wrapping her arms around herself. "Please don't go into the study. It was my father's."

"Your father's?"

"He's gone now. Dead."

"Sympathies, loov."

"Thank you." She nodded. "It was a while ago."

He hesitated a moment, only a moment, then said, "You should have the room then. Your father don't need it now."

Edwina looked away, as if around them she might see something besides the dark landing. "The whole house was his," she said. "I've taken over all the rest, made it my own, but I've left his study as it was." She murmured, "I use it as the masculine place to take my ladies, to show them how to be comfortable in a man's world." She laughed without humor. "A good joke, don't you think? I'm not very comfortable in such a world myself. Except in that room. My carefully preserved upper-class male habitat." Like a museum, she thought.

She'd said too much already. "Good night." She walked past him, into the study, ostensibly to put out the light. Then she thought to ask, "You have everything, yes?"

He nodded. The question, she realized, was just an excuse to look at him in better light. He stood just beyond the doorway in the corridor, partly in light, partly in shadow. The study's electric bulb threw sharp definition up the front of him: Her father's trousers were too short; they came to the top of his boots. Chances were, under the long shirttail, the trousers weren't buttoned. The vest without doubt couldn't be. No cravat, no collar.

None of this stopped Mick Tremore from being handsome, however. His jaw was square, chiseled. He had a straight, high-bridged nose—a Roman nose that, with his deep brow, shadowed his eyes like a ledge. He was striking, there was no doubt about it. Elegant, she thought again. Not just good-looking. Handsome in a polished way that defied explanation. The luck of heritage, an accident of features. Whatever made him so, it was a stroke of good fortune for her—and for Jeremy Lamont. It was much easier to pass a man off as a gentleman when he lined up with preconceptions of what a splendid one looked like.

Which, she realized, in another sense was not a stroke of luck for her at all.

"Good night," she said again.

She went into the study, but delayed pulling the chain on the light. She made herself dawdle, reshelving a book, realigning a vase. She didn't let herself look back at him, not once. Even though she knew he watched her, waiting. It was at least a full minute before she heard his footfalls turn then walk the short distance to his room at this end of the hall.

Good. Once he was gone, she put the light out, then went back to bed.

Edwina gave herself a good talking-to as she lay back down into her sheets.

He was lying. Don't believe him. Long and loovly, indeed. He was romanticizing, at the very least.

She herself was no romantic. She knew her own narrow face, the thin blade of her nose with its bony bump on the bridge that was fine for holding up her spectacles but did nothing for her womanly charms. She'd long ago given up on the freckles that covered her skin, from her face down her neck, right down her body over the tops of her toes. She had no breasts to speak of, while she had too much bottom to be symmetrical. And her height, well, it went without saying it was as far from feminine as was Gargantua.

Homely. Hopeless. How could any man look at her and even think to— She grew warm lying there in her bed, staring into the dark. To what?

Kiss her. He'd kissed her. Goodness, it was a night for saying things to herself she had never voiced before. *Kiss.* She sighed.

Why had he done that? Had she misinterpreted? Maybe it wasn't a kiss. Had her mouth looked dirty?

Had she looked as if she needed air? Was he trying to figure out how to say something by feeling the movement of her lips? Was there any reasonable explanation for Mr. Tremore to have touched her like that, put his mouth—his mustache—on her?

Lying there, she grew faintly frightened again—a state, it was safe to say, in which she lived almost perpetually. The only place Edwina felt utterly safe was downstairs in her laboratory, where she wasn't so much safe as lost to herself, unaware of anything else but her work. It didn't matter though. Tomorrow, like yesterday and the day before, she'd simply cover her fear by working hard, holding to the rules: immersing herself in the day and what ought to be done. All the while trying to quell worries like, What had she done to make him act like that? Would he ignore tonight tomorrow? Should she? Would he make fun of her now? Was he angry at her? She could have said things better. . . .

And if Mr. Tremore, or anyone at all, did any one of these things—ignored her or became angry or made fun—she felt responsible. She might spend weeks trying to figure out what she had done to deserve it. As if the next time, she could avoid the roughness of life by doing something differently herself.

Often, as now, she chastised herself—how spinsterish to agonize over what couldn't be controlled anyway—yet she couldn't stop her thinking. It was too old a habit. A superstition pounded into her from her youth: the belief that if she were just a good enough, smart enough girl, if she could just think about it long enough, she'd figure out the "right" thing to do, and then life would be kind to her.

No, a woman who looked like she did—who thought as she did—could not afford to be romantic. That was why Edwina was practical. And responsible. And hardworking.

And up all night thinking about what Mr. Tremore

had said and done and how sincere he had seemed when he said it and did it. And what could it possibly mean? And would he do it again? And did she want him to?

Chapter 5

❧

Mick stretched. He lay on a feather mattress. Sweet. Slowly, he lifted his eyelids, opening his eyes on shadows from bed curtains, a glow coming through their edges. It was a finer room than usual, but the light was the same as when he always woke up. Same time every day. Daybreak. No matter where he was, the sun found him and nudged him awake.

He swung his legs off the high bed, then had to step over Magic to walk to the window. He pushed open the shutters. The day's light poured in. It brought with it a lot of quiet. London at dawn was about as still as she ever got. Hardly a sound. A dog somewhere, not so lazy as Magic, barked far off. Nearby, a cart rolled on cobbles. Nothing else. Mick rested his palms on the wood sill, leaning straight-armed to look out.

Miss Bollash's back garden was damp with dew. Pretty. Her neighbors' houses were silent and still. No one. He loved this time of day—like he had the world to himself. Being alive felt good. Life was in order. It made sense.

Of course, he knew an hour from now he probably wouldn't feel the same. Most days usually fell apart, one way or another. But he knew, too, if he was alive at sunrise tomorrow the new morning'd feel like a gift. No noise in the day yet, no noise in his head.

Magic came over and bumped against Mick's leg.

The dog got his first scratch, while Mick rubbed the back of one knuckle down his mustache. It felt different on his face the way Milton trimmed it. Different, but all right. Miss Bollash sure wanted it off. Wasn't happening. It wouldn't earn him a shilling more to shave it. It wouldn't make him talk better, give him a better profession, wouldn't give him or his a better life in any way. So it stayed, because he liked it—he wasn't even certain he'd know himself without it. He'd had a mustache of one kind or another for a dozen years.

And taking it off would not make him more a gent, that was sure. Bloody hell, the Prince of Wales had one. Miss Bollash didn't want it off for that.

Standing there at the window, scratching Magic, it came to him: She wanted it off for herself.

He couldn't think why. But, well, well, well, he thought. It made him smile. She still couldn't have it off. But wasn't that just the most interesting thing now?

Down the hall, Edwina awakened with a lurch, her mind filling with consciousness and the day's worries simultaneously, like water down a slough. Before the day was even in focus before her eyes, she already had a pounding sense of everything to do and no time to do it. A normal morning. It was her habit, to gain control of her daily panic, to lay in bed and make lists, organize her concerns, tame them if she could with a plan—often an overambitious, overwhelming plan but nonetheless something to go by.

This morning, though, she lay there trying to dredge up the worry that had disturbed her sleep. What was it? Something new, something she hadn't thought of until her sleeping mind had hit upon it. What? What? She racked her brain.

Mr. Tremore. All her worst fears revolved around him, surely. What about him? She reviewed the worst that lay ahead. (Ignoring staunchly what worry of him that lay behind in a dim midnight hallway.) Changing his sound, his accent itself, was going to be the hardest work, though it could be changed; in time he could do it. His grammar and diction would be easier, though only slightly. Beyond these, he required regular coaching in acceptable upper-class social behavior, and they had to come up with a plausible background for him: enough detail to be convincing if anyone asked, to make him fit in, yet without filling in enough that people could verify specifics.

The new problem suddenly came to her. "O-o-oh," she groaned, throwing her arm up over her eyes. "Crumbs, crumbs, crumbs."

No matter what she did, no matter how well she coached him, after dinner on the night of the ball, the ladies would retire to the drawing room while the men had their port and cigars. She could offer him no help when it came to how gentlemen behaved on their own: She didn't know. He was going to have to invent his way along himself for as long as forty-five minutes.

Edwina was at the top of the upstairs landing when she first heard the laughter. It was faint but coming from below her in her own house. A laugh she had never heard before, though the voice in it sounded somehow familiar.

By the bottom of the stairs, she knew who it was. Her day-help who came to cook and clean, Monday through Friday: Mrs. Reed. The woman was laughing herself silly. The sound was coming from the serving kitchen off the dining room, a little half-kitchen where breakfast was prepared and served and where, years ago, banquets had been kept hot, course at a time. The laughter now was infectious, so round and rippling and from-the-belly it made Edwina's own mouth draw up as she imagined what might be the cause.

When she opened the door, though, she expected anything but what she saw: Mr. Tremore stealing a sausage over Mrs. Reed's head from her skillet. He complained it was hot, *yike*, as he popped it into his mouth, while the woman did battle for her sausages with a spatula. Mrs. Reed was wiping her eyes from laughing so hard. Mr. Tremore took another, letting out a triumphant crow, then bent, swooping the woman up, taking her into his arms.

"Oh, sir," the cook said in reprimand, though it was a reprimand that relished itself. He danced Mrs. Reed away from the stove, his cheek pressed to hers—which was saying something, since he had to bend down a good foot and a half to get it there. The cook was enjoying herself as Edwina had never imagined the woman could—Mrs. Reed was always so quiet with her.

Edwina stood there in the doorway, watching an alien merriment—nothing like she'd ever seen in her father's house, nothing that had ever existed in her own. While the source of it—an unexpectedly good dancer, if a person liked a two-step jig—led a woman around the kitchen to the rhythm of his own humming. Mr. Tremore's deep voice carried a clear tune. He moved well, guiding Mrs. Reed confidently, round and round, with her fussing with him to stop, as she laughed and rushed her feet after his to keep up.

Edwina frowned. The game seemed to be an ongoing invention of Mr. Tremore's. Part of her wanted to stop it; part of her was oh-so-curious to watch.

To stop it, of course, would make her the spoiler, and she already felt dour enough standing on the fringe. So the part of her that was curious watched and listened to laughter as it filled the close room. It made the little serving kitchen alive in a way she'd never have predicted. Its warming ovens, closed and dark, its bare shelves empty of the huge serving dishes they had once held—neither looked the worse today for disuse. The room's double window was thrown open, the flower box outside bursting with color, red and pink and yellow and coral coming over the sill. And there was Mr. Tremore dancing in the window's wide beam of sunlight.

The back of his vest, a silvery green, was bowed so he could wrap his long, white-shirted arm around the waist of a woman who was head-and-shoulders shorter and several feet wider, not to mention more than twice his age. His black hair shone silky and soft in the light, sharp against the white of his collar.

His clothes from Henley's had arrived apparently. Everything fit. All was new and better in quality than what her butler had found for him last night. And all quite suited Mr. Tremore. She could have believed, standing here watching him, that he was perhaps an easygoing country gentleman—there were such things. Men who remained in their native counties, landowners who talked like the locals—she knew because she occasionally trained their daughters to speak more like the *ton* if they wished to go a Season in London.

Mr. Tremore saw Edwina and slowed.

Mrs. Reed caught on and looked over her shoulder. In the end, Edwina didn't have to say a thing. Her presence alone was enough to end the amusement. Her cook and houseguest let go of each other, parting, straightening. Mrs. Reed began to make apologies, clearing her throat. She set the spatula down and adjusted her apron.

"It's all right," Edwina said, though she couldn't decide how she felt about what she'd witnessed. It was silliness, foolish enough that they were both embarrassed to be caught at it. It was nothing. It accomplished nothing. Yet she envied their lighthearted good time.

She wished she could think of anything to say but what she felt she must: "Mr. Tremore should have his meals in the dining room, all the proper silver set out. We'll do full service, at least until he catches on and is comfortable with it. Could you ask Milton to serve, please, Mrs. Reed?"

"Yes, miss."

A positively stupid thought came to mind as Mrs. Reed waddled out to get Milton: Mr. Tremore had kissed the woman. Not out of passion or lust, God forbid. No, but a bussed cheek, a peck; either was possible. Even likely. And both were aggravating somehow to envision. This overly curious, probably dishonest Cockney-Cornish ratcatcher certainly liked the ladies. Inside of twenty-four hours, with only two women under the same roof, the odds were he'd kissed them both. The skinny spinster and the heavyset cook.

He wasn't very particular, Edwina thought.

Mr. Tremore said nothing as she led him out into the dining room. "You sit here," she said, touching the high-backed chair opposite hers. When he went to sit in it though, she added, "After you hold my chair for me."

He came around. As she sat, he murmured from behind, "We was just havin' fun."

"I know."

He went back around a table more than twenty feet long. Once it had held a line of elaborate candelabra, bowls of flowers, platters of food. Once the dozen chairs on his side, the other dozen on hers, had been filled regularly with guests. Mr. Tremore sat opposite her, into one of the empty chairs, and eyed her.

He explained further, "She don't understand what I say every time. You be the only one here who does."

"So you had to dance with her?"

"She knew stealing sausages. I was telling her I liked the smell of her cooking."

"I see." She tried to. Yet there seemed any number of other ways to convey one's appreciation. She didn't dance with people over sausage, no matter how delicious it was.

They said nothing more till the porridge arrived, then he picked up the wrong spoon.

"The larger one," she said.

He frowned down at the mass of silverware surrounding the plate, as if it were a riddle of metal and shape. Good, she thought, for no explicable reason. He found the porridge spoon, picked it up.

"No," she said. He held it wrong. She got up from the table, came around, and took it out of his fist.

Frowning, he gave his fingers up to her, relaxing them completely into her ministration. She found her-

self in sudden, disconcerting possession of a man's
willing hand. Large, warm, heavy. Smooth-fingered. A
strong hand with neat joints. That hadn't the first idea
how to balance a spoon. She quickly put the instrument
into his correct grasp.

As she sat down again, she pressed her palms once—
they'd grown damp—onto the starchy-dry linen of her
napkin in her lap, then she looked across the table.

He was still holding the spoon out, staring at how
she'd wrapped his fingers around it, a look of distress
on his face.

After this, breakfast was silent.

Mr. Tremore picked up a corner of leftover toast
from his plate. Porridge had been followed by eggs,
tomatoes, and sausages with fried bread. He'd eaten a
good bit, though Edwina had the feeling he'd have
eaten more if getting the food into his mouth hadn't
been such an ordeal. The utensils had proved frustrat-
ing.

By the end, Edwina had let him be. Better he had
half a lesson and ate something.

She only wished she could make him more realistic.
When she mentioned her fear regarding his being alone
with the gentlemen after dinner on the night of the ball,
he said, "Won't be a problem." With the toast he
mopped up the remnants of eggs and tomato as efficiently as if no one would wash the plate between here
and dinner. "I'll listen," he said, "and see what all
the other blokes get 'emselves into."

"Nothing," she said. "Gentlemen don't get themselves into anything. That's what makes them gentlemen."

He was going to argue, but, as if he thought better
of it, he picked up his knife from his plate. He reached
for the jam—

"No, the spoon."

He exchanged the knife for the spoon, then used it
to scoop out jam, after which he flipped the spoon over

to spread jam with the back. "Then I won't say anything either."

"Well, they talk about *something*. Put the spoon
down—you use the knife to spread it."

He shot her a contrary frown, as if she were in-
venting all this just to confound him. He answered,
"Whatever they do, I'll do."

"They may ask you questions."

"I'll answer 'em."

"No, no." She shook her head. He didn't take her
concern as seriously as he should, acting as if it were
little more than a few details he'd pull together when
the time came. "It's a time when men relax," she tried
to explain. "They drink brandy and smoke cigars and,
oh—" What did they do exactly? She didn't know.
They behaved like men. With frustration, she said,
"You're liable to answer like a—a ratcatcher—"

He laughed. "It be fact that I will. But I'll talk
pretty, as pretty as you show me, and no one'll know
the difference. Gents ain't as smart as all that, truth be
known. And you got rats."

"Excuse me?" Edwina frowned at him.

"You got rats," he repeated. "In your house or
nearby."

"I do not."

"Yes, you do. Not many, not a problem yet—not
so you see them unless you know what to look for.
But you got a hole in a corner baseboard over there,
and you got sounds under the floorboards. I be tellin'
you: There be a nest of them somewhere."

"Oh, fine," she said, tossing her napkin onto her
plate. The gentlemen she knew were all easily smart
enough to pick out a ratcatcher among them if he
started talking about noises under the floorboards.
"You have to stop thinking—talking—like a ratcatcher, Mr. Tremore."

She felt unappreciated—keen to improve him, while
he seemed to dispute her changes were even improvements. She told him, "This is more than an adventure:
more than a month of sporting about in fine clothes. It

could change your life forever, make it better.''

"It could make it different," he contradicted. "Maybe better, maybe not." He lifted his chin enough that his eyes came out of the shadow of his brow.

Fair, level eyes. It made her nervous to meet them. She glanced down, focusing on the table as he reached for the jam again. He mounded more on his last corner of toast—he did it just right, the spoon, then the knife.

His hands were surprisingly graceful. They weren't calloused as one might have expected, though his left was scared, the marks of a bite. They were aesthetic hands, attractive, with long, straight fingers. Unlike her own funny digits that thickened at the joints and turned slightly up at the tips. She stared at her hands in her lap.

"You want that I do somethin' about it?"

She jerked, looked. "About what?"

"The rats," he said brightly. "For free. No charge."

"No." She pressed her lips between her teeth, then remembered to say, "Thank you. No, thank you." She took a breath. "You have to begin to think like a viscount, Mr. Tremore. What would a viscount see if he were sitting here? Not a hole in the floorboard."

He snorted. "I hate to tell you, loovey, but from where I be sittin', unless he be blind, he'd see a hole, a hole what, if it didn't make him think of rats, he'd be stupid." He shrugged genially, as if the next were an earnest concession. " 'Course," he said, "I think a good many gents be as bloody stupid as blocks, so you could be right."

She frowned, shaking her head. It was the bath all over again. She wanted to pick him up and dunk him, headfirst, in English upper-class manners and vocabulary and sounds. While he sat there, his mind heavily entrenched in his own ways; rough, uncouth, unmovable.

She pushed back from the table. "Fine," she said. She sighed as she stood up. "Meet me in my lab, if you will. Please hurry. I have a student at noon, and you and I have a lot to do.''

She felt as if they had a mountain to level, with only a porridge spoon held correctly to do it.

Chapter 6

❧

$\mathcal{M}$r. Tremore failed all morning. Then he failed all afternoon till tea. Failure, of course, was a difficult thing for anyone. Edwina tried to tell him that to get very little right at first was quite normal, yet it seemed particularly hard on him.

He balked at recording his vowels and consonants on a gramophone-recorder. Why record them until they were right? She explained the need for a record of progress. While he maintained that saying things into a machine—wrong, he emphasized—only made him feel like "a blewdy ahrss."

The best that could be said for the day was that he got to where he could *hear* himself being wrong.

"This is real progress, Mr. Tremore."

He didn't believe it. He'd expected perhaps to speak like a "gent" by the end of the afternoon. When, instead, by the end of the afternoon he spoke like a man becoming—necessarily—self-conscious about each sound he uttered.

That evening after dinner, Jeremy Lamont paid a call, no doubt to inspect how the odds on his bet were shaping up. He asked a few pointed questions, asked to see the furnishings he and his brother had provided Mr. Tremore, then wanted to observe the lessons themselves, hear Mr. Tremore speak. Edwina and Mr. Tremore accommodated him, of course, but she could have told him that in one day no miracles would happen.

"And when might his progress be noticeable?" Mr. Lamont asked.

"It's noticeable now, but not to you," she told him. "There is little you can do. Why don't you visit, say, during the fifth week, the week before the ball. You will get a very good idea then whether Mr. Tremore is able to learn a sufficient amount for your purposes."

Mr. Lamont asked a few more questions, mostly about "tricks" to make Mr. Tremore "seem more genteel," then left.

Not so unusual really. A client paying attention. To be expected. Yet his visit left Edwina uneasy.

Then again, she told herself, she was always uneasy about something. Perhaps she just had a lot on her mind. She was still finagling her finances to pay for a new coal furnace. A carriage horse had a tendon problem that was taking money and time. Her bank's balance on her account was different from hers, and she hadn't been able to figure out why. So what was so different about today's uneasiness? She would have thought she'd be used to the state of mind by now.

At the end of the day, Edwina had a habit she used sometimes to calm herself. Perhaps once or twice a week, it was her secret that she carried a pitcher of water to her evening primroses that grew wild at the back of her garden behind her house. The plants bloomed at night, so, if anyone asked, she was outside to see them, to smell them, and of course to nurture them. But in fact she nurtured them in a way she would have been hard pressed to explain to anyone.

She liked to go out and sing to them. Oh, it wasn't really even singing. She couldn't carry a tune very well. She hummed in rhythm to words she whispered as she confided her worries to the primroses and the night.

"The Misters Lamont, la, la, even the nicer one, are so strange," she sang. "But they pay their way, and I shouldn't complain.'' She sang some more, about the bill for the coal furnace and the horse with the limp, then moved on to Mr. Tremore's retroflexed R's. She was just working up the courage to sing on a more personal theme regarding Mr. Tremore, when from the dark another voice off to her right suddenly, quietly joined in.

She jumped, drew back. It was Mr. Tremore himself. He was on the bench under the wisteria, sitting in the shadows.

She didn't hear what he sang at first; she was too busy cringing, trying to figure out an explanation. There was none. She withdrew to the shadows, silent, utterly silent, the only safety she knew while she waited for him to berate her.

He stood up more into the light, and his voice became clearer. ''I hope, la, la, he's taking good care of my dogs, la, la . . .''

He was imitating her, making fun of her, she thought. Inside, Edwina died a little. Her throat tightened and her stomach grew hot, as if it were trying to digest something thick and burning.

Never had anyone caught her in this childish consolation. She couldn't even rally enough defense to demand why he was out here in the dark himself. What was he doing roaming her house—and now the grounds to her house—in the dead of night?

She wanted to hide when he stepped fully from the shadows, his handsomeness itself assailing her. So innocently, he came into the moonlight of her back garden, his white shirt brighter than the moon itself, his face shadowed and planed.

''I did drills today, la, la, that was too hard and my tongue wouldn't do right,'' he said.

She frowned. He wasn't smiling. He didn't seem to be taunting her. Yet . . . no, it couldn't be. She didn't trust her own judgment.

Yet he appeared to be trying her plant-singing out.

He sang his own song to the plant and the stars and the dark, his tune echoing hers, though his voice carried the rhythm into more of a melody. With his hand, he rustled the leaves of the hedge that shaded the primroses, as she had. Then, stranger still, he looked at her and sang the words to her.

To her.

"I hope tomorrow is easier, and I get something right," he sang, his words so soft that she had to strain to hear them.

Edwina didn't know how to react to his appropriating of her foolishness. She said nothing.

He stopped. They stared at each other. He opened his mouth as if to speak.

But all she could do was turn quickly and walk toward her back door.

She didn't want him to explain or make excuses, if he was being kind. If he was being something else, she didn't want to know.

Mick watched as the tall woman with delicate-like feelings marched away. The moon was just behind the house, so he saw her only for a few seconds before she fell into house's shadow. She was movement in the dark, then the latch of her back door clicked, and she was gone.

Begger me, he thought, but she was an easy girl to chase away. What an odd one Win was.

She sang to the moon. Or to plants or to something out here. She wouldn't sing to him, even though he'd invited her to. He didn't think he would ever see anything more tender or sad than the way she told her problems to no one: to leaves. And he couldn't think of anything more brave than carrying on anyway with a such a load. She was strong, Winnie Bollash. As strong a woman as he knew. Capable-like.

And the most vulnerable creature he'd ever met.

Chapter 7

*T*hey spent all the next day doing tests. It was late in the evening when they began the last of these, with Edwina striking a tuning fork into vibration. "Tell me when the sounds stops for you."

She went to touch it behind Mr. Tremore's ear, but he pulled back sharply. "What you be doin'?"

"It's a hearing test. Though let's fix some of your grammar while we do it. Two birds with one stone. I'd like you to stop using *be* with every pronoun—"

"Every what?"

"It doesn't matter. It's not *What you be doing*. It's *What are you doing*. You *are*, we *are*, I *am*, he or she *is*."

He wasn't listening. He tilted his head, watching her, frowning as she bounced the tuning fork again in her palm.

She reached toward him. "Say when you stop hearing it—"

He drew back again the moment the fork touched his mastoid. "What you got there?"

She paused, looked across the table at him. "It's a way of testing your hearing. Everything I have to teach you is based on your ability to hear it, so I have to be sure you can hear what I say."

He pulled his mouth to the side, slanting his mustache. "So I could do this wrong, too? Hear things wrong?"

"No." She laughed. "You could have poor hearing, I suppose, but there would be nothing you could do about it."

He interpreted her answer as yes, he could fail here, too. He shook his head, then caught her hand when she reached to touch him again with the tuning fork. He said, "Let's do somethin' else. Let's talk. That's what you said we'd be doin' a lot of." From nowhere, he said, "Milton says you be gentry. Are you a"—he hesitated—"a baroness or somethin'?"

"No." What in the world? "I have no title." Then, yes, she thought. Conversation to distract him. Absently, she corrected herself as she set the fork humming again. "Oh, I'm still technically, I suppose, Lady Edwina Bollash, daughter of the sixth Marquess of Sissingley." He withdrew slightly, but let her put the fork on his bone. "Say, will you, when it stops humming."

After a few seconds, he nodded.

She quickly put the fork to her own ear. Nothing. "Good," she said, then struck it again, holding it this time to her ear first, continuing. "When my father died, someone else inherited the marquisate. I don't use the courtesy title. There's no point." At her ear, the hum of the tuning fork faded.

She quickly moved the instrument toward Mr. Tremore. "Do you hear any—" She went to take his chin as she did with her lady students, but as her fingers grazed his jaw the feeling of stubble—more than a dozen hours beyond a shave—startled her somehow. She withdrew her hand, lowering it, burying it in her skirt as she stopped the tuning fork against her bosom. For a moment, the fork hummed against her chest.

She sat there a little bit taken aback. She'd done this a thousand times. It was quite ordinary.

"What?" he asked.

"Sorry." She shook her head, laughing nervously, and struck the fork again. "Let's have another go at that. Tell me if you hear anything when I touch it behind your ear."

They were both silent as she performed the second

part of the test, this time without touching his chin. It went smoothly.

"Good," she reported again.

"You was rich?" he asked.

She lifted her eyes to him. "Pardon?"

"When your father was alive, you was rich?"

"My father was. But I'm not poor now."

"I can see that. But I can see your house ain't what it was. Was it ever fancy and right?"

She pondered the question. Right. Was this house ever right? "I suppose. Though the really fine one is—well, you'll see it. It's where the Duke of Arles holds his annual ball now: in the house where I was born, my family's old estate."

"The duke inherited your house?" The look on Mr. Tremore's face said he could hardly believe that fact.

She could hardly believe it herself some days. Still, twelve years later, she'd wake up some mornings and be surprised all over again that Xavier had everything, all she'd ever known growing up, while she had ended up here, a place she had only visited in her youth, a house in which she had only ever spent the night when her father had made trips to London, because he had papers to present.

She picked up a smaller tuning fork, struck it. "You'll tell me please again when you no longer hear the sound."

When she reached toward him, he caught her hand, taking the fork from her. "What happened to your old house?"

He was delaying after a long day of strange procedures and drills, all of which he'd trudged through but disliked. She answered anyway, mostly to be done with it, to be past the awkward questions. "Exactly as you said: When my father died the next male in line inherited his title, that person being my father's cousin. He wasn't a duke yet. That came three days later, when my grandfather, the fourth Duke of Arles, died, too. My cousin Xavier inherited it all. He became the Duke of Arles as well as Marquess of Sissingley and a host of lesser honors.'' She shrugged. ''Quite normal. Lines pass through their firstborn sons.'' Indeed. Daughters of marquesses married to acquire land and money, only she hadn't.

Here was as far as she ever went aloud. Her history embarrassed her. She murmured, ''Please give that to me.'' She held out her hand for the tuning fork.

Mr. Tremore watched her a moment, then struck the tines on his palm as she'd done. He held it to his ear, listened, then handed it back, tines first. When she grasped it, her fingers vibrated.

Within the hour, they finished up the last of the initial record-keeping and testing and began in earnest on articulation. Which left Mr. Tremore really at sea. They'd hardly started when he wanted to quit.

''I ain't used to bein' wrong at anything so much as you say I be here.''

She could have countered that she wasn't used to a lot of what was happening either. A man in her house. Tuning forks handed back to her, humming. A student who leaned back on the rear legs of his chair and twitched a big, bristly mustache at her every time she said something he didn't want to hear.

She told him anyway, ''It's to be expected that you'll say everything wrong at first. We're *looking* for what you say wrong. You just have to keep at it.'' She explained, ''To learn a new sound, we'll steep your ears in it. You listen and listen, then try it. I observe the movement of your lips and jaw, infer the position of your tongue and palate, the openness of your throat passage. By watching, I can often tell you what you're doing wrong, then help you get your organs of speech into the right position to produce the desired sound.''

He smiled slightly at the term *organs of speech*. It was a game to him. He was bored.

She felt lost, a woman swimming in knowledge she didn't know how to get into him. She continued, ''Occasionally I won't be able to tell by simply looking why your pronunciation is off. But there are other means of determining the problem. For throat sounds, for instance, there's the laryngoscope." She opened the table drawer and produced a small mirror fixed obliquely to a handle.

He glanced at it, and his smile became unsure, a half-smile of misgiving.

"You see, I hold this inside your mouth at the back and reflect a ray of light down your throat. This way, I can see in the mirror just how your throat is opening and closing."

He laughed uncomfortably, but kept listening.

"I can also objectively tell the positions of your tongue by exploring your mouth with my fingers—"

"Wait." He held up his hand, chortling now. "You gonna be puttin' your fingers in me mouth?"

"Perhaps. Most likely, just my little finger against your gum so I can feel the position of your tongue."

His eyebrows drew up at that. He leaned back in his chair, folding his arms across his chest, smiling, shaking his head. "Well, this be gettin' good."

"*Is,*" she said. "This *is* getting good."

"Bloody right, it is."

She squinted. *Is.* He used it correctly. But he had the wrong idea. "We'll see if you still feel that way after the palatagraphic."

"That'd be what?"

"*What is that?*" she advised.

"All right, what is that?"

"A thin artificial palate that goes into your mouth with some chalk dust on it. You say a sound, then I infer the position of your tongue on your palate from the contact marks."

"So you're gonna be in my mouth a lot tonight? Do I got that right?"

Impatiently, she told him, "Mr. Tremore, I'm not used to your bawdy suggestions with regard to what is my job and a serious business—"

"Bawdy?"

"Vulgar. Indecent."

"I know what *bawdy* means," he said. "I just be surprised you find me enjoyin' your finger in me mouth vulgar. You be the one puttin' it there.'' He shook his head, laughing at her. ''You know, loovey, what men and women get up to ain't indecent. It's about the most decent thing on the English island. Even the good Queen went at it. The whole world knows she was keen for Albert, and she got nine children, so that many times at least.''

Edwina was unable to say anything for a moment. Nothing seemed more inappropriate than his implicating the Queen in one of his ribald digressions. ''Sir,'' she said, ''I don't know where to begin in telling you that what m-men''—she actually stammered—''men and women g-get up to—''

''Easy, loov. You be a virgin, I know that.'' He said it without batting an eyelash, as if this presumption of his, all the more annoying for being accurate, were supposed to console her.

Edwina opened her mouth, shut it, didn't know what to say for a good half a minute. Finally, she told him, ''Gentlemen, sir, don't speak of such things.''

He looked at her, tilting his head. With his arms crossed, his vest pulled across the back of his shoulders. Then he raised one arm off the vest and stroked his mustache, once, twice, with the back of his knuckle. ''That be a fact?''

''Yes,'' she insisted.

''I bet gentlemen know the word *virgin.*''

''Well, yes''—she struggled a moment—''I'm sure they do. But they don't say it.''

He leaned toward her a little. ''Then how to do they learn it? Someone says it.''

Edwina pressed her lips together, a little annoyed, a little turned-around. ''Well, they probably say it among other gentlemen—''

''This mornin' you told me you didn't know what gentlemen talked about when they be alone.''

''I don't.'' She couldn't find her bearings in the stupid conversation. ''So this must be one of the topics,'' she said quickly, ''since they certainly don't speak of it around ladies. May we get back to the lesson now?''

"Suit yourself.'' He shrugged. "Looks like we got somethin' for me to say at least in a few weeks, when the ladies leave after dinner. I'll just open the conversation up with virgins.''

She stared at him. A second later—one heartstopping second later—she realized he was having her on, teasing her. His mouth drew up in that lopsided way it had, a full, toothsome smile that dimpled only one cheek.

Edwina didn't know whether to be offended or not. She could hardly credit it. Normally, she hated to be tormented. Yet she didn't feel hurt now. It made her feel . . . warm . . . foolish but not unpleasant. He'd somehow managed the miracle of turning her upside down, just for fun, without making her feel bad about it.

He grinned wider, then took her deeper into confusion. "You ain't never known a man, I know that. Not even kissed many.''

What an outrageous—"One," she said, "you," then wished she hadn't. It called attention to the fact that no one else had ever wanted to, not even for the silliest, most lighthearted of reasons.

But that wasn't how he took it.

Mr. Tremor's expression changed. It became genuinely taken aback. He dropped his teasing mien and looked straight at her. Very seriously, he said with amazement in his voice, "Well, beggar me. That be just plain sweet, Miss Bollash. I feel right proud you let me.''

She was too surprised to give his words the horselaugh they deserved. She sat there for several stupefied seconds before she found the refuge she knew best: speech. "Now, you see, Mr. Tremore," she said, "it would be better if you didn't say *beggar me* anymore.''

He tilted his head, frowning slightly. "Wha'd'you want me to say?''

"Try: 'I'm astonished.' ''

He laughed, though at the end, still smiling, he raised one brow—a look that certainly could have passed for ironic amusement—and said, "All right: I'm astonished."

He repeated the words exactly as she'd said them, so naturally and perfectly she was without response for a second. "Yes." She blinked and looked down. "Yes, that's right."

Then he really took her breath away. He murmured, "*You* astonish me."

Edwina looked up, frowning, squinting like a woman trying to understand the mechanism of a trick, a sleight of hand. Well-dressed, sitting there with his white-sleeved arm folded across his dark-vested chest, Mick Tremore looked so much the part: the English lord. With his sounding the part, too, well—he stopped her in her tracks. As if all this talk about catching rats and Cornwall were the false part, the real part being what sat before her: a confident, well-dressed fellow whom she'd managed to astonish.

Oh, this was awful. It was painful. She couldn't keep doing it. And it was only the beginning. She had to find a way to make him stay who he was, for herself to see him properly and stop catching glimpses of this other man, this ghostly . . . what? viscount? who could inhabit his skin.

Her mouth went dry. Her skin grew hot. For several seconds Edwina looked at an English lord with graceful hands, one finger of which he used to stroke an unusually thick mustache in what was coming to be a characteristic gesture. Sometimes he did it with the back of his knuckle, sometimes with the inside of his finger as now. In either event, it always made him look pensive. Pensive and faintly wicked. She remembered how surprising it felt, soft and coarse, both, when it touched her mouth.

Oh, dear. Edwina lowered her eyes and put her hand to her throat, her palm circling her own neck, her collar, where her fingers found tiny steel beads on tulle over silk. An old dress. A dress made as stylish as

possible again. A dress bought when the idea of courting was still a ridiculous possibility. When she'd had
money and consequently had the interest of suitors.

What had she been saying? She couldn't remember.
It was no use. There was no getting back to what
they'd been talking about before all this, no getting
back to whatever it was she'd been trying to accomplish. She sat there staring at a tuning fork on the table.
Inside, she felt like that, as if someone had lightly
struck her and now she resonated from the contact,
vibrating with something she didn't understand, that
wasn't visible, yet that worked on her from the inside
out while she fiddled with the beads on her collar.

Beyond the windows of the room, it had grown quite
dark. The night, opaque at the glass, reflected the room
back on itself. Only a distant street lamp indicated anything existed outside her laboratory. It was late. She
didn't usually work so long. A bad idea. Time to call
an end to it. They'd do better tomorrow.

"Well," she said. "That's enough, I think." She
stood shakily. Her knees felt weak. "I think we should
go to bed now."

As the words left her mouth, and Edwina heard
them, she thought, No, I didn't say that. Not aloud.
Mr. Tremore lowered his eyes. Or she thought he did;
his eyes fell into the shadow of his deep, jutting brow.
"I think we should go to bed, too," he said.

She blinked, frowned, swallowed. She wanted to
snap at him, chastise him—for what? For saying exactly what she had just said. Only he didn't mean it as
she had. He was being—

What?

She'd assume he wasn't. Pretend he wasn't. Excuse
yourself, Winnie. Go to bed.

Only, for the life of her, she couldn't. Her arms, her
legs wouldn't move. Instead, heat rose up into her face
as if the door to a furnace had opened. Her cheeks,
neck, shoulders grew hot from an embarrassment she
couldn't contain. She'd said something risqué. Accidentally.

Mr. Tremore said nothing. He remained quiet. She was now, presumably, supposed to be grateful for his silence.

Fine. She attempted to speak. "W-well, yes, we may, um, could—" She swallowed wrong, choked. Her eyes teared instantly. Edwina found herself caught in mortified coughs and stammers, then was further obliged to feel, grudgingly, out-and-out indebted as Mr. Tremore took over, making excuses for her.

"A slip of the tongue, loov. It can embarrass the best of us. It's all right. I know what you meant."

Their eyes met, held. How odd. His angular brow or perhaps her own discomfort in meeting his eyes for very long had kept the color of his eyes a secret till this moment. She'd known they were fair, but they were more than fair. They were green. Not a hazel, but a true, fair beryllium green, steel-gray green around a black pupil, the iris ringed in a thin line of dark, vivid mossy green. Stunning eyes. Another detail she would just as soon not be aware of.

She was developing a schoolgirl infatuation for a ratcatcher.

Well, she simply wouldn't allow it. Though her body demonstrated that some things could not be controlled: The bright embarrassment in her face spread down her arms, her body. Everywhere. She must have looked apoplectic, because the object of her discomposure reached across the table and patted her hand, then gently squeezed the backs of her fingers—his were strong and warm, sure of themselves.

He said, "Go on to bed now, loovey. I won't even walk up with you. You be doin' all right, Winnie. A good girl. Just a little shook up. It'll be okay in the mornin'. When you come down, I'll be sittin' at breakfast nice as you please—no dancin' with Molly Reed this time."

Molly Reed? Was this Mrs. Reed's first name? If so, Edwina had never heard it till this moment.

She felt momentarily disoriented. As if he were unearthing startling objects, dropping them before her, out of familiar terrain, terrain that was her own.

Oh, enough, she thought. She was about to take what was offered, a clean exit.

But Milton interrupted. He came to the door. "Is everything all right, m'lady?"

"Yes." She frowned around at him, a plea for rescue.

As if nothing were amiss, he went on. "I took Mrs. Reed home. Her son's horse threw a shoe. I've locked up. Is there anything else you need?"

She shook her head. If there was, she couldn't define it well enough to ask for it.

"Oh," Milton added, "and the dresses from the seamstress arrived early this evening. I put the box on the table in your sitting room."

She nodded. What dresses? Oh, yes.

As if in echo, across from her a voice asked, "What dresses?"

"What?" She looked down.

Mr. Tremore's smile was gone, replaced by a strange, quizzical look. "New dresses?"

"No, old ones." She shook her head; it was of no consequence. "Brought up to date."

"Where?"

"Pardon me?"

"Where did you have 'em fixed?" It was apparently of consequence to him.

She frowned, wet her lips. "The seamstress's, Milly-something, off Queen's Gate." She remembered he knew at least the shop assistant there and couldn't resist asking, "How well do you know the ladies of that shop? Are they friends of yours?" *Until yesterday*, she wanted to add.

He didn't say yea or nay, though, only sitting back in his chair to stare at her, his attention so unwavering it could only be called rude.

After a moment, he shook his head, smiling slightly, shook his head some more, then looked down. He seemed almost embarrassed. Well, there was a change. *He* looked discomposed. One strange outcome for certain: He tried to speak, then couldn't. The man who loved talk was completely without words.

Chapter 8

ℳick spent the better part of the next week gawking at Winnie Bollash's skirts, half-hoping his stares would burn a hole through them. God knew, for all that was going through his head—while he ogled the way the fabric of her skirts moved when she crossed her legs or when she stood or sat or stretched her long self out—hell, if a man's hot thoughts and stares counted for anything, her skirts should've bloody well been on fire by now.

They sat side by side today in her laboratory. He was going through a drill of vowels—she'd given him a pencil to point down the page, so he could follow along, sound at a time, with what she'd written out. He was supposed to mark the sounds he thought he was ready to record for the stupid gramophone.

Lessons. They'd been going at all kinds of tricks Winnie Bollash knew to make a man talk different, ten and twelve hours a day for a week. They'd had things in his mouth. Her taking notes. Him saying sounds that weren't even words. Or sitting alone much of the time repeating exercises for so long, that were so boring, even Magic got up and left.

They worked at a table together now, her to his right, to his left a tall window that looked out onto the front street of her fine London neighborhood. For eight days, he'd woke up in the same bed, each day surprised to find himself there, each day amazed anew to get up and walk around a house where, from any window a man looked, he could see tall houses made of brick, clean glass blinking at their windows, flower boxes, trees neatly shaped, hedges, iron gates. He didn't feel like he belonged here, that he deserved this life—who did? he wondered—but he was happy that, for a change, the injustice of life was working for him, not against him.

He tapped the pencil on the page, looking at the sounds he was supposed to be saying to himself. He should've mentioned they were written out in a way that didn't make much sense to him. He was bored. He'd spent the morning on *is*'s, *am*'s, and *are*'s, *was*'s, and *were*'s. Yesterday, *ing*'s and *th*'s. He couldn't keep them all straight. He was ready for some amusement to break up the dreariness.

Winnie looked at him, at his hand tapping the pencil. His heart gave a little leap. She was going to talk to him. He loved to talk to her. He liked the sound of her, the way her voice was soft and classy, smooth and fine. He liked the words she used and how she used them.

The words she used this time though, as she glanced over the tops of her eyeglasses, were: "You should really shave your mustache, Mr. Tremore. It doesn't have the refined air we are trying to cultivate for you."

He rolled his eyes, but she didn't see. She went back to writing. Bloody hell. She had only told him a dozen times to take a razor to the fine growth of hair on his lip. "I like it," he muttered.

He watched her touch the tip of her pen to her tongue to make the ink flow better. Without looking at him, she said, "It's not stylish."

"It's thick. Not many men can grow a mustache like it."

"Not many men would want to."

"Oh, I don't know about that." He touched the hair that grew under his nose. "It's funny, though, you think you got the right to get rid of it, like you can reach over and tweak my lip. Kind of brassy of you, when you think about it.''

She looked up from her writing, her pen stopped over the page. ''Brassy?''

''Full of yourself. Cocky, you know?''

She squinched up her face like she could, then laughed not unkindly, which made him feel a little bad. ''I'm not the least bit''—she paused—''brassy, as you put it.''

He was being testy, he knew, but he just felt . . . itchy or something lately. ''Well, no,'' he conceded. ''You're a nice woman. Gentle-like. You mean well. But you sure think you run everything.''

''Ha.'' She put the pen down and looked at him. ''I don't think anything of a sort. If I run anything, it's my own legs. I'm usually running as fast as I can, figuratively at least. I'm scared most of the time.'' She made another face, sheepish, like she wished she hadn't admitted it. He liked her face, its funny features that could move so many ways, bend. She had a thousand expressions.

But one predominant state of mind. He said, ''Scared 'cause the world ain't working to your plan. Scared someone's gonna find out and blame you for it.''

''That's not true. And it's *isn't*.''

''What?''

''*Pardon*?''

''Oh.'' She was fixing him again. *Isn't*. Right. He said, ''Scared we all isn't falling into your line.''

''*Aren't*.''

Mick stopped talking, finding a back tooth to push his tongue against, twisting his mouth. Twisting his mustache at her. Stupid. All these different words for the same thing.

He pitched the pencil onto the sheets of paper in front of him. It tapped end over end once, making a light mark, then clattered still. He sighed. ''All I can say, loov, is it must be hell running the whole blooming place. Especially when so much of it depends on things that are about as dependable as, oh, just one damn roll of the craps after another.''

Whatever he was trying to tell her, Edwina didn't understand it. Though she knew, when he made a faint grin and lifted his eyebrows at her, he was trying to jolly her out of any offense.

He picked up his pencil again, flipping it over in his hand, playing with it, then beat on the edge of the table. *Tap tap tap tap.* . . . He kept the rhythm going lightly as he said, '' 'Course the chanciness is damn exciting, you gotta admit.'' He threw her an unaccountable smile. "Like now. Either of us could do *any*-thing in the next second.''

It was involuntary; she drew back. More of the capricious philosophies of Mr. Mick Tremore. She was always dodging them.

She might or might not, she thought, have him speaking and acting like a viscount by the end of next month, yet she had come to believe quite firmly that Mr. Tremore could grab hold of the lapels of a regius professor of philosophy on the street, expound in his face on one amusing topic after another, then let the fellow go, dizzy with his own sense of unoriginality when it came to words and theories on life.

"Speak for yourself," she said. "I couldn't do any-thing"—she paused, then used his word for it—"chancy.''

"Yes, you could.''

"Well, I could, but I won't.''

He laughed. "Well, you might surprise yourself one day.''

His sureness of himself irked her. Like the mustache that he twitched slightly. He knew she didn't like it; he used it to tease her.

Fine. What a pointless conversation. She picked up her pen, going back to the task of writing out his progress for the morning. Out the corner of her eye, though, she could see him.

He'd leaned back on the rear legs of his chair, lifting the front ones off the floor. He rocked there beside her as he bent his head sideways, tilting it, looking under the table. He'd been doing this all week, making her nervous with it. As if there were a mouse or worse, something under there that she should be aware of. It was never anything though. Or nothing he wanted to mention; she'd asked already more than once.

She phrased the question differently today. "What *are* you doing?"

Illogically, he came back with, "I bet you have the longest, prettiest legs."

"*Limbs,*" she corrected. "A gentleman refers to that part of a lady as her limbs, her lower limbs, though it is rather poor form to speak of them at all. You shouldn't."

He laughed. "Limbs? Like a bloody tree?" His pencil continued to tap lightly, an annoying tattoo of ticks. "No, you got legs under there. Long ones. And I'd give just about anything to see 'em."

Goodness. She was without words again, nothing readily available to say to yet another of his impertinent comments.

And he knew it was impertinent. He was tormenting her. That much knowledge she had gained of him. He liked to torture her for amusement, like a child pulling legs off a bug. Though something about him today felt at more extreme loose ends, more bored than usual, capable of "chancy" mischief.

He tipped back further on the rear legs of his chair, giving the waving front leg a quick double tap of the pencil, *ta-tick,* on his way to dropping his arm down, out of sight. His position was quite precarious, she was thinking—

She felt the tickle up her ankle before she understood what it was. His pencil. He ran the tip of it, quick as you please, up her anklebone along the leather of her shoe. It flipped the hem of her dress up.

She brushed it down. "Stop that."

He bounced the pencil once off the leg of the table, *tick ta-tick,* then puffed his top lip out, squelching air between lip and teeth to make a strange little rude sound; it bristled his mustache. Oh, that mustache.

Then she caught the word: *anything*?

To see her legs? Her legs were nothing. Two sticks that bent so she could walk on them. He wanted to see these?

For anything?

She wouldn't let him see them, of course. But she wasn't past provoking him in return: pointing out that, while some people wanted to see what they shouldn't, others were forced to look at what they'd certainly like to be rid of. "Well, there is a solution here then, Mr. Tremore. You can see my legs, when you shave your mustache."

She meant it as a kind of joke. A taunt to get back at him.

Joke or not, though, his pencil not only stopped, it dropped. There was a tiny clatter on the floor, a faint sound of rolling, then silence—as, along with the pencil, Mr. Tremore's entire body came to a motionless standstill. He was caught in that awful, boyishly crude pose, leaning back on the legs of his chair, a recalcitrant look on his face.

He opened his mouth as if to say something, then just wet his lips.

Edwina wasn't sure where the knowledge came from, but she understood with sudden, sure insight: He was keen to see a pair of legs that no one else cared a fig about. Long, rangy legs, their proportions to her body about as graceful as those of the legs on a colt.

As to her joke—oh, my. His expression said he was considering it as a genuine offer, an idea that made her more uncomfortable than she would have thought possible. His stillness, the look on his face . . . The combination made her run her hand over the tops of her knees, hold her dress against her shins.

He wet his lips again as if trying to lubricate speech. "Pardon?" he said finally. He spoke it perfectly, exactly as she'd asked him to. Only now it unsettled her.

Not enough though to relinquish the advantage she seemed to have gained over him. "You heard me," she said. A little thrill shot through her as she pushed her way into the dare that—fascinatingly, genuinely—rattled him. She had at last set him on his ear as he did her so often. Ha ha ha, she thought. She wanted to clap her hands in delight.

She spoke now in earnest what seemed suddenly a wonderful exchange: "If you shave off your mustache, I'll hike my skirt and you can watch—how far? To my knees?" The hair on the back of her neck stood up.

"Above your knees," he said immediately. His amazed face scowled in a way that said they weren't even talking unless they got well past her knees in the debate.

"How far?"

"All the way up."

She frowned, then cautioned, "Just my legs though."

"Right. To the tops of your thighs."

"But I'm keeping my knickers—"

"Then I'm only takin' off half the mustache."

His mustache! "You'll take it off?"

He looked at her, thought about it. "You'll lift your skirts and let me see your legs?" He added, "Without your knickers."

"No, no." Instantly, she shook her head. "Certainly not. I won't take my knickers off."

He knew when he'd gone past the limit. "All right," he agreed quickly. "With your knickers on, but all the way up to the tops of your thighs."

They were silent a moment. How had they come to such a quick, insane place? Were they seriously negotiating for what was both trivial to discuss—hair on a lip, looking at legs, silly if she thought about it—yet in some ineffable way so significant they neither one should have been bargaining with what he or she had to lose?

Modesty and mustache.

Yet, Winnie thought smugly, when she dropped her skirts down again, her loss would be over and his lip would be bare. "Yes," she said.

"How long?"

"How long what?"

"How long can I look?"

She pinched her mouth. Oh, now he wanted all afternoon to stare at her. Well, he wasn't getting it. "A minute."

"Then no." He shook his head. "Longer than a minute."

"How long?"

"Fifteen minutes."

Blood rushed, making her arms, her hands, her cheeks hot. "I can't stand there for fifteen minutes, you dolt! That's absurd! Just standing there with my skirts up? My knickers hanging out?"

It was meant to be a ridiculous image. His face changed though. His expression relaxed into it. Oh, she hated to see that. She'd lost ground somewhere. He was winning again. His mouth drew up on one side, indenting his cheek with that single, deep dimple. A slow, sly smile spread into his features. "Yes, fifteen minutes. And I get to touch your legs—"

"Now wait one instant, Mr. Tremore—"

He stopped her by coming forward onto the legs of his chair with a clunk as he pointed his finger at her. "You, Miss Bollash, want me to shave off my—well, my masculinity. The least I get for that is to know what those legs feel like."

She balked. No, this was not at all what she'd had in mind. Her idea was getting quite out of hand.

He wiggled his mouth at her then, making the mustache come alive on his lip. Oh, she hated that thing. Why? Why did she dislike it so much?

"All right," she said before he could ask for anything else. "But only ten minutes. And, if you have to, you can touch my legs." She restricted, "At the end," then cautioned sharply, "but just my legs. If you touch anything else—"

He grinned widely, crookedly. "Agreed. Just your legs." He laughed, showing a lot of good teeth. "And ten minutes is all right, but now. I want to see 'em right now.'' With the flat of his hand, he patted the tabletop. ''Hop up here, loov. Let's see what's under those skirts.''

Chapter 9

The way Edwina and Mr. Tremore worked it, since neither one trusted the other very well, was that he could see her legs now for five minutes, but not touch them. (Oh, so absurd! she thought, as she stood up shakily—and somehow euphorically—from her chair. She could hardly believe they were discussing the plan, let alone acting on it!) Then they would go upstairs together, where at his washbasin and mirror she'd watch him shave his mustache. Oh, yes! After which, he'd get to see her legs for the last five minutes. And touch them at the very end.

"Once," she said.

"Once." He repeated the word, but was so merry about the whole business, she didn't think he heard her. He stood briskly.

To her surprise, his hands landed on her waist, and then the ground came right out from under her. Simultaneously, as he lifted her up and over him, she said, "And I'm not getting on any table—"

She stood on one, looking down at him.

A strange perspective. Below her, she watched him drag his chair back a few feet. "I can't see everything proper unless it's at eye level," he said. He turned, grinning, and plopped himself into the chair, folding his arms over his chest.

And so he was: eye level with her skirts, about four

feet away. She glanced over the edge of her lesson table. The floor seemed a chasm, the table a cliff. This wasn't right. It wasn't what she'd imagined. What *had* she imagined?

His lip lathered up, a straight razor neatly cutting through shaving soap foam. That was as far as her fancies had taken her.

The face of reality was a man with a sloping grin, his thick black mustache slanted at a triumphant angle, his spine scooted down in his chair, his legs wide, knees bent, his arms crossed over his well-cut vest.

"So?" he asked. When she gave him a frustrated look, he said, "Your skirts. Lift 'em up. Or are you already backin' out?" His arm rose off his chest so his finger could stroke the hair on his lip. He prodded, "The sooner you do it, loov, the sooner we go upstairs and get to what you fancy so damn much."

She nodded. Yes, of course. She put her hands in her skirts, grabbed fabric. Five minutes wasn't so long. The clock on the mantel behind him said twenty till eleven. At a quarter till, she'd be done, or half done at least.

Yet getting her skirt up was so much more difficult than she would have thought. He watched intently—he wasn't going to miss a second, his eyes not even attempting to look at her face. She wasn't accustomed to a man's eyes openly fixing themselves on, well, *there* at the hem of her dress. It gave her a funny feeling, a frisson . . . not up her spine exactly, but a light downward ripple into her belly.

"You need some help, Winnie?"

She threw him a frown. She was going to say, *Miss Bollash,* but then she only wet her lips. She didn't bother. All her instruction in the matter so far hadn't done any good.

Just do it, she told herself. "No, no help."

Still she couldn't get her hands going. It was his fault. He was trying to—

Oh, bosh. It occurred to her. His triumphant smile. The challenging way he'd taken over. Mr. Tremore didn't believe her. He was having a good time because he thought he was calling a bluff.

The idea that he thought she couldn't do it made her feel positively audacious.

Without looking down, she made her hands work. Her fingers balled up fabric into her fists, bunching.

She watched him, still slouched in his chair, as a tension overtook him, his humor replaced with surprise—and an anticipation that was hard to miss. The way Edwina stared expectantly sometimes at the curtain as the big, bold first notes of the overture to a favorite opera sounded. She felt like that—kettle drums, cellos, heavy strings swelling, rising to sing in her veins. Yes. Do it. Shock him. An odd thrill hummed her blood and tickled her chest.

She looked down at herself. There was an inch of shoe showing. Well! That wasn't so hard! She watched as her hands gathered up more, feeling the scrunch of silk and horsehair and linen.

An inch more of shoe leather appeared. The room grew still, not a sound except the slide and rustle of fabric. More and more of it accumulated, till it was too much to hold in her fists. She had to catch it against her forearms and thighs, gathering, catching, gathering. Till she was looking at all the laces to the tops of her shoes and an inch of shins.

Skin. She had to stem a nervous giggle. It was so silly, yet exhilarating somehow now that she was at it.

When her skirts were at her knees, a faint draft brushed against her legs. It moved up under her skirts. A giddy sensation. She wouldn't look at Mr. Tremore, though she knew he was there. She heard him shift in his chair, clear his throat.

She saw the knee lace of her own knickers at the same time as she heard a soft, kind of whistling word. "Ch-e-e-e-sus." Mr. Tremore. Excitement shot through her. Her stomach rolled over. Anxiety and pleasure. The combination brought such a pinching delight.

It was so strong, the feeling. Stronger than anything

she could remember. From standing on a table and lifting her skirts till her legs showed from the knees down.

Yes, more. She wet her lips again, gathering fabric as quickly as she could, not stopping, as if she were digging through it. Up, up, up, and there she was: all her legs in view. The last little bit, where she brought her skirts in a ball against her hips, gave her the most peculiar little sensation, a kind of electrical charge at her belly. A warm, melting tingle that felt actually, physically, present inside her—right there, under the bunch of skirts, as if a response to them somehow.

Good. Done. And quite successfully, she thought, elation lifting her, taking her up. Yes, yes, yes. Now all she had to do was stand here for a few minutes and—

"No, no," he said.

She jerked her head, frowned down over the table at him.

Mr. Tremore stared at her legs, with a kind of . . . involved expression, completely engaged by the sight, yet . . . uncomfortable. And dissatisfied.

"You, ah—" He moved his head back a degree, but not his eyes. They didn't leave her legs. "Your stockings," he said. "You have to take them off."

"I do not." She straightened, dropping her skirt. "We never talked about stockings."

He scowled at the dropped skirts, then lifted his scowl to her face. "We said *legs*. I was looking at stockings."

"You were looking at legs. You had a good, clear view of exactly what we discussed."

"We discussed legs, not stockings."

She glared. So was he telling her that he wouldn't shave his mustache now, unless he got to add more to his side of the bargain? Why, the conniving—

"It has to be legs," he said. "Really your legs."

She pressed her lips together. She'd gone this far. It hadn't been bad. And the stupid man was looking for a way out. Well, she wouldn't give it to him. "Turn around," she said.

"I don't have to turn around."

"You do. We didn't say anything about watching me take anything off. Turn around. I'll tell you when I'm ready."

He protested briefly, but then stood enough to swing a leg back and around. He straddled the chair, his back to her. Winnie bent over hurriedly, reaching up under her petticoats, pushing the edge of her knickers out of the way enough to get at the new garters the shopkeeper had sent. She quickly slid them down her legs, one then the other, pushing her stockings along with them to her ankles.

She stood, then pulled her skirts back against herself to stare at what she'd wrought: her silk stocking waded in a clumping ring about the ankles of her high-laced shoes. It looked stupid, foolish. Good, she thought at first. Then no. A kind of vanity took hold. There was no point, she told herself, in looking any more foolish than she already would.

She squatted, sitting back onto the table with a bounce, lifting her foot immodestly to work at the ties of one shoe, then the other. There. Bare feet. She wiggled her toes. That looked . . . better. She stared at her foot. Better? It looked *something*.

"Are you ready yet? What's taking so long? I could take them off myself in less than a minute."

"Just wait. I almost have it." She got her feet under her, but as she raised up, unbending, she realized she could see his reflection in the window glass—his mustache a vivid bar at his mouth—which meant presumably he was looking at her reflection. They stared at each other in the glass.

Anger prickled the hairs up her arms. But its result was her digging in. No. She would not call it off, not slow it down, not give him one single excuse. She straightened completely, pulling her dignity up around her. "All right." She looked at the mantel clock behind him. "It's five minutes till eleven. You have till eleven o'clock." She'd be generous.

Because she fully intended to be merciless in the end.

His eyes lingered on the clock as he came around to face her. The game began again. He sat back, facing her, crossing his legs as if casually, one knee over the other—he did that in a way that couldn't be taught, in a rare way. Delicate, a refined air, particular and graceful, without being the least effeminate. Masculine, in fact. She didn't know where he'd learned to do such a thing, but it added to the illusion of a gentleman.

Though no gentleman would do what he did after his crossed his legs. He laced his fingers together behind his head, elbows out, leaned back, stretched, and stared at her skirts again: waiting.

She made herself do it faster this time. Get them up; get it done. But she did the wrong thing, as it turned out. Instead of watching herself, her legs, she watched him. And what she saw not only fascinated, it all but undid her.

The sight of her bare legs affected him in a way he couldn't disguise. He tried to be nonchalant about it— the raised arms behind his head, his legs resting out. But after only a few moments, he'd grown tense enough that the posture no longer served him. He lowered his arms, leaning forward, elbows onto the tops of his thighs, staring as if his life depended on memorizing every inch of her bareness his eyes could cover.

She had power over him. Power that made her mouth dry. It made that feeling low in her belly roil around like something alive.

It warmed her to have his eyes on her like this. It made her face, her skin hot. As if the sun beat on her legs, as if its rays could insinuate themselves up into her. His gaze felt so tangible it seemed to touch her, brush her calves, push against the knickers at her thighs. It made gooseflesh run down the backs of her knees then up her shins, the sensation traveling further up and up into the center of her between her legs. The same, strange place again.

She shifted on her feet, feeling the table under her naked soles. They stuck slightly to the wood, the contact cool, humid from her feet having just come from her shoes.

The feeling was more discomposing than she could have dreamed. His eyes ran up and down her legs, making her aware of how long they were, tree-like, yet somehow his appreciation was candid: burning. There was no other word. She shifted on her bare feet, unable to make herself be still. She could feel her heart thudding. How long had it been pounding like this? Was it healthy for it to pump at such a rate for so long a time as it seemed? Her breathing felt short; she couldn't get quite enough air. Or no, more as if she needed a greater amount than usual. Her palms grew hot and sticky where they clutched the wads of silk, making her dress damp.

The clock ticked. She and Mr. Tremore said nothing. His intense regard only broke once. He became briefly distracted by her shoes, stockings, and garters sitting beside her, fascinated by her pile of clothes for a moment.

She raised her eyes to the clock, trying not to think. Only a minute to go, with him having his eyes on her bare legs, the silence in the room becoming heavy. Her bare legs, she thought. Even she had never looked at them so much. No one had. No one else had ever been so interested.

Just before the clock began to strike, he broke the stillness to ask, "Winnie, do you know how beautiful your legs are?"

She looked down, agitated, fidgety, wondering if he and she were talking about the same pair of legs.

Then he murmured, "I can't wait to touch them."

And her stomach rose up into chest, turned upside down, then melted, sinking, into her pelvis.

Nothing she could do about it: He somehow had more control over her than she did. Their eyes met.

She stared down from the height of the table at him, into light, greenish eyes beneath black eyebrows, coloring so unusual . . . including a mustache, glossy with health. With her gaze fixed to his, she felt that low place in her body roll again, the place between her legs, and as if in unison with her stomach, the goose-bump feeling lower slowly somersaulted over.

"I want to touch them with my mouth," he said softly, tentative. He knew he was on shaky ground, nothing they'd discussed. He wanted to woo a change into their contract.

No words. Winnie raised her eyes to stare across the room at her wall of books. Then didn't see them. Her vision blurred. She couldn't see for the heat at her eyes.

He continued. "I want to kiss the backs of your legs, behind your knees and up."

She shook her head. It was the closest she could come to contradicting him. *Once.* They'd said he could touch her legs once. He could put his hand on one leg. Then he had to take it away.

A lot of kissing up the backs of her legs wasn't— Dear God, her head grew light, so light she thought she might faint. It was too much. She felt overwhelmed, unwell. . . .

The clock began to chime—a sobering, saving toll of grace.

Done!

Joy came into her chest with a burst of relief. It came out her mouth with gusto. "Your turn!" she announced.

She dropped hems and petticoats with a loud rustle of silk and linen and lace. Heavens, the sweet charity of being covered again. Who would have thought that to have one's legs bare, from only the knees down really—after all, she had on her knickers—could be such an ordeal?

"Not till the last chime," he said from his chair. Like some almighty emperor from the throne. "Bring 'em up again, Winnie."

"No."

They hassled back and forth as the last chimes struck. In the end, she had to pull her skirts up, let him look for ten more seconds, before she could get him moving toward the staircase.

Chapter 10

$\mathcal{E}$dwina watched over Mr. Tremore's shoulder in the mirror, his reflection above the washbasin. She watched him touch his mustache. It was brief, just the tips of his fingers lightly combing it downward, almost with affection. She felt a small twinge of guilt. Ever so small. Then he rattled the shaving brush in the cup again and slopped lather onto his lip. He picked up the straight razor, taking hold of his face to make the skin taut. He rolled his lip under his teeth, then—*scritch*—he took the first swipe.

Oh! Edwina wanted to pat her hands together. Skin under the mustache! White, tender skin. She was gleeful to see it. She could barely be still for her feet's urge to dance.

He took another stroke of mustache off, glancing over at her, a deep frown. He returned his attention to the basin to sling the razor once, slopping foam into the bowl, then wiped the edge of the razor on a towel, raised his head, and scraped again. To get at the edge, he had to twist his mouth and hold his cheek, then had to make another contortion to get under his nose and over the curve of his teeth. Stroke, *scritch*, stroke. It didn't take more than half a dozen good passes, before the thick, bothersome mustache was in the basin mixed with a lot of shaving-soap lather.

Edwina looked down. Seeing it there, she felt as if

she'd vanquished a dragon. Or a caterpillar at the very least; something that had been eating holes through her.

Mr. Tremore laid the razor down, then bent over the basin as he poured water from the pitcher. He splashed his face, rinsing over the bowl. Then rose up partway and stopped. He looked at his own face in the mirror.

He startled, blinked. They both did. He slowly rose, staring at his image in the glass.

Goodness, he looked different. Sharper. Cleaner. Smoother, of course. But unpredictably somehow . . . more severe in his handsomeness. Mick Tremore, clean-shaven, looked like an idealized drawing for a shaving-lotion advertisement.

With the mustache gone, his eyes became his predominant feature, and they, of course, were stunning. Light, mossy green eyes set beneath a jutting brow in a plane perpendicular to a long, straight nose. The bones of his face came forth, a near-patrician facial architecture of strong, masculine angles and planes. Oh, she'd been so right to insist, Edwina thought. So right to get rid of that animal tuft.

Mr. Tremore stared into the mirror, his unusual eyes focused on the lower half of his face. He put his hand over the wet, fresh-shaved skin, dragging his palm down his mouth, frowning. He pressed his lips, moving them, stretched his upper lip.

Whatever it felt like, he didn't dally with the sensation. He turned around just like that—they hadn't been in his bedroom a full minute, hadn't passed a dozen seconds beyond removing his mustache, when he pointed to the wood chair by the washbasin and said, "Get on that where I can get a good look. Then raise 'em up, Win."

Act II. Panic. She took a step back. "You're bossy."

"I'm not bossy. We're negotiating. I know what I want. Get on the chair."

"How did you get that right suddenly, all the *I'm*'s and *We're*'s. You're saying them correctly almost every time now."

"I've been listening to you. Stop stalling. We can be done in five minutes. Get on the chair."

"No." What she meant was she wasn't standing on anything.

How he took the reluctance in her tone though was, she wanted to back out of her second half of their agreement.

His face took on a look of genuine anger, a look, she realized, she'd never seen on him. It made her back up another step and talk faster than normal. "I'm not standing on the chair. The table downstairs—" She swallowed. "I didn't like it. It was too—" Awkward somehow. In some extreme sense.

Standing on the table downstairs, she thought, had made the strangeness at the end, the eerie feeling that had made her hot and light-headed. "I'm not doing that again," she reiterated. "You have to look where you are."

He twisted his mouth, an instant's displeasure, then pulled the chair he'd indicated around, straddling it backward. He dropped himself into the seat, bracing his arms on the back. "Fine," he said.

It was her word. He said it exactly as she often did. The man was a parrot today, soaking up more than she wanted at the moment. She backed a step further, staring into his newly revealed, somehow sharper features. He didn't look as kind without his mustache. She almost missed it for a moment. He didn't look himself.

"Take up your skirt," he said.

She let out a huff. "Don't make it any cruder than it is."

"I can make it any way I want: It's my turn."

He touched his lip again, and his brow drew into a deep, preoccupied crease. One elbow braced on the chair back, he absently fiddled with the newly shaved skin.

Edwina hadn't been aware she was retreating further until her bare heel stepped rudely into the baseboard. By then the weight and balance of her substantial body was already in motion. She collided, her shoulders hitting the wall.

"You gonna start, or do you need some help?"

She brushed at her skirts, getting herself settled on her feet, wishing somehow for more time, a delay, which wasn't of course going to happen. Get on with it, she told herself. "No, I don't need any help." She grabbed her skirts, two handfuls, looking down at them.

"Good," he said. "Because I want to get to the last minute as quick as I can."

The last minute? Oh. Her stomach dropped. The touching part. She wouldn't think about it. She lifted her eyes—she would look at his clean lip and do what she'd done before.

It was harder this time. She had the memory of the odd, tingling embarrassment that in the last instant had just about leveled her. Added to this now was knowing that the odd sensation his eyes made on her would become somehow the concrete feel of his hand. How was she supposed to manage *that*? Just stand here? Let him walk up and put his— Oh dear heaven, she thought.

She stared at his lip and kept telling herself it was worth it: as she gathered up her skirts. She began again, taking the fabric up more and more into her fists. The air was warmer than downstairs. She felt a draft on her legs that was almost balmy as her hands claimed scrunching silk and underlinens. When her fists couldn't hold any more, she pressed the scroopy stiffness of her skirts back against her knickers, hiking, pushing skirts up under her forearms. Skirts rising, rising . . . bare feet then shins. When she saw her knickers, where they began at her knees—

She suddenly remembered what he'd said he wanted, the part about kissing the backs of her legs. No. She looked at him. "You can't—you have to—" She couldn't say it. "You can't use your—"

"Mouth," he finished for her. He laughed, a release. Of sorts. It wasn't a particularly nice laugh—dry, ironic. There was a subtlety to him she hadn't given him credit for till now. He understood nuance. And perhaps even some sort of double entendre she couldn't grasp: "All right, loov. I won't put my mouth under your skirts where you don't want it. It ain't my intention to make you unhappy."

Ain't. The word let her breathe. Thank God he still said it occasionally. Still her Mick. Funny, joking Mick. Who wasn't joking now. He bit the inside of his mouth, a movement that sucked his lower lip in at the edge. His eyes were hooded, half-closed from watching the show that was lower to the ground than before. Looking, looking, not a moment's reprieve . . .

Winnie got the whole wad of her skirts pulled up into her arms and against her hips. She didn't know how long she'd stood there, fretting and rubbing her thumbs at the silk, standing with her skirts up in front of a man who gave the sight his full concentration. She only jerked to greater consciousness when he rose, swinging one leg back and off the chair, standing up to his full, rather imposing height. He seemed huge when he came toward her.

"What are you doing?" she blurted.

"I'm going to touch your legs. We agreed—"

"No, we didn't." The wishful lie choked out.

"Yes, we did."

"Once," she recanted plaintively. "We said you could touch one leg once."

He didn't answer but bent down on one knee in front of her. She looked down on his head, his glossy hair. He'd put himself at her legs, within inches. "Turn around," he said.

"No."

He glanced up. "Winnie, my mustache is in the washbasin. If you think I put it there for some child's game, you're wrong. I guess we said once, but it's gonna be a long 'once.' I'm touchin' you all the way up your leg. If you say I can't use my mouth, I won't. But turn around. I'm touchin' your legs at the back."

"*Leg,*" she said.

"All right, *leg*. But I'm sliding my hand up the whole, damn, gorgeous length, from your sweet heel there"—he pointed—"up the back of your calf, the inside of your knee, all the way up the back of your thigh"—his finger drew an imaginary upward path in the air that gave her goose bumps, then, when his hand got to hip level, his hands took real hold of her hips, turned her around by them, pointing in the process, still without touching—"to the curve right here under your bum. Thank you."

She was facing the wall.

She leaned her head against it, with the "curve under her bum" tingling. God help her, he hadn't done anything yet, and she was in a state. Goose bumps kept running up her legs in waves. Her belly felt as if she'd swallowed something animate that squirmed to get out.

While uncertainty made every single sensation acute. She waited, a woman up in the air, kept aloft on emotions she hated—dread and suspense.

Yet there was another feeling here niggling, as she stood against the wall waiting for Mick Tremore to do something he shouldn't. Why did she allow him the leeway to turn her, to even consider touching her? She couldn't answer the question. She didn't *like* what was happening, she promised herself. She wanted it to be over. The tension it brought was abominable.

Yet as she stood there, waiting, tortured, unhappy, anxious, she was somehow also . . . thrilled beyond words.

Nothing she had known of life till this moment had ever been this exciting.

Mick, on the other hand, was fairly clear about what was happening. He had hold of a guilty virgin he was pushing a little harder than he should. He tried to calm her. He tried to feel bad about it. Winnie here was getting fairly wrung out, and he was the culprit, challenging a hesitant, fretful woman . . . who, buggeration, come to think of it, couldn't be all that timid, since she'd found the courage to have his mustache.

Anger again. It kept shooting through him in

bursts, bright and startling like fireworks in the night sky on St. Agnes's birthday. He told himself it was just that Winnie didn't know exactly what she was doing here, how hard she was being on him. She didn't have a lot of experience in matters between men and women.

He murmured, "Just be still," thinking that would help her get through it—he couldn't make himself feel bad enough to let her off.

He put his hand to her ankle, and, with the contact, his shoulders jerked. "H-h-h-h—" he said, unable to hold it back: her aspirated H. Here was how to get him to make the sound. From pleasure. Pleasure honed on the sight of her bare legs so that it cut into him like the edge of a knife. Her skin was so bloody smooth . . . ten times smoother than his. Her ankle was narrow, the calf a long swell—

She jerked, pulled away, taking her leg with her as she turned around. "There," she said. "You did it. Your ten minutes are over." She let go of her skirts.

He caught them and stood up, carrying them to her waist.

He pushed the wad of dress at her, putting pressure against her stomach. "I hate a cheater, Winnie. Let's do that again. I know you're scared, but you can get through this. Here. Take your skirts."

She refused them. "You're done," she whispered, a little hiss.

"No, I'm not. You've been trying to short me on this idea from the first second you thought of it. Now, you notice, please, I came upstairs and took my mustache off in under a minute. I didn't dodge or argue or give you a moment of trouble. Now hold up your skirts and bear the last minute of the bargain *you* invented."

He held the bundle of skirts against her belly, leaning into them, letting her feel his existence on the other side of all the silky stuff of her clothes. He was scaring her, he knew. Winnie didn't like not to be in charge. Well, stuff her, he thought.

Except that was the point, of course. He couldn't.

And the idea of "stuffing her" was pretty much running wild through his head. Ho-o-o-o, he wanted to have at her. He wanted to lay her so bad his eyes were hot at the backs from being so close to the burning thoughts in his head. He was trying to be rational, trying not to act as crazy as he felt—galled, goaded, teased, and naked. A feeling he'd known the instant he raised his head and stared into the mirror at his own bare lip. Stuff her, he thought again.

But since he couldn't, he descended down her body, inches away without touching, to do what she'd said he could.

Winnie watched him go, then lost sight of him. She could only stand rigid and stare at his shoulders over the bunch of silk she clutched. She felt his head brush against the wad of her skirts, then nestle into them a little. She could feel the warmth of his closeness at her legs, a sensation so extremely pleasurable it was horrible. She was breathing with small vocalized gasps at the end of each breath, embarrassing mews she'd never made before. What was wrong with her? Her mouth was parchment from her trying to find air.

Mick meanwhile turned his head, and his cheek brushed where the hem of a petticoat hung down. The linen was still warm, fragrant from her body. Clean, sweet, starchy. A womanly smell that stirred up a lust the likes of which he hadn't felt since he was a boy just discovering the female sex. In half a second, he lifted in his trousers, all the way out to a full, stiff erection. Oh, bloody hell, he thought. What was he going to do with this? From here, touching her, and not having her, should be one great, big, old Buckingham Palace of torment. Halls and gardens and monuments to it.

No sooner had he grazed her calf, though, than she jerked and twisted away again.

She let out a panicked breath. "Enough. That's it. We're done."

Rage. It stood up with him, pure and clean. He couldn't remember the last time he'd known such a potent, simple emotion. "You cheat," he said. He stepped against her dress before it could fall all the way. He bent his face toward hers, almost touching her nose with his, eye to eye. He dropped his hands with force on the wall at either side of her shoulders—he watched her jump as his palms hit, the daylights all but leaping out of her.

She pulled back, hit her head on the wall. Old Winnie was going to brain herself before she accepted that right here was where her game had got her to and she wasn't going backward: She was going forward.

Forward into what? Mick stood there, blinking, panting, furious, flummoxed. He winced over how hard her head had clunked on the plaster—then the crack to her fool head knocked some sense into *him*.

He wasn't getting to touch her leg. She couldn't do it.

Mick wanted to howl at the injustice. He'd grazed her leg, thought about touching her. Hell, where he'd got to was worse than not touching her at all. He rolled his lips together into his teeth, feeling his upper lip stretch, cold, numb, and bare as a baby's.

They argued with their strength for a minute. Winnie was a sizeable girl. When she shoved him, he knew it. A big girl. The way her hands grabbed his shoulders, though, and pushed—hard, businesslike, not joking—it took more wind from his sails.

He started looking for options.

While Winnie was all but choking from how narrow hers were. Mick was all around her. She shoved, but his weight didn't budge. It didn't even lift.

In fact, she felt him shift. He stepped his feet apart, making himself as heavy and immovable as a boulder, then whispered into her ear, "So what is the penalty for breakin' faith?"

Her heart leaped into her windpipe. "I didn't—"

"Oh, yes, loovey. Let's see. I think the knickers. They have to go."

"*Ac-k-k!*" That was all that would come out Winnie's mouth at first. Then, ''N-no, absolutely not, you—''

''Now, now. You cheated. Or you've tried and tried to. You have to pay.''

''No,'' she said. Her voice sounded pathetic, even to herself. What he was doing genuinely frightened her. It was too much. He asked too much.

He took pity. ''All right, Win. You can buy your knickers back.''

She let her anxious eyes find his. His face was so close, and oh, God, she'd somehow gotten her hands flat against his chest. It was wide, the muscles curved, warm, as hard as the wall behind her. And hair! God help her, at the edge of her thumb she could feel the light cushioning of hair that ran between contours of muscle. His body made her dizzy, near delirious: as if one of the statues she'd admired had grown warm under her hands, then started to breathe.

''H-how?'' she asked.

''Cooperate for a minute.'' He put his nose near her cheek, brushed it against her. She could hear the sound of air, his smelling her. He brushed his mouth along the same place, his clean, freshly shaved mouth. It set off a series of shivers, little quakes through her.

She took her cheek away, bending her neck, and he put his lips onto the arch of it, lightly brushing his dry mouth up to where her jaw met neck at the back of her ear. They both grew still.

Winnie because she was afraid to move. He, she realized, to take the time to consider how and what to ask of her: The toad, the miserable, mean toad was making it all up as he went along.

He slowly told her, ''I'll kiss you . . . I mean, really kiss you this time, Win . . . and you let me. You open your mouth—''

''Open my mouth!''

''Sh-h-h. I knew that was gonna get you goin'. Stop. Just listen. Don't fight me. You let me show you. You open your mouth and let me in. Let me kiss you like I want to.'' His face drew back, shadowed, but it smiled faintly. She watched the slightly crooked bend of lips that seemed almost familiar. His slanting lips without their mustache were full and neatly made, plump, perfectly chiseled like those of a wicked cherub, lips as no man should own. "That's it. Then I let you go, and we're done."

Oh, she wanted to be done. Finished, over with. Her chest hurt from a kind of thudding exhaustion, as if she'd been running for hours. She let his words console her, *then we're done.* Nor did she miss that he was letting her out of the most onerous part of her bargain, the leg-touching part that simply felt too wrong. She surveyed herself. Her blood pulsed at the insides of her elbows; her arms felt weak. Her whole body was like that, beating, beating, hot, squirming with energy while wanting to lie down, wanting to rest, to languish from an insane ennui.

God, oh, God, just to get it over with, she nodded her head, a quick jerk.

"Close your eyes and relax."

Oh, *that* would be easy. In the end though, she only nodded again as if she were going to be able to do it. She closed her eyes and tried to contain her wriggling restlessness.

His palm spread at the back of her shoulders, then his fingers combed up her nape into the back of her hair. Ooh, so pleasant . . . she wouldn't have thought . . . His hands spreading on her felt much nicer than she could have imagined.

He was gentle. As one hand cupped her skull, his other flattened against the small of her back and brought her against him. It was a gentleness, however, that didn't stop an insane pitch of panic when he brushed his lips across hers, then whispered, "Open."

She did slightly, and he pressed his mouth over hers—she could feel the strength in him, his holding it back, a constraint that was palpable. It brought a sharp, ambiguous zing: fright for the size of his strength, a brawn she sensed that could break her in half; paired with a mind-numbing, knee-bending urge to be wrapped in it, surrounded by it, invaded with it. His mouth coaxed hers open further. Then, turning his head, he pushed his tongue deeply inside, between her teeth, against her palate, the insides of her cheeks, pushing against her own tongue—a full, openmouthed takeover of what Winnie had never questioned was her space alone.

For a moment, her back stiffened, and she jerked in his arms. His tongue in her mouth was revolting . . . well, not revolting exactly. She eased a little. Shocking. It was simply shocking then, after a moment . . . interesting. It was warm, very warm to feel his tongue move in her mouth . . . and, well, it was an extraordinarily intimate thing to feel his strength *there,* his tongue against hers. She could taste him— with sudden vividness she remembered the orange he'd eaten at breakfast an hour ago.

The man with the tangy kiss drew her from the wall, sliding his hand down over her buttocks, and pulled her, full length, up against him. The kiss was instantly more potent. She didn't know a kiss could be like this: teeth, lips, tongue . . . oh, heaven, his tongue was bold. It went deep. It stirred up an awareness, warm, liquid. It made her tense, yet it felt . . . surprisingly right.

Then "right" and "interesting" slowly insinuated themselves into "fascinating." She grew aware of how solid he was, aware of his weight and substance, of how deeply and languorously he kissed her, how he put his whole body into it. He leaned them both back into the wall again, pressing her there, as if he wanted to be closer, though heaven knew he was as close as another human being could be. Hips, chest, arms around her, moving, pressing, sliding. She found herself pushing back as he kissed her, though not with struggle. A resistance that added something. A cooperation on her own that made her bones quiver.

With her rumpled skirts still caught between them, she could feel the brush of his wool trousers against her bare shins. She felt his hands dig into her buttocks, push her. They encouraged her to meet the force of him. He wanted the kiss to have a slow, deliberate rhythm—and her shivers became a kind of vertigo that raced her heart and spun her head.

His hands pulled her buttocks into him, pressing the wad of dress between them as, bending his knees, he flexed his hips forward and pushed. He did it again. Then again. While he groaned inside their kiss, satisfaction, as his tongue did a slow, rhythmic penetration of her mouth.

The horrible part was, though she had a vague idea what he imitated, she couldn't stop wanting the next full press of his hips, the next plunge in her mouth. She wanted him to kiss her just as he did, to touch her, and she wanted it with a vehemence that made her ashamed while it stole the strength from her legs; they wanted to fold.

She heard him draw a ragged breath as he lifted his mouth away, turned his head the other direction, then kissed her again. The sound of his rattled breathing matched her own. Then, as if her spinning inability to get air weren't enough, she felt his hand play delicately at edge of her raised skirts: looking for what he'd asked for, the feel of her leg.

Her leg? She thought the kiss was instead of her leg. No. No, no. Then another, distant voice in her head said with grave curiosity, Yes.

Her emotions pitched. Fear, pleasure, panic, anticipation. Yet this time she let him without a moment's reproof.

His hand went up under her dress. Through the fine-weave linen of her knickers, she felt his palm lay itself, spread-fingered, onto the back of her thigh. With the touch, an acute, stomach-knotting jolt of pleasure shot through her so strongly it made her shiver and jump in spasm. Then the smooth warmth of his palm tentatively stroked her thigh up under the curve of her buttocks.

Oh, dear. So wrong. A man she hadn't known two weeks was rubbing his sublime hand under her near-naked backside. So wrong it made her stomach flip. So right she couldn't swallow.

He slid his hand lower, rubbing down her thigh, the back, the side, the front, the inside . . . ooh, the inside of her thigh. Bliss. Oh, to be touched by Mick Tremore. Pure sensory rapture. It set every hair of her body on end. Ecstatic. Dreadful in its power, its climb, its pure, blinding brightness.

This strong pleasure spread, expanded, threatening to usurp every logical thought. It ruled from that low place in her abdomen, as if she were possessed there by a demon. Something was taking her over, turning her over into the hands of a commanding instinct she hadn't known she possessed. A vaguely terrifying "something," for it was a stranger. A fierce, frightening feeling that left the rest of her powerless. She shifted, made an instant of struggle.

"Sh-h-h," he said and stoked her where she liked, in the curve beneath her buttocks. The place that seemed safer. Only it wasn't that safe.

The strange new awareness in her tugged, pulling her toward what seemed a dark pit, a place where she dare not go further, dare not let herself fall. She feared her own unknown self. She was afraid of following him where he wanted, of not coming out again. Or not coming out the same: changed forever.

Her senses singing, full-voiced, Winnie stood shaking—seemingly complacently in Mick's arms—as she quietly grew frantic: poised on an overpowering brink of too much, too new, too strong, too different from any other experience she knew, her emotions carrying her to the edge of pure, guilty terror.

While Mick fought a singing urge of his own: He wanted to move his hand an inch toward the center of her body and touch what was so close and so on his mind. He *wanted* to lose control, take her with him. They were in a bedroom, ten feet from a bed.

He fought the urge valiantly. It was leagues beyond their agreement. He liked kissing her. He kissed her and kissed her there against the wall, pressing her and tonguing her first one way, then, turning his head, another, like he could put all his male self into the single act of penetrating her female mouth. He rubbed his body as close as he could to hers. He smoothed his hand along the contours of long, comely thigh. Soft along the inside, female. While the singing thought kept whispering, What you want is right there. An inch away. Have it. Touch her.

In the end, he wanted to so badly he simply couldn't *not* do it. He ran his hand all the way up to where her thigh gave into the delicate indentation, where her leg joined her torso. He drew his fingers along the bend to the ridge of tendon, then simply shifted his hand. He took firm, cupping possession of her between her legs, holding of her, feeling her. It was worth it: She was wet. Her knickers were soaked. Her body was ready, no denying how ready, his—

Winnie's head jerked. She let out a sharp yelp. It took him aback a little when, from here, she became a sudden tangle of arms and flailing legs and fists coming at him. With all her considerable strength, she was suddenly a whirling, thrashing animal, drawing its last ounce of spit to save itself.

Mick got a good, strong barefoot kick to his shin and a fist to the side of his face that about took off his jaw before he could catch her arms, draw them down, and step back. He half-expected her to come at him again. She was that crazy. He guarded himself, hands and forearms up, breathing like a freight train.

But instead of more fight, Winnie turned to the wall, putting both her hands on herself where he'd touched her. Her head bent. Her shoulders hunched. And she burst out in sobs.

Mick couldn't've been more surprised if she'd pulled out a gun and shot him.

But, well, of course, he thought. He should've known. Winnie was the guiltiest, scaredest woman. He reached, touched her shoulder. "Sh-h-h," he said. "It's all right. I'm sorry. I shouldn't've done that."

So, so sorry. She cried like a child. A child who

knew for sure she was getting no supper, getting a beating, sent to the orphanage, put up for adoption. He felt awful.

He put both his hands on her shoulders, rubbed up and down her arms. "It's all right. It's right normal, Win. It's what men and women do. But I shouldn't've. I—" He tried to turn her around and just hold her. She wouldn't let him though, so he only hugged her from the back, wrapping himself around her as he stroked his hand down one arm.

As he petted her, his own hand ended up near his face. He caught the smell of her there. He closed his eyes and resisted one second. But it was irresistible. He put his nose into his palm and breathed in the smell of Winnie's female sex, then discovered a place where his two fingers met at the palm that was still wet from touching her. God bless, he held her there, soothing her, while behind her he opened his mouth on his own hand and touched his tongue between his fingers, tasting her. He shuddered.

How buggered-up was this? he asked himself. He wanted to bend his mouth into the curve of her neck. He wanted to rub her buttocks with an erection so hard and taut there was a delicate possibility for disaster. He had no business with Winnie in his arms here, no business consoling her, telling her that everything was going to be all right and that he was sorry—while he stood behind her, wanting to run his hand under her beautiful round bum, between her legs, get rid of the knickers, rip them if he had to, so he could put his hand directly onto her flesh, put his fingers into her, slide—

Mick, my boy, you ain't buggered-up. You are out of your bloody lunatic mind. Winnie would come at you like the Furies if she even knew what you were thinking. If she didn't kill herself first.

So, standing there with every one of his senses full of Winnie Bollash, Mick determined that all he wanted of her was bad for her. And, one of the hardest steps he ever took, he let go of her, stepped back, getting himself clear of her long, sweet body. Backing one footstep then two away, he left her alone at the wall.

Watching her there made him feel so small. If only it made his cock small, too, but it didn't. That part of him nosed rod-straight against his trousers, still trying to do his thinking for him—Winnie had forgot to let go of her skirts. Her bare legs were bent together, one pressed against the wall, as she clutched her dress to her hips and cried and cried and cried. She was inconsolable.

He tried anyway though. He said, "Winnie, it's no secret now I want you. Let me be the one. Come lie down with me on the bed over there." He shook his head. He wanted to say all manner of things he was fairly certain a gentleman didn't say. How he wanted to put himself inside her. How he wanted to eat the freckles off her long legs. How he wanted to kiss her mouth till their tongues were sore and their lips were raw and make love to her till neither one of them could stand up straight. And then, after that, exhausted, he'd crawl down her body and kiss her between her legs like he'd done her mouth, long and deep, then fall asleep with his face there.

Wisely, he didn't mention these things. To him, they were beautiful. Poetry. To Winnie, he was right sure, they were crude. He wouldn't've been surprised if, on telling her all he might want from her, she bent right over and got sick.

Especially given that her next sobbing words were, "Y-you said you wouldn't t-touch me anywhere else."

There wasn't really any defense for what he'd done. Well, hardly any. He told her, "You liked it, Winnie."

"I did not."

More meekly, he chided, "All right, but you almost did. You would've, if you'd've let yourself. And God bless, Win . . ." He shook his head, a man who had bewildered himself, then spoke softly. "I bloody loved it. I bloody effing loved it." He looked at her with utter seriousness, trying to say what he felt. "I want to do it again. I can't tell you how much. I won't. I won't come near you again, if that's what you want. But Lord, Win.'' He shook his head. "You're amazing. You are the best handful of woman I've ever held in my arms, and I've held a few, loovey. But nothing like you. Nothing.''

It didn't cheer her up. She cried like she was dying.

Mick put his hand to his lip, finding only damned, half-numb, smooth-shaven skin. Buggeration. He held his hand there, his thumb at his jaw, his fingers over his lips and mouth like he could cover it up, like he could hide what he'd done.

"What am I supposed to do, Win?'' he asked

She said nothing, but just sobbed there, her shoulders shaking.

He pushed his hand back through his hair, feeling it between his fingers, wanting to pull it out. "Should I leave?''

She didn't answer him.

"I mean, really leave. Take Magic and Freddie and go. I can forget about the hundred pounds. I'll earn it another way.'' He couldn't, of course, but that was a different matter.

She said nothing, though she took a long, sloppy sniff of air.

He tried to tease her out of all her tears. "You want that I marry you?'' He laughed at how stupid that was Like she'd marry a ratcatcher.

She stopped her crying for a minute, long enough for another big, wet hiccup of misery. Then she looked at him, sort of out from under her pretty red hair what was coming down, and whispered, strong, mean, angry, "Don't laugh at me anymore. Stop it. Stop all your teasing! I'm not a joke!''

Right. If she'd've had the strength, she'd've slapped him. Right.

Married. Winnie should've been married. She was a fine woman. Nurturing, kind. She surely as hell shouldn't have been clinging to a wall because some Cornish miner's son had stuck his hand where it didn't belong.

Right, he thought again. A marrying joke. Pretty insulting to offer to make her miserable like she was for the rest of her life. But, see, he hadn't meant the insult toward her. He was making fun of *himself.*

Oh, he was good enough for her. It wasn't that. He just wasn't good enough in her mind, and not in the minds of the rest of the world either. He knew it, accepted it, and wasn't even bitter about it. It was just the way things were. But Winnie thought the joke was on *her.* She always thought it was her, no matter what happened. She carried the world on her shoulders, responsible for every little thing that happened in it. Or even for what didn't happen sometimes like it should.

In her mind, Winnie ruled the world. And a fine old burden it was, considering she ruled a fickle place that ran on havoc.

And sweet Win here wanted a man, *needed* a man, but she didn't know how to get one. Or how to get one she wanted, since she wouldn't let herself have the one she accidentally got.

Mick forced a long, breathy sigh down his nose. The whole business made him just plain tired. His solution was easy. His solutions were always easy. As far as he was concerned, it was one of those situations where to shag her silly, he was fairly sure, would be a big favor to her. He half-wished he had the nerve to do it: just lay her down and get her past it. It'd be good for her. At least in one way. Of course, it might kill her in another.

Good thing it wasn't his job to worry over it.

"Okay," he said. "I'll go take Magic for a walk. Whatever you want me to do, put it in a note. Leave it by the basin. I'll come back. I'll read it. I'll do it." He couldn't resist a sarcastic snort. "Just don't use too many big words, all right, Win? So I don't have any trouble understanding what you want from me."

Mick couldn't find Magic at first. He went down the hall, calling him, then he had to hunt through Maj's favorite rooms. When he finally did find the stupid dog, he wanted to shoot him. He was in Winnie's laboratory, having a grand ol' time, chewing the elastic out of a fancy silk garter.

Chapter 11

The note Mick found was short:

Mr. Tremore,

Please let's not think about or discuss this morning further. We must go on as if it never happened. I'll meet you in the laboratory for our regularly scheduled lesson at three this afternoon. We have a great deal to do and too little time to do it.

Edwina Bollash

That afternoon, Edwina told Mr. Tremore, "The lady steps up into the carriage first. Offer me your hand." He did, though it took a moment for her to lay her fingers into his. With premeditated care, she grasped his extended hand. It was dry, warm, and unhesitant.

She paused with her foot on the step to her carriage. The vehicle didn't budge. It couldn't. No horse was attached. She had brought Mr. Tremore out to the carriage house in order to practice in her unhitched coach.

"Once I'm up," she told him, "you'll follow me in. You sit opposite me with your back to the horses, or where the horses would be. You never sit beside a lady in a carriage, other than your own wife or daughter;

you always sit opposite, always facing the direction from whence you are coming."

"Backward," he clarified. "I face backward."

"Correct."

He was paying attention, which was good. He could see apparently the immediate value in what they were doing.

She'd brought him out to the carriage house, knowing he'd learn more surely by doing than talking. She wanted him to begin moving through the night of the ball in his mind, knowing where to put himself, how to dance his way, so to speak, through the rules of politeness and protocol.

Also, if she were honest, she'd brought him out here because she couldn't face watching his mouth in the usual way of their lessons. She couldn't bring herself to stare at it for the rest of the afternoon, fussing over how he put his tongue against his teeth when all she could remember was how, earlier, he'd put it against hers.

She held on to his palm for balance as the vehicle rocked on its springs toward her slightly. She went up the steps. Mr. Tremore's fingers were strong in their grip of hers, helpful, steady. Nonetheless, she was eager to get her hand away. She let go the second she grasped the door frame.

Then, just as she ducked under the doorway, she was suddenly halted. She made a horrible leap, literally and figuratively—for she jumped as if he'd yanked hold of the entire back of her dress, meaning to ravish her there on the steps of her coach. Behind her, she heard him say, "Sorry." Her skirts released.

He'd simply tramped on them.

She laughed nervously. "It happens occasionally." She tried to regain herself by backing out from under the carriage doorway and turning to stand up again. Edwina balanced on the top step, gripping the door frame on either side, both hands, in order to hold herself on the precarious little tread. She smiled down at him, or tried to. "And 'sorry' is perfectly fine." She did achieve a kind of smile, she thought. "Some gentlemen have more trouble than others with ladies' trains and sweepers." She paused, took a breath, then recuperated enough to say sincerely, "Let's try again, shall we? I don't doubt that you shall get it perfectly next try."

He did. On the second attempt, Edwina made it uneventfully into the carriage and onto her seat, then watched the athletic Mr. Tremore hoist himself through the doorway with an energy and lightness that defied explanation, especially for such a large man. She was going to correct him, make him get in more sedately, but then thought better of it. The ladies she knew would probably enjoy watching him do that, swing in like some sort of primitive.

He sat opposite her as instructed, then leaned to reach for the door.

"No," she said. "Don't get it. A footman will close it on the night of the ball. Let him. You must become accustomed to people doing things for you. There will be servants everywhere."

He looked uncomfortable with the information, but sat back, leaving the door swung out on its hinges.

There they sat in the open-doored carriage in an open carriage house—they'd left the carriage house doors open as well to let in the daylight. A horse nickered down at the far end in its stall, the sound punctuating the tension of their first "lesson" since this morning. Winnie drew in a breath and took in the smell of hay and horses and well-oiled tack, while a rosy kind of light spun dust motes through the carriage doorway in a beam that ended in Mr. Tremore's lap.

She swung her head away, looking quickly out the window of her marooned carriage. Through the opening, she stared down a hay-lined corridor of horse stalls, most of them empty now. Without looking at him, she began again. "At the ball," she said, "when you enter the house or any room in it, you let the ladies of your party go in ahead—"

"There'll be ladies with us?"

"Possibly. The Misters Lamont, I imagine, will take you to the ball. They may bring wives or the ladies on whom they pay call."

"And you?"

"What about me?"

"Won't you be with us?"

"No," she said, turning to look at him with surprise. "I'm just your teacher."

"I want you there."

"Well, I can't go."

"Why not?"

She paused, frowned. She didn't know how to explain; she didn't *want* to. "My cousin doesn't wish me there." She quickly added, "Nor do I wish to be in his house. As I was saying," she began again, "you open the door for any woman with whom you are walking, allowing her to pass through the doorway, then—"

"Why don't you want to go? It sounds like your sort of fun. All these rules, and you're good at them."

She made an impatient face. "I don't like my cousin, and he doesn't—"

"What's he like?"

"Who? Xavier?"

"Is that his name?"

"Yes. And he's very old, very charming, and very well-connected. You'll probably like him. Most people do."

"Not if he doesn't like you."

She opened her mouth, then closed it again without speaking. She wasn't sure whether to applaud or laugh at his loyalty. "All right, then you'll kowtow because you'll be afraid of him. Those who don't like him, fear him. He is powerful."

"You don't."

"Pardon?"

"You're not afraid of him."

She did laugh then, short and abrupt. "Yes, I am. That's why I don't go. May we continue please?" Without waiting for an answer, she said, "Above all, at the ball, please see to it that you do not allow yourself to be alone with a woman under thirty. Never. Not for a minute. It would be disastrous. A lady under thirty may be with a gentleman only in the company of a chaperone. Otherwise—"

"How old are you?" He leaned back, put one arm along the top of the seat, making himself perfectly comfortable. He could do that. Wherever Mick Tremore went—she envied the ability—he could make himself at ease.

She scowled a moment. "Nor does a gentleman ask a lady her age."

"Then how's he supposed to know if she needs a chaperone?"

She turned her scowl into a quick, fierce scrutiny, but his expression seemed to honestly question the logic. She muttered, "I'll be thirty. Thirty on the twenty-ninth."

"Of April?" This month.

"Yes." Her birthday was in three weeks.

He leaned back into the seat, smiling. "Then you need a chaperone."

"I most certainly do. But I can't afford one and my family doesn't care. I promise you, though, that the families of those ladies attending the duke's ball will ruin you if you take one of them aside—"

He laughed. "What? Will they cut my vast fortune out from under me?"

"No." He'd best understand. "They would find what mattered to you, then they'd take your ferrets, take your dogs, have you beaten, then thrown into jail. It would take you years to get out, if you ever could."

He sobered.

She tilted her head, looked at him directly. "Mr. Tremore," she said, "the people we are going to fool are the most powerful people in England." She let that sink in. "That's what I'm trying to tell you. Fooling them is one thing. But if you compromise one of their daughters, put her in a position to have to marry you, only to discover that you are entirely inappropriate for marriage, well, they will have your hide.''

And mine, too, she might have added.

She let the picture she'd painted for him fade into silence. She didn't want to unnerve him, only be sure he was warned fairly.

The peculiar thing was, she wasn't afraid they would fail. She was afraid, in her worst moments recently, that he would succeed too well.

She looked at his clean-shaven face, his tall, well-favored looks. As if in complicity with her fears, he leaned just then, and light cut across the side of his face and shoulders, delineating how perfectly handsome he was. A tremor ran through her.

Heaven above, to pass him off, she had to teach him to be halfway consistent with his manners and speech—and, if she could, this man was going to stop hearts. On the night of the ball, he would walk into that room and doctors were going to have to be called, because women were going to faint dead away, have seizures, heart attacks. He was the sort of man who sent female hearts pounding, sent windpipes into asthmatic fibrillations, who addled brains till nothing but nonsense came out.

God help the female upper class. Because if he polished up half as well as she was beginning to think he could, every woman in the ballroom, when he walked in, was going to become a raving idiot. Mindless giggles and fluttering fans would travel along with him like an epidemic of smallpox—no woman would go without a slight case; some, if allowed, would develop a fatal instance.

This singularly handsome man nodded now, then murmured, ''I wish you were coming with me.''

Oh, yes, that's what he needed. A gawky, six-foot-tall woman, whom Xavier had turned out into the streets, walking behind him like a lovesick calf.

A lovesick calf. Oh, dear. Edwina looked down. The shadows on her side of the carriage thankfully hid her, for she'd made herself blush. Poor fool, she was fascinated by the man who Mick Tremore was becoming.

Or no. Idiot that she was, she was fascinated by the man who *resisted* becoming exactly as she tried to make him. Fascinated by him, appalled at herself. A confusion that was becoming typical of her attitude toward him. Excited, boggled, frightened—unable to stop herself from wanting to stare at him, yet unable to look at him for more than a few seconds.

She could be one of them if she weren't careful, she realized. One of the brainless, fluttering nincompoops she was perpetually trying to educate to be better, stronger, more self-sufficient—sanguine yet open-eyed about what society truly had in mind for a woman.

Her gaze rested on her own folded hands in her lap. What had she been saying? She couldn't remember. She lifted her face, looked toward him, then spoke to the place where the coach ceiling came within inches of his head.

She began again. "When the carriage arrives, you alight first with the gentlemen, seeing to the ladies of your party, if you are the last man out." Yes, yes, out. She needed to get out of the carriage. Bringing him into it hadn't been the good idea she'd thought. "The footman holds the door. You step down, turn, offer your hand."

He said nothing.

"Do you have this then?" She glanced at him.

He leaned forward, his arms onto his thighs—and the beam through the doorway suddenly lit up the entire side of him. It made the sleeve of his shirt stark white, the silk of his vest sheen softly, and gave a round sleekness to the craggy breadth of his shoulders.

He nodded solemnly. Then let out a soft laugh. "No. I don't have it." He shook his head almost fondly. "But you'll repeat it when I do it wrong. You love to tell me rules."

Possibly, she did. At the end, though, there was a surprisingly gentle moment that broke any rules Edwina knew.

He stood below her on the ground, offering his hand

up to her exactly right, convincingly a gentleman. She gave him her hand, her fingers bending over the side of his as he pressed his thumb to her knuckles. Perfect, perfect. He did so much so well so quickly sometimes. Then he said from nowhere, "You all right then?"

When she'd stepped down, level with him, he squeezed her hand and held it. They stood, hand in hand, for a few seconds longer than was necessary.

What could he possibly mean? she thought. Here she was standing next to him, tidy, full of good information, in control of herself—doing her work with grave dignity. But, odder still, for one instant she wanted to answer his question by throwing her forehead onto his chest and wailing, *No, no! I'm not all right at all!*

She said, of course, "Yes. I'm fine."

He smiled, making a quick, little nod. "Good." He smiled wider, though his sideways, slanting good humor was almost a wince when he added, "Glad to hear it, loov." He nodded again. "No worse for wear?"

Ah. "No worse for wear," she repeated.

If she harbored any resentment for his part in their rough morning, she forgave him completely in that instant. She looked at his smooth lip and smiled.

"Good," he said again. "Good." And he meant it. Relief settled tangibly on him "So shall we go in and do your vowels again then?"

She smiled perfunctorily, while thinking, Oh, no! She couldn't decide how to avoid spending this afternoon and all subsequent afternoons, evenings, and mornings for the next four weeks watching his mouth form sounds. She nodded, full of deceit. "Yes. Shall we?"

Chapter 12

*A*s Edwina and Mr. Tremore crunched along the gravel drive that led back to the house, she asked herself, So what in the world were you thinking, when you suggested your game in the first place? That it would be innocent? That you could throw him out if it wasn't?

You misled yourself, Winnie. You set yourself up for a month of discomfort.

Indeed. The best that could be made of the situation, she thought, was to pretend that she hadn't made a horrible, indecent fool of herself and that he hadn't behaved like a bull in a mating paddock. This morning didn't exist. She wished he hadn't referred to it, even obliquely.

She wanted the idiosyncratic structure of his speech. She wanted to take it apart and rebuild it—something that could well yield a paper to read before the Royal Philological Society. It was a once-in-a-lifetime project that, on top of everything else, was free, since she was being paid to do it. He needed the money he could earn if he carried the bet off, and he might gain in the process a way to speak himself into a better station in life. They both had losses if they stopped and advantages if they did not. Yes, here they were, treading along toward the house and an arrangement they neither could afford to back out of, not without great cost.

Moreover, either one of them would have been hard-pressed to explain what had gone wrong with a bet in which the Lamonts now had a great deal invested:

At the house, they discovered a pocket watch had arrived—Mr. Tremore held it up, delighting in it. It chimed in pairs, *ding-ding, ding-ding*. Inside the boxes that had arrived with it—that he and she opened instantly like curious children there in the hallway—were two pairs of day boots, some men's formal evening slippers, a pair of dark kid gloves, a pair of white formal ones, and two top hats, one for evening made of black silk and one for day, a dark brown thing made of beaver felt that was luscious to touch. Edwina hadn't seen anything like it up close in a dozen years.

Surprised by the man's day hat (for what purpose did the Lamonts think he needed it?), she raised it from its box, then stood there holding it balanced on her fingertips inside the crown. She turned it, imagining it on the head of a man who knew how to wear it. The crown was high, rigid, and perfect, with a black band, while the felt of the crown and brim were softer than the underbelly of a cat. It was lined in silk.

As she held the hat up, examining it, Mr. Tremore abandoned the watch. "Well, I'll be buggered," he said, coming over. Then he corrected himself, laughing. "What an astonishing hat." It came out half-right—he found the *an* properly, but missed the H. *An astonishing 'at.*

He plucked it off her fingers and set it onto his head. The astonishing hat fit him perfectly, of course; it had been made for him. But the way he set it on his head was the truly astonishing part: at an ever-so-slight angle, instinctively debonaire. Well, Edwina thought. She had wanted to see the hat on a man who knew how to wear it, and here he was.

She stepped out of the way, so he could see himself in the hallway mirror. His expression in reflection liked what he saw, then she watched a ripple of displeasure pass over his face as his eyes dropped to his upper lip.

He truly did look different wearing a top hat—and no mustache.

"I'm sorry," she murmured.

He glanced at her. "About the mustache? Don't be. You didn't shave it off."

"I made you do it. I made us both feel awful."

He turned toward her, taking the hat off with a flourish of his wrist. The man loved style and show, and, honest to goodness, he actually had a little. He had a way about him. "You do this with everything, don't you, Winnie?"

"Do what?"

He shook his head. "All this thinking," he said. "It's like a superstition with you."

"Superstition?"

"Like throwing salt over your shoulder."

"Now, see here—"

"Winnie," he said, "let me tell you about my mum. Grand lady. Great mother. But a superstitious loon when it came to God. When I made her mad, she'd say"—he did a full Cornish accent quite well—"'Yee be a bad boy, Mick, but yee'll git what yee deserve. God'll see to it.' Then I'd fall and skin my knee and she'd say, real smug-like, 'See?' like God had shoved me down, not my own clumsiness or hurry. In the end, she died spitting up stuff from her lungs."

He looked down a moment, frowned. Then continued, "Hard and ugly for her, you know. I told her she didn't deserve it, but she cried and cried, full of teary regret. Oh, the confessions we got. She was sure she had done something wrong or hadn't done something right. But, you see, none of us believed bad of her. It was impossible. She was the gentlest woman. Couldn't hit us. The only weapon she had, when we were bad, was to promise us damnation. While us children just rolled our eyes at her, 'cause, see, not a one of us believed we were mortal: We felt so safe in her care."

He grew quiet for a few seconds, then said, "Don't die like that, Winnie. Or live like that either. Like you can know every little thing before it happens or can explain a mess away by retelling it to yourself a hundred times.''

She frowned at him. ''Sometimes, Mr. Tremore, it's *good* to question oneself—''

He leaned toward her. ''Winnie, what I did, I was lookin' for a way to do. You just gave me the chance. Maybe not even that much. It's over. Let it go. You worry too much over everything.''

''I care about details and my own behavior. I like to look at what I can, then rethink—''

He interrupted, shaking his head sadly. ''No, the nits and picks will give you the miseries, if you let them. They'll weigh you down like stones, make you sad and dotty. They did my mum. You didn't do anything so awful, so can we go on now? You're a good girl, Winnie Bollash. Kind and decent. Right generous with yourself. You ain't a snoot like I said when I first got here. I take it back.'' He grinned then added, teasing, ''Or mostly you ain't.''

''Aren't.''

''Right.'' Mrs. Reed came into the hallway just then, humming and dusting knickknacks on a shelf a dozen feet from them. They both listened to her till she disappeared again. Mick lowered his voice, in deference to the intrusion, but he brought the conversation right back. ''Serious now,'' he asked, ''do you believe some word you say or don't say can shave the hair off my lip? You didn't do it—I did. And when I want to, I'll grow it back again.'' He laughed softly, then winked at her. ''Which is better than you can say, Miss Bollash. 'Cause I'll always know you have the prettiest legs in all of England. Any time I want to see them, all I do is close my eyes.''

Oh, the cheek of him. Winnie smiled when she shouldn't have, then couldn't let him get away with being so self-satisfied. She said, ''No, Mr. Tremore, imagination is a fine thing, but we both know there is nothing like reality. I can see your mustache is gone right here—'' She touched his face above his lip before she thought not to. Taking her hand back quickly, she said, "I know reality. You have only what you are able to remember and daydream."

His eyebrows raised. He touched his own lip where her fingers had been the second before. He looked surprised, then not. He laughed, this time letting out that deep, low rumble he could make in his chest. It came forth through his easy, sideways smile. "Why, Miss Bollash," he said, "are you flirting with me?"

No. But heat began immediately to seep into her cheeks. She couldn't stop it. She couched her face, hiding it and the beginnings of a smile. "No, of course not."

"You are," he insisted.

"No." She shook her head vehemently, but the smile kept coming.

His finger touched under her chin, and he lifted her face to make her look at him. "You are," he said quietly, with utter seriousness. "Watch out, Miss Bollash. I like to flirt, but I like better where it gets me—and you don't."

She tried to absorb his admonishment as she stared into his eyes, shadowed there in the hallway. Smoky green eyes that made her heart thud; they took her breath away. He was right, of course. *You watch out, Miss Bollash.*

Yet she couldn't make herself stop smiling slightly. He found her attractive. She truly might be attractive. She'd been turning that idea over and over in her mind since this morning. It wasn't just words any longer. She had felt how attractive he found her. And, oh, she discovered, what a greed she had for that notion. Attractive. In her way. To the right man.

Mr. Tremore broke in on this sweet thought by saying, "Don't dally with me, Winnie. I'll lead you down the path. Sooner or later, I'll have you." Then he used a word she'd used once half an hour ago: Carefully, thoughtfully at each syllable, he said, "In-ap-pro-pri-ate." After a pause, he took the word for his own by saying, "As inap*pro*priate as that'd be."

In that moment she understood: Mick Tremore was

smarter, more attractive, and more aware of himself that she had ever supposed. And these marks in his character made him powerful. She was to be wary of that power; he understood it. She *was* wary. But she was something else, too. Her chin balanced on his fingers, she felt nothing ambiguous in one particular fact: Her blood came alive, as with nothing and no one else, when he stood near her.

That evening a tradition, born of cowardice, began. After dinner, Edwina still couldn't look a man in the mouth who was promising to lead her "down the path." Hunting for a way to sidestep their usual focus on his organs of speech, she came up with what possibly would become her best idea for re-tailoring his words, even his thoughts.

"I'd like to go into the library tonight, where I'll read to you aloud." She suggested brightly, "We'll douse you in the sounds of proper English, while we educate you in the classics."

In the library, she drew down a book, and began to read to him—he on the sofa, she in a chair at the other side of an unlit fireplace.

She expected to read to him for only an hour or so. But as she began the stories—with Dryden's translation of Ovid's *Metamorphoses* Mr. Tremore grew silent, rapt. He listened to the rhythm of English in heroic couplets, chosen so he'd hear the music of the language in a different way than prose exercises. Eventually, he scooted himself down onto the floor and lay nearer on the hearth rug, one arm over his head, the other fiddling with the brim of the hat on his chest—he'd worn it through dinner; he loved it.

While she read, he and she didn't argue. They didn't challenge each other. He stopped her occasionally for words he didn't know. That was the limit to his objection. He wouldn't let her speak a word, if he couldn't guess the sense behind it, not without her telling him the meaning—there were some they both had to look up. Winnie read for three hours through two different authors—he asked enough questions that she took down Bullfinch's *Mythology*—until at last she grew hoarse.

At the end, he must have drifted off to sleep. She wasn't certain when. The hat had covered his eyes for the last half hour. Something now though in the rhythm of his breathing, the movement of his chest, made her stop reading. He said nothing, when up till this point, if she stopped, he lifted the hat and encouraged her to continue.

He lay there now on the hearth rug, completely relaxed, his dog stretched out beside him, both sleeping peacefully. Edwina sighed and smiled at the sight of the two of them, motionless, quiet. A rare state for either.

She closed the book in her lap, resting her hand on it. Then the pressure, the odd pressure as she stared at him, made her draw in a breath. Hesitantly, then intentionally, she pressed on the book, over where he had touched her today. There. Winnie had never imagined he might want to do that. It had been shocking: humiliating for him to know that animal part of her, to know her—

She couldn't proceed further in her thinking . . . but, oh, the feeling his hand had left on her. It was a constant battle not to remember the strong curve of his fingers, the feel of his hand when he curved it to—

Enough. She really had to *not* think about it. Yet more and more there seemed a bevy of things she was not supposed to think about—and by virtue of trying to remember not to, she hardly thought of anything else.

Shaking her head at herself, Winnie stood and walked to the bookshelf, where, as she replaced her book, the hair on her arms suddenly pricked with the full irony of what she'd been reading. The spine that she pushed into place read *Bulfinch's Mythology: The Age of Fable,* the last tale that she had pronounced aloud beginning:

Pygmalion was a sculptor who made with wonderful

skill from ivory a perfect semblance of a maiden that seemed to be alive. . . .

Winnie glanced at the man asleep on her hearth. She was vain of how clever she was at teaching phonetics, how smartly she could break down the vowels and diphthongs of upper-class English, manufacture its inflections, feed its vocabulary, instruct on the human considerations that were its manners. That was partly what had gotten them here, her vanity. She was good at it.

An art so perfect, he fell in love with his counterfeit creation. . . .

Yet, today, she had stepped beyond her art, and she knew it. She pushed Mr. Tremore to embody her own conception of what a man should be—or rather what a gentleman should be, she corrected herself. She was limning out her own personal conception of what a gentleman should look like and say and how he should behave, while Mr. Tremore was grabbing up the notion, running like a racehorse with it, embodying her ideal more perfectly by the day.

And smoke roiled up . . . and Pygmalion made sacrifices on the altars of Venus. . . .

Part II

Winnie

The festival of Venus was at hand. . . . Victims were offered, the altars smoked. . . . When Pygmalion had performed his part of the solemnities, he stood before the altar and timidly said, "Ye gods, who can do all things, give me, I pray you, for my wife"— he dared not say "my ivory virgin," but said instead—"one like my ivory virgin."

"Pygmalion," *The Age of Fable*
THOMAS BULLFINCH, LONDON, 1855

Chapter 13

*W*hen Winnie was seventeen years old, her father died. This was eleven years after her mother had left them, only to die on some foreign continent—her mother had traveled so much after her departure that no one had been able to keep up with her. The letter announcing her death had been forwarded a number of times, leaving Winnie and her father with only the information that Lady Sissingley had died of pneumonia in Africa, India, or, possibly, China.

Winnie had been raised by a series of governesses and a father who—though he loved her, she was sure—was preoccupied with his own work. He was a linguistics scholar of some stature. Before he died, he'd written more than a hundred monographs on language related topics and two textbooks. He was the foremost British theoretician on RP, received pronunciation—that is, the sounds that originated in upper-class mouths, how these sounds were formed, how they were perceived in the ear, and what subtle changes were happening to them as they were being transmitted via the public schools to the English middle class.

When Lionel Bollash—Regius Professor Bollash, Marquess of Sissingley by courtesy of being the fourth Duke of Arles's only son—died, everyone expected that his daughter would be taken into the household of his second cousin, Milford Xavier Bollash, who, up to that point, had been merely the grandnephew of the fourth duke, second in line, part of the family, but with no title other than the courtesty of "Lord" before his name.

To everyone's astonishment, however, when Xavier succeeded to the marquisate—inheriting not only Edwina's father's title, but every one of her family's possessions, the money, goods, and entailed estates that composed the full honor of being heir apparent to the duchy—he did not welcome her into his household. Winnie had barely absorbed the implications, however, when another calamity befell the family.

The hale and hearty fourth Duke of Arles, Winnie's grandfather and someone she might have counted on to lean on Xavier to sponsor her at least through a Season, to be of nominal support, while out on a walk at the ripe old age of one-hundred-three, was struck by lightning and smote dead on the spot. He followed his son to the grave by a delay of only three days. Xavier acquired the duchy of Arles in the same week he succeeded to the already vast and lucrative holdings of the Sissingley marquisate, ascending to the full roll call of honors: the fifth Duke of Arles, Marquess of Sissingley, Count of Grennewick, Viscount Berwick—oh, there were more; she couldn't even remember them all.

At which point, Xavier told the seventeen-year-old Winnie quite plainly that, not only was she not residing under his roof, but: "There is no point in sponsoring you for a Season in London either, my dear. You are unmarriageable. You have no property to speak of. Heaven knows you aren't pretty. And, as if these facts weren't enough, you ruin what little femininity you have by mimicking your dotty father's obsession with how people talk."

He told her this by way of excusing himself for using her dowry to buy an elaborate custom, crested brougham with eight matching bays and uniform livery for his footmen and coachman.

The day he packed her into this coach to send her off, one-way, he added, "You may as well be a man."

If only she had been, she would have been in line ahead of him.

But she was a girl, a funny-looking girl who, grieving for a father and grandfather, was ill-prepared. She— nor her father nor grandfather, she was sure—had considered for a moment that a cousin would not see to her at least modestly. She hadn't fully believed it, even as he was saying he wouldn't, till she was riding away in the coach with Milton, her butler, on her way to his sister's house. Her butler's sister's house, for goodness sakes.

Of course, by Arles's standards, he *had* seen to her: A year and a half later, when the Home Office caught wind of her situation (as it turned out, what Xavier had done wasn't quite legal) and said he must make restitution of her dowry—property he had sold, money he had already spent—he resigned claim to the only thing he didn't know what to do with: her father's library on human speech and the building it was housed in, the marquess's town house in Knightsbridge.

What was Arles like? Mr. Tremore had asked. Besides greedy? Old, but spry. When he had inherited the world, Xavier was already in his late seventies. All her life, he had stood at the self-assured center of her family. The witty one, the clever one, the one who entertained them all, the one who had the parties and the friends and connections. He loved power and influence; he cultivated them. He wanted to be adored and, generally, was.

Edwina had actually admired him. She had circled the little planet of her father—a father who floated in the solitary ethers of academia—in awe of her brighter, more gregarious second cousin, once removed. An obscure little moon to Xavier's sun.

She used what she'd acquired of her father's things and her father's knowledge to make ends meet in a way her father never could have imagined. Lionel Bollash had had no head for business; he hadn't needed one, having enjoyed, as his father before him and every other previous Marquess of Sissingley, one of the most lucrative entailments in the empire. Edwina had come through, though; she was even proud of herself. She was happiest when she was working. She loved what she did.

Nonetheless, she retained a degree of rancor for Xavier and an odd sense of shame.

One of her first students, who knew of events, said, "Oh, it was perhaps for the best. These things happen." It was meant as consolation. Yet Edwina could not surmount a sense of horror to hear the words.

For the best? As if, given the choice, she should have wished all this to befall her? Sought it on purpose? Since it was so good?

No, she personally thought she could have done without it.

Oddly enough, the parents of the same student, when the duke had first dispossessed Edwina, had been outraged. People in general at the time were outraged. Then they weren't. Life went on. It took a year or more, but eventually everyone returned to making their morning calls on Xavier's wife, to seeking his support, to asking him to donate to the missionary fund, to invest in their projects. And they never stopped decking themselves out and going to his annual ball.

A ball that Edwina herself had never attended—she'd been too young, then too strained a relation. Nor could she call at Xavier's house. He wouldn't have allowed it; she wouldn't have wanted to. Which made her feel more or less marooned, a little red boat in a dry basin at low tide. She could send other little boats out upon the sea of English high society. She could teach them to sail, to skim along the water with style and grace. While her own sails only luffed in the wind.

The next morning, Mick lathered up his chin and cheeks, but left his upper lip dry. In one night, he already had a dark shadow of stubble on his lip. He twisted his mouth, holding his cheek taut with his fingers, and shaved as usual: both cheeks, his chin, his jaw, his lower face, save the place under his nose.

He rinsed, stood up, then, as he toweled himself dry, stared into the mirror. The dark hair across his lip looked like dirt on his mouth. He'd looked better clean-shaven. In a few days, he'd look fine again, he supposed. His old self. But his new self stood there, cogitating, unhappy with an itchy lip that looked as if he'd been drinking stout and forgot to wipe his mouth.

So which self should I be? he asked.

Then the question unnerved him.

Which self? There weren't two of him.

Get rid of the thing, he told himself. Don't make it complicated. Winnie liked him better without it. Anything that reminded her that his sex was the opposite, the mate, to hers alarmed her. Fine, he could go delicate with her. He could become the most gentlemanly gentleman she'd ever known. All her ladylike rules were a lot of bung, but he was beginning to understand why gents went through the ordeal.

He stared into the mirror, turning his head. A barber had come in last week and taken a razor to the hair at the back of his neck. There was a clean line where his hair met his collar, nothing scraggily on his neck. Neat. His shirt collar was high on his throat, snug. It half choked him sometimes to wear it. Milton had been showing him how to tie a necktie, but he'd made a tangle of it today. It draped, wrinkled from effort, on either side of his neck down his vest.

Outside he was looking more and more like—what was it they wanted him to be? A viscount? But inside he still felt like Mick from Cornwall who lived underneath a shoemaker's shop in London next door to the Waste Market.

Winnie liked the result, and that made half of him— the lower half of him—want to go on. He'd done crazier things to get up close to a woman he liked. The other half of him, though, hesitated

More and more, he spoke differently. He acted different, too. But the strange thing was, sometimes he thought different lately. Differently. Hell, he worried over whether to say *different* or *differently*, when how the hell much could it matter? And why did he care?

He thought things like, Wouldn't it be nice to have a respectable woman like Winnie Bollash? When what he wanted of Winnie, of course, was for her to be unrespectable with him. No, no, he corrected, not Winnie Bollash. He didn't want her; he couldn't have her. But . . . oh, a seamstress's assistant maybe. A woman *like* Winnie Bollash. Good-hearted, smart, hardworking. And faithful. Of the half dozen highborn women he'd been with, every one of them had been married. But Winnie . . . a woman *like* Winnie would be loyal. Hell, there she was yesterday, steadfastly trampling along beside him after he'd scared half the wits from her just hours before. And grit. She had grit.

He picked up the razor again, then spoke to the fellow on the other side of the mirror, taking exaggerated care with pronunciation. "I rahther think you should take the mustache off, old man. Jolly good idea."

Stupid toff. Except he liked that his room was dry. In the cellar under the shoemaker's, half the time when it rained, water seeped through the walls. He liked not being exhausted at the end of the day. Eating well and regularly had its advantages. And new words—especially finding new words, more particular words, and being *understood* when he said them—were bloody marvelous.

It felt surprisingly good not to be misunderstood most of the time—to have a thought, a feeling, and say it, then have others grasp what he was trying to get across. Expressing himself easily relieved a tension in him he hadn't known was there. And it was useful, being able to tell people what he wanted. Milton understood what he said lately, and Molly Reed laughed at his jokes. Useful and enjoyable. And it would most surely be a help, when he next had to explain to some fancy housekeeper that he wasn't begging at her kitchen door, but offering to rid her of a chronic problem in London.

Useful. Mick looked down at the sharp razor itself,

pearl-handled. It was the smoothest-feeling blade he'd ever held. He liked the feel of it on his skin. It cut clean.

He looked at the hand that had hold of it. There wasn't a mark on it, not a scratch or bite, because the hand didn't dive into the rat holes of life. If he wasn't careful, he'd have himself do-nothing gentleman's hands. Yes, hands that had time to think—but look what he thought. How to trade his good ol' flavor-savor mustache for a look at a pair of legs he wasn't supposed to touch. On a woman he couldn't have.

The really stupid part, though, was he picked up the shaving brush, clacked it around in the soap cup again, then lathered his lip up. He razored the damn beginnings of mustache off, shaving his lip again for Winnie. Because he was hoping for another damn, pointless look.

Ironically, down the hall, Winnie was also standing before a mirror. She had, however, a slightly different prospect. Ten feet from the mirror, she looked at the full-length reflection of her body, stark naked.

She could never remember taking off her clothes by the light of day before, simply to look at herself. She had never thought not to, she had simply never done it. This morning, though, with her nightgown off, before she drew a stitch over her head, she turned to the mirror to survey herself.

Her body. She was immediately struck by how long her legs were. She'd never thought of them. But yes, they were long, and their muscles were good, well-proportioned. Her legs were firm. They were pretty. It was the first time she could honestly like any part of herself. They'd always been covered up. She'd never looked. Now that she had—well, marvelous: The only part of her that was pretty was one that no one would see, not even the faintest shape.

And the rest of her—oh. Her breasts were two little funnels on her chest. Her waist was small, but her hips and buttocks offset any advantage that brought. They were too full, making her into a pear.

Her eyes settled at the top of her legs, at the apex between. The hair there was dense, tight-curling, and dark cherry blond, only slightly deeper in hue than the hair on her head. Winnie touched it. It was wiry. Like—

Like a mustache.

She tried to envision what Mick Tremore looked like here. She couldn't. The small bits she'd seen on stone cherubs, the baby penises (there, she'd thought the word!), had always seemed so vulnerable. Cherub male parts in the flesh, she always thought, would look like little snails without shells—an idea that most certainly didn't suit Mr. Tremore. Adult stone men had fig leaves where their widges should be. She was sure that was wrong. Which left only imagination.

And a word. She formed it silently with her mouth. *Widge.* Her lips looked as if they were blowing a kiss. What did one look like? And hair. Did a widge wear a mustache?

She found herself feeling uneasy, silly, peculiar— giggling as she donned her clothes for the day. Just as she was getting her hair up, there was a knock at her door.

She jumped guiltily, then thought, Oh, goodness, Mr. Tremore was so forward. There he was outside in her sitting room, knocking on her bedroom door.

When she opened it, though, it was Milton. "May I come in, m'lady?" He looked grave.

"Yes. Certainly. Is something wrong?"

He frowned. He stammered. "I— Well, yes—" He finally said, "I've been with your family"—he cleared his throat—"for a very long time, and I have never intruded, my lady." She waited for him to go on. It took him a moment. "I was there on the night you were born."

"Yes, Milton. What's the point? What is bothering you?"

"Well." He drew his small frame up and stiffened

his mouth. "Well," he repeated, "Mrs. Reed and I were discussing it, and we think—" He blurted the rest. "We think it would be better if Mr. Tremore moved downstairs with me."

Edwina sank down into the chair by her bed. She stared at him. "Why?"

He frowned. "My lady, you are living upstairs with a man—well, who is— We didn't think— No one thought— But, well, now— And he clearly finds you—"

"You think it's immodest of me to have him staying above stairs, his room on the same floor as mine?"

"Yes, m'lady."

Goodness, such a judgment from Milton, who tended to be generous with her. Winnie nodded, expressing her understanding.

"There are eight empty rooms below stairs," he proceeded to tell her. "Mr. Tremore could have any of them. I can make one up, tell him, help him move—"

"No." She shook her head quickly. "I'll tell him."

Milton was right, of course. She couldn't have a . . . a gentleman sleeping under her roof, just him and herself alone upstairs. Why hadn't she thought of it in this light before?

She repeated, "I'll tell him. I'll explain." She glanced at Milton, the most loyal family she had. "I appreciate it," she said. "Thank you for saying."

He nodded. "Your best interests," he murmured. "I've watched you grow up into a fine young woman, Lady Bollash." The form of address for the eldest daughter of a marquess; he had never made the transition, always addressing her with the same respect. He continued, "I am proud to work for you. I don't wish to see you"—he hesitated again—"unhappy when he goes. I'd stay by you, it's not that—"

Ah. It wasn't for form's sake that he wanted to move Mr. Tremore, not for the sake of gossip or appearances. He feared she'd succumb to ruin itself.

"It's—" He continued, "Well, I do think, if Mr.

Tremore were to sleep downstairs in the room next to mine, it would be better.''

"Yes, it would be." She nodded again, then repeated herself. "I'll tell him."

Winnie was going to make short work of the obligation. She would go downstairs, find Mr. Tremore, and tell him straight off. She'd explain that he'd become—what? A man. He'd become a man to her and to the others around them.

How awful. She couldn't say that. What had he been before?

God knew. She only knew that now he fit a different pattern. It didn't matter if a ratcatcher was given her finest room. But it mattered if Mick slept within tiptoe of her bed, especially given that she stood before it recently, looking at her own naked body while wondering about his.

It mattered. And she'd say.

Then she hedged. At the foot of the stairs, she veered toward her laboratory. There, she sat and stared blankly at her notes, trying to think how to phrase it.

Chapter 14

ᴡᴤᴇ

*W*innie intended to mention to Mick all that day that it would be better, all things considered, if he moved himself and his things downstairs. She intended to, but didn't do it. She didn't know why she hesitated. It was her house. She could make the decision. Yet there never seemed an appropriate moment.

Moreover, Mick was moodier than usual, unsettled. It was a new or at least a less often seen side to him. All day long, he seemed lost in thought. She set him up to do his drills and exercises on his own, using a mirror and a gramophone. When she checked on him half an hour later, though, he only sat, staring into space, running his finger over his bare lip—surprisingly, it had been shaved again. The muscle at the side of his jaw, the one that squared it so perfectly, flexed morning till night. In the end, she simply funked the task of speaking to him about moving downstairs. She'd do it tomorrow, she promised herself.

Then tomorrow came, and she couldn't find him.

Mick occasionally left for short periods of time. "To attend to my business," he always said quite formally. Edwina was never sure exactly what he did. He had animals to which he attended, she knew. He had friends, she suspected, he taunted with his new wealth and manners.

She heard him return about noon. She was down the

hall from her lab in the library, reading, when she became aware of him knocking around in the mudroom at the back of the house in a way Milton never did—Mick usually had mud *on* him. She could hear his kicking off wellies, as if he'd come up through the back garden.

A few minutes later, she recognized his footfalls in the hallway, coming toward her, though his tread was a bit heavier and more jangly than usual.

Then he appeared into the doorway and announced, "It's the carriage house."

"What's the carriage house?"

"The rats. That's where they are. They have a nest. Let's go get 'em."

She laughed. "You want me to catch rats with you?"

"It's fun," he said. He grinned, the most relaxed she'd seen him in a day or two. Fun. He was the Mick Tremore again who thought everything, life itself, was fun.

She sat back in her chair, smiling despite herself. It wasn't such a bad way to see things, she decided. She wished her existence were fun or at least that she thought it was as often as he did. "It's work," she contradicted. And he was dressed for work. He was wearing heavy boots and old clothes.

He came over, lifted her, or tried to, by the arm. "True, but exciting work. Come on. You don't have to help or watch, but you should see what I'm talking about. It's your carriage house."

She let herself be stood up by the arm, then raised one eyebrow at him. "Do you kill them?"

"The rats? Of course."

She frowned. "Is it bloody?"

"Not for me, though I'm sure the rats think otherwise—the dogs and ferrets get messy." He made a mock-exasperated face. "Winnie, they're rats. They're dirty, ugly rats, who each have fifty or sixty babies a year, and those babies start dropping babies by two months. You figure it out. That's a lot of little things scooting around, eating your horses' oats, burrowing into your walls, getting up into your carriage—"

"Ewww," she shuddered, then wrinkled her nose. "Still, they're animals."

He laughed with that rumble that always caught her up into it somehow and made her want to smile back. "You're right, loov." She'd told him a number of times that it wasn't *loov* but *love,* and in either case that it was an unseemly form of address, yet still he insisted on using it. He said, pulling her forward, "We should go buy them cheese, leave it for them each night, maybe put a little bow on it. Oh, come on." He used her arm to turn her and put her ahead of him, then he pushed at her back.

When, over her shoulder, she threw him a worried look, he only wiggled his eyebrows in that funny way he could when he was thrilled with himself. "Shiver me timbers, mate," he said gleefully. He did his old accent, only thicker: Cornwall, the land of pirates, with a Cockney twist. "We'll pint th' carrich 'ouse wiv ther blewd."

It was a relief to see him in fine spirits again.

She went out with him to the carriage house, thinking, Yes, here was the opportunity. While he was doing something that made him feel good, she'd tell him he was moving downstairs. Why was she making it such a tribulation? It wasn't. He'd shrug; he wouldn't even care.

At the end of her drive in front of the carriage house, she saw a donkey cart. He'd borrowed it from a friend to transport his dogs and ferrets. In the back of the cart, Mick's entire retinue barked and kicked up a commotion the moment he and she came into view.

From the wood cart, he unloaded half a dozen box-carriers, two ferrets to a box. Five small dogs clambered down, but not until Mick whistled for them. Magic jumped at his heels. The little dog was alert in a new way, more excited. Into the carriage house Winnie went, following this animal act—Mick with carriers under both arms, more dangling off his hands, dogs nipping at his heels, a bevy of small beasts to whom, it seemed, he sang. Whether to control them somehow—for they seemed to follow with it—or as an expression of his own absorbed contentment, he hummed a low tune, the Pied Piper.

Inside the carriage house, he squatted, setting boxfuls of ferrets onto the floor. The dogs continued to make a ruckus. But when he moved his hand through the air at them and said, "Hey," every one of them quieted and sat—six motley little terrier faces looking up at him expectantly. "You wait," he told them.

She watched him move—he stooped, stood, bent to slide a ferret box across the floor, motioned to a dog, each of which listened with rapt attention—as he explained to her.

"Ratting's a sport where I come from. A useful sport that neighbors do together. Growing up, I ratted barns, poultry houses, and mines with sometimes as many as a dozen men. . . ."

He said more, but she heard only bits. She watched, mesmerized. Methodically, he sat dogs at intervals, then slid ferret boxes, turned them, looked, turned one a few more degrees. Periodically, he assessed the space, the placement, as if he had an analytical plan. All the while, he jangled—tools swung from his hips as he moved, off a wide leather belt he'd strapped on: collars with bells, a coil of string, secateurs, a long, slender wood club, a short metal cosh.

Over the edge of the belt against his hip was folded a pair of old leather gloves. He wore heavy boots. They clunked as he walked. His trousers were tucked into them, while into the trousers was tucked a tight-fitting knit shirt, faded red, open at the neck. Old work clothes, similar to those the day she'd first seen him, though these had considerable more dignity, all fascinated properly, no one chasing him: Mick in control.

He was graceful and precise. He knew what he was doing.

He finished some sort of explanation. ". . . but only if you station the dogs in good tactical positions," he said. "Then you're ready to send the ferrets into the likely places. They raid the nest. What escapes them has to face the dogs. And me—I try to get any who get by the first two lines of attack.''

It was a battlefield to him, a war to be waged with his animal army. Winnie shuddered again. She must have made a sound, for he stopped and looked around. ''You're gonna go before I start. But I just wanted you to know, I guess, it's gonna be better when I'm done.'' As if she'd argued with him he said, ''It's none worse than foxhunting. In fact, the terriers cut their teeth on foxes. Magic here'll go to ground for fox *or* rat, follow the darn thing right under the earth, then stay there barking till you dig him and the animal out.''

She grimaced. ''Heavens, if I even saw a rat—'' She looked at him. ''What's it like?''

''See them?'' He laughed at her timid curiosity. ''They're going to be jumping out of the woodwork, leaping everywhere.'' He shook his head. ''It'll be about as crazy as you can imagine for a few minutes, all of us chasing each other, with rats making us wild. It isn't pretty, Win, but it sure is exciting. You'd be safe up in the loft, if you wanted to watch.''

''Safe?''

''Brown rats don't like heights.''

''Um, no, thank you.''

''It's a shame,'' he teased her. ''You're missing about the most exciting thing you'll ever see in your life.''

She doubted that. She suspected she was looking at the most exciting thing in her life. A man with coshes and belled collars hanging off him, in hobnailed boots that clacked like thunder on her floor, who wanted to make her carriage house ''better.''

''What?'' he said. ''Why are you staring at me like that?'' He smiled, then, as if she'd accused him of something, said, ''All right, I brought you out here because I wanted you to see how good I am at it. If you stayed, you'd be impressed.'' His face drew up further into his recklessly confident, left-tilting grin.

''I am impressed.'' She smiled back, if a little un-easily. Rats. Ugh. ''I'm sure you're enormously competent.'' She shook her head. ''You're good at a lot of things.''

He tilted his head with interest. ''You're always fixing me.''

''You're good at a lot of things,'' she repeated.

''Do you think so?'' He liked the idea.

''Yes.''

She looked around. With a little shiver she could imagine his battle plan come to life. Yet it was too earthy and frightening to let her mind go very far with it. Though it would be triumphant, she didn't doubt. ''So you have—'' She didn't know what to call them then found, ''customers and places you go?''

''Ace,'' he said, having fun with her.

''How do you remember where you've been and haven't been and who needs it done and how much you charge?''

He glanced over his shoulder as if she were crazy. ''I don't remember it. I write it down.''

''Where?'' she asked. She envisioned scraps of paper or the back of his hand.

She received another glance that mocked her doltish lack of imagination. ''In a book, Win.''

''A ledger?''

He rolled his eyes. ''You could call it that. I'm a businessman. I have a hundred regular customers, and every year I have to sell myself to a hundred new ones. I write down their addresses, where I've been, what they've said. I add up what I make—last year, I earned sixty-four pounds. That's not too bad for a bloke''— he corrected—''for a fellow like me. Damn good, in fact.''

It was indeed. She was stunned. And he kept records?

He went on. ''Joe there is Magic's son. The fellow with the cart has a bitch Maj is fond of. I traded first pick of the litter next time for second, in exchange for the use of his cart today.''

''That was nice of you.''

''No, it wasn't. That's what I'm trying to tell you.

It's my business. I have to keep the fellow happy and making a living, or I don't get to use his cart; he couldn't afford to keep it. . . ."

He kept going, keen to talk about his work. He was proud of it. And Winnie surprised herself with how fascinating she found the ins and outs of ratcatching.

Mick took out a ferret, snapped on a belled collar, ". . . because this is the one going under the boards, and I want to know where she is." He held the little animal up. Her dark coat was glossy, mink-colored. "Pretty, isn't she?"

As he dropped it back into its box for the moment, Winnie thought, no, not the ferret, the *man* was beautiful, long-armed, long-legged, physical, robustly reeking of health. Even in rat clothes.

A ratcatcher. He *was* one. Imagine. And he'd kissed her: once gently, once with so much passion it had made her cry.

Oh, dear, dear, she reprimanded herself. Don't find him exciting. Or, no, why not hire a chimney sweep to clean the chimney, then kiss him, too? She could call the glazier to fix the front window and perhaps have a hug. And the plumber was a nice man—*smirk, smirk, smirk*. Oh, Edwina, she thought, get hold of yourself.

Rats, she thought. Goodness. Time to leave. He was set up, ready to begin. She turned. "Well—" she said.

Mick watched her and knew she was about to go. For no better reason than he wanted to hold her there, he said, "Watch this."

He raised his arm over Magic, snapped his fingers. And ol' Magic did his old magic. Just for fun, just because Mick wanted him to, he started to jump.

Now Magic wasn't a good-looking dog. He had a white body, a whiskery-looking snout from the white fur flecking into brown, a short, shaggy coat, and a wizened little face. A scruffy little dog, barely a foot high at the withers. But Maj had the heart of a giant. If he did something, he put his whole, fearless self into it.

He jumped more than five feet into the air. Straight up. Then, his neat little feet no sooner touching the ground, he went up, straight up again. It delighted Mick to see the energy the dog put into it. Over and over. He wouldn't stop till Mick told him to. If Mick should die someday between when he told the dog to jump and the stop signal, Maj would jump himself to death.

Mick smiled at Win, at her face beaming with wonder. "It's like he has springs in his back legs," he said. "Have you ever seen anything like it? He's jumping five times his height. If I could do that, I could leap this carriage house."

She shook her head, glued now to the sight. He felt exhilarated, seeing her there, her expression amused, absorbed. Oh, he wanted to charm her. He wanted to woo her, make her stay. He just wasn't sure how to do it. Not by setting rats loose on her.

For Maj's sake, he gave a nod of his head, and the dog settled to earth, bright-eyed, happy, ready to go again the second he might be asked. Mick fed him a piece of apple from his pocket, something the dog loved, his payment—though had there been no payment that would have been all right, too; often there wasn't.

Mick knew Win wasn't listening as he told her about the dog; he was barely listening to himself. He wanted to say, *Don't go. Just stay. Stay and keep looking at me like that.* He rattled on instead, "Only once did a rat ever mess with this fierce little fellow, and the bite only made Magic madder. . . ."

He glanced at Winnie. She was enjoying the dog's antics, but she was dancing on her feet a little. The ratting made her nervous. She didn't like the atmosphere. She didn't want to watch rats killed.

Why had he brought her out here? He could have predicted her reaction.

He knew the answer, of course. Her face was the answer. Because he was so damn good at this that it was obvious even in the way he laid out his attack—

and he was so damn awkward at everything else she was teaching him. He wanted to be . . . skillful, elegant at something in front of her. Ha. Elegant at being a ratcatcher. Now, there was a way to impress the ladies.

Thing was, it often did impress them. More than once, a lady had watched from over her upstairs banister as he got rid of the brown rats below. Brown rats on the ground floor, the milder black rats in the upper stories; it never varied. It was the order of the rat world. A few cats could take care of the black rats upstairs, but Mick was the man for the meaner ones who dominated the more accessible turf. More than once, a lady had watched him do the deed, shrieking in disgust but riveted. Then he'd clean himself up in her scullery or mudroom, and been invited for a cup of tea or a glass of claret, where one thing led to another.

"I have to go," Winnie said.

He looked up at her. "I know. I'll wash and change, then meet you for the afternoon lesson. I'll be on time."

"That would be good." She took a step, then rotated back. "Oh, and I have to tell you something. Milton," she said, as if the man should be forgiven for something, tolerated. Then she shook her head. "No, not Milton. Me—"

Mick waited. The blood in his body knew before he did. It reacted to her expression or reluctance or something. It started to pump hard, rush. He was going to be told something bad.

She said, "Um, I'd, uh—like you to move your things downstairs to the room next to Milton's. He'll help you do it."

More for her to deny it, he asked, "You want me to move into the servants' quarters?"

She shook her head no, but she confirmed it. "You'll be with Milton," like it was a big privilege, "the room down one from his."

"Right."

Defensively, she added what he already knew. "I

like Milton. He's more than a servant. He lives down-stairs because he prefers to and because it's proper.''

''And because he's your butler.''

She frowned, opened her mouth, then said nothing, like she was angry with at him for saying it out loud.

While the reality of it raced around inside him. He knew why he was being moved. Mick the rake, banished. Maybe she could remember not to kiss the help, if the East End hooligan-help lived a few feet further away from her. Bloody hell, she was welcome to try.

He didn't dare say anything for a moment. And he didn't want her to see his disappointment, so he turned his back, waving away her tongue-tied, irritated confusion. ''No need to explain,'' he said. He stooped down and stroked his dog. ''I'm as good as there, Miss Bollash. I'll do it as soon as we finish here. You better go now. I'm gonna start.''

He stood, dusted his hands on his trousers, pulled his gloves off his belt.

Just then, a ferret down the way made an angry little sound at her coworker in the carrier. There was a hiss and a little *bonk* of soft bodies.

And, like that, Winnie was on him. Her weight hit him. She grabbed his shoulders and half-climbed his back to his neck. She all but knocked him down, before he got a leg-hold of her with her clutching him by his chin and a handful of ear.

''Ferrets,'' he muttered as best he could with her arm under his jaw.

Her body relaxed a little, though she didn't relinquish her higher position. She had her legs wrapped around him like a vise, skirts and all.

''Just ferrets,'' he assured her.

He torqued at the waist and slowly pulled her down him, trying to lower a sizeable woman from an awkward position without dropping her. Oh, it was right odd and delicious, the feel of easing her down. He jerked when her parted legs slid for a second over the top of his thigh. She leaped, too, from the contact of their bodies, though she was more taken aback. Him, he was getting used to the jumps and jolts of their pleasure. It was a fierce thing. No help for it; it slammed them around.

He peeled her off him, his blood hopping. He could feel the place where her breasts had pressed into his back, the place where she'd straddled his thigh. Christ, he thought. He shifted her around in front of him, lowering her by her spectacular bum, down onto her feet.

And there she was, her face an inch away from his for a second, her body all but up against him. She paused, looking up. If he blew on her, her eyelashes would've fluttered from his breath. For one blistering moment, he was sure she was waiting—waiting for him to do what he normally might. If he wanted to kiss a woman who got this close, he didn't usually hesitate.

This time, though, he murmured down into her face, "It'd be my fault again, wouldn't it?"

"What would?" She wet her lips, staying right there, waiting.

Hell, he thought. He didn't do half bad, when he had some distance. But when she was this close, it just made him angry she wouldn't admit it. He asked bluntly, "Do you want me to kiss you?"

"No!" she said instantly. Though the shock in her face, he would've guessed, was more for having her mind read than from the idea.

He turned her loose, pushing her away. "Fine. If you ever do, just remember I like a little participation. A little share in the responsibility, Miss Bollash. If you want me to kiss you, it'd be right damn nice if you'd say so. Otherwise"—he reverted intentionally—"you ain't havin' a kiss from me."

She glared and pressed her lips so hard together, they turned white. Her face was full of havoc—frustration, vexation, bewilderment—for what had just happened.

Then the mean witch of a woman said, "Instead of *right*—*right nice* or *right fine*—you should say *quite* or *rather* or even *ratherish.*"

He gave a snort. He wanted to hoot. "I'm not saying *ratherish.*"

Then he wanted to laugh outright. Here they were, him and Winnie, going at it again. Jesus, the woman was thick. Didn't she feel it? Hell, he wanted to shove her against the wall between bridle straps, pull up her skirts— Or no, maybe in the carriage, flat out on the seat or— Jesus, he couldn't think how to do it or, rather, he could think of a hundred ways he wanted to. He wanted to have her, just have her—maybe the floor would do, if the dogs and ferrets didn't mind.

He made himself ask instead, "What do you want me to say? What was the rest?"

She corrected him again. "*Pardon.* Remember you're supposed to say *pardon* when you want someone to repeat themselves."

He raised his brow with theatrical impatience and said, "Pardon, Miss Bollash? What the bloody foke do you want me to say instead of *right damn fine*?"

She stared fixedly. "*Quite fine.* Or *rather fine.*"

"*Rather,*" he repeated. Rahther. Mick could hear himself saying it right. He looked at Winnie. She waited for the whole phrase. Stupid woman. She was happier fixing him than admiring him. It was her way of connecting, her way of shagging him blind. "Rahther fine, Miss Bollash."

He wondered if maybe he still said it wrong though, because she blinked at him, stared. But then she said, "Well. Yes. That's quite good." She laughed. "Right damn fine, in fact." She had a bloody wonderful laugh when she let it out, which wasn't often. Then she murmured, without explanation, "I'm sorry."

Another apology, though he wasn't sure for what. But without a word more of explanation, she turned and bolted.

He watched her run from the carriage house, up her back garden, all the way to her back door and inside her house without stopping.

Bloody wonderful, Mick. You're a prize.

He pushed his hand back through his hair, then held

a handful of it, closing his eyes. He breathed, only breathed, for a minute, letting his mind, his blood calm. God bless, the woman made him crazy.

He took it out on the rats.

He rid the place of them in short order—ferrets chasing and diving, dogs jumping, rats screeching and running everywhere. Ten minutes of pandemonium, which suited his mood perfectly.

At the end of it, he sat on the floor in the midst of mayhem. He took an accounting: several dozen dead rats, with a ferret and a dog bit, the dog pretty badly. Right, he thought. Right.

"She could have a point, you know," he told the little dog softly as he cleaned out its wound. "It's awful, isn't it? Look what they did to you."

Another reason to have brought Winnie out here struck him. Yes, he'd wanted to show her how good he was at something, but—maybe more so—he'd come out here to prove in his own mind he was still himself.

Only to succeed in proving he wasn't: The dog didn't agree with him. He hopped right up the moment Mick let him, ready to do it all again. Stupid dog. Something always got ripped up by rat teeth, and though not often, more than he liked, that something on occasion was Mick Tremore. He had a place on his hand where a rat got it, a place on his shin. Ratting might be good sport, but as a line of work it was right disgusting.

Rather disgusting.

He let out a breath, a laugh, down his nose. It was *extremely* disgusting, which had never bothered him before. It was dangerous, but he'd never thought he had a choice. And there was the problem. Choices. New ones could be there for him, if he just looked.

Mick sacked rats with a hook, not touching them, then rallied his whole brood of animals and washed them out back. In cold water at the pump. He washed his dogs and ferrets to protect them from the diseases and vermin rats carried, the same as he'd wash himself.

As he poured cold water on Magic, though, he couldn't help be glad he had a hot tub to look forward to.

Then he heard himself thinking. Bloody hell, was he even liking baths these days? He was. He hated to pull the plug on the tub. He usually lay back and soaked himself wrinkled.

Being here in this house was having a more drastic effect on him than he had expected. He'd begun to like things he couldn't afford. Tubs. Gallons of hot water pumped in at a spigot. Steamy rooms just for bathing.

He'd begun to want a woman he couldn't have.

It was funny how he trusted Winnie. He'd gotten used to her fixing him. He trusted her to look at him, then say, to listen and correct what might give him away in a few weeks. And lately, he'd begun to make notes in his head, things he liked that he was learning and intended to keep, things he would abandon the moment they were finished. He was getting more from her than a way to win a bet. He was getting new ideas. And Winnie was like a kind mirror. He could look into her and adjust himself to suit himself.

When she wasn't being stiff-necked, she was the friend he most wanted to talk to, who he couldn't wait to see each day. She came into his mind with the first ray of consciousness at daybreak. He nodded off, smiling over her with his last, heavy-eyed blink before sleep. Sweet Win. Funny Win. Clever Win. Frightened, brave, careful, meticulous Winnie, trying to avoid the bite of the world by pretending it didn't have teeth.

No, he wasn't his old self. He wasn't sure what he was, except different. And to know it, to see himself a different way, was like looking for the first time at his bare lip again. It rattled him. It ran him off his rails. He felt turned around by the vague, untried choices that lay before him. He wasn't certain what he was beyond a ratcatcher who chummed with Rezzo and the others. He couldn't say for sure where he was going, and it was right unusual—no, *rather* unusual— to feel so directionless. Which made him remember suddenly a swarm of words from his and Winnie's nightly reading, reading he liked so much, on one hand, while, on the other, it made him curse his good memory: disconcerting, confounding, addling, perplexing.

What was a ratcatcher going to do with these words?

After he was finished, he went to calm Freddie, his ferret who no longer worked but rather stayed in her cage at the rear of the carriage house. She had to have been "disconcerted" herself by what had gone on. Freddie was thirteen year old, when ferrets only lived ten or twelve years. She was feeble and near-blind. When he'd thought she was dying, he'd carried her in his pocket and made up excuses to people to have her with him. In her day, though, she'd been the bravest, craftiest ferret, the best of her kind. She'd fed him and his kin rabbits in Cornwall. She'd given him work when he'd brought her to London: She'd given him self-respect.

These days, she was getting around pretty well again. She was less thin. Her new surroundings agreed with her. So Mick stroked her and cooed and told her of all the rats that had gone under today as he fed her the liver of the healthiest kill. It cheered her, he could tell. While petting her, seeing her look good, certainly cheered him.

Chapter 15

Mr. Tremore wasn't very genteel about the move. He came in that afternoon, cleaned himself up, then threw his things into his bed's counterpane, yanked it all up by the corners into a knapsack, and hauled it and himself downstairs. He wouldn't take the room next to Milton's. He took the one farthest from the butler's, which happened also to be the smallest, but "more private, more my own." It was a room that would have belonged to the scullery, had there been one, a miserly piece of space with only one high window that looked out onto the sidewalk in front—onto the glow of a street lamp by night; by day, the feet of London passersby.

Fine, Winnie thought. At least they would get along better now. And so they did, in their way. She'd silenced him. It was an eerie silence though, much happening beneath it, invisible, undiscussed. Fine, she thought again. Just as well.

It took another few days for her finally, fully to return to her side of the table, to sit across from Mick and work with him—something, as she began again, she realized, she enjoyed too much to give up.

Mick wasn't educated very well, though not as badly as she'd first thought. The country school he'd been to in Cornwall had done a decent job on basic reading. Heavens, though, had he made the most of a fundamental education. His mind loved wordplay. It made teaching him language a pleasure. He was a classic case of the student, though less knowledgeable, keeping the teacher on her toes. He was always one step ahead of her, always leaping in directions she had never considered.

In particular, he took to the vocabulary exercises she gave him. Of course, he ended up acquiring favorite words, then couldn't be pried away from them. *Diabolical* was a standard he only moved from when he discovered others. Along with his avidity came, also, a mystery. From nowhere, he started using words she hadn't taught or read to him. He brought them like gifts, coming up with them on his own.

"Junoesque," he said one day.

She looked up and across the table. He was staring at her in that thoughtful way he had, contemplative.

He continued. "Callipygian."

She blinked. He couldn't possibly know the word's meaning.

But he did: "Having well-shaped buttocks."

"It has pear-shaped connotations. A large bum."

He smiled. "I know. Large and well-shaped. I wish I knew a word for a large, well-shaped bum that goes into legs yards long and with more curves than an orchestra of violins."

She didn't know where to look for a moment. Boldly, she tried to hold his eyes. Well, she thought. An orchestra of violins. The Venus Callipygus. His references were certainly changing, if not the direction of his mind.

She lost the battle of eye contact when her gaze dropped a degree, to his lip where a mustache had been. It remained clean-shaven, but felt now somehow like a joke. He could shave the mustache, but a big, bristling masculinity remained in him.

There was a kind of virile swagger to everything Mick Tremore said and did, indomitable, in all his teasing and talk, his daily rituals, in his smallest duty or whim. It permeated even his silence. He had a masculine sense of himself that couldn't be tamed or turned into something else. He hadn't lost the animality in his mustache; he was only becoming more polite about it.

The odd thing was—a new perspective on herself that set her teeth on edge—she was fascinated by the very thing she abhorred, that she wished she could tone down: the unchecked, all but unvarnished, potent male energy of him. She half-relished the odd, anxious chagrin it brought. He seemed lately more complicated than anyone had realized, while—never mind the polish he was acquiring—she was more entranced by his raw edge than she liked to admit. And by the directness that went with it. And his good heart.

The mystery of how he learned the words was solved a night later.

Winnie awoke at two in the morning with a start and discovered herself to be crying—a frenzy of soft little sobs. After a few seconds, she was able to get hold of it, though her heart raced as she wiped her face. She lay there, puzzled. She'd been dreaming; she couldn't remember of what. She tried to grasp the content, yet was only able to recapture a sense of fury and deprivation—a wanting, a howling for something someone wouldn't let her have.

Sleep, she told herself irritably as she slid from bed. Something was keeping her from it lately. She hadn't slept decently in a fortnight, though tonight was the worst. Happy at least to be free of the mental debris of her dream, she went downstairs for a glass of milk.

Coming back upstairs from the kitchen, she saw light at the end of the ground-floor hallway. It came from her library. She didn't think about what she was doing any more than would a moth. She padded silently, then pushed open the door.

And there he was. Mick, sitting in an overstuffed chair beside a reading lamp. He jumped when he saw her: caught. He had a book in his lap.

She walked in. They stared at each other. More dense silence, full of matter neither wanted to discuss.

Finally, he shrugged, smiled, and offered an explanation. "I like reading. I thought I should read as much as I could, since I doubt I'll get another chance at so many books." He held out one hand, a gesture of bewilderment. "Twelve days," he said.

That many days till the ball. Yes, where had the time gone? The days, the hours lately seemed to go by in blinks.

He added, "I'll catch up on my sleep after I'm gone."

He'd said it: what Winnie had been avoiding thinking about. In twelve days they would no longer have any excuse to spend day in and day out in each other's company, no matter how strangely they were getting along.

She asked, "Do you have any trouble with your reading?"

"Yes. All the time." He laughed. He was still dressed from the day, though his cravat was loosened and his vest was open. The halo of the reading lamp put a slight golden glow to his white shirt. "I'm getting better though. It's mostly vocabulary."

"How do you manage?" It seemed impossible he could be teaching himself the words he'd been saying.

From the table beside him, from under the bright lamp, he lifted a collection of papers, half a dozen sheets, offering them.

On them were written words in a tight scrawl—*callipygian, Junoesque*, simpler words, too, *identity, banished*, more, pages of them—and marks. Beside each word, he wrote down the title of the book where he found it, sometimes abbreviating it, a page number, then how many lines from the top or bottom with an arrow pointing up or down, indicating the exact location in the book where the word occurred.

"I look them up at the end of the night, then I go back to the pages and read the words again when they mean something to me. I go over them the next night. If I forget any, I look them up again." By way of apology, an excuse for such excessiveness, he shrugged again, helpless, and said, "I like words."

That, she knew. She smiled faintly. "Diabolical," she murmured.

"Felonious."

"Nefarious."

He blinked, smiling with wonder. He didn't know that one, but he liked it. He added, "Black-hearted."

She laughed. "All right. It's not that you don't know words, but you use them strangely."

"I like to play with them." From the beginning, he'd liked grand-sounding words that he could say majestically.

Or amusing words. Widge, she thought. "I know," she acknowledged. "But for the night of the ball you have to play with them less obviously. And you can't use certain ones."

His brow creased. A contemplation came over his face, a meditative look that would have suited a Cambridge don. His features, when still and serious, simply gave the impression of insight, judgment, sharp mental activity. It wasn't true necessarily, she told herself. His mind could be as blank as a stone at the moment, but the structure of his face—the way the ridge of his brow tended to knit, the clarity and focus of his eyes, the high forehead—lent itself to the notion that he was intelligent, possibly profound.

She stared at his handsome face. The word *astute* leaped to mind, and it was from more than just the look of him. Canny, street-smart, cunning. She held his eyes and knew he was a sharp customer.

And that he was sizing her up.

She broke her gaze away, turning her head. "We'll give you some expressions." She cleared her throat. "Things to say, to remember for that night." She looked down at the sheets of paper he'd handed her, paging through them for something to do. "Actually, as we continue to fix your grammar and pronunciation, the way you like to use words may not stand out so baldly."

When she glanced up, he was still watching her, a

disturbingly secure look on his face, a look that wanted to bore into her. He didn't think he used words badly. Differently, he might have said. Cleverly. And he wouldn't have been wrong.

It was she who judged too harshly, who jumped to wrong conclusions about him. She hadn't taken his measure correctly, not from the first moment. With condescension, she'd occasionally told herself that Mick was smart, clever.

No. Mick was brilliant. She'd never had a student learn so much as fast as he did. His abilities were outright eerie at times. He was smarter than she was.

She handed back his papers, then snugged her dressing gown up tight around her throat, crossing her arms over herself.

As he stared at her—his keen eyes a green found in the sea, the color of grass-bottomed inlets—she actually felt her face warm. For no better reason than his looking at her. She could feel her skin heating. She turned away from him, putting her palm to her face. A casual way to hide from him. Her hand felt cool on her cheek. Blushing. She couldn't believe she was blushing. Again. For nothing. He'd done nothing to warrant it.

He just sat there in the light of the reading lamp, Mick lit up, the rest of the world dark, watching, silent, though out the side of her vision she saw him tilt his head. The way his dog Magic did when a human being baffled him by one behavior or another.

Well, good. She baffled herself. She might as well baffle him, too.

Chapter 16

After almost five weeks of instruction, Mr. Tremore had all but mastered the structure of proper English and was well on his way to reshaping his diction to an impressive degree. One lesson, though, Winnie delayed as long as possible. She might have avoided it completely, but since he was going to a ball, he had to learn to dance something beyond a jig around the kitchen.

She always taught her girls in the upstairs music room, a little room originally for the purpose of small gatherings of instruments and dinner guests that had occasionally, when her mother was alive and in the house, turned into extemporaneous dancing. Now it was a bare room, except for a big, black grand piano with a lot of broken strings and hardened pads. The bulky piano stood scooted back in a corner, unused and slowly falling apart. Other than this, the hardwood floor was wide-open and spacious, if a little dusty. All in all, though hardly the size of a ballroom, there was still plenty of area across which to move.

Dancing lessons were not usually a chore to Winnie. She loved to dance, and teaching foreign ladies or the gauche daughters of lawyers how to do it was her best opportunity to indulge herself in the entertainment. It was normally a favorite lesson. She brought in her gramophone, setting it on the closed piano lid, then cranked it up and ran full-volume the recordings she'd made of a trio playing Strauss.

With Mr. Tremore, she started the music, then went to position him. "Here now. You stand not exactly in front," she said, "but a little bit off, so our legs can go—" In between. She couldn't say it.

Then she didn't need to; he already knew. He took her hand into his and put himself automatically at the proper angle. She grasped the upper portion of his arm, the one he put round her waist. He knew to do that, too. She stood there for a moment in the marvel of it. The embrace of a dance—her own arm resting up his to the edge of his stone-hard shoulder, his palm flat to the small of her back.

She had to reverse her usual instructions. She told him, "You step forward, taking me with you to the count of three. . . ."

She had to step backward, the opposite direction she usually went, onto the opposite foot. He tightened his grip, moved her, and suddenly everything seemed upside down. *She* slipped, missed the step. She thought something rolled underfoot. Like a stone loose on the floor, though she couldn't imagine where that would come from. So perhaps it was simply that she was her usual off-kilter self with him.

Before she could put anything right, something more went wrong. On the piano beside them, the gramophone found a scratch, and the needle stuck. "Oh, bosh," she said.

She took herself out of his arms to hunt through her stack of cylinders for a better recording. Oddly, a sound intruded into the silence of the room, and she looked up.

As Mr. Tremore waited, he made a faint jingle. A light, metallic *clink*. She stared at him a moment. He stood with one hand in the pocket of his trousers, the other tapping his leg.

Tap-clink-tap. How annoying.

He dressed the part of gentleman; no more ratting clothes, now that her carriage house was "better" than before. Today, green tweedy trousers, neat, worsted wool, lightweight in anticipation of summer, creased with a turnup. His vest, a light, muted brownish gray, fit snugly, it, too, cut for a warmer season. Low, it showed two studs, his cravat, which he had finally learned to tie, parted, folded, and tucked to expose the starched front of his shirt.

No, he appeared perfectly the gentleman. He had pulled together every last thread and seam of the look of an upper-class Englishman. He understood the style of one. But—*clink, clink, clink*—she frowned down the length of him again. What made that irritating sound?

Though in concept, Mr. Tremore was coming along nicely, in the flesh, she found more and more he galled her these days. His perfections disturbed her. His silence exasperated. She especially took exception to the way he faced her now and then with regard to some of her improvements that he didn't seem to value as improvements: with an insolent self-assurance, as if he knew something she didn't. Worse, she resented her own horrible fascination with him at moments—the fact that, without his saying a word or lifting a finger, he could taunt and attract and make the hair on her arms lift.

Today the tension in him was palpable. It needed to tap.

Her temper was short. "Stop it," she said.

He looked right at her and continued, *jing jing jing*. In fact, if she weren't mistaken, he did it a little harder.

It didn't matter, she told herself. She went back to her cylinders, lifting one then another to read the scrawl on her own recordings—all the while thinking that the jingle was something in his pocket. What was in there? What did men usually keep in their pockets?

She remembered all the "usual" things Mr. Tremore possessed. Long, slinky animals that became fierce and dived into dark places. Coshes and bells. Bells? Would he keep bells in his pockets? She wanted suddenly to go through his trousers—go over to him and turn his pockets inside out, to be sure he didn't have anything, she told herself, that would give them both away later. And she'd like to reach into his vest where a chain indicated she'd find, held by a vest pocket firmly against his abdomen, the chiming watch he so liked—

That was the sound. His watch chain clinking against the stone button of his vest as he moved his arm a fraction, whapping his hand on the side of his thigh. The sound and movement momentarily arrested her, captivated by his tapping his leg in idle impatience.

She shook her head free of it, then found another Strauss she liked that was slow enough for a beginner. She put it on, went back to stand before her student, then was unsettled again when he took hold of her as if he knew what he were doing.

He didn't exactly. It took them four attempts till they were finally moving. Or moving of sorts. He knew how to lead, yet still he and she weren't graceful. He didn't know the rhythm. He was used to dancing differently. He kept wanting her to put her arm all the way onto his shoulder so her hand would be at the back of his neck—till she finally told him, as inoffensively as possible, that his way of dancing was indecent. It put the couple too close.

He snorted and glanced her over, as if she invented the criterion. But he kept at the lesson, waltzing her way. While, every time the music and the room grew quiet, as if to punctuate their dance's ceasing, she could hear the faint chime of him clink to a stop.

When she went over to crank the gramophone for perhaps the sixth or seventh time, he followed her, poking through the cylinders himself. She doubted he could read her handwriting or, if he could, that he would be familiar enough to make sense of the names of composers or musical compositions. But he pulled one out after a moment and said, "This."

She looked at what he handed her. No, he didn't know the piece; he only liked the name. The "Thunder and Lightning Polka." Typical.

"It's not a waltz." She went to set it back into the box.

He caught her wrist. "I know that. But I know how to dance it better than a waltz, and you, I'd bet, don't. It might get us over your trying to steer me."

She looked at him, raising one eyebrow. "I don't steer you—"

"You do. Like a pushcart."

"I don't steer you like a pushcart!" Did she? She was both offended and taken aback.

"It's a damn wrestling match we're doing here, Winnie. Your wanting to lead is why we're having so much trouble."

"No, it's not. It's your inexperience—"

"My experience with a woman who's afraid to let me control her, who wants to mop the floor with me." Then with barely a breath between, he said, "All right, a waltz, but take off your shoes."

"Pardon?" She drew back. "I won't."

"Take off your shoes. You'll slide better. I can move you easier. It'll help."

It also made her shorter. Her head came to just under his nose when she stepped forward in her stockinged feet to take his hand again. He pushed his advantage of her having less traction, her barely being able to keep her balance at places as he turned her on the smooth floor. It made her more fidgety still that she'd let him talk her into taking off her shoes. It didn't seem smart all at once.

Though he was right, it was good for their dancing.

No, it was wonderful for it. It put her somehow in a different state of mind. Eventually she followed, letting him find the movement he needed. Then, once he had the basic feel of the waltz, it was a fight to keep him from doing it double-time, spinning her—partly from delight (he was pleased to learn that some waltzes had a fast, spinning finish), though partly, she suspected, from his liking that he could make her body move with his, make her physically follow his will.

He was better at the spins than the slower movements. There, he needed practice. Practice with the slight bend in the knees, the left and right swooping turns of an English waltz. It was practice that seduced them both. He liked to dance. She loved to. He became increasingly good at waltzing, taking her round and round the room, moving her with a growing confidence she could feel in him, a masculine confidence that danced her backward into a state of breathless appreciation of it. She waltzed in the large, dark shadow of her own awareness of him, a shadow so large she quaked to think of the dread attraction that cast it.

Dancing put him at his zenith. He didn't speak very much. He moved well. He looked marvelous—an uncommonly good imitation of English peerage on the wing. How dare he, she thought, irrationally. How dare he turn her like this: on her ear with his astounding adaptions, so vastly outstripping anything anyone expected of him, so far exceeding merely looking the part. How could she expect to stay stable through such a waltzing, vertiginous reality wherein what she heard and saw breathing before her contradicted what she knew to be true.

A ratcatcher! she told herself. A ratcatcher from the worst streets in London, formerly from the poorest district in Cornwall, with nothing to travel on but a rural education and a cocky, crooked smile.

As she cranked the gramophone for the dozenth time at least, he asked beside her, "Do you want to stop?"

"No," she said too quickly.

"Neither do I. Your face is pink though." He gave her a wry look. Two people having fun in a strained kind of way. With his having a seeming admiration for a face pinked from exertion and a strange stimulation.

It made Winnie laugh, despite herself.

Which made Mick laugh too, against his better judgment.

The tension between them broke slightly, though only for the moment. They had been like this for days, so he didn't expect it to go.

Oh, they were getting along like cats and dogs. Him

chasing, wanting to grab her by the neck, her spitting and hissing every chance she got. If they didn't sleep together soon, they were going to kill each other. Except he couldn't explain that to her. She wouldn't hear it, even if she understood somewhere inside the truth of it.

Still, to enjoy her smile, even for a moment, was lovely—with its contradiction of shyness and slightly crooked teeth, of faint freckles and eyeglasses and downcast humor. Despite all their pushing and shoving at each other, despite the less than conventionally pretty elements of her person, the total of Winnie Bollash pleased him like no other woman in the longest while. When her mouth drew up into a wide smile, it made her eyes come alive.

Then her spectacles caught the light from the window, reflecting. The lenses blinked at him, obscuring what was behind them. On impulse, he reached and unhooked her eyeglasses, lifting them off.

With her, of course, grabbing and protesting. He won by the length of his arm; he held them overhead. Then, setting them down on the piano, he took hold of her and danced her away from them.

"I can't see." Worse and worse, Winnie thought. Barefoot and blind.

"What's this called?" He let go of her hand—it was like being left out on a limb, twirled in a blur. He touched the lace yoke of her dress at her collarbone before his hand came back to hers to guide her.

"What?"

"The word. Give me the word for it." He stared at her collarbone. With her spectacles off, her whole world was muted, narrow. Her myopic eyes could bring nothing into focus but him.

"Um, ah—Lace."

He raised a rueful eyebrow, the way he did when she didn't give him enough credit.

Only that wasn't the problem. It was a matter of trying to think when he put his finger on her collarbone as he waltzed her backward and stared down at her, nothing but a fuzzy room turning behind him.

"No," he said. "The stuff underneath, here"—again he let go, leaving her hand in the air, to point—"that you can hardly see."

She looked down, then missed a step. He put his finger in a hole between lace rosettes.

For a few seconds, she couldn't have told him her own name. Then she let out a light breath. "*Ah-h-h.*" A sound that was mostly air. "Tulle," she said. "The lace is crocheted onto silk tulle."

"Silk tulle," he repeated. Perfectly. "Silk tulle the color of flesh." Every sound correct. Then he grinned faintly and added, "Blimey." She blinked. She wanted to hit him. He was having her on, playing with his old accent. While she tried to keep her equilibrium on a dusty floor in her bare feet, blind, with only his arm for balance, and his teasing humor.

"And your dress—" He arched back, his eyes drawing an X on the front of her, tracing where her dress crossed between her breasts. "What's it called when a dress does that? I like it."

"It's, um, ah"—she looked down, trying to think what he meant—"a surplice bodice." She scowled up. "You don't need this much information about ladies' clothes."

He was going to say more, but the gramophone groaned into its slowdown, preparing to stop. "Excuse me," she said.

On the piano, she found her spectacles. She put them on, shaking, angry. It took her two tries to hook the left earpiece back into her hair and over her ear. She tried to calm herself by hunting through her cylinders. Not a word registered. She couldn't read a name on one of them. While behind her, he said, "We dance at the Bull and Tun." Conversationally, he added, "You know, you've never danced till you've danced with someone you like who's kissing your mouth as you go." He added, "Let me know if you want to try it."

She turned to look at him, ready to knock him down.

With narrow eyes, she watched him tap the side of his leg again, standing there in the center of the room as if having a casual dialogue on the various styles of dancing.

Dancing with your mouth on someone's. No, she did not want to try it, thank you. She put the same cylinder on again. They could dance to the same thing over and over.

He waited as she got the music going. Then he took her hand and put his palm at her back as if nothing unusual had been said.

Good enough. She'd ignore it, too. She'd ignore the choler she felt; yes, she didn't doubt her face was red. She told him, "Let's practice the pivots."

They were fast, so he was good at them.

He was fast, she thought. In every sense.

She didn't like the idea of him dancing with his mouth on some woman. Or some woman's mouth on him. It wasn't proper. It wasn't decent. And she certainly didn't want him to do that to her.

Though she wondered for a second what it would feel like. *Let him know?*

She remembered in the carriage house that he'd said she had to tell him if she wanted him to kiss her, that he wasn't going to unless she did. Tell him? She couldn't. Even if she'd wanted him to, which she didn't, she could never have been so bold. For a lady to say something so forward was beyond the pale of decorum.

Besides, wasn't he the one who'd threatened in a hallway to take her "where flirting led"? So why was he making such a to-do over a kiss? Dryly, she told him as they danced, "All this commotion from a man who, at one point, wanted to lead me 'down the path.' "

"Ah"—he laughed, taking her through a smooth turn—"so that's what you're hoping for. Not just kisses."

"I didn't say that—"

"No. You said *I* wanted it. But that's the way your mind works, isn't it, *Miss* Bollash?"

She hated when he said her name like that. She said, "Don't be vulgar—"

"Why? That's what you like so much about me. If I were a real gentleman, you couldn't blame me as easily. Hooligan Mick. Low-class Mick. Who has the poor taste to make you feel what you don't want to think about."

"Damn you!" She stomped her foot, which ended their dance. They came to halt. *Damn.* She never cursed. She was horrified to hear it come out of her mouth.

They stood there at the far edge of the floor, the tinny music across it continuing on without them.

He laughed, surprised by her cursing and thoroughly pleased with himself. "Nice," he said, with chuckling, wicked approval. "Congratulations, Win—"

She slapped him. Without thinking. Not once, but twice. She whacked the air with all her might and caught his cheek, a sharp smack. It was no accident. She meant to get it. Then, just because the contact felt so *damn* satisfying, she did it again. She would have hit him a third time, but he stopped her. He grabbed her arm.

He stood above her, for a second as angry as she was, both of them engrossed in one another in this unholy way.

He slowly lowered her arm, then let go, though the air was charged. They neither would let the other break his or her eyes away. Until Winnie happened to see out the corner of hers a red splotch on his cheek. The place where she'd struck him began to glow, more intense by the moment. She watched her own angry handprint, the spread of fingers, the impression of palm, appear vividly on the side of his face.

"Oh," she said as she watched it get redder and redder. "Oh," with dismay. What had she done? She had never hit anyone in her life. Why Mick? Why him? "Oh, Lord, does it hurt?"

She frowned and winced and put her hand to his cheek. The handprint was hot. She caressed it, running her fingertips over the frightful mark she'd made on him. She put her other hand up and caressed his face, both palms.

He jerked as she embraced his jaw, but then let her touch him freely. Once her hands were there, they wouldn't stop.

His cheeks were smooth with the faint grit of a shave that was half a day old. His jawbone was hard, angular; his eyes, the regard in their greenish depth, as fervid as the imprint she'd put on his skin. Her fingers fluttered over this face, her palms smoothing and cupping the topography of it, the planes and hollows. Regretfully, she retraced the livid red blotch up a cheek that had high, perfect bones. She drew the pads of her fingers down the cartilage of a narrow, straight nose, then along a mouth that—

He captured one hand and pressed it to his mouth, breathing into her palm, his hand clasping the back of hers. Then, licking a warmth into the center of her palm, he kissed the inside of her hand. As he had her mouth so many days before.

Winnie was speechless. She wouldn't have thought it were possible—he kissed her hand with a wet, open-mouthed kiss, with the push of his tongue, as he groaned and closed his eyes.

Goose bumps . . . chills . . . the hair at the back of her neck, up her arms lifted. Her belly rolled. The room did a slow rotation around them, while Winnie stood still.

Paralyzed. She wanted to take her hand away, but it wouldn't respond to her own volition, as if it didn't belong to her. When he raised his head, she made a fist, and he kissed her knuckles. She closed her eyes. Lord help her.

She used her other hand to reach and take her arm away from him. "I'm—" She could barely speak. "I'm not—not going"—her murmur broke again before she could finish—"down your path."

"Too late," he whispered. "You're already on it." He added in a tone that sounded more resigned than happy about it, "Too late for both of us."

The voice of the gramophone grew slow and low again, then rasped to a stop with her standing there, staring up at him.

Then, clutching her tingling hand to her chest, she walked across the floor in her bare, stockinged feet. At the piano, she cranked the gramophone, round and round and round briskly. She wound it too tightly. The music started again at a high pitch, a crazy tempo.

She walked back to Mick, into position, then had to stand there in front of him, both of them waiting for the machine's music to gain some semblance of sanity.

The odd thing was, once it did, she couldn't. She was reluctant to put her arm on him, to reach up and touch him at all. The music played. Nothing happened. Until he slipped his hand under her arm, as if to begin dancing.

But his hand instead ran lightly down her back, the hollow of her spine, and he said, "Let's have your skirts up again, Win."

She couldn't have heard right. She let out a quick, nervous laugh when he actually took hold of a handful.

When she stopped him, he shook his head in reprimand. He said, "Be good, Win. Do what I say."

She let go, a reflex.

Good. She'd been good all her life. A good girl who felt muscles tense in the pit of her stomach when he invited her to be good his way.

He whispered, "So what did they tell you when you were bad, Winnie?"

"What?" She looked up at him, blinking. Her heart began to thud at the base of her throat.

As if he knew, with the edge of his thumb he touched her there, then traced her neck up the tendon to behind her ear.

She shivered and murmured, "Give me your hand. Put your hand at my back where it belongs. We're supposed to be dancing."

"Tell me about 'supposed to be,'" he whispered. "When you didn't do what you were supposed to, what did they tell you?'' His face came closer. ''What happened when you did what *you* wanted? What do I need to say to let you do what you'd like?'' He changed tack. He said, ''What I'd like is to kiss you. I would. But I'd like you to want it. Do you?''

''N-n—'' She got that far, then stopped. She didn't know. She was reeling again, caught in the strange energy of him. She wet her lips. No, she didn't want it.

The music played behind them, its own little world, getting away from them. While he waited. Then touched her collarbone again, tracing it with his fingertip. She let him. The touch of his finger, so light, up then down her neck, was unearthly. Sublime.

She bit her lip, closed her eyes.

Then heard him say, ''Fine,'' very softly, as he'd said once before. ''When you can say what you want, you can have it.''

Just like that, he stopped.

She opened her eyes to see him walk across the room himself to the gramophone. It was groaning again. He cranked it, then two seconds later was pushing her backward into pivots around the floor, the jangle of a recorded violin moving them.

Let him know? she thought.

Kissing him, she remembered, ''really kissing him,'' as he called it, had been . . . exciting. Such a surprisingly powerful and tender connection to him. Unforgettable. As she spun backward round the room—as he let go of the counting, gathering himself into the rhythm alone without it, incorporating it into himself—she remembered how vital it felt when his mouth opened hers and he breathed into it.

She was supposed to ask for this?

She couldn't. She murmured, ''You want too much.''

He danced and answered with his usual candor. ''You criticize me and cry, Win. You curse me and slap me and move me downstairs.'' He shook his head at her. "Is it too much to want that you take a look at what you're doing?"

She was saved from having to think about what he meant. Just then, as they moved across the dusty floor, the ball of her foot stepped squarely on a small and sharp object.

"Ah— Wait— I've tramped on something." She halted them, hopping on one foot as she grabbed the other one under her skirt.

The music kept going, though it wasn't as pronounced to Winnie as the sound of their breathing, both slightly breathless from waltzing and talking, both.

She was clutching his arm, holding her foot, trying to figure out what she'd done, while he supported her balance. He was close. His arm remained around her back. Her hand gripped his wide shoulder.

Yes, she thought, she wanted him to kiss her. Yes.

But she didn't want to say. How unfair. She frowned, then scowled. How miserably unfair. She stood there sluicing her eyes sideways at him, flat-footed in one stockinged foot. She opened her mouth, closed it, skewed it to the side, then looked up, scrutinizing him.

Chapter 17

Holding Winnie, with her standing on one foot by the piano at the side of the music-room floor, Mick watched her screwed-up face—her brow furrowed downward, her mouth twisted up. She was trying to say something—

By God, she was going to say it! he thought. He just knew she was. She clutched his back. He let her hang onto him. God bless, they were all over each other today.

He could almost see her mind review the problem—how to get kissed without admitting she wanted it—from a thousand angles, trying to process each one.

She opened her mouth.

He leaned forward so as to hear every syllable or to grab a shred of one, at least, if she couldn't get it all out.

Then Winnie said, "My foot hurts," and folded. Her long frame simply collapsed downward into her dress like a deflating balloon onto the floor.

Mick stood above her, stymied, not sure if this were a good sign or not. After a moment, he sat down beside her, tried to reach under her dress for her foot, then got his hand slapped for it.

Glumly, he protested, "I was going to look at your foot, see if I could find anything. Is it a splinter?"

"No, I tramped on something larger than that."

"This?" he asked, rotating to lean out onto one arm and pluck a small black screw off the floor. He showed her.

She nodded. "It has to be from the piano. I slipped on it earlier, I think. I should have stopped. Look, it cut through my stocking." It made a pinprick of blood at the round swell of the ball, as if she'd tramped full force, all her weight.

He dropped the screw into her hand, then took her foot. Like everything else, they fought over it, but he won by massaging his thumb up her arch.

"Oh," she said. Then "Oh," again. "Oh, crumbs. What you're doing feels wonderful."

She leaned back as, reluctantly, there on the floor, she let him take her foot into his lap. She stared at the screw in her hand. "I think it's from the music stand. It fell off last week."

He rubbed her foot down the bottom strongly to the heel, then rotated her ankle.

"Oh," she said again. "That feels impossibly good."

He said, "So, when you were bad, what did they tell you? What did they do?"

Her eyes blinked up from where they were policing his possession of her foot, taken by surprise to find the game on again. "Who?"

"Your parents."

"My parents didn't say anything."

"Truly? Not a word?" He was puzzled. "Someone then. Someone else."

She frowned and looked away.

"A governess," he suggested.

She whipped her eyes around to him, as if he'd read her mind.

"So what did she say? What did she do?"

"I had a lot of governesses." She frowned then said quickly, "Miss Nibitsky."

"Ah, Miss Nibitsky," he repeated, sliding his hand up her leg a little, kneading the back of her lower calf.

"So what did Miss Nibitsky say when you were horrid?"

"She'd say, 'You little brat, if you don't do what I say, I'll break all your toys.' " Then she laughed shyly and looked down. "I've never told anyone that. How peculiar to say it to a grown man."

"No, no." He shook his head, surprised, interested. "Would she break them?"

She answered with a shrug. "I just stopped playing with anything I liked in her presence. One year, she canceled my birthday. She said I simply couldn't turn six. I'd have to wait till the following year."

"What a wretched woman." He didn't like any of this. He withdrew a little. He rubbed the bottoms of her toes and asked, "Didn't you tell someone?"

"Who? If I said anything to my father, he waved me away vaguely. If I told my mother, she got angry; she didn't believe me."

Mick frowned and tried to get hold of his original notion. "Then what?" he asked. "What if you still wouldn't listen?" There must have been gentler reproofs, he told himself. He wanted to use them, to see if he could counter all that held Winnie back with reasons to go forward expressed as rigidly. He rubbed up her ankle, playing at the hem of her dress. "What if you were just a little bit bad?"

She said nothing. He stopped, tilted his head. He had to look for her face. When he found it, the look on it—it was bloody terrible. "There was no 'little bit bad'?" he asked. Then he guessed more than he liked: "She hurt you," he said, "really hurt you."

Winnie defended her upbringing quickly, yet it shocked him. She said, "She only used a cane once. She said that, if I were a boy, I'd be in boarding school by now, where in a blink, when children were as bad as I was, they sent them to the headmaster who made them stand on a pulpit and—" Her voice broke. She stopped.

Mick let go of her foot and smoothed her dress down. He leaned back onto his arm, putting his hand up to his mouth, a finger across his bare lip.

"What's wrong?" she asked, as if she'd offended him.

In a way, she had. It was his turn to feel sick. He, who could cosh a rat bloody senseless, was revolted by Winnie's childhood. It was a good thing her story took place a long time ago, because, if he ever saw this Nibitsky woman, he would want to do her violence.

"Did your parents know?" he asked.

"I think so."

All Mick knew about boarding schools was that they turned out snobs. He hadn't known about their discipline habits, and certainly had had no idea about evil governesses, though he understood what caning was from stories of orphanages and poorhouses.

"It wasn't really so—" She tried to shrug it off.

He was too distressed on her behalf to let her. He said, "No, Win. English gentlemen and gentlewomen don't deserve the word *gentle*, to put such fear into their own children. Or to pay someone else to do it. The upper class is"—he looked for something to say that was sufficiently disgusting, then found it in his growing stockpile of words—"barbaric."

"I was a frightened child before she ever—"

"I'm sure. All the worse."

She looked at him as it seemed to dawn on her. "It *is* horrid, isn't it, what she did?" She frowned at him. "Have I made you loathe me then?"

"No!" He laughed, then slid her around and pulled her up against him. "Sh-h-h," he said. "Oh, Winnie."

He felt homesick all at once, a sweet, sharp longing for rocky moors and jagged coastline, where a boy was never more than twenty miles from the sea no matter where he stood. And always on solid ground with his family.

"Let me tell you about Cornwall," he said. He scooted her till she sat in the cove of his legs, nestled her into his arms, and kissed the top of her head.

He did: He told her of playing in Celtic ruins, ducking through half-tumbled-down archways, unmindful of the hands that built them. His castles. He told her of running along the sea with several of his brothers, then sisters, too, as more children came along, until he was running in a pack of fourteen wild siblings, some of them barely nine months apart.

"That's a lot of children," Winnie said.

"Mum was Catholic. She didn't believe in preventing a child the Lord wanted her to have. She even took in one He didn't put on her. My brother Brad isn't even hers. His mother died, then his father beat him, so he came and lived with us, the wild Tremore brood. He fit right in."

"If your mother couldn't manage you all, did your father do it?" Winnie wanted to know.

"God, no. My father left after the fourth or fifth one, I think."

She puzzled over the information. "Then how did the sixth one and the rest come about?"

He got a good chuckle out of that. "God did it," he said. "That's what my mother would say. The rest were all immaculate conception. She was a crazy one, my mum. Or else she thought we were." He laughed again, fondly. "She did her best. She tried to put the fear of God in all of us, and always succeeded for a while with the littlest ones. But they'd come to me, crying, scared, you know, and I'd explain. 'No, God won't punish you. He loves you. And your mum does, too, only she's angry with you and can't give you the good swipe you deserve.'

"Being the oldest, I thought it my duty to put them on to her, wise them up, you know? No use scaring little children with a lot of talk about damnation. Then I'd say, 'But see, I can take a swipe at you, so do as you're told. Your mum's too kindhearted to hit you. That's why she invents all these things.' " He laughed. "It worked. We all helped her."

"You especially," Winnie said.

He ran his mouth down an inch of her crown, feeling her hair against his lips. "Yes, me especially. I pretty much ruled the roost as the oldest. It was my job to use that the right way, to help the rest with it.''

She thought for a minute, then said, relaxed now, her body fitting sweetly against his chest, between his legs, ''That explains why you act as if you're king sometimes then.'' She was teasing him.

''I am king,'' he said. ''King of the life of Mick Tremore. And you, my pretty thing, are queen. Queen of yourself.''

''Why did you leave if you liked Cornwall so much?''

''To feed us. After my mother died, we about starved to death.'' He laughed. ''I'll be honest, Win. I think some of my brothers and sisters were the result of my mother's enterprise.'' It was funny to him, sad, too; his mother struggling to feed her brood, but doing it in a way that only made her more children. ''Anyway, with just myself and three brothers working in the mines, trying to feed fourteen, it wasn't enough. So I put my younger brothers and sisters with aunts and uncles then came to the city. I brought Freddie, a great ferret. You met her.''

''Yes, you said she's your best.''

''Was. I lied a little. She's old now.'' He paused, thinking. ''Because of her, though, I sent home money my very first week, enough to buy food and a bit of clothes, something the younger ones sorely needed. We wouldn't have made it another winter. Freddie saved us. That's why I have to take good care of her, right to the end.''

''Fourteen,'' Win repeated. ''That's a big family.''

''It is, but I managed and the older ones help now. Five brothers, eight sisters. My youngest sister is eleven. I support the ones who can't support themselves yet, with a bit left over for me after I give extra to the three aunts and an uncle who care for them. It works out. Don't know what I'd do without family.''

''Or them without you,'' she pointed out.

He laughed. ''I guess.'' Then he corrected himself. ''I imagine.'' He refined it. ''I rather imagine.'' He made a snort, a vocalized breath that heard—but wasn't certain it liked—how upperclass he sounded. "Anyway," he continued, "it wouldn't even have occurred to me to keep the money all to myself." He made indirect reference to her cousin. "I mean, how could I enjoy it, knowing I had so much when they had so little?"

If she understood his expressed loyalty, she didn't acknowledge it.

They sat on the floor there in the dancing room, saying nothing for several minutes, just sitting together. He liked it. He brushed his lips across the top of her hair again. It was silky. Like the rest of her. It smelled lemony.

When he started wanting to eat it, to lick her neck, to pull her backward and down, roll on top of her . . . bloody hell, at that point, he slid away and stood up. "He doesn't *sound* pleasant, this cousin of yours." He was contradicting what she'd told him earlier, that he would like Xavier.

On the floor, she spun around on her skirts, pulling her knees against her chest. She arched her long, pretty neck to look up at him directly and said, "He tells good jokes," then laughed, shaking her head.

She bent it again, down till all he could see was the interesting way she held her hair up. With two sticks. It fascinated him. He couldn't understand how her hair didn't fall down. It looked heavy enough. It was abundant, shining; a light, coppery red. Lots and lots of colorful hair. Pretty.

She continued, "Someone said recently that he's changed. Not so funny, more solemn. But he wasn't when I last knew him. The day he inherited every last bit of family land, he was jubilant, the most miserably happy eighty-some-year-old man I've ever seen. Shortly after, by the way, he married a woman who was about my age now, a woman whom he'd adored for a dozen years. Can you imagine? That would make Vivian, let's see, about forty now. And I wish I could say she was a conniving, spoiled shrew who was only after his money, but the woman I met a dozen years ago was quite sweet. Shy. Obedient. People tell me she still is. The daughter of a rich Italian family, oh, with some title or other. Something high-and-mighty, since Xavier wouldn't have anything less. Very beautiful. She's with him still. She'll be there beside him the day he dies.''

Mick sympathized. ''That must annoy the hell out of you.''

She laughed again, squeezing her knees. ''Sometimes it does. It's as if one person, always one person, is dealt all the aces.''

''It only looks like aces from here, Win. You don't know. You can't see—you can't play his hand, only yours.''

She nodded. She was lost a moment, then looked at him. ''Mick,'' she said. It was the first time she had ever used his given name, and it made his chest expand to hear it. It made him warm. ''You are the most generous man I have ever met.''

He liked that even better. He smiled widely. Then told her, ''I'm not generous. It's just—'' He shrugged. ''Why blame people when they can't help their nature?''

She contemplated that a moment. Then she suddenly reached her arms out and lay straight back, all the way onto the floor.

''The ceiling is peeling,'' she said, then let out a long, delighted bubble of laughter, the sound of genuine humor.

Looking down at her, Mick thought: He'd stood too quickly. If he were down there now, he'd have stretched out beside her.

Before he could think of a way down to her, though, she reached up, holding her hands toward him, asking to be pulled to her feet.

He drew her up—and she made a little shriek. ''Oh,'' she said, ''my stomach lifts when you move me sometimes.'' Quickly, ''So can you waltz, do you think?''

"No," he said gravely. "Or not like someone who's been doing it all his life. I need more practice." Dishonest again. Though not quite in the same formal manner as her way, he waltzed all the time at the Bull and Tun. He'd pretended not to know, just to spend the afternoon dancing with her.

And he wanted to "move" her some more. He held out his hand.

She put hers into it, and he took her into his arms in the proper manner, in the way she allowed. He began counting. "One, two, three. One, two, three." No music. Or just the music of the two them together, his whispering in her ear as he spun her around.

She felt so loose in his arms, warm and smiling. Oh, he liked her like this: waltzing in the byways of one of life's finer moments, in one of its little contentments.

They danced through supper, till their feet hurt. Sometimes they used her gramophone, but often, when it *grog*ged slowly to silence, he took over. He made up waltzes, humming to her, loving the feel of her in his arms, her laughing and dancing with him.

At the end, he made a ballocks of it, of course. Somehow their mouths got close. When he drew closer, her eyes widened. They filled with wonder— she was perpetually amazed by his interest. And confused by it: Her eyes filled with that funny fear of hers, too. She braced herself, ready for him to push her into it, but not ready to invite him in. Her posture shot a jab of frustration through him, with enough pinch to it to make him wince. Damn her anyway.

"Winnie," he said. "I want to kiss you. I want to do a lot of things, and I've been about as forthright as a man gets about it. But it can't be all me every time. Me pushing, me seducing, me making you do what we both know you want to do anyway. I can't keep chasing you and chasing you, even if you like it, without your giving back, letting me know you want *me*. Own up to it."

Her expression wouldn't. Her mouth grew into that tight pucker she could make. She didn't offer a word.

"Do you or not?"

"Do I what?"

He'd start at the most basic. "Want me to kiss you," he said.

She frowned down. She wanted him to.

"Say it," he said. "Say, 'Kiss me.' "

She opened her mouth, then closed it, shaking her head as if he'd asked her to fly up to the ceiling.

He continued, torturing them both. "Say, 'Touch me, Mick.' Oh, God, Win, I'd like to hear you say it. Say, 'Hold me, undress me, touch me, come inside me—' "

He had to look away. His mouth went dry saying the words. To the piano, he muttered a string of epithets under his breath, cursing himself, but her, too.

It rallied her sizeable frustration and rage. Starchy again, she said, "Most gentlemen don't swear as you do in front of a lady."

"Most gentlemen don't go through what I go through with you."

"You go through nothing—"

"I go through your tying my privates in knots, with you wanting to lather them up, me dodging, so as to keep you from shaving them off in a pique, trying to make me tame enough to get near." What a speech. He was half-sorry he said it.

Then sorrier it hadn't been worse, when she said with sarcastic wonder, "Oh! Oh, yes!" With emphasis, "That was splendid! You are quite getting the hang of being a gentleman. Why don't you just stick your hand between my legs?"

That did it. He leaned toward her. "Well, you'd never have gotten any part of man stuck there otherwise. You're terrified of sexual relations. Hell, you're foking terrified of life. Whatever brought you to this place, *Miss* Bollash," he said, "it killed off every speck of spontaneity and adventure in you, if you ever had any to begin with."

She blinked, and the fight in her rose up. She came back with, "Spontaneity and adventure? What big words, Mr. Tremore, for *randy*. For being a rat who wants to climb up into the flounce and froufrou of every silk petticoat."

He saw red. He wanted blood. "Not yours," he said. "I'd rather be gnawed to death, thank you, than have to deal with what's under your petticoat. Every bloody moment'd be anxious. I'd be ready to shoot myself, trying to tow a line you'd snap in my face every ten seconds."

He'd gotten her, a direct hit. He wasn't proud of it the second it happened. Her face fell. He'd confirmed to sweet Winnie, who thought no man wanted her, that he didn't either.

He took a breath, then said quickly, "That's a lie. Winnie Bollash, I want you so badly, you're making me say things I don't mean." Then that was wrong, too. "No, you aren't making me do anything. I'm wagging my own tongue. Winnie, I'm sensitive about the fancy ladies I've slept with. Oh, they all wanted me. For the day. I'm a good time, but nothing more. I'm tired of it." He took a breath, looked around, then stepped back and shoved his hands in his pockets. "You're right, I'm wrong. I wouldn't enjoy being a good time to you either in pretty short order. It would make me feel terrible." He shook his head, then looked at her.

She was wide-eyed.

"I'm going back downstairs now," he said. "Bloody hell," he muttered, exasperated. "If you need me, pull the bell cord. It'll ring below stairs, and I'll hear it. Me and your butler. Other than that, I'm staying away from you. That should suit everyone. Even me," he added.

Chapter 18

❧

$\mathcal{E}$dwina, Mick, Jeremy, and Emile Lamont awaited tea in her father's upstairs study. On the rare occasions when gentlemen called, she always felt it more gracious to speak to them in the room where her father had conferred with his colleagues. A room of large, heavy chairs and dark wood, of bookcases full of philology and linguistics as well as a bit of poetry and fiction that, she presumed, appealed to men. *Moby-Dick. The Strange Case of Dr. Jekyll and Mr. Hyde.* Richard Burton's *Arabian Nights*. The most delicate accouterment of the room was a cut-crystal brandy decanter that sat in a polished niche with two matching snifters set upside down.

Jeremy and Emile Lamont had arrived at a propitious time. She and Mick had been arguing over a bill that had come in the morning's post. It was from the tailor, for every piece of clothing Mick owned at present, and the bill was addressed to Miss Edwina Bollash.

Mick, of course, had rolled his eyes. "I think we should take as much back as the tailor will allow. Those two fellows—" He referred to the Lamonts, and, though he left the thought unfinished, there was no doubt about his feelings for them. "We could end up having to pay for all this. They're up to something, Win."

She only shook her head. "You can't take anything back," she told him. "It's all custom-made. Besides, the bill is a mistake, a simple mistake."

And, of course, it was. These things happened.

Though Winnie realized how much Mick's suspicions were coloring her own thinking by the magnitude of her relief when Jeremy Lamont said, "Dear, dear!" He turned the envelope over, frowning down at her address on it. "They confused the address to which they shipped the parcels with the address where they were to send the bill." He looked at her with what seemed genuine regret. "I am so sorry. What an embarrassing confusion. Here."

He reached into his ever-deep pocket and took out the ever-full notecase. It was, as before, packed with bills.

He counted out several, then looked up at Winnie. "And how much do we owe *you*, Miss Bollash, to date?"

She glanced at Mick. Emile sat off to the side, Mick stood by the window, his hostility so dense in the air, it all but left a haze.

He had greeted them at the door a few minutes before like an ogre guarding its lair, then had been actually offended by their astoundment.

They kept looking at him now, then passing looks between each other. There was no doubt that Jeremy in particular was thrilled by Mick's sound and appearance.

Winnie's own accounts were prepared. It was a matter of retrieving them from her sitting room, which she did. She hurried. Leaving the three of them alone in the study together felt chancy somehow.

When she returned, all three men were exactly as she'd left them, as if in her absence they had not moved or spoken, but only glared at each other. Oh, dear, oh, dear. She presented the list of her fees and expenses. She'd computed them carefully, hour by hour, and was prepared to go over them. She'd been generous, if anything.

Jeremy glanced at them, then, without question, counted out more crisp notes of British pounds sterling. He set a stack on them on the mantel, saying, "I've put in twenty pounds extra to cover anything that might come up till we're back. Emile and I are going to the coast for a few days, but we'll return the day before the ball. We'll bring the invitation then."

He looked at Mick over his shoulder, then, putting a monocle to his eye, he studied the man in the center of the room, up then down, walking around him. To which Mick responded by folding his arms over his chest and looking faintly truculent.

"I must say," Jeremy told her, "*Emile's* money is extremely well spent." He chuckled and glanced at his brother, a goad referring to the fact that the loser was to reimburse the winner of their bet.

Emile remained in the far chair, though he studied Mick with no less interest, only less kindness. He said, "He hasn't done it yet, you know. Though I admit," he said grudgingly, "Miss Bollash has wrought a miracle. If I didn't know those clothes and that face, I'd say it was a different man."

It. "He," she corrected. "He's in the clothes you picked for him. They're excellent—"

"No, no," Jeremy insisted, "he greeted me at the door. His manner is completely different, and what I've heard him say sounds marvelous. You're brilliant, Miss Bollash."

Her pride puffed a little. Yes, she was doing first-rate work, it was true.

Mick snorted. "Right," he said. "You all have done a bloody fine job."

Ah. Winnie said quickly, "No, *we* all." To the Misters Lamont, she declared, "Mr. Tremore is the most able student I have ever taught. He is at the heart of the change."

Any rapprochement among the men her words might have won, however, was immediately lost when Jeremy said, as if he spoke to a trained monkey, "Say something. Talk."

Mick made a sideways pull of his mouth, then held out his hand. "Lemmy see them notes there, Cap'n. Pass 'em over, eh?" He put Cornwall into his voice as thickly as he could.

Alarmed, Jeremy turned to Winnie. "He sounded better when I first came in."

"He's annoyed with you." She scowled.

Mick said, "I can speak for myself. Let me see the notes, mate." He pointed to the money Jeremy had stacked over the fireplace.

Jeremy raised an eyebrow in affront.

Mick looked at him levelly, unmoved.

A kind of tension grew.

Happily, Milton dissipated some of it by walking in just then with the tea tray.

As tea and biscuits were served, Jeremy sat. He balanced his hands in front of him on the ferrule of his cane. To Mick, he said, "I'm leaving the money here. Feel free to examine it, Mr. Tremore. Oh—" He threw a concerned glance at Winnie. "Which reminds me. We have to find a better name. I was thinking Michael Frederick Edgerton, the Viscount Tremore. It's not a real title, but has the advantage that if anyone calls him 'Tremore,' he'll respond. Meanwhile, if we are called upon to do so, we can claim the title for a remote viscountcy in Cornwall. Hardly anyone pays attention to that provincial tip of England." He turned to Mick and repeated, as if trying it out, "Michael?"

Mick snorted. "It won't be hard to answer to. It's my name. Michael Tremore."

"Well." He looked at his brother, as if to say, More surprise, more delight. Their evident pleasure seemed to grow by the second. "He does talk well, doesn't he? Isn't it amazing the change it makes?" To Mick, he said, "Perfect then. Michael it is." To Winnie, "You must call him 'Michael' from now on so as to be sure he's accustomed to it."

Michael, Winnie thought. Michael. Something inside squirmed, uncomfortable. He was Mick to her. It was hard to think of him differently.

"Say something," Emile said from his chair again. "Make him speak more. I want to hear it."

Mick turned toward him. For a moment, Winnie was frightened as to what he might say. God knew he could still be profane. She said quickly, "Read something, if you please." She pulled down a book and pushed Mick toward the desk.

He sat, disgruntled, but he opened the book. He began to read aloud a passage they'd read the night before. Everything, and then some, that a person might want to know about whales. He wasn't perfect with it—most of the sounds were right, but he struggled over a word here and there before he recognized it.

Still, he was amazingly convincing.

Listening to him, again Winnie felt that ghostly sensation. Another man, Emile had said. It was true. Mick's family in Cornwall, the friends he spoke of in London, the way he could mimic his old accent—his real life, she reminded herself—seemed sometimes just another one of his extravagant stories, another of his jokes. Here was the real man. Michael Whomever-They-Wanted-to-Call-Him, soon to be the Viscount Whatever, world traveler, humanitarian, bon vivant, and wealthy member of English nobility.

And would-be suitor to Lady Edwina Henrietta Bollash, only child to the Marquess of Sissingley. Ah, now there was a lovely fantasy. Soon she'd be gathering pumpkins and mice, hoping for a fairy godmother to come along and turn them into a coach and eight.

Yes, someone, please turn my ratcatcher into a prince for me.

The someones who all but had stared at Mick—or rather, Michael—as he closed the book with a snap of its cover, a grip in one hand that would have allowed him to throw the volume across the room.

She quickly took it as Jeremy began, "That was"—he stood, as if for an ovation—"that was simply, well"—he could barely find words—"marvelous . . . unbelievable." Looking at his brother: "Can you credit

it, Emile? Did you hear? Better and better—oh, I like
it!''

Emile stood. Mick did, too. Nothing. There was
nothing for anyone to disagree about, yet Winnie felt
it expedient to get the Lamonts out the door as quickly
as possible. She took Jeremy's arm. Emile followed.
''You wait here,'' she told Mick, who wore consternation all over his face.

At the doorway, though, he stopped them by calling,
''Will the invitation work to take her to the ball, too?''

She turned, sending him a sharp frown. ''I don't
need an invitation.''

All three men paused to look at her. It was her tone.

She explained, ''I'm invited every year. I send my
regrets. Xavier only invites me for form's sake.''

''Surprise him,'' Mick said. ''Go.'' When she only
scowled at the suggestion, he argued with her name
alone, ''Winnie—''

''*Winnie?*'' Emile repeated, lifting an amused eyebrow.

''Shut up,'' Mick told him.

The room grew icy-quiet for a moment. Then Emile
smirked and began, ''Oh, no. This is too good to—''
He stopped.

Mick glowered at him, a look of open, hateful ani-
mosity from a man a head taller and five stones heavier
at least.

He presented enough threat that Emile raised his
hands, a surrender. ''Goodness,'' he said. He longed
to say something more; his face twitched with it for a
moment. Then he seemed to think better of it. ''Well,''
he risked saying. ''What an amazing afternoon.''

Winnie hastily ushered the Lamonts out, thanking
Jeremy profusely for the payments, seeing that he and
his brother had their hats, canes, and gloves in their
hands, then closed the door on them, as happy to see
them go as she had been to see them arrive.

When she returned to her father's study, Mick was
still there: holding one of the banknotes up to the light.

He said, ''It's good.''

More relief—a sense of out-and-out deliverance. Which said a great deal about her own doubts.

He destroyed her peace of mind, though, by adding, "Extremely good. Better than what Rezzo and I ever came up with. It's on the right paper."

"Oh, stop it," she said, walking briskly over to him. She snatched the note away, then took the whole pile from the mantel into her possession.

He looked at her, offended. "Look at it, Winnie. It's all new. Not an old bill among the pack." He added, emphasizing the last diphthong, "Fresh-sh-sh."

She looked at the money in her hand. They were new bills, but no, she would not be impressed by the fact. She frowned at him. "The Bank of England does occasionally print new ones, you know."

"Then hand the whole stack over to two blokes who throw it around like"—he corrected—"as if it were water?"

"They're rich. Besides, we aren't. What could they possibly want from us?"

"What they're getting, I'd have to say."

That made her stop and think, then ask, "What are they getting?"

He lifted one shoulder. "I don't know. Your skill. Me, all decked out like a lord. It has to do with that ball." He paused, then said, "Winnie, I want you to go with me." More quietly, "Don't send me alone. You know the people I'll be mingling with." He re-phrased again. "With *whom* I'll be mingling. Things could happen I don't understand, and you'll know what they mean."

After a moment, she said pathetically, "I can't." Then, "If you're afraid, we'll tell them it's off. We'll stop."

He shook his head. "I don't think we can. I know this game. Jeremy is the good one, Emile, the bad. If we try to back out, there will be pressure. Jeremy will shake his head and apologize, while trying to hold his brother back, but he won't succeed. Emile will make threats and—well, I'm not sure how far he'll go. They have a lot invested in their game. They've gone to a great deal of trouble.''

"If they become unpleasant, you could—" She didn't finish. What did she envision? Mick, the hero? Rushing in to protect her from anyone who became harsh with her?

"Thank you," he said, as if she'd made perfect sense. He smiled. "And yes, I bloody well could. But I don't want to stop them yet. I want to ruin them. I don't like being set up. I want to see what they're up to and shove it down their throats." He grinned lopsidedly. "Come with me. Do it with me."

"I can't." She tried a practical reason. "I don't have a dress."

"Let's find you one. What do you have in your wardrobe?"

A dress. In all her life, Winnie had never purchased an evening gown. She didn't even own one to alter. She'd been too young to have one when she'd been of a monied family. Now, of course, she couldn't afford one that would be appropriate. She ignored Mick's suggestion.

Besides, he was seeing shadows. There was nothing wrong going on here, aside from a little prank on her cousin who would never know. It was a bet, she told herself. A stupid, competitive wager between two rich brothers, nothing more. Mick was judging others by the fact that he'd run too many ''games'' himself. A classic case of the kettle calling every pot black.

He wouldn't let it rest, though. More ideas, more questions. "You must have connections. Can you ask someone about them?"

She looked at him, frowning at his concern. For no other reason than to please him, she nodded. "All right. I stay in touch with several of my former students. I'll ask them. I'll see what they know of the Misters Emile and Jeremy Lamont."

That very evening, she sent Milton with several inquiries. By morning, she had two responses. No, her contacts in the realm of high society knew nothing one way or another of a Lamont family, not good nor bad. By default, the Lamonts were in the clear.

Then after elevenses tea, she received a third correspondence. It was from the Duchess of Wychwood, a delightful young woman, recently wed, and a student of Edwina's just the summer past.

Particularly happy to hear from the girl, Edwina quickly tore open what unfolded out into a lovely, long letter—or lovely until the last few sentences, which made her frown and reread them:

> *As to your new clients, I'm afraid I have no recollection of any Emile or Jeremy or Sir Leopold Lamont, not does my mother. Mother mentions, though, that she heard of gentlemen twins in Brighton last season—she doesn't know their name—who ran some dubious investments out of the pocket of a cousin of the Marquis de Lataille. I sincerely hope your Misters Lamont are not the same men.*

Oh, crumbs, Edwina thought. All right, she reasoned, it didn't matter so much that no one knew the Lamonts; her lofty friends wouldn't necessarily know every member of every minor family of consequence. But this other—

No, no, she told herself, she would not believe the worst. There were many sets of twin brothers in England. Why, the two who'd caused trouble in Brighton could be any of them.

Besides, she reassured herself, there was no profit in taking a bogus nobleman to the Duke of Arle's ball for an evening.

Another voice whispered though: Profit or not, if the bet isn't legitimate, you have no reason to continue teaching Mick. You must stop; your association with him is over, here and now: sooner than expected.

She would lose their final week.

As she folded the letter, with its last dreadful sentences, back into its envelope, a part of her knew perfectly well that Lady Wychwood had just told her the Lamonts might well be as Mick suspected: some sort of confidence men involving him and herself in a fraudulent scheme of unknowable depth.

But there was the problem: the knowing part of Edwina didn't care what the truth was or what the risks were. She wanted the last days with Mick Tremore. They were hers. She'd counted on having them, and she would, come what may.

Chapter 19

"*If* I have to say that one more blasted time, I'm going to pukc." Thoroughly exasperated, Mick twisted his mouth and looked at Winnie across a table on which—it was too splendid an image to forget—she'd once stood with her long legs showing.

"Well." She blinked and cranked her head at him. "That was perfect," she said. "Especially if you could think of something a little more genteel to threaten than puking." She laughed. She let go, a small, light peal of genuine delight. "Oh," she said, "you did the H just as it should be and every vowel perfect. *Hahff to, blahs-sted,*" she repeated. "You didn't even curse too badly, and the grammar was perfect. That was wonderful. And quite natural."

"Truly?" He laughcd too. Though mostly at her. Her nose wrinkled when she laughed. It wiggled at the tip.

He'd said he'd stay away from her, but he couldn't. And she wouldn't let him anyway. No matter where he went in her house, she chased him down, then insisted they "get on with it." And so he put up with her "it," whatever "it" was she was doing to him. Any contact seemed better than none. He put up with her moods and seemingly unassailable, stiff-necked propriety, and watched and waited and hoped.

''What a lovely nose you have,'' he said. He reached, thinking to touch it.

She pulled back. Her laughter stopped. Her eyes, a look in them, grew wary, almost hurt. He realized that she thought he was playing with her in an unkind way.

''I mean it,'' he said. ''I love your nose.''

Love. He'd said it. Though only for her nose. It was only her nose he loved.

Her eyes grew larger, wider behind her eyeglasses. She looked afraid, yet full of hope. She was dying to believe him about something she couldn't see in herself.

''I don't like my nose,'' she said.

''You're so hard on yourself. I think your nose is the best nose I've ever met.''

She gave a little snort. ''You see? The best nose. Honestly. You aren't supposed to notice a woman's nose.''

''Why not?''

''It's supposed to blend in, be part of the overall beauty of her well-proportioned face.''

''Yours is part of your overall beauty.''

She made a face at him, complete with tongue stuck out.

Which made him laugh outright. It took him a moment to recover.

While she watched him with her wide blue saucereyes, perfectly solemn, attentive. As he calmed, she asked, ''Do you really think I'm hard on myself?''

''Yes.''

''How?''

''You don't let yourself see how good you are. To begin with, how striking your looks are.'' *Striking*. It was a new word. He hadn't even planned on saying it. It simply came out.

She didn't seem to notice. She merely shrugged. ''No one before you has seen me as striking.''

''I doubt that. I'd bet dozens of men have eyed you.''

''None that said anything.''

"And if they did, you'd probably criticize their taste in women. That's what you do to me."

"I do?"

"If I say you're pretty, you tell me I'm wrong."

She looked puzzled for a moment. "Well, the people who were supposed to love me best never thought I was very presentable." She cast her eyes down. "My mother thought I was 'a fright of a child.' My father didn't see me at all. If you'd asked him what color my eyes were, he wouldn't have known."

"There must have been other people."

She shrugged. "Milton."

"There you go—"

"Look, Mr. Tremore—"

"Mick," he told her. She said it occasionally, though she tried not to.

"No, Michael, we've decided. Remember: Michael."

He nodded. "Right. Michael."

"Michael," she said, then realized she'd lost the volley of given names. She broke off, as if she couldn't remember what she'd been about to say. She exhaled a long, loud breath. "Don't be foolish, Mr. Tremore. My nose is huge."

He laughed. "Yes, it's a good-sized smeller, loov. If it weren't so pretty, I might have sympathy for you."

"Pretty?" She let out an insulted breath.

"Yes." This time, when he reached, she let him run his finger down the ridge of her nose before she jerked back. "So thin and delicate," he told her, "with long nostrils, and the nicest, slightest curve to it. It's upper-class, you know. You have a very classy nose, missus. Calls attention right away to your breeding. Wish I had one like that."

She twisted her mouth as if to say that, if he weren't out-and-out insincere, he was certainly misguided. "I have a funny face."

"Funny?" He stared. "I suppose. Your face *is* amusing. Like a pretty puppy's. You have a witty face, a lively mug of a face, Win. As if God made everyone else's then came back to you and gave you a few extra touches, to make you stand out; you're more interesting to look at than most women, Win.''

''I'm not pretty,'' she complained woefully.

He frowned. ''All right, perhaps you're not. But your face is much more riveting than a pretty one. Pretty faces are a guinea a dozen. So predictable. I'm tired of pretty faces already. Your face, though, I'd never tire of.''

That put a *clunk* in the conversation. Why had he said it? He shouldn't have. Of course he wouldn't tire of her face. He wasn't going to see it after three days more, was he?

Three days till a ball, when, it had only recently occurred to him, he wasn't even sure what a ball was. A lot of dancing, he thought. Saturday, though, he'd find out.

He changed the subject. ''Let's go somewhere. Let's put me to the test. Let's take that pretty face of yours out of the house.'' He wiggled his eyebrows wickedly and leaned forward. ''Let's go back to the tearoom,'' he said.

She let out one of her gasping laughs. ''No! They'd know you.''

''No, they wouldn't.'' He sat up straight, touching his mouth. ''I have no mustache. I have a new haircut, all new clothes. I talk completely differently. How could they possibly know me?'' He raised one eyebrow. ''I'm not at all the same,'' then winked. ''But I'll know them, and it would be great entertainment to see some of the fools who chased me wait on me all afternoon.''

He grabbed her hand and stood. He tried to lead her up and away from the table. ''Come on,'' he said. He remembered brightly, ''Oh, and I can wear that top hat, the one we like.'' The idea was sounding better by the moment. Then he thought of something else and turned too quickly—she ran right into him. He smiled down the few inches into her face and said, ''No big hat. No big hat for you, all right?'' His wagged his finger. ''A little hat, if you have one. Or no hat. I want to see your funny face.''

She squinched it at him, but her eyes behind her lenses were smiling. He laughed again, so amused by her. Oh, her sweet face . . . her dear face with all its infinite movements and twists.

She said, ''No, sir. I'll wear any hat I choose, thank you. Now get out of my way. I want to dress for the occasion.''

Winnie chose a little straw hat she hadn't worn in years, one with a small, forward brim. It was out of date, yet not too bad. Milly had put a new flower on it at the side and new ribbons. It was cheerful; yellow straw, little yellow roses, with dark green grosgrain.

Indeed, not too bad. Like Winnie herself. Not too bad from this angle or that, especially in a not-too-bad little hat. Yes, she had a strong, healthy, if quirky, sort of femininity, she thought. No nonsense. And then, of course, there were her legs, which were beautiful, she was coming to think. No matter what she believed, though, the amazing part was, when she looked in Mick's face, there was no mistaking his sincerity: *He* thought her pretty, and she could have looked at that information on his face all day long.

She looked forward to staring at it across a tea table at Abernathy's. Her heart was light, though her nerves were frayed. She wasn't certain he was ready for public inspection. She wasn't certain she was, for that matter. She had never gone to tea with a man, other than her own father.

For all her own nerviness, Mick seemed perfectly calm, happy, in fact. Charming. He asked Mr. Abernathy for a table for two, please. ''Yes, sir,'' the man said, and Mick laughed out loud.

Winnie loved watching him act the gentleman, yet it terrified her to see him do it, too. Like watching someone on a high wire, someone she had put there, who carried somehow her fondest hopes, high, high up in the air overhead. She wanted to stand under him with a giant net. No, she wanted to get up there with him, hold onto his shirt, tie strings around each of his ankles. Don't fall. Don't let anything bad happen.

As they walked behind Mr. Abernathy into his main tearoom, entering its refined air of soft chatter and long-fronded palms, questions popped into her mind. Did he know not to remove his hat? Not to raise his voice? Had she told him every single rule regarding a gentleman's behavior in public? Probably not. Could he extemporize his way through the moments that depended on what she'd forgotten to tell him?

"Will this do?" asked Mr. Abernathy. He was seating patrons himself today.

The teahouse wasn't crowded, though it was relatively full. He sat Winnie and Mick at a small table near the door. Good for a quick exit, she thought, then sat nervously, laughing at herself.

They ordered tea and cake. The first five minutes went well, and she relaxed a little. Mick was beyond gentlemanly. He was attentive. He touched her hand at one point, and she blushed.

In the heat that flushed through her, her mind warmed to a little fantasy. Suppose they went to tea together next Wednesday, too, after the ball was over? Suppose they went to tea next Wednesday, or perhaps the opera?

Oh, yes, she answered herself. Imagine that—because that is the only way you'll see it, in imagination. Mick at the opera. Pah. He wouldn't like it. It wasn't his sort of entertainment. No, they had no future, not even one of Wednesday-afternoon teas. He didn't fit into her life—passing him off for an afternoon or an evening wasn't the same as passing him off for a lifetime. And she was hardly suited to catching rats—she'd proven that, when she'd all but climbed him like a pole then run away from fright.

She watched Mick raise his teacup to his mouth, ever so beautifully, especially when she remembered the last time she'd seem him do it in this tearoom. But then his cup stayed in front of his mouth without his drinking. His eyes grew still and intent as he stared fixedly over the cup across the room.

"Oh, no," he murmured. Then, "Don't look. But brace yourself. We have a visitor."

The baroness from the seamstress's shop six weeks ago, the one who had bought Winnie her garters, came straight over to their table.

Ignoring Winnie, she said to Mick, "Lady Randolf Lawnhurst, the Baroness of Whitting." She added coquettishly, "Blanche," then extended her arm toward him, her hand dropped at the wrist. "And we know each other, I do believe." Her face was smiling, though puzzled, one eyebrow was arched high in question. With relief, he realized, she couldn't remember the circumstances under which she knew him.

Mick started to rise, being a gentlemen at the moment, when he would rather have told her to go jump in the Thames.

She stopped him. "No, no, don't get up. I don't mean to intrude." She already had, of course. "It's just that I'm sure we've met, yet I can't remember where." She was asking him to explain her own confused memory.

Settling back into his chair, Mick smiled and shook his head. In his best, most posh syllables told her, "I'm sorry. I don't believe I've had the pleasure." He tried to look dismayed, disarmed.

"Oh, but I'm sure—"

"No," he insisted, smiling, "I don't think so."

She tilted her head, frowned, then smiled, then frowned, like neon flickering in a glass tube, off and on, off and on, all the while studying him. She shook her head, then her smile widened as she announced cheerfully, "You're wrong. I know you, I'm certain."

Ah, well. Since she was certain. "You do look familiar," he allowed.

Winnie made a sound, a surprised, censuring little click of her tongue. She was alarmed, no doubt, at hearing him go in this direction.

While the baroness openly flirted with him, flapping

her eyelashes, rolling her shoulders under her boa. "Are you from here?" she asked.

"No," he said quickly.

"Where are you from?"

He blurted what was as far away as he could think of. "Paris."

Under the table, Winnie kicked him.

He laughed at the heady sensation of two women taking after him at once.

"Paris?" The baroness was delighted. "I love Paris! Where in Paris?"

He knew of only one landmark in that city, so he said it pleasantly. "The Eiffel Tower."

Behind the baroness, out of her line of vision, Winnie put her hand over her mouth, her eyes widening, part horror, part mirthful disbelief she held back.

"The Eiffel Tower," the baroness said, perplexed. "You live in the Eiffel Tower?"

He could hear in her tone this was wrong. "No, no," he amended, "I was suggesting we might have met there."

She thought the information over, as if trying to make his hypothesis plausible. "When did you last visit the Eiffel Tower?"

"Oh, I go there all the time," he said. When he saw on the baroness's face that this wasn't right either, he thought to add, "I know it's foolish. Even trite, since, well, the most common of persons knows of the place. But I can't help myself. It's simply so—" He had no idea what he was talking about.

She finished for him. "Yes, so amazing. And the fountains—"

"Oh, yes, especially the fountains. And—" And what? What to contribute to the conversation? He held out his hand. "And the tower itself."

"Oh, yes. A marvel. Those French."

"Indeed." He smiled and said, "Well, it was lovely meeting you again."

She blinked, seemingly at a dead end. Thank God. "Yes," she said. "Very nice to see you." She turned to go. He thought he was free of her trouble, but she turned all the way, full circle, and came back after only moving away a foot. "Your name," she said and smiled. "I don't remember your name. Please remind me." She eyed him with an interest that was a shade warmer than was polite and so reminiscent of their last encounter he wanted to shake her.

Remind her indeed. He dare not. If he repeated the name *Tremore,* she might remember its context. He looked down at his teaspoon, turning it over. He read the names off the back and flipped them over. "Bartonreed," he said. "Michael Edgerton, the Viscount of Bartonreed."

"Bartonreed," she repeated blankly. She couldn't seem to think of anything further to ask. "Well, then, Lord Bartonreed." She wanted more information, but had run out of latitude to acquire it. "A pleasure," she said.

Once she'd left, Winnie leaned forward and whispered, "You gave her the wrong name!"

"I couldn't give her *Tremore.* She knows it."

"She knows it!" she repeated, though her tone was more emphatic. It questioned him.

He didn't want to explain. Besides, they were past the problem.

Winnie, of course, didn't like to miss a chance to worry. "Oh, crumbs, oh, crumbs," she said. She put her long fingers to her mouth, pressing them, then spoke over the tips. "Now you have to remember 'Bartonreed'—where did you come up with that?—and answer to it. Will you be able to?"

"I'm sure. But we can go ahead and use—"

"No, we can't. She's the wife of the Master of the Hounds for the Queen. She'll be at the ball."

"Oh, bloody hell," he said and sat back. He did laugh this time, and richly. Bloody hell.

Winnie, though, was losing her sense of humor. "Stop it," she said. "You're going to mess this up."

"No, I won't."

She leaned toward him, her face furrowing, squinching up and down both, as it could. Intently, she asked him, "Do you know what it would be like to fail in front of the *bon ton*?"

"The *bon ton*?"

"Yes. Every. Single. Family in England that matters?"

He raised his brow. "Every single person at the ball matters to you?"

"Well, no." She made a befuddled frown, then shook her head. "Oh, I don't know. Some do; most don't. They all mattered to my parents."

"Ah," he said. He laughed gently at her. "Loovey, how sweet. I'll do my best. I'd love for your parents to be proud of me—and proud of you, too—even though they're dead."

She let out a laugh at this, a *squawk*, half of distress for being teased, half of release, then nodded, biting her lips together. She admitted, "I'm so nervous."

"I can see that." She nearly always was, bless her.

He hoped her nervousness this time didn't make her put her fingers into things beyond good judgment. He hoped she'd leave him be so he could do what he needed to his way. But she either would, or she wouldn't. He would deal with her as she came.

For now, he signaled the waiter, asking for milk instead of cream for his tea. As the waiter left, however, Mick watched trouble circle back around to them.

Smiling, a look of triumph on her face, the baroness left her own party once more to bear down on Mick and Winnie's table.

He leaned forward and whispered, "Finish your tea, loov. She's found something more to say to us."

The baroness walked up to their table again, wagging a thoughtful finger at Mick, and said, "Niece." That was the word she used, though he was fairly certain she meant a place, when she continued, "In Nice at the Hotel Negresco. You were on the floor." She frowned, as if it were painful to draw so hard on a memory that resisted. She bridged her flawed recollection with an invention of her own. "Yes," she said with certainty now, "you were the one who found my cat. Positively heroic, you were." She frowned, then smiled, doing that flicker of uncertainty again. Then, as if perfectly logical, she let loose a torrent of what he thought to be French.

He nodded politely till she finished, then took a chance saying, "Excuse me, but my fiancée doesn't speak French. May I present Miss Edwina Bollash. We're to be married in June." That should shut the woman up and make her leave him alone.

But, no, she was fascinated. "Miss Bollash? Lady Bollash?" she corrected. "Lionel Bollash's daughter?" The baroness was surprised, but riveted.

Next to Winnie, however, the woman looked calm.

Win had been startled apoplectic by his announcement. "Michael," she began, then laughed, then couldn't get whatever else she was going to say out for a few seconds. "You're, um—ah, not supposed to say that. That is, *tell* people yet." To the baroness, apologetically, she said, "It's not official. We haven't announced it. We aren't really."

Mick reached across and patted her hand. "Winnie, my dove, don't start again. You promised. Don't say you're making me wait longer, because I can't. I can't wait to make you my own."

Win's jaw dropped. No halfway about it, her mouth looked unhinged for a second. Then she giggled, blushed, and looked away. The perfect picture of a sweet, shy bride.

Oh, to have it be true, he thought. Wouldn't that be something?

The baroness turned and studied Winnie now with rapt curiosity. She glanced at Mick, then once more attempted to speak to him in French.

He held up his hand, shaking his head, a man being firm. "In English, Lady Whitting. Please."

Lady Whitting, ha! He was enjoying himself! Nonetheless, he thought they should cut their tea short. His luck was holding, but he had no idea what the baroness might latch onto next.

To Winnie, he said, "Are you finished, darling?" He took out the chiming watch that he loved to look at for any reason, and that he was probably going to have to return. Too bad. He popped its cover. *Ding-ding, ding-ding. . . .* It continued to chime till the hour exactly. Four o'clock. "Goodness," he said. "I had no idea it was so late. We have to meet Lord Rezzo at five. We'd best be going." He stood. To Winnie: "Dear one, you gather your things, while I take care of the bill."

She grabbed his forearm. "You can't pay," she hissed, though suppressed laughter was now making her all but delirious. She tried to speak under her breath, but her voice carried anyway. "You have no money," she said.

"Of course, I do, dear heart. I have a fresh twenty." He turned toward her fully, wiggling his eyebrows, a gesture only she saw. "A very, very fresh-sh-sh"—he let the sound run—"twenty. Let's go see how it spends."

"Michael!" she said with giddy panic.

But he freed himself from her and backed with a slight bow from the table. Behind the baroness—who followed him, looking disappointed and bewildered—he watched Winnie put her hands over her face, aggrieved, laughing, hiding. He called to her. "Winnie, gather your things. We're leaving."

Indeed, they'd best be gone. He wondered if the baroness were truly going to the ball on Saturday. Or if any of the other upper-class women he knew, several of them more intimately, would be there. Bloody hell, what a shock to realize he might actually know people at the gathering. An ugly shock. He laughed. A challenging shock.

Outside, down the street, with Winnie's hand safely in his, he caught sight of an omnibus. A number six. Perfect. "Come on," he said. He started to run, pulling Winnie along.

She followed, still laughing, a gamine making her escape. He could hear her, delighted by their strange encounter, drunk on it. "Where are we going?" she called.

"We're trying to catch that bus." He pointed and tugged, encouraging her to move faster.

"My carriage—"

"One problem at a time, loovey. Come on, be quick."

She wasn't as quick as he was. She held her hat and clopped down the pavement behind him, skirts kicking up around her wonderful legs.

They weren't going to make it. The omnibus stopped. One man got off, two women got on. Mick called to the driver, but he and Winnie were still too far for anyone at the bus to hear him. Mick slowed. Still a block away, the horses of the ominbus lurched forward.

"There'll be another," he said.

Then a woman across the street, closer to the vehicle, called to the driver. The omnibus slowed and Mick said, "Come on. Run."

Winnie did. She remembered the breathless chase he'd led the first day she'd set eyes on him. Now she ran with him, and it thrilled her. No other word to describe it. *Thrill*. Feeling his dry, warm hand around hers, his pulling her through traffic, then his arm about her back, her waist, lifting her, propelling her up a curb, taking her with him, then boosting her up the steps of the bus when she hesitated—oh, it was so bold and simply too much fun. She started laughing hard somewhere along the way, uncontrollably; she couldn't stop.

In this condition, Mick wound him and her both all the way up the steps to the roof of the bus, the bench seat. From the top, she stood on her knees and waved to Georges, the coachman she shared with two neighbors. He saw her, then a second later, her own carriage pulled away from the curb to follow. She turned around and slid down into the seat, and Mick's arm—he'd braced it on the bench back—slid down, too. He gripped her around the shoulders. He squeezed her to him as both he and she laughed without reserve.

As they clopped past Hyde Park, then along the side and around Buckingham Palace, the two of them laughed like fools, recapping the baroness's confusion and surprise till they were slouched against the seat and each other, gripping the arm pieces to hold themselves up, till Winnie was wheezing from it. She couldn't catch her breath from the wild run topped off by laughing too much.

When he became concerned with her breathing, she waved her hand. "It's all right. Asthma. It'll go away as soon as I settle down." She tried to get hold of herself, drawing in deep breaths, then letting them out slowly, with giggles.

As she wheezed her way into sanity again, Mick frowned, smiled, shook his head, then touched her cheek. "Oh, you are a mess, my sweet duck. Such a sweet mess."

He turned in the seat, his shoulder against the bench, his chest close enough to her arm that she could feel his humidity and warmth. He wanted to kiss her. She was becoming aware of the signs, how he moved close, how he watched her face, her mouth. Then she remembered that he wanted her to say it, to tell him. He waited.

Oh, dear, if she were honest, she'd admit she loved all this kissing business. She could do it forever, give up eating, sleeping, just kiss his mouth, maybe lie down beside him, press her body against him. Just the kissing. She remembered it sometimes so vividly from that time in his room that memory brought a near-perfect echo of sensation, a lovely ripple of the same, if muted, pleasure.

Sometimes, too, she remembered the other thing he'd done. The way his hand had sought her lower, the way he'd so fiercely seemed to want to touch her there. When she thought of it now, it wasn't so awful. Only intimate. Very, very intimate.

Yes, she wanted him to kiss her, quick and strong; hard, as he had that time when his mustache was just freshly off. She wanted to say it. *Kiss me.* She wet her lips, opened her mouth—and her mind went blank. She sat there like a nit, nothing coming out but horrid, faint asthmatic wheezing. Which made her close her eyes in despair as a wave of the old feeling returned: a sense of being the least appealing woman on earth.

Why did she have to ask? Pretty women didn't, she was sure. If she were only pretty enough, only a more powerfully attractive female, she'd have kisses bestowed . . . kisses everywhere : . . that would arrive on their own.

Since they wouldn't, though, she tried valiantly to get past her misgivings about her own worth so as to ask for what she wanted. The concept was simple enough. Yet she tried all the way down Birdcage Walk and onto Whitehall to no effect, save a lot of wheezing.

As they approached Trafalgar, Mick laughed beside her, then his lips brushed her cheek. "You're hopeless, Winnie," he said. "But it's a stupid game. Arrogance made me invent it, and I'm suffering now for it. We both are. I'm kissing you anyway. Just let me."

Then he lifted her chin, brought her face to his, and breathed into her mouth as if he could supply her oxygen.

God above. He may as well have. He certainly did something to the flow of her blood. It began to pound. Oh, yes.

He kissed her in front of all of London, on the rooftop of a horse-drawn omnibus as they trotted by Lord Nelson looking down on them from his granite column.

In front of the world, clever, handsome, humorous Mick kissed her, while her heart thudded and her belly squirmed and something low inside melted. Then better still, Mick moved her around, pulling her legs over him, and scooted her up into his lap.

Goodness. Oh, goodness. He pulled her against him as he kissed her strongly. She let him; she helped. She put her arms about his lovely, sturdy neck, reached tentatively into his hair, and kissed him back. She devoured him.

His soft hair. His hot, tender-wet mouth, reaching, wanting hers. He scooted himself down a bit, till her weight rested against his chest, until she lay against a hard, broad wall of muscle. Then something new and strange. Where she sat she could feel through her skirts the vague outline of him under her. He grew hard, becoming a noticeable, rounded ridge.

The sensation wasn't repellent, though she had believed somewhere it would be. Someone had left her with that impression, but, whoever they were, they were wrong. It was . . . mesmerizing. She could sense the length of him against her buttocks as well as a kind of heaviness, a substantive presence. He was changing right there under her, growing longer and thicker, information she acquired through the unlikely source of her bum, while he kissed her mouth. Heavens, what a sensation. She didn't know what to make of it. Too much to assimilate, too different from what, all her life, she'd thought a man would be: both more sleek—elegant—and more formidable.

It was the formidable part, of course, that gave her pause. She backed away from his face, looking into it, both of them knowing what she was feeling. The size of him felt threatening when paired with what she knew of simple biology, with where he was supposed to put something that large. She couldn't imagine it.

She was saved from having to, then, when the conductor interrupted. " 'Ay, lovebirds.'' She and Mick both looked around to see the man's head up over the top of the steps. "How far, mate?" he asked. A Cockney. *'Ow far, mite?*

"Aldwych."

"Four P for two." *Far pee.*

Mick leaned to dig four pence from his pocket as Winnie slid herself back onto the seat, a more ladylike location. Goodness, what had come over her? she thought. In front of anyone who wanted to look up on top of a bus. Could people know? Could they tell what had been under her backside? She thought she should be embarrassed. She *was* embarrassed, she told herself.

Still, she hummed tunelessly to herself as they headed east.

When she asked Mick at one point where they were going, he said, "My part of town."

At first, this quieted her. She worried he meant Whitechapel. She'd been there once with her father; they'd gone to listen to voices. The sounds in that district, of purest, richest Cockney, were wonderful, but the atmosphere of Whitechapel was frightening. At the heart of the East End, it was a hard place of ragtag children, poverty, and narrow, sunless streets. It had been a seedy part of town; then, three years after her visit with her father, Jack the Ripper had made it notorious.

As they lurched through traffic, though, she felt Mick's arm bump her shoulder blades—it was stretched out along the bench back behind her. After that, it didn't matter where he was taking them; she wanted to go. She felt oddly confident of him: If he thought he could guide them without danger, then she would believe that he could.

It was a pretty, midweek late afternoon. London was still bustling as shops prepared to close for the day, people out on the streets, in transit; coming or going. The light breeze on the top of the bus was beautiful; the view was excellent. They left behind the spire of St. Martin-in-the-Fields, then passed Covent Garden, like a tourist's ride. Then at Aldwych, they got off.

"We have to walk from here."

They shooed pink-footed pigeons out of the way as they cut through a small churchyard. The smell of flowers wafted from somewhere, as if from a whole market of them, then this changed abruptly into the pungent smells of a brewery. Then music. Distant, but jolly.

They followed the music into back streets, and Winnie became turned around. They were burrowing their way into what was not a bad area so much as working-class: close flats, children playing in front of an eel-and-pie shop, a heavy cart-horse slipping on wet cobbles where a sewer drained, stomping and jangling its trappings.

And all the while, Mick held her hand, leading her along. His part of town. His warm, embracing hand around hers. He could have led her to hell, and it would have been fine; pleasant, in fact.

Then she thought, How prescient. For he stopped, held out his arm, gesturing toward an overhead, swinging sign halfway down the block. The Bull and Tun. The music was coming from there. It was loud—a tinny piano played with a violin that sounded as though a gypsy worked it, along with some sort of percussion, perhaps a sack of tins. What the trio lacked in nuance they made up for in volume, as they played a lively, if slightly off-key rendition, of a cancan from *Orpheus in Hades*. Hell, indeed.

"Dancing," Mick said and smiled as if he offered a gift. "I can't guarantee what kind, but some of the people inside will dance before the night's over. Let's be two of them, Win."

Chapter 20

🌹

The Bull and Tun was little more than a large room with a bar and foot rail at one end. Its furnishings were simple—wood tables and chairs, the walls covered with ale signs, certificates of inspection, a dart board, all proudly displayed along with a large photograph of the Queen and a smaller one of the Prince of Wales. The public house's wood floors hadn't seen wax in a very long time. The brass at its rails was dented but shining. Nonetheless, the place had an air of goodwill that was attractive. As Mick and Winnie came in, a dozen people greeted them. Several greeted him by name. He was a regular.

At the back, the musical trio caroused through the Offenbach rearranged to suit working-class tastes. A man with a bald spot on his head played the piano so hard his hands bounced off the keys. A swarthy man with baggy eyes sawed a bow back and forth on a violin. A rather talented young man rattled sticks across glasses and cans and anything else he could hit. If people got within reach, he'd play their buttons.

Patrons sat at long tables together, elbow to elbow, though there were still places available. On a small section of open floor, a dozen men and women did a fairly robust polka to the French music. Mick's dance.

He wanted to join them. "We have to dance soon. It will be too crowded later."

First, though, he introduced her to a small, wiry fellow named Rezzo, then several other men whose names she hadn't heard before, and two women, Nancy and Marie. Marie liked him, Winnie knew immediately, though Mick didn't seem to be even faintly acquainted with the fact.

He was well-liked. And well-known—his friends wanted his jokes and philosophies, telling him, "No, no, do the voices, do the accents." They liked him to talk in dialects. It was odd, but during his introductions, she'd heard him attempt to sprinkle his speech with some of his old accent, to blend in, she supposed, but then he stopped. His friends teased him a little about the way his voice sounded these days; her, too, as if he and she had both been somewhere that flavored them differently, like pies in the larder set too close to the basil.

Accent or not, his friends wanted his reactions and ideas; they engaged him in conversation. If anyone knew what he did for a living, it wasn't a subject of interest. Here, Mick was the fellow who—someone let the fact out—danced well with all the ladies and spouted colorful stories with a clearsighted outlook that everyone loved to hear.

She looked at him among them. He wasn't like them. His clothes were too smart, his speech and manner too polished. She looked at his hair, so dark and shining. It was well-cut. His eyes, oh, his beautiful eyes. Their steely green was so much finer than any other eyes here. Perhaps he never had been one of them, she thought, then laughed. Perhaps she was prejudiced. She thought him handsomer than any of the others. Cleverer. Taller, of course . . . kinder, friendlier, funnier. . . . The list went on.

After ten minutes of chatting with friends, with two men buying both him and Winnie drinks—Mick ale and Winnie lemonade—Mick wanted to dance. "In an hour, we won't be able to."

For him, it was simply a matter of dancing, of course. He was familiar with the way of the place, good on his feet, good at quick steps. Winnie was less able. It took a few attempts at each new rhythm to be graceful with it—though Mick exclaimed over and over how quickly she caught on and how good she was once she did. Still, she had good, if self-conscious, fun. He was always a pleasure to dance with.

Then a fast waltz played, and he leaped right into it.

With surprise and recognition, Winnie accused, "You knew how to waltz!"

He shrugged, smiled, and spun her to the music, left then right. "Not all the same steps and not the dignified way you do it, but yes." He laughed, then teased, "Still, you had so much fun telling me how, I was happy to cooperate."

"And what else could you do before I ever tried to teach it to you?" She teased him back. "Could you talk like a lord all along?"

He grinned crookedly and said nothing, as if it were possible.

She remembered all the difficulty they'd had getting him to this point. Still, there were moments when she could almost believe their struggle had never happened. The sounds coming from his mouth tonight were so clearly upper-class—even if his knowledge about Paris was sketchy. Oh, she laughed to think of that foolish woman at the teahouse, flirting with him when there was no point.

He was hers.

She began to think this: hers. As they danced among his friends, and the floor grew more crowded. He was the only Cornishman, but not the only one from remote places. There were gypsy and Irish and Jew. She could hear in the voices that they danced among the grandchildren of the potato famine, the children of European pograms, all come to England for haven. And though Winnie knew that just a few blocks further east, it wasn't very safe at all, here felt haven to her, too. Here was light and laughter and ale and song.

And music. With Mick dancing her around to it. A rare opportunity. She warmed to the unusual music and the quick tempos. She danced, having her own little ball in a pub on the west edge of the East End in London. She danced with Mick till they were bumping up against backs and shoulders, till they didn't have a square foot to move, till, when they wanted a drink to wet their throats, it took half an hour of wedging and working their way to get the fifteen feet to the bar. The room grew hot from the bodies alone. And still, people kept coming in. On a Wednesday night.

They brought tables from the back, filling the dance floor with them. The dancing was over, Winnie thought. Until the woman introduced as Nancy grabbed her arm and said, "Those of us who don't want to stop dancing, get up on the stage." She pointed.

The "stage" was three long wood tables put end to end. Several men, Mick one of them, helped maneuver the wood furniture into position. He saved Winnie and himself seats at the "stage." They pulled up chairs.

When the music started again, Nancy, her friend Marie, and two other women climbed up onto the three contiguous tabletops and began to move to the music. Though this dancing was different.

The girl, Nancy, swung her skirts, then kicked them up in back. She put her fists on her hips, still holding handfuls of skirt, and moved in a way that was provocative and sly, but rhythmic and beautiful to watch. The others showed their petticoats, too, laughing, dancing.

Winnie watched the four girls dance till they were all perspiring, then watched with utter astoundment—horrified, but fascinated—as each and every one of them, one by one, shrugged out of their blouses. Not that they didn't have a great deal on underneath; there was much corsetry and underlinens, all very lacy and pretty. They exposed nothing indecent, or not exactly. But removing their blouses left their arms bare.

She looked to see what Mick made of this. He wasn't even paying attention. His head was bent in cheerful conversation with the fellow next to him; Mick was uninterested, as if he'd seen it all before.

Winnie hadn't. She couldn't decide what to make of it.

"Would you like something to eat?" Mick called over the music. Before she could say, he was up and answering his own question. "I'll bring you something."

As he left, Nancy's friend, Marie, climbed down, using his chair. On her way past, she smiled at Winnie and said, "All the single women are allowed to dance up here. Come join us."

Winnie drew back.

The girl added, "If you want to."

"I don't," Winnie said quickly. She pressed her lips together and shook her head.

Oddly enough, though, she didn't disapprove exactly. Or yes, she did, a little, but she also admired the dancers. She admired the girls' boldness, their joie de vivre, their openhearted laughter and friendly manner.

"We're not whores," Marie called down to her, reaching over Winnie's head to accept a drink Nancy brought.

"Oh, no, I wasn't thinking that." Though, of course, the idea had been in the back of Winnie's mind.

"I work in a garment factory," Nancy said, "and Marie sells apples and flowers. We're good girls." She laughed. "But we love the fellows. And love to dance."

Yes. Winnie loved to dance, too. She tapped her feet to the music.

Other than toe-tapping, though, she had the presence of mind to sit, ladylike, and watch as Nancy, having swilled a half pint of ale in a single draft, stepped back up, from the floor to a chair to the tabletop again.

The piano went from a double-quick polka to a music-hall rendition of another of Offenbach's can-

cans, while underneath the table Winnie danced her toes in little steps.

On the tabletops, the girls broke into high kicks. Amazing. And bawdy. And slightly awe-inspiring. They bounced their knees into the air and circled their legs—their pretty, stockinged legs half-covered in lacy knickers. It made Winnie's heart pound to see it.

The oldest girl up there, she would guess, probably Nancy, was still at least five years younger than herself. They were all pretty girls, one dark, another petite, another slightly plump; Nancy herself was fair, slender, and shapely.

From nowhere, Winnie remembered her mother. In the six years she had known the woman, Helen Bollash had paid as little attention as she could to her daughter, and when her attention came, it was inevitably harsh. Winnie had understood intuitively before she could talk that her mother didn't like children. The Marchioness of Sissingly had been young when she'd had her only child, eighteen; twenty-four when she'd left; then dead at twenty-six.

Winnie had never heard the word applied to her mother, but she didn't doubt that some said it: Her mother had been *wild*. Or as Mick would call it: spontaneous with a strong sense of adventure.

She wished she had a dash of her mother in her now, for, she felt sure, Helen Bollash would have thrown her head back at the suggestion of dancing in her camisole and shaking her skirt, of showing her legs. She'd have laughed sweetly, even squealed with delight, then leaped upon the tabletop. Her mother would have danced. And her father, even if he'd been sitting at the table, wouldn't have noticed—he wasn't indulgent so much as blind. Lionel Bollash was aware of his wife only insofar as she had a beautiful voice that spoke with clear, upper-class syllables. Lady Sissingly could even curse like a lord, but when she did, it came out with such soft, round sounds, with such dignity that people doubted they'd heard correctly. She couldn't have said *that*.

Spontaneity and adventure.

Winnie watched. As she had watched her mother. She watched other people have an unconventionally good time, afraid to have it herself.

Finally, Nancy, with a stroke of insight, said, "Come on, love," and held out her hands, reaching down toward Winnie. "Come on. You don't have to take your blouse off. Just get up with us and dance. It's fun."

"I can't."

From behind, Mick spoke as he sat down into his chair, pulling it forward. "She can," he said. "She will. I can see her knees moving." He laughed.

She twisted, frowning around at him "You're always watching my skirts."

He grinned, unapologetic. "I damn well am. I can't stop myself. Here," he said. He'd brought her fish and chips and a lemon shandy—lemonade and beer. More money; he shouldn't be spending it.

She sipped the shandy, her second of the night. Mick took a long draft of ale as he tipped back on the rear legs of his chair, then casually laid his arm across the back of Winnie's, wrapping his fingers around her chair back's far spindle, a possessiveness that somehow made her spine prickle with pleasure.

They watched for a while like that, eating their fish and chips, a social couple; something she had never known and was keenly aware of. She couldn't sit back in her chair all the way for being nervous she'd lean into his arm, yet she loved knowing his arm was there.

Meanwhile, the girls entertained them, dancing for all they were worth. They were good. The music thumped in Winnie's chest. Now and then, Mick rubbed his thumb against her shoulder, a little brush in musical time.

"Come on," Nancy said when she came down for the third time. "I can see you moving to it. You don't have to do anything you don't want to, but come dance with us, dearie."

Winnie was susceptible enough to the girl's coaching that she leaned forward in her chair, wanting to get up, shy, uncertain. Then Nancy grabbed her at the elbows, Mick planted his palms squarely under her bum, and Winnie was levitated up onto the tabletop.

She straightened herself, turned, and looked down. Heavens, a tabletop again! The room below her was crowded, hardly an inch between people to move. Full of faces . . . strangers . . . who suddenly applauded a lady who would play their game. *A lie-dy who 'ill ply,* a man's voice called out.

And the music pounded; the crowd stomped. Winnie stood there a moment, dumbfounded, while the other dancing feet around her made the table hop under the soles of her shoes, making the rhythm of the music shake up her legs. She could feel it.

Slowly—to please everyone, then she'd get down, she told herself—she allowed herself to be moved by all that was going on around her. When she took her first step, the men and women below her hooted goodnaturedly.

"Come on, duckie! Let's see whot you're myde uv!"

Yes, her mother would have reveled in the attention, the same attention that embarrassed Winnie. She blushed. She looked for Mick.

He was just below, leaning back in his chair, precariously balanced and perfectly confident. His face smiled up at her, ready to accept anything she wanted. He'd get her down, if she asked for help. *Take me away.* He'd clap his hands in time to her movement, if she let loose and danced.

She shifted on her feet, making small, halfhearted movements, listening to an Irishman at an old English piano play a French bouffe song that had been turned into a fine East End rhythm. Her feet moved a little more earnestly. Then she raised her skirt enough to watch her own toes.

She danced—not like the others, not without restraint—but as she danced by herself sometimes at home, with demure little steps. But the music wasn't really for that, so she matched it a little better. Her steps grew daring. She made a little kick, then a small twirl, then a crossed-over step that became a kind of deep curtsy, from which to recover she had to swoop herself up; she ended with a spin.

When she found Mick's face again, he was laughing, enjoying himself: enjoying her. He liked it. And his laughter, her own movement, her own feelings as she did it, these made her feel light—not the large, sometimes cumbersome woman she was, but light on her toes; light in her mind.

She must have been interesting to watch, because after a few minutes, Nancy and Marie and the other two stepped back and the whole room began to clap. Winnie was flustered when she realized they clapped to the music for her, encouraging her to turn and move and leap. Well. All right. She did it.

She danced. She danced down the tables then back. She kicked a beer over on purpose. The splash was perfect. It went with a jangle of the piano that made the little crowd roar with approval. She danced till her dress was sticking to her, till her hair was coming down in strings. She even kicked her foot high once and showed her legs—that was a truly popular step. The men—it seemed all the men in the room—made such a fuss. More than the commotion they made for Nancy or Marie or the others.

When she looked for Mick, he winked at her, wiggled his eyebrows, then dropped his gaze again and watched her legs the way he could. She would swear that the glow on his face was from pride and possessiveness and anticipation. His. She felt like his, and it was a good feeling. And he, oh, he who was the finest man in the room; he was so hers. The tallest, handsomest, friendliest . . . warmest, earthiest. . . .

Anticipation. Her stomach rolled over again in that way it had weeks ago now, when she'd stood on a table in a room alone with him. Then more so, when he'd pressed her to a wall. She grabbed her skirts as the music went into a cancan again, raising them to shake

them to the tempo and see how high she could kick.
The whole tavern roared. The other men, no doubt,
thought the whole thing saucy, a devilish good time,
but when she saw Mick's face, it was something else.
To everyone else, it was rollicking. But to him—she
could feel it—he was watching a change happen,
watching her do what she could sense in her blood:
ease up.

Anticipation, she thought again. His gaze followed
up her body once more till their eyes held . . . and, oh,
the heat in his stare. His eyes, his lovely smoky eyes—
green yet not, gray yet more—they wouldn't let hers
go. Their intensity promised something.

What? Oh, what? she thought. She gave him a ques-
tioning look, saying wordlessly, *Why do you stare at
me like that?* Her heart felt gay all at once.

Nancy grabbed her. "Your hair is falling down."
She tried to repin a piece that lay on Winnie's shoulder, then leaned to her and said, "Take off your jacket
and blouse, dearie. No one cares here, and it's cooler.
You have plenty on to cover yourself. Take it off or
at least unfasten the collar."

Practical advice perhaps, but no, thank you.

Except, well, the collar. Yes. She let Nancy fiddle
with it. Yes, it would feel good to release the high
neck. Winnie tried to hold her feet still long enough
for the girl to ease the hooks of the boned collar up
her throat.

The fabric fell free, and Nancy quickly untied the
little jabot and undid a few top buttons for good measure. Air found the moisture on Winnie's skin, cooling
her. It felt wonderful.

"Come on, dearie," Nancy chided as she pulled at
Winnie's coat, a little mutton-sleeved bolero that was
showing dark, damp splotches. "Gawd love us,"
Nancy said, "but you have on more clothes than a nun
on a winter's night. Here." She peeled the coat from
Winnie's arms, turning her around as she did it, three
hundred sixty degrees.

When Winnie faced the room again, she was oh-so-much cooler. And freer.

Nancy pinched two fingers' worth of blouse, pulling it from where it stuck to Winnie's chest. "If you get rid of this, your arms won't be so hot."

If she got rid of her blouse, she'd feel naked—despite, it was true, a camisole over a corset over a chemise corset liner over a ruffled bust-improver. She wore too much.

On her own, Winnie unbuttoned the sleeves of her blouse and rolled them back. Oh, to have air on her arms! She danced more and harder, till she had to stop from asthma. She took a break, stepping down.

Her blouse was wringing wet. She could see through it to her skin and her corset liner where its ruffles came up over her corset to show in the low V of her camisole. A fine lot of good her blouse did her.

"Are you stopping?" Mick asked. "Do you want a drink?"

"No, and yes, please!" The wheezing eased a little. All she had to do was rest, then she could go back up again. Oh, she never wanted to stop.

When he turned and pushed into the crowd, she put her own fingers to the buttons up the front. She popped them through the buttonholes, one, two, three, four. . . . She tapped her feet and hummed as she did it. Winnie took off her blouse and lay it over Mick's chair.

Yes, much better. And her arms weren't completely bare. The wide neck of her chemise, after all, ended in the little cap sleeves. She stretched her neck, her long neck, and put her hand to her bare throat. She felt exceptionally good, if a little tipsy. She was slightly drunk, she realized.

Not so drunk though that, as she stood there alone, she didn't know it when a man came up and flirted with her. He actually flirted with her! And she flirted back. Not because she liked him—she couldn't have remembered a single detail about him, if asked. He said his name, and she promptly forgot it. No, she flirted with him to see if she could and because, with Mick gone, she wanted to practice for when he came back.

And because she was full of herself.

She wanted to crow. Goodness, she was having a good time as her mother used to. And so far it hadn't killed her. How grand! Oh, how grand it was simply to do what she felt like doing! How grand to be alive tonight!

Chapter 21

"Coo, ain't you fancy tonight," said Charlie behind the bar.

Mick smiled as he ordered another ale and shandy, trying some of his old patter with Charlie. It didn't work any better with him than it did with anyone else.

Oh, his mates were nice to him. He liked them; they liked him still. He laughed and talked to them, just as always. But when he tried to talk like them, it sounded wrong. Not for them, but for him. He didn't like his own voice when the same words came out that, a month ago, would have passed by his ear unnoticed.

A part of him must want to be a gentleman of some sort, he decided. He liked the new way he sounded; he even liked his new manners to some extent. He enjoyed bringing a sense of refinement to his life.

He might become a kind of gentleman after all. He'd spoken to Milton, asking him what other occupations the butler thought Mick might be able to do, and the butler had encouraged him with a few interesting ideas. He could work in a shop, maybe own one someday. He could go into service; at the right house with the right pay, this had the advantage of fine living arrangements. There were other things he could do, none that caught his fancy, but Mick was fairly certain he could find something to do with his new self that suited him.

It was a little daydream these days that he'd do

something that suited Winnie as well. They'll go off, find a little cottage, and live together forever as man and wife. Why not? He was honest and hardworking and smart. She could do worse, and she fancied him, he was sure of it. Of course, the two of them together, really together, wasn't a practical idea, but it certainly made a good daydream.

Standing at the bar now, waiting for his drinks, Mick turned to watch the room again, to watch its endless mixture of people and find Winnie among them—at which point he found himself staring at Why-not: Winnie, with her damn blouse off, talking to a toff out slumming.

Mick had seen the man come in. It happened occasionally. An upper-class fellow wandered over from Covent Garden after an opera or such, looking for a little . . . mud. The bloke was chatting Winnie up, probably thinking her a tavern wench. Ha, he was in for a surprise.

Mick, though, got a surprise, too. Winnie answered the fellow in a friendly manner, instead of with her usual tartness, and, of course, the moment she opened her mouth and her sweet, soft voice came out—the smooth-as-cream upper-class tune in it—well, anyone could see the fellow's response from across the room. The man liked his surprise.

Mick didn't like his: Suddenly Winnie and the toff over by the dancing stage were having a fine old talk, two peas in a pod. She was laughing with the man, smiling at him, wagging her finger at something he said.

Charlie put the drinks down, a *thunk-thunk,* as Mick turned and left them behind.

He cut straight through the crowd, shoving people, using his size to get through. Damn it, he didn't like the way the man nodded and leaned toward her.

As Mick came up to them, the arsehole asked her, "So, having a little 'outing,' are we?" *We*? He and Winnie were no *we,* and Mick was about to tell him so.

He could have saved himself the worry. The second

Win saw him, her face lit. She turned toward him, ignoring the other man. "Where are the drinks?" she asked.

He didn't have them. She laughed. Never mind. She grabbed Rezzo's beer from him, took a swill, then wiped her lips demurely with her fingertips. All was forgiven. Mick was confused. What had just happened?

Then more amazing: Winnie leaned forward onto her toes and planted a quick, damp kiss on his cheek. As she clambered back up onto his chair, then the table, he was left holding his face where her wet, cool mouth had touched him. Stunned. Oh, Win. . . .

She began her dancing again. He laughed. A madwoman. Mad to dance. She couldn't get enough. She was too eager to be about her own entertainment than to be bothered with a toff out on the town. Mick let it go. She danced. He watched. So did the toff, he noticed. So did a lot of the men. Who wouldn't? Whenever she'd stop long enough to get a drink of water, the fancy fellow, though, tried to make conversation.

Mick listened to him ramble, paying less attention to what he said than how he said it. He put *bloody* into the middle of everything: hoo-bloody-rah, abso-bloody-lutely. When he asked Winnie to step out front with him "where it isn't so noisy," Mick interceded. He put his hand over the fellow's reaching arm and said, "Not bloody likely."

The man looked at him. Mick realized he assumed they were the same, two toffs wanting the same bit of wild skirt, a lady out for a good time. Hell, the man couldn't have been more wrong about everything, though it made Mick frown at Winnie. Something was different about her, something nice, something he liked. Though somehow it worried him, too.

Then she became reassuringly the same. With all the starchiness she was capable of, Winnie said to the man, as if he were insane to have imagined differently, "I'm not going anywhere with you." She looked perfectly startled to have to inform him of the fact.

Thank you, loovey, Mick thought.

The fellow accepted her decision, though he handed her a quinine, which Mick might have complained about if he hadn't forgotten his own drinks at the bar and Winnie hadn't looked so thirsty. While she drank it, in under a minute, the toff mentioned he was in London for a horse auction, obviously trying to impress her.

Mick folded his arms. Hell. In the minute, offhand, in passing, they talked about breeding horses—for Ascot as opposed to good carriage horses—what it took to breed good hunting dogs, and where to buy a Van Dyke, whatever that was.

Winnie could talk to the fellow about these things. She knew all about them; she had lived in his world. Lived there still to a degree. He said to himself, She's the daughter of a marquess, for godssake, Mick. You're thinking you'll just up and marry a marquess's daughter? Then what? Haul her off to the country in a donkey cart? If you can find a donkey cheap enough?

What was so god-bless special about her anyway? Yes, she was quite the classy lady. Sweet, kind to people; kind to him. She was about as intelligent a woman as he'd ever known, and he liked that about her. He liked that she was sensitive and careful, even if she was so careful sometimes she made herself crazy. And pretty, Lord, she was pretty to him—in a unique way that no other woman could duplicate.

A smooth-skinned, strong-featured face. Very English. Beautiful coloring. An elegant height. Substantial. With pretty little breasts. A fine, grand bottom. And, of course, the damnedest legs a man might ever know. Lord, he'd like to see those legs, bare again, just one more time before he died.

He loved Winnie's body. It was odd, but Mick could no long remember if he'd always liked this shape in a woman, then Winnie came along and filled the bill. Or if he liked this shape because it was the shape of Winnie Bollash.

When he came down to it, he just didn't know. It was a mystery to him why he liked her so well, why he wanted her. A mystery usually summed up with the phrase: *I'm in love with the woman.*

And there it was, for better or worse. His worry. He was in love with Winnie—with Lady Edwina Bollash— a lady he couldn't carry off and have forever. It was going to break his heart to leave her. But he was going to have to, and that was a fact. He was going to have to leave her to the likes of the toff.

By midnight, the crowd had thinned enough that in a cramped, crowded way, couples, now most of them to one degree or another drunk, clung to each other in what might have been called dancing. That section of the floor swayed again to the music, slowing along with the girls who moved more languorously on the tabletops—only three survived: Nancy, a girl named Lolly, and Win, his sweet Win. Mick didn't know if Winnie were aware of it or not, but her own movements had become willowy, softly undulant. Sultry. He was riveted.

The lordly fellow hung on, too. He wouldn't leave, and he wouldn't stop staring. It hadn't bothered Mick that any man in the room looked at her, not up to this point. He was damn proud to know her, to watch her make herself happy in a way that didn't hurt anyone— in a way, in fact, that made a lot of other people damn blissful. The men in the room were pretty much mesmerized by tall Win moving her long body.

Now, though, even though the upper-class fellow was being perfectly polite about his interest, Mick wanted to throttle him. For no good reason at all. Or no, for the simple reason that he had the good taste to watch the prettiest woman in the room dance better than anyone else. Winnie certainly had a way of moving to music. She'd said it was Strauss in her blood, but tonight it was gypsy. Sweet gypsy Win.

He realized after a while that he and the other fellow were standing shoulder to shoulder, watching her, though his own shoulder was a good six inches higher.

The other man noticed, too. "Can't help but observe," he said, "we both have good taste." Then he asked, "Is she yours then, mate?" He didn't own the word *mate;* it wasn't his. He was being chummy, trying to adopt the vernacular of the place—possibly because he'd noticed Mick had command of it.

"Yes," Mick said. It was simpler than explaining.

Then stupid Winnie, fresh from huffing and puffing her way off the table, stepped down and chimed in, "I'm not his. I'm not anyone's." She looked right at Mick when she said it, as if he should contradict, but how could he? She wasn't.

The fellow arched a self-important, condescending eyebrow at Mick and shifted his gaze to her, smiling. "May I buy you a drink then?"

"No," she said cheerfully. "I'm drinking with him."

"I could buy you something much fancier. I'm a baron's son." The awkward announcement, if it were true, was meant to convey he had money, connections, a way of wooing beyond the Bull and Tun.

Mick told him, just as cheerfully as Winnie, "You could be the son of a whore, and no one would care."

The other man jerked, blinked at him. Mick halfhoped he would rise to the insult. He would have been happy to level the arsehole. He hadn't hit anyone in years, and tonight felt like a splendid night for it. He was angry over something—over something larger than a stupid nob making eyes at Winnie. Still, whatever it was, he'd be only too happy to take it out on a mouthy fellow with more gall than a monkey pulling his own tail.

Now, it was Mick's experience that other men didn't lightly test out the truth behind his mean look. He didn't even have to make it all that hateful. It was one of the joys of being a tall, powerfully built man that his confrontations rarely escalated into physical matches of brawn. He was usually the declared winner by virtue of the other fellow taking a good look at him. So he let this other fellow study him.

Then Winnie pushed him. "Stop. Don't cause trouble." Oh, fine, now *he* was causing trouble. She looked down at his hands, both fisted together, and frowned. "Whatever happened to the drinks you were bringing us?"

Ah, the ale and shandy he'd left on the bar half an hour ago. They'd be gone by now. He tried to sidestep his way around her question. He didn't want to leave her, not now. But she was hot and thirsty, and there was no getting around her saying so.

"Go on," she told him and pushed him in the chest again. She used her full, flat palm, which he caught and held against him a moment, rubbing it up his shirt-front an inch, holding it to him. *Yes, touch me, Win.*

It felt so good, her hand on him. Better still, the way her eyes met his made him feel like a bloody king. The male grit and gripe of him relieved in one direction and expanded in another. He wanted her. He wanted her right now. If there hadn't been a law against it, he'd have thrown her on the table and had her. That is, if there hadn't been a law and a lot of people and if Winnie herself weren't, almost certainly, opposed to the idea.

Unaware of the way his mind worked, she absently wet her lips and curved them up for him, her expression glowing—full of promise he doubted she understood, that she didn't mean.

"All right," he said. A drink for Winnie.

He went, watching her and the fancy, irksome fellow over heads and between shoulders as he shoved his way to the bar. Winnie didn't even look at the man, though, horse's arse that he was, he remained at her side, trying to get her to. At the bar, Mick played the same sort of game, torturing himself by looking for them through the crowd as he waited for the drinks. He tapped his fingers, hurried Charlie up, grabbed the mugs, then pushed his way straight back across the room.

Just as he came up, Winnie managed to rid herself of the upper-class nuisance. Yes, a nuisance, Mick thought. That's all the man was to her. Lord Baron's Son moved off, wisely shifting his interest to Nancy, telling her something that made her spill her beer laughing. Anticlimactic. One of Mick's newer words. It was perfectly accurate.

He was left with no place to put all the crazy feelings that raced around inside him.

He handed Win a half pint of straight ale. "Here," he said. "Drink up. You look as if you could use it."

She waved her hand in front of her face, an exaggerated fanning gesture, and smiled. "Hot," she said.

Wisps of hair clung to her neck. Sweat ran down her throat in two neat rivulets, one of them sliding between her breasts as he watched, making him curve the tip of his tongue to the back of his teeth. Yes, Winnie was roasting, he thought. He watched her chug the ale a little quicker than she should. As she drained it, he caught her eye over the rim of the mug. He tipped his head sideways, a nod toward the door at the back. Night air.

She nodded quickly. "Oh, yes, that sounds good."

He set his own drink down, untouched, and took her hand. It felt thin and fragile, soft. He rubbed his fingers over the knuckles as he led her through the room to the back. There, he pushed the door open, then leaned, holding it to let her go first. She brushed his chest as she walked past, out into the night, out onto the stoop, then down the one step to the ground; she walked into the dark.

He followed. It was surprisingly cool outside, quieter, though the music still rattled behind them. He came closer to her as his eyes adjusted, then saw the glimmer of her bare arms as she wrapped them around herself in front. He watched her silhouette from the back. Her pale neck in the moonlight that came between buildings into the alley. Without all her clothes up around it, her neck was long and slender, supple. Her shoulders were rounded. He knew from the shadows and her posture that the muscles of her back were lean and strong; she would have a beautiful back.

He reached, rubbed his palms over her shoulders and down her bare arms, to her elbows. She shivered, making a lovely, light sigh, then surprised him by stepping back against him. Ooh, more promises, Win. With her nestled there in his arms, he took his right hand and lifted a strand of hair that had fallen to her left shoulder. He brushed it back up then gently continued, pushing her head over to make an open place, opening up the vulnerable curve of her neck.

He bent his head into the exposed crook and kissed her there as he pulled her strongly into him, wrapping his arms around her. He more or less ate her neck— lips, teeth, tongue—all the way up to the edge of her jaw where it met the back of her ear, then all the way down again to where her collarbone met her shoulder. It was a delicious stretch of skin.

She shuddered and gave him access while molding her back against his chest.

His, he wanted to say. *Me. Only me.* But he didn't have the right.

Just a compelling inclination. A relentless drive down one narrow train of thought that carried him, again and again and again, to the same conclusion. He needed to have her. He needed to put himself inside Winnie, into the sweet, dark privacy of her, and stroke himself there till he came—h-h-o, God help him.

Putting words to his strongest wish made his head swim. It made the world tilt under his feet. He told himself, Time to think with something other than what was coming to attention in his trousers. Get yourself on the straight and narrow here, Mick. Winnie wouldn't like all this.

But he kept kissing her neck, because Winnie wasn't the same tonight, and any fool could see it.

God help him.

He wanted a woman who could talk about horse auctions and Van-whatever-they-weres, who could teach a man to talk till his friends hardly knew him. Yes, God help him, he thought.

Because all he could think about was how to get this woman back further into the dark.

Chapter 22

*T*he back door of the Bull and Tun gave onto a little alley lit only by the tavern sign's gaslight on the street, an illumination so faint Winnie hadn't noticed it till her eyes had gotten used to the dark. She stood at the edge of the alley, in front of a small, one-step stoop. There was a similar stoop down thirty feet, its door giving into another part of the public house, the dim filtered glow from it indicating it was a kitchen. Behind her, she didn't know what Mick was doing or why he'd stepped back. She turned, rubbing her arms, trying to find him in the shadows. He'd stooped. She couldn't see his movement. Then she realized he was anchoring the door open with a rock, letting some of the heat out for everyone else. The pub had become a furnace inside. How considerate of him, she thought. She waited, her neck feeling bare for his having left it, her arms and back cool from his absence, but she knew he wouldn't leave her here alone for long.

He'd brought her outside to kiss her, and she didn't even have to ask.

The music was softer here in the alley, though the rhythm was just as toe-tapping. Winnie felt a surge of happiness as a breeze blew her chemise flat to her; it clung to her corset where it was wet from the perspiration of her body. She turned to stare back into the tavern a moment, through the doorway, grateful to be out of the humid heat of bodies.

Another wave of good cheer came over her. She felt lucky all at once, though she couldn't have said why. She felt fortunate somehow, blessed by life. The breeze whipped up again, cool, blissful on her skin. She could look up and down the alley; it was open, a little pass-through delivery road at the back of the Bull and Tun. A smell wafted on the wind. Winnie located it vaguely in the dark—ten feet away was a huge bin of bottles and pub accouterments, not the kitchen bin but the bar bin. Its smell was as yeasty as a brewery, earthy in a way that wasn't bad yet was strong enough to encourage her to move away.

She had to laugh at herself. Lucky. Lucky to be standing in an alley, damp, not quite wearing enough clothes for the night, while smelling old beer bottles and tap tubing.

Oh, yes, and this: Lucky to be caught around the waist by a long, muscular arm. She let out a delighted, long laugh as Mick took hold of her again.

"Come here," he said.

He pulled her into the dark that he'd made by opening the door. It cut off the light from the tavern sign at the street, while the light from the kitchen wasn't enough to make it into the corner between stoop and wall. Oh, yes, so considerate. He'd made them a private, invisible niche.

This was where he first kissed her in earnest, really kissed her. He took her by the hips and guided her, backing her up against the bricks, putting her where he wanted, into this wedge of lightless space. Then he bought his body, his mouth up against her. No sight, Mick blocking off the all light. There was only the feel of him and the heat from dancing hard and the rich, organic taste of his mouth, malt blended with hops.

Oh, glorious, she thought, as his tongue touched hers. He pressed her mouth open, and she didn't even have to tell him she wanted him to. But she did, oh, she did. He kissed her openmouthed again, as he had that time in his bedroom. Exactly right, without asking. Oh, yes! It was perfect. A big, lush kiss with the full of his mouth, his hands down her back, his body pressed to her. How strange, how right. She didn't know what she was supposed to do from here, but she would let him figure it out, let him lead the way. She wanted more. More, Mick.

While Mick thought, What naïveté. He could feel her willingness to go beyond a kiss—just as he could sense her ignorance of what "beyond" meant.

He tried to tell her. "Winnie." He pulled back from kissing her neck. "Do you know I want your skirts up again? I want your skirts up and these"—he pulled at the ribbons and lace at her shoulders—"all these"—she wore all manner of covers and corsets and liners and lace—"down. I want your clothes around your waist."

His honesty took her aback, though she laughed at it. "You can't have that," she said.

"I think I can. That's what I'm saying. The time to change your mind is now."

She laughed again, so confident of herself in her innocence. "Fine, then," she said. "Let me go. I'll go in." When he said nothing, she said, "You agree not to then?"

"I agree not to make you do anything you don't want to."

This reassured her. Though he kept her pinned there in the dark corner between door and wall. He knew what business he was about.

Oh, he wanted to lick her body, gently bite the insides of her thighs—taste them, eat his way up. He had no idea what he was going to do exactly. He only knew that the flashing images in his mind were full of sexuality; he was steaming with it. He suspected he would shag her here, that when they went back inside, it would be without her virginity. She didn't take him seriously though.

So much for warning her. He kissed her again.

Again, she opened to it; she warmed to his deep kiss, a woman of growing experience.

He should be warning himself, he thought. God bless, the large, bold physicality of tall Winnie. So undeniable in sheer physical presence. If she had any idea how appealing she was, it would give her far too much the upper hand. He'd never tell her, he promised himself. She'd never guess. He'd never let her know the degree of attraction he felt.

As if he could keep it a secret. Delicately, as he kissed her, he rubbed his thumbs along the bone of her shoulder, till he managed to slide lace and ribbons and gauzy stuff down. Flesh. He shivered. He bent his head to kiss her bare shoulder. Then she jumped and caught her breath as he peeled the neckline a fraction lower and exposed a firm little breast.

"O-o-oh," she said in her soft upper-class voice. "Oh-h-h." As if exclaiming at a tea party. He loved the sweet, proper sound of her.

He loved making nonsense of it. Her breast jutted over the top of her rigid corset. It was tiny in his large hand, soft against the calluses at the inside of his knuckles. Kneading it made her go into a panting kind of flurry, not one of prohibiting him so much as trying to take all the newness of it in. He squeezed and tugged the nipple between his thumb and palm. So sweet. So small, and soft as down. God, how lovely she was.

She put her hand to his, trying quietly to inhibit it as she murmured complaint. "Too small," she said. Her breast embarrassed her.

"Just right. A mouthful." He bent his head and swallowed it up.

She leaped, started with a kind of mild, willing panic. He could feel her heart. It beat so hard he could count the thuds through his lips when he took her breast all the way into his open mouth, pressing his lips to her chest. All the while, she whispered a kind of litany into the dark, "Oh, God. Oh god, Oh god, ohgod, ohgod, ohgod. . . ."

From here, he tried to raise her skirts, but she

wouldn't let him. She still had enough presence of mind to say, "No," quite clearly. It echoed softly in the dark.

All right. He pulled her floundering hands to his shoulders, laying them at the back of his neck to show her what to do with them. He bent his head again, suckling and nipping at the one breast, then, pushing the gauzy fabric and ribbons off the opposite shoulder, he exposed the other to the night air and his mouth. He wet first one, then the other with kissing. Her breasts, two perfect little bon-bon–sized bites he tormented with his tongue.

"Lord," she said, then repeated that, too, as if her mind when aroused were prone to sticking like a needle in the groove of her gramophone. "Lord. Lord, lord, lordlord, lordlord. . . ."

She became unintelligible, guttural, just sounds in her throat as he teased the soft little tip with his teeth.

She arched, knocking her head on the wall.

"Easy there," he whispered.

"Oh, stop, Mick. I can't—I don't—"

He used his knee to open her legs—and she helped, a tentative little piece of cooperation. He leaned into her and, even with all their clothes between them, his body found the right place. Through their clothes, it dropped into the small cove of her sex, as if it had found home. He let out a long, deep groan, growl-like in his attempt to keep himself from calling out. God in heaven, he'd found paradise.

He wanted the impossible. More. "Straddle your legs." He breathed out soft laughter at his own nerve at what he was willing to say to Win. But he wanted it. "Do it," he said. "As if there were a horse under you. Make your legs wide, loovey, and bring one up. Here."

She let him find the back of her thigh through her dress, then lift her leg up and around his waist. He wrapped her long, luscious leg around and behind him, then pressed her heel into his buttocks. "Like that," he said. "Ooh, yes, like that." His head swam in carnal pleasure. He reeled from it.

If he could have gotten her skirts up, fine gentleman that he was, he would have had intercourse right then. He'd have plunged in, burying himself in her. Instead, he-didn't-know-how-many layers of fabric, skirts, petticoats, trousers prevented it. He was left with pressing his erection along her, rocking, stroking the full length of his penis in the slight depression of her female sex, through clothes and all.

He stroked himself, up then back, driving himself along her, till he throbbed, hot and swollen, almost painful. He let out a groan, and it could have passed for anguish.

In a way, it was. "Aa-a-h!"

So harsh, their passion. So strong. If he could ever get her to release herself into it, they would climb mountains of it, sink into oceans of it, cleave the earth, if they weren't careful. The attraction between them was huge.

He tried to raise her skirts again.

"Someone will see," she protested.

Not unless someone walked outside, he thought, who could see in the dark.

He made note though: her objection was no longer her own, but belonged to "someone" else.

He might have simply proceeded from there to have her. In his arms, she trembled and shook. He sensed her will shift.

He owned it.

But the word *alley* sobered him. A miserable, rational voice said, Listen, Gentleman Mick, the reality is: you don't take a virgin for her first time, a kind, gentle lady who's been sheltered most of her life from the facts of men and women, in an alley behind a tavern. Whether you love her or not, you don't do it. If you love her, especially you don't.

Right. Yet another voice demanded, Now. Have her now. Just a little coaching, a little wooing, and she's yours.

Reality. He hated it. Someone truly could see, if they came out with a lantern. No, he should walk her back inside. He should be satisfied for now—Winnie had surrendered. Out of respect for that, he should take her home and make love to her properly, where there was privacy and dignity and sweetness.

Yet something prevented him from letting go of the moment. Somehow, now, right now, it wasn't enough. His body—no, his spirit felt arched, taut and bent to the point of breaking. A voice howled, Not enough!

Before he could move from this place, he wanted to possess her in some way. He felt hungry for it, famished, emaciated, needy. Like a beggar in the street; give me. Like a thief; I want.

He began to make promises to himself. And to her. "Let me touch you," he said, gathering her skirts again slowly, trying not to frighten her into shoving them down. He put his foot on the edge of the stoop to better support her raised leg. "I want to touch you, then we'll go."

Winnie mumbled something. She made no sense. Her leg grew slack, relaxed over his. She was trying to pull the shoulder of her camisole up, but only succeeded in pulling the ribbon out of its casing. She wasn't able to pull herself together. And despite all good intentions, Mick didn't want to help her.

Not enough. It was heaven to hear the sound of her fluster. Winnie, undone, breathing like a woman aroused, talking like a woman in a stupor. Touch her. The thing he hadn't been allowed to do before. Do it now. Touch her between her legs. And not just through her knickers. Touch her, really touch her.

What insanity. What an outrageous thing to want of her in an alley. As a token. Yet he'd never known her as she was, without her lists and organization and proper demeanor. How to keep her like this? How to never let her back into the safe place of her propriety?

Take her now. Yes, that would do it. You have her where you want her. Take her now. What if whatever had changed her here tonight is gone tomorrow? Or, worse, is gone by the time you get her into the car-riage? What if it disappears between here and home? Take her.

No. No. Though, as a kind of compromise—a re-ward for his heroic self-denial—he kissed her again while, through her skirts, he grazed the front of her body. Through fabric, he touched across the private female place with the tips of his fingers. She jumped, but she didn't pull her leg away from him. He kissed her deeper, and she dug her heel into his buttocks, moaning softly.

He slid his hand along her raised leg, going along it up under her skirts. Along a silk-stockinged calf that went forever, up underneath the humid warmth of her to a knee inside the wide leg of her knickers. Though it was as wide as a small skirt, her knickers snugged toward her hips. He smoothed his hand across her knickers at her abdomen, then around. He explored where they met her corset with the flat of his hand, front and back, trying to understand the construction of her underdrawers, while he fought a head-spinning delirium of lust. Her knickers buttoned down the back, he realized. Down the back all the way under the crotch to midway in front.

Well. What innovation. With the tips of his fingers, he found the strategic buttons and began flipping them through the buttonholes, opening her knickers down the low curve of her backside and under.

Then he slid his hand inside, touching the bare curve of buttocks, the cleft where the two moons of her rounded together—and the earth beneath his feet shifted under him. He gripped her as his hand found her bare bottom, the flesh soft, dewy, and smooth, like the petals of flowers. Oh, the pleasure of touching her. He thought he would die of it.

While Winnie felt herself alive with it. Her pleasure was nervous: excited, astounded; unknowing, appre-hensive. Before, Mick had touched her through her knickers. Now his hand was inside them. Lord, what did that mean? This wasn't wild. It was impossible, unimaginable. And pleasure, oh, the pleasure of it.

He reached behind her and tugged her knickers out from under her corset. He found the rest of the buttons at the back. With one hand, he undid them completely, then folded them forward onto her own leg. Then, with no leave or hesitation, he slid his hand over her knickers, under her body, between her legs. His palm took possession of her naked pudendum.

She jumped then grew utterly still. Shame. That was what the word meant. *Pudendus*, the Latin for *worthy of shame*. And she felt it. Shameful, how her body sang at his touch. She wanted to close her legs for the disgrace of it, take her leg down; yet his elbow clamped her leg to his waist, holding it there, and she was glad.

"Let me," he whispered so softly it was without voice, just his air forming the words at her ear. More hushed sounds, he told her, "It will be all right." So quiet, she could hear the faint contact of his perfectly articulated T's.

She nodded, though her body kept spasming in strange reaction. Yes. If he wanted to, she trusted him. She let him have his hand under her skirts, her underthings down, her legs open to him; free rein.

Indeed, who else might she give this to but Mick? Who else could she follow into the world and all its experiences? Who else but the man she watched with unceasing interest? Whom she delighted in? The man who made her laugh and feel good, who responded sometimes more honestly than she did to her own hurt and joys?

Who else but the man she loved?

She let him slide his hand over her, inward, cupping, then out. In truth, she would have let Mick lay her down onto the cobbles of the alley, put his weight on her and do whatever a man did to a woman. All resistance left—she felt it go as if her veins opened—as he cupped his hand to her. If he had chosen to murder her in this moment, she would not have put up a fight.

She leaped slightly when his fingers burrowed slightly, then nearly climbed up over his back as they found her. So new, the sensation. And powerful. All her senses, her mind drew into focus on the spot where he pressed her flesh apart. His fingers touched inner layers. Slick. She was slick. Why? She was messy. That couldn't be right—

"Aa-ah," she said, her muscles jumping and jerking. His thumb found a sweet, secret place that, when he touched it, made her see stars. Little, ecstatic exclamation points of sensation.

She knew nothing of her body here. To find it all so sensitive amazed her. To discover he knew all about her body, more than she did, astounded even more. Thank God he did though. He stroked her exactly right; he knew better than she how to stir up pleasure, more than pleasure, a hypnotic, physical joy so compelling it absorbed every corner of her mind. She tried to analyze it, understand, but couldn't make her attention do anything for longer than a second. Her mind wanted to feel, simply feel, nothing else.

"Let go, Win," he murmured. "Stop thinking."

His head bent, his silky hair touching her chest as he lightly bit the tip of her breast. Then he slid his finger deeply into her, all the way inside her.

"H-hah, h-hah—" She jerked as her diaphragm sent spasms of air through her lungs. "H-ho, H-hooh—"

He drew his finger out, pulling more wetness along her flesh. Her knee buckled. He had to support her. He touched what she wasn't sure she'd even known about, didn't think about, a part of her own body she had never looked at or touched. Absurd. His finger hit upon where his thumb had been before. More star-bright bits sparked in her mind. By comparison, they darkened everything else. Sensation became only this. The dark fog of his knowing fingers, sliding, warm . . . making sparks of perfect pleasure along her nerve endings, bliss so pure and glistening it was blinding. It obliterated the rest of her senses, incapacitated all other awareness. A steady heat built, one made up of these sparks . . . snapping, becoming more and sharper . . . a rising rapture taking her up and up to God knew where.

She knew a tension . . . something coiling in her belly, tighter, stronger. Then it suddenly released in an instant of crystal-clear, physical euphoria at the center of her, a spilling of this so intense she let out a cry.

She tried to hold back her own voice, but sounds, soft animal noises erupted from her mouth, noises as she could never remember speaking. Low groans, strained mewlings that, had she allowed it, would have come out nearer to screams. Her body jerked from the effort of holding it back. The pleasure was so acute. . . .

Once, as a child, she'd been stung by bees. Half a dozen minute, quick, angry stings that hit her nerves, shooting their little pinpoints of pain everywhere. Her pleasure was like that, though it spread more evenly, more liquid somehow, as if pinpoint droplets of stinging ecstasy dropped into her, a thousand tiny droplets of it hitting her then expanding across the surface of her senses until sensation ringed and rippled to silence.

She calmed slowly, smoothing out into a glassy peacefulness. She shivered once, then curved into Mick's chest. He kissed the crown of her head as he straightened her skirts, fixed her camisole at her shoulders; putting her right. She stood there inside his arms for a full minute at least, perhaps more, letting him rearrange her—aware that she had never in all her adult life known such a thorough trust.

Another person, a man—Mick, dear Mick—had done this to her. She'd given over all her defenses, and it had been just fine. Better than fine. Better than anything she could have thought of on her own.

"I'm taking you home," he murmured. "I'm taking you home and making love to you all night, Winnie." He lifted her face to him by her chin and kissed her mouth again, intimately but so gently this time. Mouth and tongue. Then softer still, he said, "Let's go rid you of your infernal virginity. I hate it. I want it gone."

Yes. She was absolutely in favor of the notion. She wanted to do away with it, too. She wanted to hand it to him like a gift. Here.

Chapter 23

Winnie followed Mick into the tavern, his warm fingers wrapped around her own as he pulled her lolling self along a bit faster than she might have chosen. She felt dreamy, unable to focus. She kept thinking, Mmmm, make love to her all night. Yes. Mick, with his strong body and knowing hands. Make love. Whatever that meant, she wanted it in all its glory.

In contrast, the man who dragged her along by the hand was a man on a mission, focused enough for both of them. Without breaking pace, he picked up her blouse and jacket and hat, his own coat. They were almost to the door when the baron's son, who'd given them a bit of trouble earlier, decided to go for broke.

"Well, well, well," he said. Winnie hadn't been aware he was near, till her grabbed her round the hips. She was pulled in two directions for a second, till Mick realized she was hung up somehow.

He turned, saw. Then even Winnie pulled back as far as his grip on her hand would allow. His face was frightening for a moment—she'd never seen such instant and open rage come over a man.

"Get your hand off her," he said.

The other man was drunk, she realized. He said, "Why don't we ask the lady? Perhaps she'd like someone who'd entertain her in the West End of town."

Winnie would never have believed what happened

next if she hadn't seen it. Mick raised one eyebrow, lifted his head a degree, then his lip, a lordly sneer if ever she'd seen one. "You?" he said with a derisive snort. His posture changed. He was acting, but what an actor he was. He could have been on the stage. His stance became at once hostile and arrogant: the full male challenge of superiority.

The other man was briefly hesitant. He hadn't expected such an aggressive and immediate confrontation after Mick's last concessions to peace. Unfortunately for him, he recovered himself. He leered at Winnie— he honestly leered, which in a strange way flattered her. She hadn't realized she was sufficiently interesting to generate a leer. Then he floored her further: "I say the lady stays. I want to see her dance again with those long, beautiful legs."

Goodness, other men thought they were pretty!

To Winnie, the young blood said, "You are without doubt, miss, the most attractive"—he laughed—"and tallest woman I have seen all evening."

Winnie wanted to hug him, give him a big kiss for saying something so nice. Though of course such behavior would never do.

Mick, as it turned out though, wanted to kill him for saying the same words. He clenched and bared his teeth, then spoke through them. "You aren't seeing anything, except possibly my fist in your face. Get out of the way."

"A baron takes precedence over—"

Mick interrupted with a snort, a truly convincing display of contempt, and talked over him to say, "What makes you think you're the only blood to slum on a Wednesday evening? What makes you think you are and I'm not, you silly pisspot?" He took a step toward the man, pulling Winnie around and behind him. "And I do believe a viscount goes in to dinner before a man who's not a baron but only a baron's son. You go in dead last. And with this lady you don't even start."

Well. He'd learned his lessons on protocol. How

nice. Though she could think of better circumstances for him to use them.

The fellow made the mistake of believing, however—now of all times—that Mick was truly a gentleman: that he had some restraint.

He moved a step toward Winnie, and Mick hit him: in the face, the stomach, then kneed him in the groin. The precious gentleman out to see the "low sights of London" saw the lowest—the floor—so fast, Winnie didn't have time to screech till he was down on it, and there was no point in saying anything.

The sound that came out of her was a high-pitched chirp.

"Come on," Mick said to her. He took her hand again. To his friends behind them, he said, "Can you get the bloke some water, help him up when he gets his breath back?"

Winnie left feeling dizzy. Two men had fought over her, a baron's son had been leveled for want of her. She'd been the toast of a tavern. She'd kissed the man she loved in an alley till her nerves were jumping like a warehouse of fireworks touched by a match.

What a perfectly wonderful night!

In the carriage, Mick kissed her fiercely. He kissed her and kissed her and kissed her, but a strange thing happened. Instead of his doing all the horrible things he'd promised, as he kissed her he grew *less* ardent.

Till he suddenly stopped and moved away. For the last five minutes of the ride home, he stared out the window, not saying a word.

She'd done something, Winnie thought. She'd made him angry. She'd upset him. She'd behaved badly. Something.

Then no. It came to her: She had done absolutely nothing she could think of and, given that to be true, she needn't feel guilty about anything. She'd had a marvelous time and given him every—and she did mean every—consideration. He was being sullen all on his own.

Jealous. When the word came to her, it made her

jubilant. Mick, so clever at everything he did, so smart and handsome, so convincingly anything he wanted to be. *He* was jealous of the baron's son—a real, if insipid, example of what he played at with more style and force than all the barons in the Doomsday Book. Well. She could deal with a little jealousy. How utterly delightful, she thought. She felt like Delilah—dangerously powerful: desired. She laughed to herself. It was the crowning cherry on top to a night of her ego's eating pure cream till it bloated.

Still, Delilah wasn't all that good for Samson. That wasn't the feeling she wanted most to know in any consistent way. What she wanted to feel again with the warm sense of herself when Mick looked at her and saw the real Winnie. She wanted him to *love* the real Winnie, the one with her ups and downs. The Winnie trying to become brave enough to reveal herself to him as completely as a person could.

She wanted an emotional corollary to what she'd done physically with Mick in the alley. She wanted the afternoon on the dance-room floor, only more and without fear. Trust. She wanted to trust him with all of herself, her body, her spirit, her emotions, her mind, right down to the most delicate, sensitive places of her human existence. She wanted to turn it over into his hands and see what he did with it. And she wanted something similar from him. She wanted to know him and touch him and have him believe in her generosity toward him.

She began to talk to him, trying to draw him out. There was no reason to be jealous. She thought it was as simple as that. She wanted closeness.

While Mick withdrew. He felt a distance coming between them with the speed of a whistling wind.

He stung from his encounter with the idiot-lord, an idiot who nonetheless was authentically what he himself only pretended to be. For all his bravado, Mick felt like a forgery. Like the money he and Rezzo had made downstairs in the Bull and Tun's cellar. Almost as good, yet no matter who accepted the tender it was still something to hide, to fight doing again, to worry over: not real.

He'd felt tonight like a king to be among his friends, like a king when he kissed Winnie. But the stupid toff had set the truth on him like a pack of dogs: In the real world, he was king of the beggars—a fake lord, a good fake, but a real ratcatcher: He would never be good enough for Winnie Bollash.

He and Winnie. Whatever they were to each other, to extend it into the realm of mating was sham. Their relationship in this regard was as fake as Lord Tremore himself: It had no future.

Unmindful of the fact, she chatted softly at him as they entered her house. The hallway was dim. There was only the sconce lit at the end to provide enough light to enter safely. He stopped her from putting on the brighter lamp on the side table. He was too depressed to want her to see him clearly.

Milton, happily, had gone to sleep already. At least they weren't required to make explanations for the careless way she laid her blouse, jacket, and hat on the side table. She hadn't bothered to put them on again, presumably too warm from her thrilling night.

Oh, he knew she was thrilled, and he was happy for her. He just wasn't too thrilled with himself or the role he played. Where was his real self? Where did this game end and where did he begin? He felt confused. And tired. And unhappy.

As Win walked to the stairs, she rambled and digressed, laughing, whispering intimate things to him. He loved her openness; he hated it. The social gap between them made it feel awful, like looking at a kindred spirit across that river Styx.

Of course, he could invite her downstairs to his room for a little lovemaking. They could have a fine old time, so long as they didn't make too much noise and wake her butler. Or he could go upstairs to her room, upstairs with a fancy woman who wanted an earthy good time, as he'd done half a dozen times.

He muttered curses under his breath as he paused at

the newel post. He didn't want either of these things, yet he could find no equal footing. Perhaps there was none. He resolved to say good night quickly. Alas, nothing seemed more appropriate than they part here, that she go up her polished staircase, while he took the service stairs down.

But at the base of her polished staircase, she touched his arm, drawing him literally closer as she laughed her way into another of her stories. He tried not to be interested, but ended up being taken in. He couldn't help it. He found Winnie, her life, endlessly entertaining.

"I was very young," she was saying. "It was Easter, and the parish church asked the children to bring tins of food for the poor. Only I misunderstood somehow. 'Bring tins,' I heard. I was fascinated by tins myself. I played with them, put holes in their shiny metal for candle holders, beat on them for music. I was allowed to have them from the cook. Anyway, I interpreted the priest's directive to mean that I was to bring empty food tins. My mother insisted I was wrong, but I was adamant.

"Then destroyed: for when I got to the church with my empty tins, everyone of course had brought full ones, which, the second I saw them, made ever so much more sense. I felt utterly bereft. I cried and cried with a sense of hopelessness for myself. How could I have made such a stupid mistake? I was humiliated. My mother was mortified. She made her usual to-do. 'I told you. But it is so like you, Winnie, not to listen to a word I say. I don't know what's to become of you. You look like a mantis and think like a mule.' Oh, what a scene she could make, what drama. I was a pigheaded child, difficult, selfish, the bane of her existence. And, that day, I agreed with her. I still do at times."

She sighed, laughing at her own story. "Though not tonight," she said. She leaned back against the rails of the balustrade, the banister slanting upward over her head. She looked inviting. Her chemise was damp, its lace lying wilted against the curve of her breast. "To-night," she said, the gypsy come-hither aura shining shyly again in her eyes: looking to be fanned to life. "Tonight I was no mantis."

"No," he said sincerely, wishing he didn't feel the truth of his words as sharply as he did. "Tonight you were the most desirable woman I have ever looked upon, ever watched move or draw breath."

Her breasts, there in the dim light of the hallway, swelled as she softly inhaled his compliment.

It was crushing to watch her. She was so full of life. Her mind was shining, bright. The beauty of it, of her here in the hallway, pierced him, the pain as exquisite as catching his fingertip in the spring of a trap: a pinch so hard it brought tears to the backs of his eyes. It ravished him; it shimmered and blurred his vision. Winnie, the beautiful, could be his.

Till the end of the week.

Then she couldn't.

Next week, he'd became a ratcatcher again. Or a valet perhaps, though now the two felt almost the same in light of the fact that neither were good enough for Edwina Bollash. Sunday morning, when the impossible magic of Emile and Jeremy Lamont evaporated, as in the fairy tale, Michael's fine horses and clothing would return to Mick's rats and rags once more. He and this remarkable woman would no longer struggle with the make-believe of him. When he walked out her door— whoever, whatever he was—the only thing certain would be that neither his "what" nor "who" would be the equal of Edwina, Princess of the Empty Tins.

She was waiting for him to respond. She expected him to kiss her.

Mick smiled, hesitated. God knew, nothing would be so sweet as to make love to Winnie the gypsy girl tonight. Nothing better, that is, than making love to her while knowing it was no magic or pretense or heedless moment: that he could make love to her as his own, his other half, his mate.

He could pretend a lot of things. He could fake

much. Yet he couldn't fake this: He couldn't pretend tonight was forever. Such a lie would have made his chest so tight no air could enter.

So he laid his palm against her face, as if he could touch for a second what was inside her bright, waiting expression. He smoothed his thumb down her soft cheek and met her glistening eyes—they were fixed on him in a way he would not easily forget. He leaned, pressed his dry lips to her forehead, drew the smell of her hair into his nose, his lungs, held it there, then pushed himself back and spun on his heels.

He turned and fled down the hall, across the dining room and into the half-kitchen, then down the stairs and into the servants' quarters where—Milton was right—he belonged.

He ran like Freddie. Too many dark, ugly things down there, Mick. And the teeth are sharp; I know. Can't knowingly jump down into a rat's nest anymore. You just got to understand.

And he did. Oh, he did. Too well.

Mick was undressing for bed, the placket of his shirt open, his trouser braces dangling, standing there in his bare feet, his back to the door, when he heard her. He turned, expecting the sound was his imagination.

But no, there Winnie was, framed in his doorway. She'd rallied the courage to follow him downstairs— now of all times suddenly uncowed by the fact that Milton was asleep only three walls away.

"Well," Mick said, then couldn't think how to follow the pointless remark. It seemed rude to ask simply, *What do you want?*

How funny: Her eyes fixed at his chest. She loved his chest, and he loved that she did. She eyed what she could see of him inside his open shirt. It was a strain for her to bring her eyes up to his face, even though, clearly, she had something to say.

Bloody hell, he thought. She was finally going to say it. Something brave and romantic. Too late, he told himself. They were past where it would do them some good. Still, he listened attentively. He waited, half-hoping, half-fearing he might finally hear "Kiss me" or "I love you." *I love you* would have been nice.

Instead, her sweet-soft, classy voice said, like silk, in her tea-party singsong, "I figured out what I want. I want you to be as naked as a statue: I want to see you in the rude with your widge hanging out."

Chapter 24

$\mathcal{M}$ick burst out laughing. He tried to contain it, then couldn't. What release. "My widge?" he said finally. And that started him all over again. "Oh, God," he said, trying to get hold of himself. He put his hand in his hair and leaned his shoulder on the bedpost. He didn't know where to look. His widge? She wanted to see his widge?

Winnie smiled at his discomposure. She liked it. It made her bold. She told him, "You promised. You told me when I could say what I wanted, I could have it."

And so he had. "Winnie—"

He didn't know what to tell her. He touched his lip, in his distress forgetting for the hundredth time his mustache was missing. He shaved it off every morning, then forgot he had, at least once a day. He brought his hand down and tried telling this unusual woman the truth. "Winnie, I'm in love with you," he said.

It was not what she was expecting. She glanced down quickly. She couldn't look at him for longer than a second at a time, but her face filled with wonder. She was happy one moment, then sad the next. She finally squinched her face and held his eyes long enough to ask mildly, "So that means you can't make love to me?"

He shook his head. "It means—" He couldn't explain it neatly. "It means I want more than I can have.

276

And having a little, a taste, might hurt worse than having nothing at all.'' He shook his head again, frowned. ''I wasn't prepared to feel as I do about you, Win.''

With a new curiosity and a kind of timid, but growing confidence, she stepped into the room. ''Mick,'' she said, ''don't worry about the future so much that you make our present less than what it should be. We could die tomorrow.'' She spouted his own philosophy. ''Anything could happen.'' She came to a stop right in front of him and whispered, ''Make love to me now. Please.''

He shook his head, then muttered, ''No escape.'' It was true. He laughed helplessly at where he'd gotten himself. Up to his eyeballs here in trouble, and only able to dig himself in deeper. Muttering, still laughing, he looked at her and repeated, ''In the rude? Honest to God, Win. With my widge hanging out? Where did you hear such a thing?''

''You said it.''

He did? He sat down on the end of the bed, bewildered.

In the end, though, he knew what to do. He lifted his arms and peeled his shirt over his head. He wore no underclothes; he hated them and no one knew the difference. Until now. Winnie looked rather amazed by the fact.

He tossed the shirt, then patted the mattress beside him. ''Right here, loovey. Put it here. The wicked widge of Michael Tremore would love to make your acquaintance.''

Winnie only stood there.

After a moment, he complained with humor, ''You tell me to make love to you. I tell you how to start, what I want you to do, then you won't do it. You are not the obedient girl you once were.''

''I know.'' She smiled and murmured, ''I want to see. Show me.''

''Aah. The widge,'' he said. He felt himself lift— from simply the sound of her voice, the cool-soft, feminine plush of her saying in her tony English, *Show me*. Yes, he was going to have something to show her. ''Close the door.''

Winnie turned and leaned against the door, watching as Mick's dexterous fingers undid the buttons of his trousers. His long-fingered hands moved with a slow grace that was almost courtly as he opened them for her. She wet her lips and watched with concupiscent curiosity. Then started at what dropped into view. He continued, shoving his trousers down his legs, not the least bit inhibited. Already barefoot and bare-chested, once he stepped out of the wool worsted, he stood naked in front of her.

A statue, yes. Warm and breathing.

She watched the rise of his chest as she walked forward. She already knew he was broad and muscular through the chest and shoulders, but she hadn't realized how narrow he was through the hips. Sturdy, but slender. His thighs were long and cut with muscle. But between his thighs—

She walked close, riveted. She said, ''*That* wouldn't fit under any fig leaf. In fact''—she looked up into his face with a sudden frown—''that won't fit anywhere I know of.''

''Oh, yes, it will.'' He laughed at her. ''And perhaps I might mention''—he mocked himself—''it ain't a widge, loov. Not now.'' When she knit her brow, he explained, ''It's a widge when it's quiet. Or when it's nosing around just a bit. At some point, though, Win, it becomes a cock: mine especially.''

Whatever he called it, it was as stiff as the boom on a ship. It stood straight up, slightly mobile in an upward-angled way. As she inspected him, he took her hand, then leaped and gasped as if surprised when he placed it on him. Covering the back of her hand with his, he put pressure, sliding her palm slowly up and down him, pushing forward with his hips. He groaned from it, a single deep rasp of breath.

Then took her by the shoulders and turned her

around toward the bed. "You can look more later. I'm sick with waiting, Winnie. I'm having."

Indeed, they were both past ready. The backs of her legs hit the bed, and he pushed her. She fell, a delicious plunge through the air that lifted her stomach and ended on bouncing bedsprings. He lifted her skirt and pushed her legs apart at the same time, then got his knee between, on the bed, as he put his hand on her, rubbing between her legs, through her knickers. He rubbed for a moment, hard, a few times, then said, "Let's have done with these. Lift up, loov."

He stripped her knickers off, just like that, then lay over her, bringing his naked weight on top of her. Oh, his body. Free of his trousers, his penis fell heavily, nestling naturally into the sensitive crevice of her. They both leaped, tensed at the contact, caught their breaths in unison. She tried to relax again, though relaxing wasn't exactly what she wanted. She closed her eyes, then found her mouth kissed. Mick's mouth touched hers and she opened it to him, then his tongue penetrated this intimate place. Tentatively, she let her tongue push into his. He groaned, twisted his head, and went at her mouth harder, his body curving to her in rhythm.

It was the last she knew of sanity.

She knew the sliding of his body, a desire for the contact of skin that became a sliding everywhere and particularly a rhythmic grind of hips. His hands went into her clothes, owning the inside of them and her naked flesh . . . then the inside of her. He reached between them and did what he'd already done once tonight. He touched her inside.

"Aah!" she called out.

He made a low sound, something near a growl of satisfaction.

Their communion became the way it always was with them: rough—not for what either one did, but from sensation itself. She wanted whatever he would do with an intensity she could never foresee. Then, with each contact, the feeling was so powerful, it seemed to knock her senses flat. She jumped and gasped through his stroking her, his rubbing his face against her cheek, his chest against her breasts . . . his hips . . . his finger moving in her. She loved it, yet her own ears might have doubted she loved anything. Sounds came out, not unlike those from an animal crying out, beaten, torn apart.

They touched each other with relative gentleness, yet they each reacted as if from violence: bombarded with pleasure.

Mick flinched and let out a long, dragging rasp of air, when all he did was open her with his fingers, then draw the head of his penis down her—she shivered with enough power to shake the bed—to where he could guide it with his hand. He was shaking himself and muttering epithets as he planted himself into position, then with a thrust of his hips—one, single, swift, elegant deflowering—he buried himself deeply into her and they both buckled up into each other as if reacting to being scorched.

"Gaw-aw-awd bah-less-s-s," he breathed out. "Be still oh be still," he warned.

Winnie couldn't have been anything else. Her body had contracted around his, arms, legs, torso, the very inside of her. It felt like what it was: her flesh torn. A strong pinch, then a burning. She lay there, aware of the fullness of him. An alien, thick pressure, a weight that was surprising, yet satisfying, indescribably satisfying.

He began to unfold himself, move again. The burning lessened through friction. He withdrew then thrust again with the sure force of passion, a thrust then pull, each time flinching, his breath rasping with his deep bass groan. While each stroke made her dizzier, consciousness itself in question at the peak of full penetration. He pushed his hips, as if he couldn't get himself deep enough, yet each time the heat of him went so deeply into her body that it moved something inside, something unearthly and wonderful.

Winnie let instinct take control. She returned Mick's strength. She savored his power and her own. She loved his movement and the vigor of him that translated into a hardness not just inside her body but everywhere along him, in his muscle and sinew and bone, while she clutched this rock-solidness in his flexed shoulders, dug her fingers into them.

A fever took hold as if it flowed in her veins, as if she had grabbed hold of an electric wire charged with pleasure. Volts and volts of it. It coursed through her, leaving her helplessly connected to it while it traveled up her nerves. It gripped her—him, too, for he called out as he convulsed—and drove them into each other. Till it grounded, like lightning, down her spine into the low center of her, between her legs, shocks of bliss. . . .

In the throbbing aftermath, she felt the ghost of Mick's masculinity inside her, as if it were thunder, rolls and rolls of it in the distance, continuous. It resounded through her veins, booming, as she lay exhausted, leveled by it. As if she were singed from the bolts of their contact. Struck. Love-struck. She understood the analogy all at once in more particular detail. Yet was bewildered to understand that it came from something so simple and seen daily: the skin and muscle and heat of Mick's male body.

Winnie had had no idea. . . .

Mick pursued sexuality the same way he pursued everything else. For the rich, full joy of it and for all he was worth. He had a penchant for whispering wicked things in Winnie's ear. Oh, the horrible-delicious things he promised to do. Attacks, atrocities, on her modesty. And he liked her up against walls and straddling him on chairs and in his arms, rolling around in bed, not to mention once rolling around in the grass of the back garden in the middle of the night. Oh, the fine old time they had.

Lovers.

They were naked for most of the next three days. Milton became so put out with them, he went to his sister's. Mrs. Reed mysteriously didn't come at all. Mick and Winnie had the house to themselves. And they put their privacy to good use.

"Look," Winnie said one afternoon. She was exasperated. "Look at these pathetic things." She glowered down at her breasts. "So small they don't round even a little. They point."

There on the bed, Mick looked as if from politeness, since she'd asked him to. His eyes, when they rested on her naked body, darkened; they became the green of a still sea reflecting black clouds overhead, the sky closed off, a black green, deep in hue. These eyes didn't miss a spot on her. If she showed naked flesh, they found it and stared.

They looked directly at her breasts now. Then Mick smiled. "Here, you complain you aren't petite, Win, when you have two somethings that are petite and don't even appreciate them."

"Petite breasts! Who wants petite breasts!"

"I do." His hands took them, one in each, curving his fingers around them as he rubbed his thumbs over the nipples, back and forth slowly. Back—"They are the sweetest little things I ever laid eyes on"—then slowly forth again—"or mouth on." He bent his head.

He opened his lips over her breast, widening his mouth enough to take the whole of it. Inside, he tongued the nipple and the area around it, while her entire breast sat enveloped in the warm, slick softness of his mouth. Then he slid his lips back up the little mound out to tip, riding the breast as he closed his mouth, sucking as he went, then nipped the tip with his teeth. She shivered. Both nipples puckered tightly.

"M-m-m," he said. He did the same trick to the other one, leaving both her breasts wet and cool to the air when he was finished, their nipples little hard pebbles of sexual awareness. "M-m-m," he said again.

"Warm little dumplings, sweet as cream."

And so it went. A man of many talents.

He could make his erect penis nod yes and no, on its own. He could move it left and right. Neither trick impressed her so much, though, as the fond relationship he had with his body that made him willing to entertain her with it.

"Imagine," she said. She took him into the grip of her fist, making Mick huff as he tried to maintain composure. "And only a moment ago you were half this size. How do you do it? How does it work?"

"H-h-ha-a-ah," he said at first. Then, "H-h-hyou do it." He grabbed her hand and pressed it to him, as if the pressure would relieve some of the delicacy of feeling. "You know how you're always worrying that you've done something you didn't mean to do?" he asked, then made a wicked laugh deep in his chest. "Well, this time, you have." He repeated, "You do it."

"I don't do anything." She teased him. She wanted him to say more.

He leaned his face into her neck and touched his tongue lightly to the spot where her jaw and ear and neck all met, then whispered, "You do. You make me hard." He bit the lobe of her ear. "Hard and long and thick as a post. You've been doing that to me for six weeks."

She laughed and lay back, happy. "I am strong," she said. It amazed and pleased her to think so. "Potent."

She was glad when he understood what she meant. "You are indeed. Heady stuff, Win. You are two-hundred proof, loovey." He whispered, "Do it some more."

*   *   *

They played like children. Adult children playing games all through the house. The time went by so quickly.

Winnie had to watch herself. By Saturday morning, she was daydreaming dangerously: of picking up and

moving somewhere, of passing Mick off forever as . . .
oh, a country gentleman. He could hunt rabbits with
ferrets as some rural squires did. He and she could find
a little cottage, live off whatever lessons she could give
to the local girls. He'd mill about, just like a true gentleman; no gainful employ.

They were in the half-kitchen behind the dining
room, when Winnie mentioned her fantasy to him, just
to see what he'd say.

He didn't react as she'd have liked. "Ah," he said.
"Like all the other fancy ladies. You want to buy a
man to play with?" He guffawed over it, thought it
hilarious, then added, "I never could understand that
about gents, why they'd *want* not to do anything, no
skill, no trade, no service to God or England."

Winnie wanted to discuss it seriously, though. She
wagged a sausage at him. They were cooking themselves breakfast.

"I don't understand what the joke is," she said.
"Don't laugh. I'm serious."

He grew grave. Without a speck of his humor, he
asked, "What? I'm supposed to do nothing? Have
nothing of my own? And you teach who"—he corrected—"whom? Country girls? Country girls don't
care how they talk. I know country girls. Milkmaids.
Farmers' wives. Daughters of shopkeepers. No. You
need a city and society mamas. I need my business or
something like it, nothing you would approve of, but
it meets my bills—and will afford me a wife one day
when I decide to have one. You think it's beneath
you."

He was gaining steam. It was apparently something
he'd thought a lot about. "I'm telling you," he said,
"useful work well done is something to be proud of.
Thing is, you're a bit of a snob, loov. Not horrible.
But the saddest part is you're a snob about you—
you're too individual to conform to bland standards.
You make yourself crazy trying to, then you don't even
like yourself. You won't even let yourself go to the

ball and have fun. You should. You should go the
duke's house, dance holes into your slippers, and
foke the bloody bastards who don't like it. Foke
them all.''

What a speech.

Winnie tried to absorb it. It made her heart race.

To lessen its impact, she tried to dismantle it. She
told him, ''I don't know what that word means, though
I'd wager you're saying it wrong.''

''Which word?'' He frowned.

''Foke.''

''Ay!'' he said quickly, turning on her with the fork
he was using to cook sausage in the pan. He waved
the implement. ''That's not nice, Win. Don't say it.''

''You say it all the time.''

''Do I?''

She laughed, a belly laugh at finding him in this rare
ignorance of himself. ''Oh, yes. And I think, when you
say *effing,* it's short for *foking.* What *does* it mean?''

He grinned sideways, then wiggled his eyebrows.
Raising one in humor, he said, ''I could show you.''
He pulled her into him and pressed his hips once.
''This.'' He moved them again, and she liked it. She
always liked it; it was such a wonder, his touch. ''It
means—'' He looked for a phrase, a good example.
''It means, Have it. Take life by the balls, Win. Take
her, have her, mean old thing that she is. Foke her silly.
Lap her up. Love her, why not?''

She giggled. ''Women don't have balls.''

He laughed, nuzzling her. He said into her hair,
''Life does. Life has it all. And I love it, Win.'' Softer,
she thought she heard, ''I love you,'' but she couldn't
have.

He wouldn't have said that. *In love*, yes. But not *I
love you.* Mick was honest. He wasn't a man to court
a woman with lies.

Then he said quite clearly, ''So how would it be,
after breakfast, before those stupid Lamonts arrive''—
they'd sent a note that said they were bringing evening

clothes, the invitation, and themselves at noon—''I take you upstairs one last time before we go and foke you silly? What do you think about that?''

She bit her lip, then answered honestly. ''It sounds very bad, terribly wicked.'' She whispered, ''Do it.''

Oh, she did revel in the secrecy of lovers. In Mick's dirty words and sweet words. In their private conversations that, murmured elsewhere, would have been horrid, beyond the pale. Yet between them in the kitchen or the music room or in the pitch dark of night, they were just right—because they spoke with different meanings to the words, meanings and sly degrees of meanings that they invented together, in a language that was just for the two of them.

A snob, though, Winnie wondered. Was she? A snob couldn't have Mick Tremore, that much she knew. So could she let go of her opinions of ratcatchers and poor Catholic Cornishmen? Surely she could.

Or was she fooling herself? It was more than snobbery to want comfort or even luxury. She looked around at a house that already had quite a bit less of both than the one she was born in. Sometimes she missed the old elegance of her upbringing. Sometimes. Could she leave even this? Her bathroom and electricity and the luxury of buying any book she took a fancy to? Even she wasn't sure.

If he asked her to go with him, would she?

Meanwhile, Mick wasn't certain that the accusation didn't work equally well for him. No matter what he told her, he had a vague sense of not being good enough for her. All her family, education, culture, money, her house and skills—the whole of her he found bloody frightening, truth be told. How did he dare to want such a smart lady, a teacher, the daughter of a marquess, granddaughter of a duke—what a laugh.

He always knew he was ambitious, but this was going some, even for him. The son of a copper miner, whose family thought he was a bloody adventuring hero for going to London and making a ratcatcher of himself so as to send home more money than anyone there had seen in years. Ha. Honest to God. Winnie Bollash. Michael Tremore, you may as well try courting the Queen.

Winnie had been to university. She owned a fancy coach and two horses of her own, plus a carriage house to keep them in. She owned a house of three stories with a lower level for the servants. She had a cook and butler, for godssake, and a third of a coachman, whom she shared with two neighbors. Mick, he'd made the most of two dozen ferrets, most of which he'd bred himself, and five dogs, all of which he'd picked up off the street. He housed every last thing he owned in the cellar where he slept, renting it off a shoemaker for nothing, in exchange for keeping his shop free of rats.

His absurd fantasy was for her to flee her high-class upbringing. She'd become the ratcatcher's wife—though he never mentioned his daydream to her. And not because she wouldn't—though, of course, she wouldn't—but because she deserved more.

The fellow at the bar haunted Mick. The toff who raised horses was more her sort. Or someone like him, but nicer. There were nice blokes, real gentlemen, who could give her a respectable place, show her off in society—Winnie could use that.

She could use a hundred years of admiration; she'd had too little in her life.

The Lamonts were late. "Happily," Mick said. Winnie knew they couldn't be late enough, so far as he was concerned.

When a box arrived just after lunch, she thought it had to do with them, but no, it had to do with Mick. When he realized it had arrived downstairs, he rushed to get it, as if relieved.

Relieved, elated, and almost fearful, he brought it

upstairs to Winnie in her bedroom and presented it. It was a gift.

"Happy birthday," he said.

Oh, dear. She herself had forgotten. No one remembered her birthday. It was an un-event.

"Thirty," he said. "You are now as old as I am. We're the same age."

He took the lid from the box, then, from the top of its tissue paper, handed her a pair of long white evening gloves. "Milly said you had to have these."

She took them, bewildered. They were kid; soft, lightweight, with twenty or more tiny buttons on each.

Then he pulled back the tissue paper and, inside, was a sunset. Winnie caught her breath.

"Tulle," he said, pleased with himself. He lifted it out, as if he could lift out light itself.

It was a dress of embroidered, glass-beaded, salmon pink tulle over darker taffeta—the beads almost as if they were dropped onto the net while liquid, on every other filament, the whole fabric glittering with tiny droplets of smooth glass. Between double shoulder straps, one to be worn just off the shoulder, the other down the arm, the little sleeves were sheer, nothing but tulle and glass beads.

She slipped her hand under one delicate sleeve. The tulle disappeared, while the beads shimmered, as if their sparkle had condensed on her skin.

"Oh, Mick. What have you done?" she asked. He had to have robbed a bank. Or stolen the dress. Or God, no: He must have paid for it with counterfeit money.

She would have to take it back. Though, for the time being, she would just look at it, hold it up to herself. The astounding thing—breathtaking, in fact—was that it seemed it might fit.

"Try it on," he said.

She looked at it, holding it against her in the mirror. No, she shouldn't try it on. She would look . . . pretentious in a beautiful dress. As if she were trying to be prettier than she was. She shook her head.

"Try it on," he insisted. "I want to see you in it."

She turned her head, gazed at him, wanting to, yet feeling hesitant. She pressed her lips together between her teeth and stared at him. In this one regard, Mick saw her so differently from how she saw herself. And, oh, how she wished he were right.

"Come on, my loovey with the wide blue saucer-eyes. Don't look so distraught. Put it on."

It was exactly long enough in the hem, exactly right. The waist was perfect, narrow, and banded in velvet, the neckline square, flat to the breast, and low. The skirt flared in front then billowed in back, a froth of rich, bronzed rose organdy embroidered with silk floss and more glass-beaded tulle. It was an enchanted dress, a spell conjured up out of nothing. She wondered again how he'd done it, then lost herself in the feel of the gloves. They fit like a second skin up her arms, with tiny, graceful little wrinkles when she bent her wrist. She'd never had anything like them. The buttons, though, were a trial to fasten. Mick had to do her right hand, his fingers working with delicate attention up the inside of her wrist. An amazing feeling. And an effect, in the end, that was stunning.

Winnie looked at herself in the mirror and felt . . . grown-up somehow. A grown-up woman in a grown-up dress.

Mick, meanwhile, walked around her, smiling and smiling and smiling as he took turns touching her and the dress, both. "It's really beautiful," he said. "I've outdone myself. I'll never pick anything more beautiful than this." He added, "Except you." He found her eyes with his and told her, "Now you have no excuse not to go with me."

She still wasn't sure she wanted to. Frowning, she told him, "You've robbed a bank."

"I did nothing illegal or immoral to get it."

She looked at her reflection, half-wanting to believe him, though to do so seemed like believing in sorcery.

She tried not to like the evening gown. ''People will stare at me in it.''

''They damn well should. I will, I can tell you that.''

She furrowed her brow with concern and self-consciousness.

''Winnie, they looked at you when you took your blouse off and shook your skirts. This at least will be a little more demure.''

He was wrong. That wasn't the problem. A ball would be very different. Especially a ball where her cousin and all his friends were there watching. Xavier, with his gregarious elegance and easy self-confidence, his upper-class hauteur and haughty manners: He would take one look at her in this dress and break out laughing.

Yet, to her own eyes, she could not deny that the dress suited her or that it was lovely beyond imagining. The color made her freckles look . . . healthy. It made her hair seem a prettier color, a kind of strawberry gold.

She brushed its skirts. The beads weren't heavy. The fabric was light, as light as air. It whispered, running through her fingers, liquid and shimmery. She had never seen anything more beautiful. Never. And her mother had owned quite a few fancy ball gowns.

''How?'' she asked, turning on Mick. How could he possibly have managed such a trick?

He waved his hands in the air, abracadabra. ''Magic,'' he said.

It took her a second, then she frowned and looked around suddenly. ''Where's your dog?''

It was a stupid question. His dog could hardly have brought this sort of dress. She realized, though, she hadn't seen the dog, not for several days.

''Where's your dog?'' she repeated, this time with a sense of horror.

He frowned. ''Win, I have something to tell you. I sold my dogs and ferrets at the beginning of week, all my cages, my carrier boxes, all my equipment as well as my customer list. I won't be needing them.

"You see," he continued, "I think I'm taking a job as a valet after we're done. Milton says his brother in Newcastle can get me a position." He let that sink in.

Her stomach went cold. He'd named a real place. He was going, and he had a destination. Newcastle.

"Milton says I have a style to me that would appeal to young gentlemen who can't match their stockings. I agree. I'd be good at taking care of a gentleman." He laughed. "Though after looking at that dress, I'd probably make a better lady's maid, but no one would hire me for that.

"Still, being a valet would be good for me, secure. Good for me and mine. And because I can write and do sums, they're talking about my balancing the gentleman's accounts and keeping track of his appointments, too. It would be at a good salary. It makes sense. Anyway, I won't be needing dogs and such to do it, and my animals weren't getting the exercise and attention they need anyway. Better for them to sell them. Better for me. Even Magic—"

"No," she said, appalled.

"He was worth the most, Win."

"He was your pet."

"He was my friend, he surely was. But you see, the place in Newcastle, they won't let me bring my dog." He stopped a second, looked at his feet. "Milton's brother said the gentleman in Newcastle has his own kennels. His dogs are pedigreed, and he wouldn't want them mixed up with mine." He smiled at her a moment, that cocky, raffish grin he had, full of male bravado. "I mentioned to Magic how I could, you know, have him done, but he said he'd rather I wouldn't. He's wild for Rezzo's bitch. He just loves her. They've been having puppies once a year for a while now, and, truth is, their puppies go like fresh jellied eels first thing in the morning. There's a list of people waiting for them. It'd be selfish to take him."

She tried to accept the dog's absence as matter-of-factly as Mick did. She looked at the dress. It was lovely. But it made her cry. She put her hand to her mouth.

"What?" he said. "What? Don't." He took her shoulders. "No," he reprimanded. "I want you to have the dress. I'm nothing but happy to give it. Won't it do?"

"Oh, yes." She cried, trying to smile, a mess. She sniffed. "Oh, yes. It's quite marvelous, Mick. Quite marvelous." But him. Oh, him. He overwhelmed her. While the dress, the way she looked in it, frightened her.

Oblivious to her distress, since she wouldn't discuss it, he smiled, happy, then—silly man—he wiggled his eyebrows over his crooked grin. He said, "I'll be taking Freddie. If she's up to it. I'll sneak her into my rooms, if I have to." He added, "Just come with me tonight."

Winnie squinched her face at the dress, then at him in the mirror and the way it had all come about. She wasn't sure she should like an evening that he'd had to give up his dog to buy.

He knew her so well, though. He said, "Win, don't struggle with it. I can't have everything. But that's not bad: A poor man learns what he values better than a rich man. I loved that dog, but I love you more; and I want a life with hot baths, books, and enough money for the last of my brothers and sisters to get a good start. I'd have sold everything anyway, even if you had a dress. But since you didn't and since I'm going to a place where I'll have more spending money, well, why shouldn't you have this present?"

He smiled. "Besides, the magic isn't gone from my life." He touched her face with the backs of his fingers, brushing her cheek lightly. "Quite the opposite. I want us to have tonight. One, magic, singular night. Do you have shoes?" he asked.

"No."

He laughed. "Dance in your stocking feet then."

She snorted, a kind of laugh finally. Mick was consoling *her* for his having sold his dog to buy her a dress. How typical of the man. How purely, endearingly typical. Oh, how she loved him.

Mick's heart was noble. Inside, he was better than a gentleman; he always had been. A kind of stunning reality hit her: Life would not be the same—it would be less—without him.

The Lamonts were very late, if they were coming at all. In the interim, Winnie told Mick about the letter from her former student, the new duchess, then told him her theory:

"If they bring an invitation, they have to be legitimate. The duke doesn't invite any but those of the oldest, most reputable families to his annual event the long-known, the bluest blood."

Yes. That was the test. She doubted that Jeremy and Emile would show themselves at her door if they couldn't procure an invitation, which would be fine. Or if they arrived and tried to travel on hers, she wouldn't allow it. In either case, neither she nor Mick would go. That would be the end of it.

And if the Lamonts did bring their own invitation?

In that instance, she told herself, she and Mick needn't worry. All his idle curiosity was pointless. No matter what the young duchess said or what Mick thought, if Xavier put invitations to his ball into the hands of the Lamonts, then the twin gentlemen with Brighton in their voices had the hardest to acquire, most eagerly sought reference that society deigned to give.

Chapter 25

As it happened, Emile and Jeremy Lamont did *not* have an invitation to the Duke of Arles's gala. Yet. But as they walked up the front walk of his London town house, they were fairly confident that, within the hour, they would be walking down it again, carrying one.

As they tapped up the wide steps of the duke's portico, they were still talking about their Cornish ratcatcher-cum-aristocrat.

"Quite the *gentilhomme*," said Emile with undisguised gloat. He was so happy with the way Tremore had cleaned up, he had to keep himself from rubbing his hands together. He could feel money coming toward them, buckets of it, dropping into his waiting arms. "I was hoping she could make him halfway presentable, but, by Jove, she's made him bloody royalty." He laughed. "He's perfect. Absolutely perfect." Jeremy joined him in chuckling yet another round over their good management.

At the door, they were greeted by the duke's butler. They'd made an appointment. The butler brought them into an entry hall, a room that was a hall in the sense of *town hall* or *public hall*—a vast, open space where people might gather. This hall, though, was by no means so paltry as those found in public buildings. It was a simple, splendid arrangement of high, coffered ceilings inlaid with gold, marble floors, and rich Persian carpets. Its furnishings were spare in number and extravagant of design: Over the central medallion of the huge Oriental rug was a gilt Louis Quinze table that held fresh flowers arranged in a crystal ship. The arrangement stood eight feet high and was at least that wide. The only other furniture in the room was a series of matching gilt and velvet benches around its perimeter, broken only by the precise geometric placement of four small, Italian tile fountains. Water burbled in these, the sound a little, liquid symphony that played peacefully in the hush of a very formal house.

The effect of the duke's house in London wasn't pretentious so much as a genuine expression of staggeringly ridiculous wealth. And this house wasn't even the grandest one he owned, merely the most convenient to the amenities of London.

Emile and Jeremy walked along behind the butler, their steps cushioned across thick carpet. He escorted them to the front library, where they waited for the duke among his books and family portraits.

"Here it is," Emile told his brother, the moment the butler left them. He indicated one of more than a dozen dark, oil-on-canvas paintings that broke up the bookcases of the room. "A portrait of the duke's son. He died years ago."

Jeremy stepped back to look at the painting. Then said, "My God." He was suitably impressed. "Tremore looks just like him! The resemblance is uncanny!"

Indeed, it was. Due to careful choosing, some similar clothes—and, more, to the miracle that Edwina Bollash had worked. Six weeks ago, no one would have believed it possible that Tremore was the son of the man in that portrait. The Cornishman had simply been too grimy and coarse. And, similarities or not, Emile knew his mark: The duke would have rejected such a fellow out of hand. Arles was a pompous old bastard. He would have sooner believed he was related to a monkey than consider himself related to an ill-spoken ratcatcher. They wouldn't have been able to get the fellow into the house.

Now, of course, Tremore was suitable to dance across the floor of the duke's ballroom at Uelle Castle. He could have a chat with the duchess—hang it, Emile thought, he could have a nice chat with the Queen herself, if she showed up tonight.

Further contemplation of his triumph, however, was cut short when the butler opened the door and an old, frail man hobbled in with the use of a cane.

Once of a stately stature, the Duke of Arles was now stooped. He moved slowly—with an hauteur, though, that was uncompromised by the indignities of age. Though he was old and infirm, people joked that he had a mind upstairs in his attic slowly becoming senile, while the one that everyone dealt with was as sharp as a bee's quill. Emile had already told his brother: Do not underestimate the old man.

Arles came into the room with the august decrepitude of ageless power. "I don't have time for this," he said.

He knew already what "this" was about. In order to gain the interview, Emile had sent him a note. It had said simply: *Your grandson is alive, and we know where he is.*

Jeremy was the one they had decided should begin. He said, ever so pleasantly, "We have found a man whom we believe is your grandson—"

Arles cut him off. "You haven't." His expression didn't change. "Is that all you have to say?"

He'd only come in as far as the chair closest the door, a man who didn't intend to enter further. He grasped the chair's back now for balance, as with his other hand, he leaned heavily onto his cane.

Emile came forward, as planned, the brute again. He asked bluntly, "Is the reward still being offered?"

"Emile," Jeremy said. He smiled his sincere smile—the best part about Jer's deception was that he believed it himself so well that he was utterly convincing. To the duke, "My brother can be so crass. I'm sorry—"

"Shut up, Jeremy. I'm not a rich man, and neither are you." Of Arles, he asked a crucial question. "There was once a reward of a hundred thousand pounds for the return of your grandson to you. Is it still available?"

The old man laughed with a dryness that ended in a slight cough. Then he said, "I haven't offered a reward for my grandson in twenty years. He's dead, you know."

"Is he?" Jeremy said. He furrowed his brow with his usual artless sympathy, and asked, "Do you hold no hope at all then?"

Arles's bony fist contracted around his cane as he pounded the end once with a sharp rap. Then he leaned on it toward them. "I can save you both a great deal of trouble. In the thirty years of my grandson's being missing"—he looked from one to the other—"I've had every swindler this side of the Atlantic try to sell me someone who looked vaguely as they imagined he might." He reached the cane, took a step away from the chair. "I don't know who you think you are, but you aren't going to get anything from me." He waved the cane once, surprisingly able to stand without it, then took a swipe through the air with it. "Except possibly the end of this. Now get out."

It was not precisely the reaction they had been hoping for.

Emile scrambled. "How old was your son in this portrait?" he asked and turned to look up. He needed time to think, time to sniff out a weakness in the old sturdy duke.

Only silence ticked by. Then behind him, he heard, "Thirty."

He turned around slowly, gauging, allowing a faint smile. "That is almost exactly the age of the man we wish to bring to you." He indicated the painting behind him. "And he doesn't look vaguely like anything: He is the spitting image of his father."

Arles's sharp, rheumy eyes narrowed. For a moment, he seemed interested, then his arm raised with a swiftness that surprised. He pointed to the door. "Get out!" he said. "Do you think you are the only ones to try to play on an old man's emotions? Do you imagine I am some sort of fool? Get out! Get out this instant!"

Emile glanced at his brother, who was already taking small sideways steps toward the door. The devil take him. His stupid brother was never any help, always the coward. Emile gnashed his teeth and said with just as much force as the high-handed old duke, "Listen to me, old man. You may have seen a lot of schemes, but this isn't one of them. I was here two months ago with a chap from your club. I saw the portrait. I heard the story. Then, last week, I met the son of the man in it. My brother and I have come to tell you. We'd like the reward, if you agree we're right. We're not rich as you are. But we aren't trying to swindle anyone. We're offering you a chance to see for yourself."

Arles was livid, but he didn't issue his command again. He listened.

Emile continued. "Michael," he said. "They even called him Michael. He is well over six feet, with your eyes and hair the color of jet—"

"Stop it!" The old man came at him. He raised his cane, swinging it this time. "Stop it!" Surprisingly, he was able to get it over his head. He thrashed the air.

It missed Emile, only because he stepped back. It clacked on a chair, splintering a piece from its carved wood.

"Get out!" he repeated. He limped forward, coming at Emile again. "Get out, you thief! You sleazy, venomous snake of a human being. How dare you start this again—"

"And his smile," Emile said, ducking another swift slice of the cane. He played his ace, the one that had taken the most patience as he'd studied men, looking for the right candidate. "It's like the one in the portrait. It's off-center. His smile lifts up on one side more than the other."

The old man hobbled to the side and pulled the bell cord, while through his teeth, he said, "Get. Out. Of my. House." He yanked the cord again, then again, then bellowed with great volume and strength, "Get out! Get out!"

That was it. Emile had played every card that he had and had lost, he thought.

Then something else, something inside the old man made him raise his eyes.

Emile turned. Jeremy looked, too. They all lifted their gazes to the large painting overhead, to its dark colors and moody look that seemed to speak across their silence.

No, Emile thought, the similarities were perhaps not so great as he was making out, though they were profound enough that their ruse was tight. What luck, he thought.

Then, no, of course it wasn't luck. He knew all the facts. Twenty-nine years ago, just before the duke's grandson's third birthday, while everyone was asleep in the house one night, someone crept in and stole the small child from his nursery. The boy disappeared, no explanation; a child kidnaped, never to be seen again— though his family searched and called out every favor that was owed them. They put pressure directly and indirectly on friend and foe alike; everyone felt their furious, hysterical conviction that they could buy or negotiate or dictate their way out of their bereavement. The duke offered a spectacular reward. Yet, still, nothing.

Which, by Emile's standards, meant the child was already long dead. Though the idea of the lost baby, even thirty years later, provided a damn lively game.

When he turned around again, the old man was still holding on to the bellpull. He seemed, for a few seconds, almost to dangle from it. Then he lowered his haughty eyes, drawing himself up again.

Quickly, Emile said, "You can assess the truth of what we're telling you without risk."

The old man raised one contemptuous eyebrow.

"Give us invitations to the ball tonight at Uelle Castle. We'll bring the fellow. We'll dance him right out into the center of your ballroom. You can look him over. If you agree with us that he's your grandson, we get the hundred thousand pounds. If not, he dances out the door, and nothing more is made of the matter.'' Emile held his hands out and smiled. What could be more simple?

''Pah,'' the duke said in a burst of air. ''If he's not, I'll have you all arrested for fraud and—''

Not if Emile had any say in the matter. He and his brother had train tickets to Southhampton and a dinner in Brussels tomorrow.

The old duke scowled, truculent, but he'd stopped arguing.

Jeremy was helpful. At last. Soothingly, he asked, ''What do you have to lose?''

The old man sent for his secretary who brought them invitations. The duke himself, by then, was long gone. There was a hiatus between when the secretary left them, before the butler came to escort them out.

In the interim, Jeremy dallied, staring up at a portrait of a man long dead. A tall man with a deep brow and strikingly black hair.

He murmured, ''You know, brother, the likeness is so amazing, it makes me wonder if we might truly have found the old fellow's grandson.''

Emile, too, paused for a moment to look up and contemplate, in awe, the possible convolutions of their own chicanery.

Then he sniffed and said, ''Yes, but he's not. Jeremy, we've bought him clothes in the same color scheme as those, in the same general style, only undated. We've cut his hair nearly the same, and, happily, Miss Bollash talked him out of his mustache. Then, too, don't forget: He *has* a family. He's from Cornwall, for godssake.

''I picked very well,'' he said, taking credit where credit was due. ''And remember what he was like when we first saw him,'' he reminded. ''A slimy Cornishman who lived among Cockneys and chased ferrets.'' He tapped his brother on the shoulder. ''Let's go, Jeremy. I want to find a servant or someone in this house who knew the child. I want to gather a bit of personal information. We have to *make* this work. We can't expect it to, or it won't.''

When his brother only stared up at the portrait, as if transfixed, Emile cuffed him along the ear.

Jeremy jerked around, scowling and holding the side of his head. ''Don't do that.''

''All right, but don't become sentimental or romantic. *We* are making the stupid ratcatcher into a duke's grandson. *We* are doing it, along with Bollash's help. Don't start believing your own hoax, idiot.''

Chapter 26

❧❦

The Lamonts arrived with the coveted invitation—a mere five hours late. They brought evening clothes for Mick, along with the tailor himself for some last-minute adjustments. Mick stood in his former room upstairs before the large, full-length mirror, his arms out, while a black tailcoat with satin facings was adjusted at the cuff.

On the bed lay a voluminous cape of black worsted with a deep velvet collar and a lining of midnight purple silk. He wore black trousers held in place by wide, white, elasticized braces. In a moment, though, he would cover them up with a white waistcoat that was cut deep to show the pleats of a white shirt. A white silk tie lay draped about his neck; he didn't know how to tie it. By a chair sat evening boots, a silk top hat, and white gloves, all ready to go.

Mick looked at himself, coming together in the mirror, as the tailor finished then packed up his needle and thread. Yes, he thought, quite the posh getup. Meanwhile, the Lamonts kept staring at him and exchanging looks.

"My God," Jeremy said finally, "he looks so like—" After a pause, he finished, "A gentleman."

He saw the tailor downstairs and out, while his brother, sitting on the windowsill, began feeding Mick a history they'd invented, "if anyone asked." A history with the oddest details. Trains. He was supposed to love trains. What did he know about trains? Aside from the fact that the fellow who wanted him to work in Newcastle had sent him a ticket for a ride on one—it had arrived in the afternoon's post.

"And purple. You love the color purple."

Mick dropped the waistcoat down his upraised arms onto his shoulders, then he turned the edge of it out to show the lining. Purple. He said, "You allowed me to select the lining, remember? I do like purple, so we have no problem there. But trains. I know nothing of trains." He shrugged, offering, "Except that in America the red car at the end is called a caboose."

Jeremy returned to the room just then, overhearing. As if the fact were an event, he asked his brother, "He knows the word *caboose*?"

"Indeed." His brother laughed.

Jeremy frowned at Mick, then his eyes widened. He said, "The lining of his vest is purple!"

Emile laughed again. "He likes the color. It's his favorite."

"You're bloody kidding," Jeremy said with genuine wonder.

Mick couldn't grasp their mood. He said, "Well, not my favorite, I don't think—" Though he had picked a lot of purple. He'd selected the lining for the cape as well, if he remembered correctly. He frowned, looking at it on the bed.

"How do you know about cabooses?" Jeremy asked. He sounded almost irritated.

Mick shook his head. "I read it somewhere, I think. Is it significant?"

"No." Emile queried, "Do you like the word?"

"*Caboose*?"

"Yes."

Mick puzzled over their fascination with the topic. "I suppose," he told them. "It has an interesting sound. *Caboos-s-se*," he repeated.

They looked flummoxed for a few seconds, as if he'd told them a joke they were having difficulty sorting out. In the mirror, Mick watched them look at each other. Emile shrugged and shook his head; Jeremy nodded—a strange little pantomime between twin brothers who were already a fairly remarkable sight.

Jeremy moved on with: "We should come up with an explanation why no one knows of the viscountcy we've invented."

"It's a Cornish viscountcy. No birth records," Mick suggested. He wrestled the bow tie, not paying much attention to anything but trying to tie it. He was making a regular mess of it. After a few moments of silence that became noteworthy for its lengthiness, he found them again in reflection, one at the window, one directly behind him.

Both had turned toward him again, both frowning deeply, identically.

Mick turned his head to face them over his shoulder. "What?"

"The birth records in Cornwall."

Since they didn't seem to understand what he was getting at, he explained, "Births aren't recorded out in the country. There could easily be a peer in Cornwall whom no one knows about, a peer whom no one is aware of until he comes to London. Perhaps he's come to sit in Parliament and reestablish the title."

Jeremy glanced at his brother, more agitated. Then he said to Mick, "Michael." As if the name itself had a bearing. "How old are you?"

"Thirty. Why?"

"Ah." This somehow relieved him. "Two years too young," he said.

"Too young for what?"

He didn't explain, but only laughed, then said, "You are incredible. The way you talk, the way you look. *What* you talk about. Goodness, even we, who know better, believed for a minute you were—" He paused, then said, "A gentleman." He said to his brother across the room, "This bloke is brilliant! And he looks so like—" Another halt, then, "A peer. He's perfect. What a find you are, Tremore!"

"Happy to please," Mick told him, though he was more mystified than anything else.

What *were* they up to with purple and trains and Michaeling him suddenly?

The Lamonts had brought their own evening clothes. They had brought not only an invitation for Mick, but invitations for themselves as well—then had been surprised to learn Winnie intended to use hers. They seemed happy enough to allow her to come with them. Perhaps they realized that she was, for Mick, an unnegotiable part of the evening.

Perfect. No, Mick didn't feel perfect. He felt annoyed with himself. He knew the Lamonts were setting the game further, deeper into what they intended to accomplish, yet for the life of him he couldn't get a foothold into what it might be. Purple. Michael. Cabooses. What idiotic game was this?

Then, on top of everything else, he went out to give Freddie a quick bite to eat, and there she was: lying on the bottom of her cage, looking tired and hungry. She hadn't eaten what he'd given her this morning. When he took her out, she was weak. She couldn't hold her head up well.

"Ah, Freddie," he said, stoking her fur. "Ah, Freddie," he crooned over and over. "Don't pick tonight, duck. Not tonight."

All three men waited at the front door for Winnie, while they took turns fussing with Mick's bow tie. Both Jeremy and Emile wore one. Emile's was pretied and hooked into place. Jeremy could tie his, but he couldn't reverse the process and make it work at Mick's neck.

"I can do it."

They all turned, looking up. And there was Winnie, standing at the top of the stairs, and, oh, what a sight.

She'd run out and bought shoes, little satin slippers that were pretty on her feet. She carried her mother's purse, with its jeweled metal frame and gold tassels that looked like acorns, made of wrapped metal threads. The only other accouterment she wore were opals, also her mother's. Mick had never seen opals until Win had taken them out this afternoon. They gleamed now at her throat, showing off her long, graceful neck. She shone like them, pale, iridescent.

As Mick's eyes rose to her face, he found another small alteration that he liked particularly well: While out buying her shoes, she'd found a jeweler who was able to mount the rimless lenses of her spectacles into a pince-nez on a satin string, a stylish solution to her nearsightedness that, as she raised the elegant article to look at him, caught pleasing light. An edge glinted warmly, playing hide-and-seek with the blue of her eyes.

Even Jeremy and Emile caught their breaths. Princess Edwina, with her hair piled up on her head. Oh, she looked the part tonight. Tall, willowy, elegant. A vision of opals and salmon-rose light and long white gloves.

Mick beamed at her. "You are gorgeous," he said. He went to the foot of the stairs and offered her his hand.

She came down only so far as the last step, though, then, looping her evening bag over her wrist, began tying his tie. Her fingers were shaking. He looked at her. She was excited. She was terrified. How very much like Winnie.

She did what no one else could—tying his tie in a few seconds—while looking as if any loud noise might make her race back up the stairs and decide not to go.

He touched her arm. "You'll do fine."

She made a face, unconsoled.

He shook his head, trying to smile reassuringly. At his timid, long-legged fairy. His tall, tetchy imp-face who had no breasts to speak of, full hips, and perfect legs. And whose idiosyncratic, capricious pieces came together somehow in a way that was so amazingly attractive his chest ached at seeing her.

Outside, they all ascended into Winnie's carriage, which then rolled out into the street at about six in the evening. They would miss dinner. They were going to be quite late, with Uelle Castle still an hour southwest of London.

In the carriage, the three men sat opposite Winnie for the first five minutes, then Mick thought, The hell with etiquette, and shifted over to sit beside her. He took her hand. She smiled briefly, letting him, then stared out the window, tense but quiet. Poor thing, he thought. Yet once they arrived, they would surely enjoy themselves: better they had this night than nothing.

Their emotions seemed to joggle along in tandem as they rode, she perhaps a little sadder, while Mick felt resigned; the two of them together in an understood bittersweet harmony. One way or another, an exciting night lay ahead. Then nothing. They wouldn't speak of it; there was no more to be said. When Mick tried to imagine his walking out her front door tomorrow morning, on his way elsewhere, he couldn't envision it. Literally, he couldn't. Nothing. As if he would step off her threshold into a void.

Eventually, from simple, baffled irritability over the fact that Emile Lamont watched him with a small, self-satisfied smile on his face, Mick said, "Why are you so happy? You're about to lose a very large bet."

The man's smile didn't change, faint but smug as he said, "Merely seeing if you can pull this off—the pure dangerous mischief of it—intoxicates me. It's worth it, even if I lose, to watch you do it." He laughed. "And of course Jeremy is going to squirm with worry all night. That's always fun."

His brother huffed, then interrupted, cutting off further exchange between Emile and Mick. Wisely perhaps. He involved Winnie in conversation, something about the Royal Enclosure at Ascot.

Mick was becoming accustomed to discussions of topics he had no knowledge of, discussions that Winnie's bearing, her accent, something about her, generated when anyone came near who could engage in what he thought of as toff conversation. It didn't bother him. He settled back, listening, the rhythm of her voice reminding him of good music played well on a fine instrument. He let the sound of it lull him into daydreams as he watched the sun set into the horizon. Whenever the carriage turned a little southward, these last, gold rays would cut across Win's face, and he'd watch her mouth.

Watch what you can see of my tongue, she'd told him as she'd shown him her teeth, making an *Eee.* Oh, yes. Whenever he listened to the tune of her voice, he wanted to lean toward her, up onto his own arms for balance, and bend down into her mouth. *Watch what you can see of my tongue.* He wanted what he could feel of it. He wanted to touch into her well-spoken *E,* into teeth with a space between, to twist his head and press himself into her clever mouth. He wanted to make her his own again for the night. Ah, tonight, he thought.

Possession. He'd tried not to want Winnie, but he did.

He wanted her so much it made him shudder to think of it. With delight. With dread. Wanting Winnie, so far above him, was as practical as wanting to walk on water. Even as he enjoyed her—the miracle of floating, the sparkles and ripples beneath his feet—he knew that to sink was inevitable. What he feared, in fact, was that he had succeeded too well, that he'd gotten out too deep with Princess Winnie of the Empty Tins and now all that was left was to drown.

There was no bridging the gap between them.

When he thought of her with her linguistics and her house and her students, it was hard to imagine a life more removed from his in Whitechapel or even his new possibilities in Newcastle.

Hard to imagine a life more removed, that is, until the place where she was born came suddenly up over the horizon.

The road curved, a zigzag that turned the carriage south along with the river. Winnie pointed. Mick leaned to look out her window: and there it was. Uelle. *Yule.* Like the pagan festival. A celebration of stone and fire, of Thor. Of power. And eternity.

Against the darkening sky, the seat of the marquisate of Sissingley rose up and onto a south bank of a bend in the river Thames. A spreading rise of yellowish stone, it extended itself out and up, the setting sun's colors sheeting up steep walls and limning a crenellated skyline of towers and sentry walks, casting the whole in an aura of a golden, pinkish orange light.

Mick blinked for a few seconds, squinting as if he might bring it into more realistic focus. *This* was the home where Winnie had lived? This was what she had lost?

The structures that made up Uelle were as numerous as those of the town where he was born. They took up more space. A massive gatehouse before a high barbican. A huge, central octagonal keep. A high-spired chapel built in the shape of a cross. Square towers set into walls with arching gates, nestled against round towers that extended upward into turrets. Behind all this, a separate, long, flag-flying hall, with high, imposing bay windows down its entire length.

It was a congeries of civilization, like an old medieval village, yet orderly, the buildings—there were corridors of them—arranged in courtyards around gardens, squared, their corners rising in massive, castellated towers. Uelle was larger than Buckingham. It was older, more a fortress, yet grand, beautiful. And more dramatic for sitting on the far side of the river, alone in the midst of darkening English countryside, meadow and hedgerow.

Princess Edwina. How astonishingly accurate. A princess, deposed, her fall from grace the scope of a chasm: come to reclaim her place, Mick hoped. If only for the night. And he would help.

He'd help, that is, if whatever Emile and Jeremy were planning didn't bind him, hand and foot.

He happened to catch glimpses of their perfectly replicated faces as they leaned forward to stare out the carriage window. Neither man had ever been here before. The fact was written all over their gaping awe;

they were as impressed as Mick by the small town of a castle toward which they all headed. So how the bloody hell had they gotten invitations? It was the question of the hour.

He hoped it wouldn't be the question of the evening. It was past time to find out.

Chapter 27

🌹

$\mathcal{U}$elle. Winnie was surprised to know it still moved her to see the old place. It was a large, squared, battlement affair overlooking the river, though to call it so was truthful without conveying the effect.

Tonight, the torches were lit. As the carriage clattered across the river, the air drifted with the smell of rosin burning at regular intervals in small iron baskets along the bridge. They didn't show up well at sunset, but she delighted to glimpse their fire; they would light up the night. She could see more cressets atop the rampart that rose up from the banks of the river, cups of flame that guttered in the wind, extending in both directions, up and down along the whole length of the castle. An architect, a century ago, had turned the rampart into the wall along a wide promenade that, all along the riverside of the castle, looked down into the Thames. The river below was already coming alive with reflections of flickering light.

After the bridge, the carriage plunged into a tunnel lit by torches, then it climbed out again at the first gate, upward into the lower ward. As they went under the gate, she called to Mick, "See the slits overhead?" He angled his gaze to look out and up, and she explained, "They're for pouring boiling oil down onto the castle's enemies." She shivered and laughed.

They passed under the iron and wood grate, a portcullis, that could be raised thirty feet into the air. Its full drop took less than thirty seconds, its iron spikes coming down with the force of two tons—guaranteeing for centuries that no one entered Uelle without invitation.

Up they climbed through a corridor of guardhouses and outbuildings, their crenels and merlons having once hidden legions of archers. It made her skin prickle. Oh, Uelle, she thought, such a lovely, shivery place—and so suitable for the duke's ball. A place built for the sake of intimidation. An elegant, embattled fortress, the home of knights from centuries past who had brought back treasures that had remained.

They pulled into a courtyard, and footmen rushed forward from the shadows to help Winnie descend into an Arabian-tiled coach entrance. Mick came down behind her as more servants scurried toward them from a dark illuminated by tall windows that bent long, bright, paned rectangles of light over bushes and ground. The sound of people and music rang from inside.

Winnie gripped the hand loop of her evening bag, clutching her own squeaky-gloved fingers. The Lamonts walked past, while she remained transfixed.

Mick hung back with her, silent, taking everything in. She wondered what he'd been expecting. Not what stood before them, it was safe to say. Unless he'd ratted Buckingham Palace, he had no reference point, nothing in his experience against which to measure this.

He wasn't silent, she feared, so much as dumbfounded.

She herself felt a stab of faintheartedness, and she *knew* the rooms they were about to enter. Though she didn't know them as they were—not lit, full of people, an orchestra playing, not as an adult admitted to partake. It was so unnerving. Poor Mick, she thought.

She heard her carriage roll away to take its place in the line of carriages that would wait all night, then before her two doormen pulled back heavy double doors.

Light and music and chatter poured out, amplified, dignified, clinking with crystal, humming with sociability. Inside would be people whom Winnie hadn't seen, save her own students, in a dozen years. Why had she chosen to return? Why now?

To see a joke as she'd imagined six weeks ago? The joke of sending—no, bringing, as it turned out—a ratcatcher to dance in her cousin's ballroom? It had seemed like such a good idea then. Now, if it were a joke, it was no longer funny.

Then, worse, when she glanced over her shoulder for reassurance, she got none: for the man she looked at wasn't a ratcatcher.

Instead, she saw a tall gentleman standing beside her, straight-postured, his top hat at an insanely right—rakish—angle, his shoulders wide as the wind off the river billowed his long dark cloak. Mick. He was shadow and light standing there in the nightfall, the back of him only a glow across his shoulders from the torches, the front of him stark, his shirt and vest a snowy contrast to the black of his evening suit.

And his face. Dear Lord, his face. The brim of his hat cast his eyes into perfect obscurity, while the light from the reception room made the rest—the angles of his cheekbones, his straight nose, the wide, masculine set of his jaw—simply and stunningly handsome. At her side was a mysterious gentleman in a cloak blown by the wind, a cloak that cast shadows across him, its lining flapping eerie bursts of vivid, sheening purple.

For a moment, she didn't know who he was, why he stood there, or why she was beside him. To be here felt unreal.

Then he asked, "Shall we?" And a smile she knew, yet didn't, crooked up sideways, devastating.

She was so taken aback, she asked, "Mick?"

The hat turned, looked right at her, responding to the name. In a whisper, she asked a question in her own mind. "Are you sure you wish to go through with it?"

Without hesitation, he said, "Damn right." She felt a strong arm loop about her waist. He whispered, "I wouldn't miss it."

His hand came up, and his head came closer. He was about to remove his hat to kiss her. But she quickly braced herself, holding him back. She felt a tension in his arm, in his chest where she pushed.

And knew: God help them both, he wasn't intimidated. He was excited.

Full of himself, she thought. His confidence panicked her. "Remember the rules—" she murmured.

"Oh, Winnie," he answered softly. "Don't you know by now? There are no rules." Then he pulled back and laughed—at her, she feared.

She was going to lecture him, bring him down to earth. But as their bodies separated, she felt something—a small, soft weight between them that rested in the lining of his cloak.

"Do you have your gloves?" she asked.

"On," he told her.

"What's that then?" She reached for the weight.

He drew back. "Freddie," he said.

"What!" Her heart lurched quite nearly out her throat. Then, with sudden relief, she put her gloved hand against her chest, onto her shoulder cape. She shook her head. He was tormenting her. "Goodness," she said, "I almost thought you were serious. Don't be so unkind. You terrify me."

He said nothing, only staring at her for a moment. Then quite seriously, he murmured, "I don't want to terrify you."

"Then don't tease me."

Nothing again. Until he said quietly, "All right."

"Are you two lovebirds coming?" Emile Lamont called from ahead. With his brother, he stood just inside the doorway.

Mick offered his arm. Winnie linked hers through it, and she marched forward.

They left their wraps with the servant in the cloak-room with only minor incident. Mick hesitated to turn his handsome new cloak over to the attendant till she encouraged him. "It's fine," she whispered. "He'll keep everything sorted and watch over it. You can leave your things. Everyone does."

That was the last of any awkwardness on his part. Shed of their wraps, he took her gloved hand and threaded it through the crook of his arm. All awkwardness became hers: She felt like a cliff-diver as they walked out to be announced. Once, she'd gone with her father to watch a man who dived from cliffs at Dover into a deep shoreline pool of the English Channel. She couldn't understand why the man kept doing it or how he did it at all without dying.

That was how she felt, as if called upon to participate in a free fall that might kill her, when she heard: "Lady Edwina Henrietta Bollash and Lord Michael Frederick Edgerton, the Viscount Bartonreed."

She and Mick walked out onto a huge landing that overlooked a monumental staircase leading down into the ballroom. Winnie drew herself up, having to remind herself to breathe.

Mick, it seemed, had to remind himself to proceed slowly. As they began down the stairs, he murmured under his breath, "Oh, look at the size of this room! Oh, my God, I can't wait to dance you out onto that floor—look at the size of that floor!"

And the number of people. Dear Lord.

And every single one of them seemed to stop and stare up.

As they made their way down, Winnie stole sideways glances at him, looking for a kindred spirit: and not finding one. He held his head up, a faint smile on his face, perfectly calm, as if he walked down a hundred twenty-seven wide marble stairs—she had counted when she rolled jacks and balls down them as a child—every day of his life. Dashing. That was the word for him. Dashing, handsome, perfectly pressed, perfectly tailored, and poised.

The poise was his own. The rest was a complicated overlayer of clothes, speech, and manners, applied to a ratcatcher whom she kept trying to see, yet couldn't. Where was Mick?

Instead, she watched the ghost who had materialized now and then in the course of Mick's instruction. Only now, the ghost had taken over his skin. When she was younger, she would have had difficulty speaking to such a man as walked beside her. Words would have stuck in her throat.

Where was Mick? She couldn't find him.

Could anyone else?

She lifted her pince-nez when she thought she recognized the Baroness of Whitting from the teahouse. Indeed, it was—the woman saw them, too, and began toward them from the far end of the room. The baroness's presence was expected. Less expected, Winnie saw two couples she was fairly certain had been in the same teahouse six weeks before on the day Mick had made his less than graceful entrance into it. Oh, dear, oh, dear. She spotted also several of her former students. One of them, the lovely young duchess, turned the moment she saw Winnie, lifting her skirts in a careful, ladylike hurry, waving as she approached—which she was not supposed to do.

Nonetheless, Winnie felt nothing but relief to see the greeting. She smiled back, trying to appear cheerful.

She wanted to enjoy herself, she really did. But how? She couldn't with so many people watching. And Mick—he was worse than the dress he had brought her. He attracted attention. People stopped to stare at him. New blood. New gossip. A new bachelor for the mamas to look over, for the papas to chat up. And for the young ladies to sigh over. By the hush, it was obvious the entire room was studying him for one reason or another. Him and the tall, freckled woman who came down the stairs on his arm.

The orchestra in its balcony overhead came to the end of one waltz, then without hesitation swirled into the notes of a new one—the opening strains in praise of another river, a beautiful blue one that flowed through Austria.

Then, on the last stair, just before she and Mick touched down into the room itself, a little gathering at the side opened up to reveal at the end of a corridor of stiff, staring people—

An empty chair. A woman came around it toward them. Vivian, if Winnie remembered correctly, Xavier's much-younger wife.

There was a carpet that ran from the stairway to the empty chair, like a pathway to homage. Only the man to whom one usually paid it at this point was nowhere in sight. Mick and Winnie followed the carpet toward the duchess, making the required approach. She met them halfway, as if to make up for, to hide, the insulting, empty chair—an indication of what the duke thought of her arrival, Winnie feared.

She brooded over what to say, how not to whimper out something meek and self-effacing to Xavier's wife. How to respond after so many years, with apparently still so much resentment between Winnie and a cousin who absented himself from his own gathering. Mick, however, solved the problem.

He bent in a low, graceful bow before the duchess and said, "Your grace. Good evening. Thank you for inviting us." He was happy to be here and said so.

Winnie followed suit with a deep curtsey, wondering with bewilderment what could be simpler. Sincere appreciation, directly expressed.

The duchess seemed relieved herself. She nodded.

Then before anyone could agonize further, Mick pulled Winnie by the hand, taking her by the waist, and drew her into a turn. He spun them both out into the room.

He smiled as he did it, as if to say, Xavier could be rude, but they needn't be. They could enjoy themselves. Well, he could anyway. Winnie looked up into his face, into his confidence and perfection and . . . frowned; she quaked. How had he done that? So unruffled. Without a moment's distress.

He reminded her of . . . someone. Of someone who made her feel timid and disheartened without lifting a finger.

He undid her tonight. He turned her around, inside out.

"What's wrong, loovey?"

She glanced up at the endearment, biting her lip. For a moment, he was her sweet Mick. "You overwhelm me," she said.

He clicked his tongue. "No, no, loov. Don't let it happen. I'm just playing. Play with me." As if to illustrate, he said in an ever-so-dramatically upper-class voice, "Aah, Miss Bollash, you do dance divinely." Then he winked at her and added, "Of course, you do have the best equipment for dancing of anyone in the room."

Her legs. The thought made her smile. Then frown, then blink, then smile and frown, both, shyly and perpetually dazed by the seeming earnestness of his admiration.

He pulled her closer, too close for etiquette, but the best distance for pivots. He took them into this step. Round and round they went till she was faintly dizzy from it, held against his starchy shirtfront, her nose filling with the warm, lemony talc scent of his fresh-shaved cheek.

He eased and led them into a fluid waltz rhythm. She kept up, moving with him smoothly, with growing satisfaction. Yes, they did move remarkably well together. Let people watch if they hadn't anything better to do. She tipped her head back, enjoying the twirl of their waltzing under a ceiling of paintings coffered deeply into other paintings, a ceiling of cherubs and gods, wreaths and battles, ornaments, clouds, all sixty feet or more overhead.

"Look up," she said. And he did. They spun in the light of old-fashioned chandeliers aflame with real, flickering candles, illumination augmented discreetly with gas jets.

"What a place," he said as they passed a woman

who waved her fan at them. The Baroness of Whitting, becoming rather bold in trying to gain their attention. Or Winnie thought it was she. She wasn't certain, she couldn't see perfectly without raising her lenses, which she pointedly refused to do. They danced past a man who, she believed, was one of the Lamonts, movement and lack of eyesight making him, too, impossible to determine precisely. They left them all behind as Mick said again, "What a place, Winnie."

Yes. She loved Uelle. Uelle itself was something. She had just breathed her first easy breath inside its walls again, just gathered her first nice moment, when Mick said, "Suppose the Lamonts brought me here to pose as someone."

She frowned, saying quickly, "They didn't."

He only laughed at her. She stared up into his crooked, handsome smile.

"Suppose," he continued, "I'm to impersonate someone. Who?"

"Oh, Mick, don't. Don't weave stories or start trouble."

"I'm not starting any. I'm going to end it." He wiggled his eyebrows in his wicked way, then told her, "I'm going to catch rats."

"No! Oh, no," she groaned. "You mustn't! Mick, I'm so nervous. Don't complicate things."

It was like pleading to a wall, though. His mind was elsewhere. He couldn't stop speculating. He said, "So this person I'm to impersonate likes purple and trains. No," he corrected, "cabooses. Purple and cabooses. Someone whose name is perhaps Michael. Do you know anyone who fits that description?"

She shook her head, lamenting his obsession with the Lamonts. "Oh, Mick, do you seriously believe Jeremy and Emile have set up something so elaborate? Then would try to carry it off here, of all places?"

He took her aback. "Without doubt, Win," he answered. Then repeated, "Purple and cabooses."

She frowned at him. "It sounds like a child."

"Yes!" he said. "A child, yes!" He thought a moment. "A child, grown up into me." He pondered the idea to a left turn then a right. "And money," he added. "There's money in it somewhere, for me being this child." He frowned, perplexed. "Can you think of anything from there?"

"No." She shook her head and danced with a man who moved as naturally as if he'd waltzed all his adult life.

He kept them dancing, turning, swooping to the music as they avoided everyone who might want their attention.

Then *Winnie* missed a step. "Wait," she said. Oh, no. She frowned. She half-hated to tell Mick, but something did occur to her. She said, "The year I was born, there was a tragedy. I only heard about it. But one of my cousins"—she thought it out particularly—"my second cousin once removed was kidnapped: Xavier's grandson." She looked up into Mick's face, pressing her lips together. She truly didn't like the rest of what she had to say. She sighed, disappointed to lend credence to his theory that the Lamonts were swindlers. "There was a very large reward," she said. "Oh—"

He broke away.

"Wait. Where are you going?"

He headed toward a doorway through which a servant had just come into the room, a servant carrying a tray of champagne. Winnie followed. He stopped the fellow long enough to take two glasses, handing one to her.

"Wait," she called again. Then repeated the question he hadn't answered, "Where are you going?"

He pointed to another servant, whose champagne tray was empty. "Wherever he goes," Mick answered. "I'm going down into the kitchen, wherever I can find a servant who might have been here thirty years ago. I want to know more about this grandson."

"Oh, Mick—"

He was gone. He disappeared between the arches into the series of anterooms that ran along one side of the ballroom.

Winnie stood there, holding a cold glass of champagne, feeling uneasy. She took a sip, then another, then a long swill. It was good. She took another drink. Then she blinked, for it seemed she saw Mick again, only walking between the same arches in the other direction. She lifted her pince-nez to confirm the oddity. It was indeed Mick, going the wrong way. He was carrying something. Food.

She called, "No. You want the door at the other end."

He started, as if surprised to see her still standing there, watching him through her spectacle lenses. Then he smiled, shrugging off his momentary fluster, and answered, "I decided to get my cloak first. I think I left something in it."

His cloak? She tilted her head, puzzled. He was taking food to his cloak?

Mick was taking food to Freddie. He stood out on the river walk in the dark, his cloak over his arm, that hand holding a plate, while his other dipped into the place in the lining he'd made for the animal. He pulled her out. She felt listless, but warm and breathing, happy to see him. And well she should be: He offered her slices of cooked liver he'd found in an antechamber that was serving it. He'd found, in fact, a virtual ferret feast: liver, some of the fattest, biggest goose liver he'd ever seen, some sort of fish row with cream, and chopped, hard-boiled egg; plus he'd brought the champagne. Surprisingly, the ailing ferret ate the liver. She loved it, then liked the fish row even better. She lapped up the thick cream, nibbled some hard-boiled egg, but wouldn't touch the bubbly wine.

"There you go, duck," he told her, pleased to see her eat. "You fight the good fight. Keep your strength up."

Once she'd finished, he settled her back into his cloak, smoothing it over his arm, feeling her weight in its lining. Then he walked around the corner, out of the dark, and smiled at the servant who held the door for him. "Fine night," he said.

The fellow looked startled, then smiled. "Yes, m'lord." The man seemed quite cheerful to have been addressed.

At the cloak counter, Mick handed the garment back to the fellow who would hang it. "No," he said sadly. "I didn't leave my notecase in it. Nor it is outside where I thought I'd dropped it. Sorry to trouble you. Hang it carefully, please."

Half an hour later, Winnie was standing with Mick, a member of Parliament, and the MP's wife, when the baroness finally caught up with them. She waved at Winnie, still several heads away, just as the MP asked Mick, "Bartonreed, how long have you been in London?"

"Six weeks." Mick didn't even hesitate.

After more than an hour, Winnie knew him to be frighteningly good, frighteningly bold in his charade. She kept watching people, waiting for someone to call him out over the hoax. No one did. No one even seemed to suspect. In fact, people liked him. As the evening had progressed, more and more he was sought out.

"Six weeks? Yet we haven't seen or heard of your being here," said the MP's wife. She smiled and batted her fan against her chest, *thwap, thwap, thwap.* "Where have you been hiding yourself?"

Mick lowered his eyes as if hesitant to say, then smiled and explained, "Lady Bollash has, um, taken most of my time."

Winnie looked at him. Oh, no, she thought. He wasn't going to begin with his courting-her nonsense again, was he?

Then worse, the Baroness of Whitting wiggled her way through the last cluster of people, calling, "Michael!" She thought to add, "And Winnie!"

The MP and his wife turned, making a place for the woman among them.

"Oh, Michael," continued the baroness. "And Win. How lovely to see you again." She leaned and bussed both their checks like old friends. With a look of smugness, she announced to the others, "Winnie and Michael are engaged. Isn't that delightful?"

"No, no—" Winnie protested.

"Unofficially," the baroness corrected, then winked, pleased with herself.

"Your lordship," the MP's wife asked, "where are you from?"

The baroness chimed in, "Paris."

The other woman frowned at her. "That's odd. He doesn't sound as if he's from Paris."

"Actually I'm not," Mick said. "I'm from Cornwall. I'm sorry"—he reached for her name then, surprisingly, found it—"Blanche. I was having you on a bit."

The baroness loved the use of her given name with its implied coziness.

The other woman didn't. She questioned Mick, "Well, you don't sound as if you're from Cornwall either."

"Ah." He looked around for a reason, then found, "That's because I was educated elsewhere."

Winnie was entranced. He simply kept going, spinning bits of the truth into long, believable threads, while no one seemed to think anything of his ludicrous answers.

"Where?" the MP asked affably.

Mick frowned at him. "Where what?"

"Where were you educated?"

He was only nonplused a moment, then smiled in Winnie's direction. "Why, um, the same place Winnie was," he said, taking her hand.

"Girton?" his wife asked. "Girton is a girls' school."

"No, not Girton," Winnie said, giggling nervously. "Cambridge. I was at Girton when Michael was at Clare. That's how we met, at Heffer's, the bookstore.

I dumped over a stack of books, and he helped me pick them up.''

Mick stared at her, then beamed.

A few minutes later, as they danced, she told him, "It was rather fun, that last bit. I saved you."

"You did."

But who would save her? She danced with a man who was bold beyond her bravest dream, who moved as easily in this crowd as the one at the Bull and Tun. Confident, elegant— It suddenly occurred to her whom he reminded her of, and the notion made her stumble and stop: Xavier. Only younger and handsomer. And kinder.

Though this fact disturbed her, Winnie managed to relax a little. The evening became pleasurable in its way. She caught up with two friends who had tried to stay in touch, but whom she had avoided because she'd been too ashamed of her circumstances. How ridiculous. It was pure fun to hear about their lives and realize she still liked them very much.

Mick disappeared again. Sometimes she spotted him among people. Sometimes he was nowhere to be found. Mostly, she enjoyed suddenly coming upon him in a crowd. She played a game, Find the Ratcatcher, as she tried to catch glimpses of the man he used to be.

He seemed to control it. He could smile out at her, call her *loovey*, then disappear behind Lord Bartonreed—a man who nonchalantly named himself after the sterling on his tea table, then carried the masquerade off as seamlessly as if he were truly the lordly fellow he pretended.

She realized it wasn't the ghost of the English lord she feared. It was the real gentleman, the sterling article she didn't feel up to.

As she watched Mick, she thought, her problem was not as she'd supposed, that she couldn't run off with a ratcatcher. Oddly enough, that didn't sound so difficult anymore. No, her problem was that she was afraid of Lord Bartonreed. The man whom everyone looked at, who could have any woman he chose, who, if he lived among these people, would be deluged with finer possibilities than an elocution and deportment teacher.

Empty tins. Empty again. Insufficient. When everyone else's seemed full.

Winnie stood talking to her former student, the young duchess, while waiting for Mick in the antechamber near the servants' door. He'd gone downstairs again. A footman had arranged for him to talk to a cook who'd been in the duke's household for years. As Winnie spoke with her friend, Jeremy Lamont caught her attention. He came toward her, looking harried, then motioned her aside with urgency. She excused herself to speak with him.

Jeremy shook his head, unhappy, then told her, "Arles wants you in his study." He pointed to a room at the other end of the long anteroom, the distress on his face compounding. He gave her a pained look. "We hadn't planned on an interview, but he wants Tremore, too. He wants to talk to him, to talk to all of us. Where is he?"

"Who? Mick?" She pretended to look around, then shrugged. That was when she saw him. She couldn't believe it.

Winnie lifted her pince-nez and frowned through the lenses. Yes, Mick entered the room at the far end, coming from the reception room again. He'd gotten to it somehow through another service stairway. The man was certainly familiar with below-stairs avenues.

Then as she stood there with Jeremy squirming, full of anxiety, a horrible feeling of her own suddenly descended into the pit of her stomach. Mick's cloak. He kept leaving and was clearly doing something more than talking to servants. She remembered once before, when his ferret had not been doing well, he'd taken the creature into his pocket.

And tonight, when she'd felt something small and soft in his cloak, he'd even admitted it. Freddie.

No, she thought. Oh, no. Not tonight, Mick. No one could overlook a ferret. Not with several people in the room who had even been in Abernathy and Freigh's when Freddie had last made herself publicly known. No, oh, no, she groaned inwardly.

To Jeremy, she said, "There he is. You go on. I'll get him."

Winnie avoided Mick instead, racing toward the cloakroom. A ferret. Only ratcatchers had ferrets. Gentlemen had . . . horses and setters or perhaps a pet parrot. But ferrets . . . Oh, they would be discovered. She would be humiliated in front of—if not *by*—a cousin who enjoyed humiliating her.

She told the man who watched over and fetched people's wraps, "I've left my face rouge in my fiancé's cloak. It's the long black one with the dark purple lining."

He wouldn't let her take it, but only come into the back to go through its tucks and pockets. Happily, someone else came along, needing the man's attention. Winnie wedged herself between a pile of hats and a rack of hanging wraps. There she ran her hand down Mick's cloak and—oh, with a plummet felt the soft little weight.

"O-o-oh, no," she groaned.

She reached into the pocket in the lining, squinching her eyes tight, clenching her teeth. She had to get it out, get rid of it, but, *ewww*, what was it like to touch? She felt around, digging down into the cloak lining, then suddenly she had it. Through her glove, it was smooth-coated, warm and wiggly—like a snake in a slippery-slick mink coat.

Ugh. She let go with a choked little breath, her hand coming out empty. She had to steel herself to try again. Calm down, she told herself. Get the thing into—what? Her purse. Would it fit into her purse? Yes. Put it in your purse, she told herself, then carry it out to Georges at the carriage. He could take it back to London, give it to Milton, who could put it in its cage, then come right back. If Georges left now, he'd return just in time to take them home.

That would do it. Perfect. She reached in again. The little thing was frightened. So was she. She rubbed the back of her gloved knuckle along it, feeling the resistence of bone, possibly a little skull. She got her fingers under its belly and lifted, aware of its little bones, the way it braced its claws, fearing her, trusting her.

With her back to the room for shelter, Winnie pulled the little animal out into view—oh, ugh, she thought again and shivered. She looked it in its little animal face, and it made a little sound, a kind of hiss at the back of its throat. Its parted mouth, the view of its tiny teeth, made Winnie shudder again. Then the ferret took a good look at her and began to run its legs, wiggling its body. It didn't like her holding it any more than she liked having it in her hand.

She lost her grip of it. Freddie dropped into her skirts, a light plop, then slid down the silk, making Winnie squeal and step back from fright. The thing looked stunned for a second. She thought she'd killed it. Oh, God. A new dread. Mick would be furious. But the second Winnie reached for the ferret again, it skittered—straight into the coats and wraps, burrowing into them.

She dug through for a few moments.

Someone—the man who checked and watched over the coats—tapped her shoulder. "Miss, may I help you find the gentleman's cloak?"

She looked up and around. "No, I have it." Indeed, she still held Mick's evening cloak. Which left her with no excuse to keep digging.

"What are you looking for then?"

She didn't dare say. "Nothing." Out the corner of her eye she saw a little brown tail-thing skitter out the door and into the main reception room. "Oh, dear God."

She threw the cloak at him and ran after the ferret. The reception hall, though, was crowded. The last she saw of Mick's ferret was its tail as it disappeared between the trouser legs of a lordly secretary from the College of Arms.

A moment later, Mick appeared at the far end of the entry room. He spotted her, but it took a minute or more for him to make his way to her. A full minute to suffer over what she had done.

Oh, what to say, what to tell him? Her apprehension grew, spiraling into gigantic proportions.

As Mick came toward her, suavely excusing himself past people, smiling as he went, she wanted to shake him. She wanted to scream, *Stop!* Stop it! Stop being as I remember Xavier, only more so. Stop being so . . . frighteningly competent and polished, so damnably fearless.

Lord, he reminded her of Xavier's hauteur when he moved, of the cocksure way that Xavier had carried himself years ago. Mick was taller and more limber, but he had something like Xavier's bumptiousness to him, a manner that everyone had put up with in Xavier because, like Mick, he had somehow managed also to be charming—and because her cousin had been the most likely heir to a duchy. No, part of her *wanted* the ratcatcher revealed. This man, this Lord Bartonreed, made the hair on her neck stand on end.

As he came nearer, she shrank back, determined to say nothing about the ferret, like a miscreant under death-sentence, waiting for the axe. He'd find out. But until then, distraught at what she'd done, she would hide there inside her own quiet.

Yet Mick was wrong to have brought the animal, wasn't he? For a moment more, she felt confused: ashamed and fearful, but angry, too. The old terror didn't quite take hold. Worse than empty tins, she reprimanded herself. You look like a mantis and think like a mule.

Yet no. She hadn't meant for this to happen. Her original intent had been to safeguard them, not expose them further. She had meant to take good care of the ferret. And besides, a voice said, you needed to be a mule to survive your upbringing. Outwardly shy and retiring, a proper young lady; inwardly as strong as a donkey.

As Mick smiled and touched her shoulder, Winnie frowned, putting the tips of her gloved fingers to her mouth. Then she brought them down and told him, "I lost your ferret."

"You what?"

"Freddie. I thought I was sending her home, but she got away from me."

"What the hell—" He didn't like it.

"Don't be angry."

"She's ill."

"She certainly ran fast enough."

He scowled. "Where did you lose her?"

"Right here somewhere."

"Why did you do it?" he asked. He bent toward her, putting himself nose to nose with her.

She whispered, vehement, "Because at least two of the couples from the teahouse six weeks ago are right here—"

"It would have been fine—"

"It would have been odd beyond measure: A gentleman does not bring a ferret to a ball."

"You don't know that." He made a harsh, put-out face. "There could be a ferret in every cloak here: You didn't look. You expect everyone to play by the same rules you do."

And *still* she didn't crumble. It amazed her. "I'm sorry," she said. "You're right. I shouldn't have done it. I should have spoken my fears to you. But I didn't. Now help me find her."

They tried; they looked. They wandered through the crowd, communicating with each other through heads to ask by facial expression, *Have you seen her yet?*

The answer was always no. Then Winnie lost sight of Mick entirely. She could find neither. Not Mick. Nor Freddie.

Someone grabbed her elbow. Emile. He hissed. "He *wants* us now. We're late. Get going."

Oh, grand. Xavier. This was all she needed. Now of all times to have to face him. But there was no help for it. She would go and placate him till Emile or Jeremy were able to bring Mick along.

When Winnie walked into the study, Jeremy was already there. Emile came in a few minutes later. He'd spoken to Mick who was coming. Shortly, he hoped. On their way here, they'd been separated when an animal of some sort had attacked the Russian caviar and crème fraiche, then beat a path through the foie gras. Mick had gone berserk trying to catch the thing.

The ferret. Since it was just the three of them, she told them about the animal, two souls with whom to lament. They all groaned.

"And Xavier will make us wait at least half an hour," she told them. "He likes to keep people dangling."

So they sat, while her stomach churned.

She felt ill. Oh, and she thought she'd been embarrassed—shamed—before. Wait till everyone heard *this*. Winnie Bollash was thrown out of the Duke of Arles's ball for having brought a ratcatcher and a ferret to it. No one would ever bring their daughters to her again, no matter how good she was at phonetics.

They only waited a few minutes, however, before the duke's study door creaked open, and a stooped old man came through it, walking slowly with the use of a cane, a woman hovering behind him.

Xavier. He was thinner and more feeble than Winnie remembered. She lifted her pince-nez and had a good look.

He was himself, yet he wasn't. She could barely credit how he'd changed. Withered and bent, he had to have help—his wife attended him—all the way to the desk, where he sat like a bag of bones dropped into the chair.

"You let go too soon," he snapped at her, his voice raw. She stepped behind him, less the trophy than Winnie had imagined, more a nursemaid. Attentive, fussing, she reached for his arm, trying to take his cane. Imperiously, he snatched it out of her reach. Then from his chair, as from a throne, he settled the cane across the desk and stared about the room, glowering at everyone.

Oddly, he didn't seem powerful so much as crotchety. Though, no doubt, he had power. Just not the kind Winnie had always accorded him: He had no power over her.

His wizened body didn't keep him from quick words. The second his eyes settled on her, anger straightened him like a rod down his spine.

"You stubborn, obnoxious girl," he said. "Like all the rest, you come to play on an old man's pain. Well"—he looked around, speaking to them all—"where is he, this Michael?" He said the name with distaste.

"He's coming," Emile told him.

"I've seen him," the old man said directly. "I looked him over when he came down the ballroom stairway, then I left. That was enough. He's an imposter." He added, "Whom I shall unmask with a few pointed questions, then have you all thrown in jail."

Jail. Winnie's heart sank. They were all going to jail.

Just then, footfalls outside the room made everyone's head turn. Just beyond the door, footsteps approached. They were Mick's; Winnie knew their confident rhythm. They tapped, separating out of the crowd in the anteroom, came closer, then paused, and the knob turned.

Mick stepped in, handsome, dashing, looking as if he could carry off anything. Ah, there was what she wanted. There was what she stood to lose that was greater still. How to have him? How to get out of all this somehow and run away with him somewhere?

He stared from one to the other, puzzled by the gathering. Then his eyes stopped on the old man behind the desk, and a look of surprise crossed his face.

After which a single word came out Mick's mouth,

with his looking more surprised still, as if it came out on its own and he couldn't hold it back.

"Poppy," he said. The way someone might ask, *Poppy, what are* you *doing here?*

Chapter 28

Xavier Bollash's chin tightened till it dimpled. He brought his lip up, mashing it against his teeth, while his glaucous, watery eyes grew fierce.

While he stared at Mick, he spoke under his breath with chilling quiet. "Get out." Then louder and firmer, "Get out." He lifted himself precariously to his feet, and, from here, he flew into rage. "Get out, get out, get out!" He pounded the desk. "Get out, all of you! He's not my grandson! This is a hoax. I won't have it!"

His pursed lips began to tremble until the movement was so violent he had to put his hand up over his mouth.

Winnie watched Mick take a step toward him, his brow furrowed in concern.

He seemed about to say something, when the old man swung his cane through the air. It cleared everything off the desk. Pens, a book, a pair of glasses moved with such force that they hit the bookcase to the side before they clattered to the floor.

Thumping his cane down, he hobble-pounded around the desk. "You! And her!" He swung his cane to point at Winnie. "Don't think I don't know what she does. This time she goes too far with her passing off her damned creations on me." To Mick, "I saw how you danced with her. The conniving witch is try-

ing to regain her lost property through a man she's
invented. Well, I'm not having it." To the room at
large, "You're all pretenders, all of you, scoundrels.
This is too much! All of you, get out!"

His wife cautiously approached him, trying to help
him without being hit by the cane, while the old man
was so unpredictable, no one else dared move. With
shuffling steps that couldn't match his rancor, he made
his way toward the door—"getting out" himself, since
no one else seemed inclined to.

He seemed infuriated by his own slow progress,
muttering as he went, "So what? So he looks like my
son. My grandson wouldn't dress like that. He
wouldn't wear a vest with such a loud lining." He
looked from one person to the next, as if he didn't
know to whom he was addressing the remark. He
frowned at Mick, stared a moment, then looked away.
"Though he might wear purple," he grumbled. "He
loved purple." At the door, he glanced at them all
again, issuing another fierce scowl, then asserted finally, as if it were proof positive: "But he wouldn't
dance all night with Winnie Bollash, not when there
was a roomful of prettier women. *My* grandson would
have taste." He stabbed at the floor again with the
walking stick as his wife opened the door.

He would no doubt have loved a clean, brisk exit. But
physical feebleness dictated he scoot a step, Vivian Bollash taking his elbow, then scoot another step. She
guided him as he stabbed at the floor for traction. Stab,
step, stab, *scoot.* Shaking with age, infirmity, and a
strong desire to deny what he obviously feared to believe, he made his feeble way out, his wife at his elbow.

After such an astounding departure, utter silence
reigned in the room for at least ten seconds. No one
had expected anything like this.

Then Emile Lamont looked at Mick and said, "That
was cute. Where did you dig that up?"

"What?" Mick looked distracted: as if trying to
grasp the meaning of a seemingly huge, unforeseen
possibility.

Could he really be Xavier's grandson? Winnie wondered.

She stepped toward him, laying her hand on his arm as she tried to explain his use of the nickname away. "He must have learned the name downstairs when he went to talk to the cook's assistant." She changed the subject. To the Lamonts, she said, "You have attempted to trick my cousin, but it didn't work—"

"Oh, it worked," Emile said. He turned more fully toward her, folding his arms and leaning a hip on the desk. "He's shaken. But he'll come around and fairly soon." To Mick, "He believes you're his—"

"No," Mick said, stepping toward him. "No. You're finished now. So am I. I was coming up here to tell Arles the whole story. The bet, how you made me seem like the grandson he still longs for, and how"—he paused—"how it just isn't true."

Emile snorted. "Right. That's why you called him that name when you came in. Because you were going to tell him the truth." He snorted again. "*Poppy*. Nice touch, Tremore—"

Mick leaped at him, grabbing him by the front of his coat, walking—slamming—the man backward with the momentum of his anger. He rammed Emile's back into the bookcases against the wall.

"Mick—" Winnie called.

He didn't listen, but lifted the struggling, furious Lamont slightly onto his toes. Into his face, Mick said, "What I 'dug up,' arsehole, is you are conning this old man for a hundred thousand pounds and using me to do it. Well, you're finished; it didn't work." He glanced over his shoulder at Jeremy, who, now pale, had stepped toward the door. "You won the bet," he told him. "Everyone here thinks I'm a viscount. Your brother owes you money—"

Emile hissed vehemently, "There was no bet, you stupid—"

"Shut up." Mick shoved him harder, til the man let out an *ooof* of breath.

"Mick, don't be—"

"I'm not hurting him, Win. Not yet anyway." To Emile, he said, "My obligation to you was to fulfil my part in a bet. I did. You owe me a hundred pounds, because I pulled it off. And then you're leaving. You are *not* using me to milk money and heartache out of an old man, no matter how much he might deserve it. And you are not staying here to cause trouble."

He let the man go and stepped back so suddenly that Emile stumbled down the length of one bookshelf. His face, when he turned, though was livid. Leaning toward Mick, he whispered, furious, "The reason you don't want us to have the hundred thousand is you see it coming out of your pocket now: You intend to con him out of the entire duchy, you ungrateful, greedy son-of-a—"

Mick grabbed him by the back of the coat, moving him toward the doorway, escorting the two brothers out.

Winnie followed, frowning. So *did* Mick hear the nickname downstairs? Was he attempting to assume a duchy? By virute of six weeks' instruction on how to be an English Lord? *Her* instruction? She wished for a moment that she didn't know him to be so . . . quick-witted, so adept at improvising and taking advantage of whatever came his way.

As Jeremy and Emile were handed their things from the cloak attendant, Jeremy stammered, "W-we'll call the police on you, Tremore. We won't let you get away with this."

"I've done nothing wrong." He pushed them toward the main front doors, then stepped out behind them into the night with Winnie following. "Have a good walk to London," he told them.

"You won't get away with this. I'll see that you—"

"You won't see that I'm anything. Tomorrow morning I'm turning over your counterfeit bills to the authorities. If you have any sense, you'll be as far from England as possible by then. Don't ever come back."

Jeremy let out a high, foolish laugh that came out in a giddy burst. He stood under the portico, silhouetted against the river torches, his hat in his hand, his cloak clutched to his chest. "You—you—" He struggled for words for a moment. "You *rat*catcher." Rather prosaically, he added, "Who do you think you are?"

There in the odd light from the riverwalk, Mick blinked, frowned, then shook his head. He looked down. "I don't know," he said, "I don't know."

In the entry alcove as they came back in, Winnie leaned toward Mick and asked, "Did the cook's assistant tell you the name?"

Mick bent his head to her, touching her back, her spine. "No," he said, "but I don't think that means anything." His voice grew more hushed as they whispered together. "She told me about the kidnapped grandson and the reward from years ago. I was going into Arles's study to tell him, to set the record straight from one end to the other. But when I saw him—" He broke off. "I can't explain it. He so reminded me of my own grandfather. That's what I used to call him. *Poppy.* The name isn't that unusual, is it?"

Winnie took his arm. Such a warm, muscular arm beneath his evening coat. Then he lifted it to put it around her shoulder, and they leaned into each other. They stood there almost as if consoling one another.

"I don't know how unusual it is," she told him. "I don't know what to think."

He brushed the crown of her head with his lips.

No, she didn't know what to think, except that she loved him, whoever he was.

When they returned to the ballroom, the most amazing thing happened. As they entered, a small commotion was already in progress. Winnie raised her pince-nez. And—egad!—she watched a small tail-thing scoot from the sidelines out among the dancers in the center of the ballroom floor.

Pandemonium. The dancing stopped. The orchestra faltered. Men called out as women screeched, lifting their skirts and trying to flee out of its way as it darted between feet and around dresses.

Winnie—Winnie herself—took off after it, leaving

Mick behind. She ran straight out into the middle of the huge dance floor and held up her arms. "Don't anyone move," she said. "You'll frighten her. It's Mick's ferret. She's gotten loose."

She glanced at Mick and saw him, his head tilted at her, smiling the sweetest smile.

Everyone grew still, exactly as she'd asked. The little thing skittered around feet, visible one moment, lost the next. A man near Mick—the very man who was part of the couple who'd been at Abernathy and Freigh's when the ferret had last gotten lose six weeks ago—said, "Oh, I hope you can get her. My pet monkey ran out of the house last month, and we never found him. I've been distraught ever since."

People bent down—though a few, mostly women, climbed onto chairs.

Someone called, "Here it is!" Then, "There it goes!"

For the most part, the gathering tried to help the new young lord in their midst locate his unusual pet.

The ferret didn't matter. Because there was something about Mick that wasn't a fake anything. And Winnie herself felt more real somehow, running around, looking for the little animal that meant so much to him.

Alas, though, Freddie eluded everyone again. Mick called her and called her, but she was either too frightened or too weak to come.

He was philosophical about it. He shrugged as they began dancing again. "It's all right," he said. "The night is won. We did it. Let's enjoy our success."

Surprisingly, it wasn't hard to do. Winnie found herself smiling and smiling at Mick. She worried for him a little, because he didn't always smile back. He was quieter than usual. But the music and the swirling rhythms of dancing seemed eventually to penetrate his mood. Indeed, the night was won. Mick made a brilliant English lord. And she celebrated a success of her own: With a freedom much as she had at the Bull and Tun, she came back to Uelle—to the ease she had known within its walls only rarely since childhood.

Somewhere near midnight, Mick said, "I want to ask you something."

They were dancing in the thick of the crowd, in a sea of shoulders that swirled in unison. Her face felt flushed from exertion. She was happy. "Ask away," she said innocently.

"Winnie," he began, "when I ask you this, I want you to understand, it's just Mick asking. As nice as this evening is, I'm not a viscount or marquess or heir to a duchy, nor do I want to be."

She only smiled. She knew who he was. Her Mick.

He halted a moment, a man facing his misgivings. Their gazes caught, eye to eye, and her smile seemed to give life again to his. After a moment, he let out a snort of humor, shrugged, then laughed outright. He said suddenly, "I love dancing with you like this." He leaned toward her, dancing much too closely, and murmured, "I love you, Win."

Goodness. Her chest filled with warmth, a rush of pure, physical joy to hear the words aloud. He loved her.

"I love you, too," she said, the silly exchange of lovers.

"I know."

She laughed. "You would, of course."

He stared fixedly at her, still smiling as he turned them in waltzing rhythm. "So I was thinking that I'm good enough for you, Winnie Bollash, good enough to ask at least. My question is, Will you marry me?"

She stared. Marry him? She'd dreamed of his asking, of her doing it. She'd played with the idea. But he was joking surely. Still, she smiled so widely at the notion, it made her cheeks hurt. Oh, this man. This bold rat-catcher she had taken in six weeks ago knew no limits, no boundaries. "You know," she said, "you remind me of someone."

"Who?" He made a put-out face. "And that is not an answer, you witch."

She laughed. A witch. Oh, yes. "You remind me of Xavier."

"No-o-o-o." He rolled his eyes. "What an awful thing to tell me." He laughed. "Here I offer to make an honest woman of you, and you say I remind you of your atrocious cousin." More seriously, though, he added, "Winnie, don't kid yourself. That's what I was saying: You're in the arms of Coornish Mick"—he used his old accent—"the soon-to-be-valet who'll have a nice income with a retirement sum one day. And the immediate use of his own cottage on a picturesque estate in a town that could possibly use a resident scholar who writes her papers in Newcastle, then has to take the train to present them in London." He took a deep breath after all that, then said, "Winnie, find a way. Make it true. Marry me."

She frowned. He wanted it to be real. Marry him. What would she do with her tutoring? What would Milton do? How would she sort herself out in a community where she was the wife of a gentleman's gentleman?

The practicalities of it boggled her mind. Yet, try as she might, the idea so pleased her, she embarrassed herself. She looked down at their feet. And, goodness, their feet. How well they moved together! In and out, in and out, between each other's legs. She shook her head, grinning foolishly. Oh, dear. What was she doing? Everything around them, people and ballroom, blurred as she looked up again to meet Mick's gaze.

She nodded. "All right."

He missed a step. "All right?" He stopped entirely, his face full of wonder. A couple ran into them before dancers knew to detour around. "All right?" he repeated.

"Yes."

He didn't know what to say. He looked about them a moment, then grabbed the first person to dance within reach. He told a surprised, elderly woman with a tiara, "We're engaged." As if she'd disputed it, he added, "No, truly. We truly, in fact, are engaged. We're to be married."

He grabbed hold of Winnie then, taking one hand tightly in his, his other palm pressed her back, and pulled her up against him, flat against him, as he danced them in pivots, round and round, double-time. Then he kissed her on the mouth, still dancing. *Dancing with your mouth on someone you like.* It was harder than she'd thought, bumpier, but nice.

He laughed at her gracelessness with it, then danced them some more. If she'd thought people would disapprove, she'd been wrong again. A little space cleared for them, and people began to applaud.

"Tell me again," Mick said. Over and over, "Tell me again, tell me again. . . ."

"Yes." And again, "Yes, yes, yes." She was delighted with his elation, his candor. More practically, she couldn't help asking, "Can't we stay in London? Do you really want to go to Newcastle? Do you really want to be a valet? I don't know what I want exactly or how to manage it all. Could you give up something so I could be in London a little—"

"Shush." He put his finger over her lips as they danced. Then, making his ridiculously fine half-smile up one side of his face, he said, "We'll bargain. Figure out what you want most, and it's yours. You're the queen of propositions, Win."

Chapter 29

❧⟨❀

*T*he next day, Winnie and Mick were awakened by the arrival of an urgent message from Vivian Bollash.

HE WANTS TO SEE YOU. HE ISN'T WELL.
PLEASE COME SOON.

Lady Arles greeted them herself at the front door of their London home. "I have something I want to show you first."

Winnie and Mick followed her through a vast entry room with thick carpet and trickling fountains. It took Mick somehow aback. He halted when he first saw it.

He murmured to Winnie, "I think I ratted this place once. I know this house."

He seemed disoriented when they entered the front library. Then out and out stunned, as was Winnie herself: In the center of the far library wall was a portrait. "Oh, my Lord," she whispered, grabbing Mick's arm as if she could hold him back from looking.

The painting, five feet high and placed prominently in view, was of a man in his thirties, a man who wore clothes from decades ago, yet who, other than that, looked so like Mick, it was hair-raising. The man in the oil portrait had Mick's long bones, his deep brow, his black hair.

And a faint, lordly version of his perfectly crooked smile.

"His eyes are blue," Mick said as if in contradiction to something.

"Xavier's are green," she murmured. "You look like this man. Exactly like him. Mick—" She left the thought unfinished.

He put his hand up over his mouth, thinking, then he turned around, scanning the books on the shelves, then the room. His eyes slid along a heavy desk the size of a grand piano to the lamp on it that dripped with crystal. A tray beside the lamp held glasses of cut crystal. He frowned at this, then looked at Vivian.

"Was there ever a decanter on that tray?"

She looked at the desk, frowned, then shook her head. "I don't know. Oh, wait. How odd." She turned again and reached toward the portrait, its frame. "Here," she said. "I've never seen a decanter in this room as long as I have been here, but Xavier won't fix the picture frame. He says his son did this."

She ran her hand over a gash in the side of the wood, then explained, "He told me his son broke a decanter on it, when he threw it against the wall. He had quite a temper apparently." She looked at Mick. "Do you suppose it's the same decanter you remember?"

Mick shook his head. "I don't know. I'm not even sure it's significant." He shrugged. "Winnie has one, too. They're not so uncommon."

They walked upstairs then into the darkened room of Xavier Bollash. They could hear him before they entered. He was cursing someone, complaining that people were always trying to trick him, take his money, that no one ever told him the truth. That no one ever loved him enough.

It was his doctor, who was packing up, leaving, disgusted with him.

"What's wrong?" Winnie asked from the doorway. Xavier was in bed. He didn't look strong enough to be sitting up, though he was.

He turned toward them. "I've had a heart attack is what's wrong."

"Oh, no," she said. Then, "I did this by bringing ferrets to your ball and by—"

He cut her off, saying, "I'm ninety-six years old, you arrogant girl. Who do you think you are? God? I'm dying because I'm old, and nothing works anymore." Then he motioned them close, to stand by his bed.

There, Winnie looked down and saw a surprise.

"My God!" Mick said.

It was Freddie. The ferret lay on the old man's chest, snoozing.

"It's yours, isn't it?" Xavier's crackly voice asked. "Do you know it only eats foie gras, crème fraiche, and Russian caviar? An expensive little beast." He laughed, rasping and coughing again as the complacent animal allowed him to pet it despite his joggling it on his chest. "What's its name?" he asked.

"Freddie."

His eyes brightened, a genuinely lively burst, and he smiled without reservation, delighted, surprised. "Freddie," he repeated, settling back again, stroking the shiny brown fur. "I should have known."

He lifted his gaze to Mick's as the small, pointed tip of his tongue came out, trying to wet lips that looked as dry as paper. His eyes grew round and glassy. "My grandson loved animals," he said. "Of course, what child doesn't? But he was marvelous with them. At two and a half, he would call; they would come to him. They weren't afraid." He closed his eyes, remembering, a beatific look of bliss coming over his face. "Oh, he was a magic child." Then he opened his eyes and scowled at Winnie. He pointed a long, boney finger at her, shakily. "Instead we were stuck with her. A girl. And an ugly one at that."

Mick didn't like the remark, but he sat down on the edge of the bed anyway. Very quietly, he began to explain, "Sir," he said, "we've come because you asked. But you have to know: I'm not your grandson. I had a mother. I have a family. I come from Cornwall.''

The intransigent old man, though, would only smile and shake his head. "No," he insisted, "you're my grandson. You're Michael. Though I called my grandson Freddie. They wouldn't name him after me, so to confound them, I called him by his middle name, my father's name." He smiled with vindictive pleasure.

Mick glanced at Winnie, glad he hadn't been raised by the fellow. Glad he had nothing to do with him. Sorry that she had.

The old man crooked his finger, inviting them both closer. When Mick leaned forward, the old man said, "You are Michael Frederick Bollash, the sixth Duke of Arles by nightfall, I would guess."

"Now, now," Mick said quickly. "Let's have none of that." He frowned. "I'm telling you: I had a real, loving mother. She always said that she nursed me too long, and I was a difficult birth."

No help at all, Winnie asked, "Mick? Don't you think it's a rather large coincidence that your name is Michael and you named your ferret Freddie?"

"Yes." He grew annoyed with both of them. "I do. A coincidence. Let's not call it more than what it is." When he looked at her, though, she believed it. She thought he was the duke's grandson. "I'm not," he told her. "I'm not."

He didn't want to be. Despite the fact that Winnie might deserve a fancier husband, he didn't want the absurd wealth he saw around him. He felt a real and sure attachment to his own family in Cornwall. Moreover, he certainly didn't want to be related to the self-centered old man lying here in bed.

Meanwhile, the self-centered old man, his eyes still closed, his mouth faintly smiling, spoke into the room as if for all posterity. He said, "My grandson's wet nurse was Cornish. I don't remember her name, but she wouldn't wean him, so we dismissed her. She was too lax, too indulgent. She went back to Cornwall." He shifted grammatical person. "And your birth *was* difficult. My daughter-in-law almost died."

The old man believed it, too.

He added, "The wet nurse was Catholic, deeply religious. We worried she would turn him into a Papist."

Mick, the Papist, remained unconvinced. There were many parallels, but many gaps. "I remember nothing, not any of this."

"Two and a half," Winnie told him. "The child was only two and a half when he disappeared, Mick."

The duke said, "She took him. We let her go months before he was kidnapped. It never occurred to me *she* might have been the one, but now it makes sense. She'd lost a child just before she came to us. She knew the house, our schedules, where to find him. He would have gone with her happily. After all these years, I remember now her saying she thought we were a terrible family, that he should have a better one." He chuckled. "Can you imagine? A Cornish wet nurse thought she was better than the heir to a duchy and all his blood, lineage, and kin." As he nodded off, he muttered, "What an idiot." He settled to sleep.

Vivian asked if they could stay for dinner. She looked harried and alone. Winnie wanted to, so Mick agreed. They stayed, taking turns sitting with the cantankerous patient upstairs. Xavier awoke several times, but seldom for very long. Mostly, he slept with short bursts of demanding one thing or another in fits.

It was Winnie's turn when he awoke, saw her, and motioned her over. Once she was beside him, he patted the bed.

She sat down nervously on the counterpane.

Just then, Vivian brought in his dinner. The moment she entered, he was distracted.

Winnie had already noticed that he never took his eyes off his young wife when she was about. He watched her with ceaseless interest, while she was polite to him. Sweet. Obedient. If he asked for water, she put her sewing down and fetched it for him. When he asked for tea, she went downstairs to brew it herself.

After she'd gone again, Xavier looked at Winnie. Then he whispered in his hoarse voice, "She doesn't love me. She never loved me.'' His teeth found the edge of his lip. His round, milky eyes filled with tears that didn't flow. Rather the tears sat in small pools in the bags of his lower lids. He wiped them away with his hand, then tried to bring all his emotion into a bitter laugh that only ended in coughing. His hand found the ferret. Odd, the way the two of them had found each other. Freddie seemed to like his attention.

Petting the animal, Xavier told Winnie, ''I've lived for a dozen years right beside what I've always wanted most, what I thought everything else would bring.'' Then he shocked her by saying, ''But, no. She's still in love with the man I stole her from.'' He added bitterly, ''Though I gave her everything. I gave her a hundred, a *thousand* times what he could have.'' He curled his lip. ''Would she even pretend though—'' Even he realized the thought was unworthy. He let it go.

How strange that she had imagined he didn't suffer. How foolish to think, because he was rich and powerful and mean as the blazes that he somehow had life by the tail.

His eyes held Winnie's. She patted his hand. He nodded once—in a kind of thank-you, though she wasn't certain for what. For a moment, his watery eyes clung to hers, hungry for something. She would have given it, if she'd known what it was.

Then she watched as Milford Xavier Bollash slipped out from behind his eyes. They glazed, staring sadly at her, seeing nothing; seeing eternity.

She reached and closed them for him.

It was only when Mick came upstairs that they noticed that Freddie had slipped away, too. The old man and the ferret had wandered off together.

Even for a man of ninety-six, for whom everyone expected that death wasn't too far away, it was a shock. Mick and Winnie stayed to help Vivian through the worst of the first twenty-four hours. Mick took care of the practicalities, organizing the servants, the particulars of the room, calling the doctor, while Winnie fixed Vivian tea with brandy in the kitchen.

As the duchess's husband had imagined, she was not struck down by his going. She was quiet. Quietly set free, Winnie suspected.

She must have been preoccupied though, because she didn't remember to give them an envelope till it was well past midnight and they were leaving.

"I almost forgot. Oh, dear. Here. He said to give you this when he died. I just didn't expect—well, you know. I didn't expect it to be today."

She handed the envelope to Mick, a letter from a dead man.

He opened it as the three of them stood in the severely formal entry room, fountains trickling. Then he had to sit on one of the stiff velvet benches.

"Dear God," he said, then handed the letter to Winnie.

I, Milford Xavier Bollash, fifth Duke of Arles, do hereby acknowledge that the man who presented himself at Uelle Castle this evening, the nineteenth of May eighteen hundred ninety-eight, as Michael Frederick Edgerton is my grandson, son of my own blood, Phillip Samuel Bollash. I do hereby recognize him as my heir and proclaim him due all hereditary honors and properties associated with the duchy of Arles, including the title, and all subsidiary titles, the Marquess of Sissingley, Viscount Berwick, Viscount of Meadborrow, Baron of Berchester.

The letter was dated yesterday evening, signed by the duke with his ducal seal, and witnessed by four men, including the lord secretary of the College of Arms and the Home Secretary himself.

That night Mick dreamed of legs, though it was an odd dream. He dreamed of fine, sturdy legs. Men's legs, women's legs. Beloved legs. Legs lost to him. New legs, strange legs. And all the legs in a dream that was overrun with them were so tall he only came to their knees.

Epilogue

*W*innie married Mick anyway, even though he was a duke.

They traveled to Cornwall for the wedding, where they were united as man and wife in a small ceremony followed by a fine, jovial dinner at Mick's aunt's house. Mick's family was in great attendance: two uncles, three aunts, two cousins, and twelve of his brothers and sisters—one brother being unable to come because he wouldn't leave his wife; she was pregnant with their third child and too close to term. The celebration afterward was a gay affair filled with Cornish voices, much dancing, and warm laughter.

Unavoidably, Winnie noticed that Mick didn't look a thing like his brothers and sisters. He was a head taller than the tallest of them. They were all brown-eyed with pinker complexions. No one seemed to notice though; they all adored him. He was fond of each, from the youngest early adolescent rapscallion to the eldest after Mick himself, a shy sister.

Not a one of them thought a thing of the fact that Winnie's few guests—Milton, several of her former students, and a few of her old friends with whom she had reconnected after the ball—kept addressing herself and her new husband as "your grace."

In general, London society was greatly put out that the new duke should be so private and remote in taking a bride. But it was a precedent. The new duke showed no desire to occupy the center of society in the way the old duke had. Very quickly, people learned the new lord prized above all else family, his wife especially, and the company of dogs, especially terriers—in the first weeks of his marriage, he acquired several from the stock of the famous Reverend Russell.

In London, Mick signed the official marriage documents with his new name, which ironically did not change his wife's name at all—other than to make her the Duchess of Arles. As a matter of course, the new duke granted the dowager duchess the use of the house in London where she had lived with her husband, "for as long as she should want to live there." No kinswoman of his, Mick determined, would struggle to have a good roof over her head. Much to the mystification of London, he granted a family in Cornwall—one by the name of Tremore—the use of the duchy's four lesser estates.

Thus Winnie Bollash, the only daughter of the Marquess of Sissingley, had a remarkable thing happen: Not only did she marry the man she adored who became the Duke of Arles, but through a circuitous route of second cousins, once removed, she regained her family home, Uelle Castle, which was where she and her husband chose to live.

Mick was out on the river promenade, waiting for her the day she came home from London, having gone to discuss and deliver a copy of her paper on Cockney speech to a playwright who was researching the concept for a play based on the myth of Pygmalion.

"Mick!" she called as her carriage rolled across the bridge. "Mick! Come see!" She had her driver pull right up onto the river walk. "Look what I've brought!" When Mick came close enough, she said the line that she had been rehearsing: "Everyone can always use a little magic."

Then she leaned out the window of the carriage, not even bothering to open the door, and handed him a warm, wiggly puppy.

"Oh, a mongrel terrier!" he said. "My favorite."

"No, a little Magic."

Then she opened the carriage door and let another dog bound out, a dog that leaped up on seeing Mick; it high-jumped five feet into the air.

"Magic!" Mick said. The dog was as pleased to see him as he was to see the animal.

Winnie stepped down from the carriage herself, saying, "He's only visiting. Rezzo won't sell him. But he gave us the puppy as a wedding present." She took the puppy from Mick, letting him deal with Magic, who was beside himself with joy; jumping, jumping. She brought the puppy against her nose, rubbing his tummy. "Ooh, he smells so good." She grinned over his little, round belly, her eyes smiling at Mick as the puppy stretched his head backward to look at him upside down. She assured him again, "He's Magic's son."

Mick nodded, too content to answer.

"How are the ledgers coming?" she asked. She knew, he was overwhelmed by them some days.

He looked up from the dogs. They had already relieved his preoccupation with all he had to learn—all he and she *both* had to learn—about running an estate. He spent hours over its books, trying to make sense of them. "Getting better," he assured her. "The whole thing is rather like breeding ferrets. Once you know who's who and what strengths are where, you start to know which assets to match up with what liabilities. We'll make a lean little animal of this estate yet."

She watched him playing with the dogs, so seemingly at ease in his bespoke clothes—he liked them and had a wardrobe of them—and new responsibilities. Still, though, she wondered if he missed the more ragtag lifestyle of making his own business pay by the seat of its pants. From nowhere, she found herself asking, "Are you happy, Mick? Really happy?"

He looked up, surprised. "Aren't you?"

"Me?" She laughed. "I've landed in heaven. I just worry."

"About what, Win? I love you. I want to be with you."

She shook her head. "No, not that. The life here—"

He winked at her. "Loovey, the life here is grand. I've ended up with my Cornish mother's love, my grandfather's money, and you in a castle on the river. What could be better?"

"Well, there's one thing that could be better," she said. She was sheepish, but grinned in spite of herself. She announced, "I'm missed my second mense, Mick."

His eyebrows went up. "Oh." He smiled, abandoning the dogs. "Oh, loovey, that's marvelous."

"Really?"

"Abso-bloody-lutely."

She cackled at that—and with delight as he scooped her up against his chest.

"M-m-m," he said, pressing his face into her hair. "I want a lot of children. I come from a very large family, so large it's two families, in fact. M-m-m," nuzzling her more, "that's wonderful, Win. Really wonderful."

How could a person be more content? she wondered. How could anything be better than this?

Then he showed her: Very softly as he nuzzled her, his mouth near her ear, he began to sing. "I'm so happy with you, la, la . . ." A plant-song. Only this time she let him sing it to her.

That night, in the huge bedroom neither one of them were quite used to, in a high new bed, on a new feather mattress, Winnie said to him in the dark, "Grow your mustache back."

Mick lay beside her, his long body still. She thought he didn't hear her at first. He looked unconscious in the moonlight as it came through the high windows. It was a balmy night. The sheer, flowing draperies that lined the heavier damask ones blew out into the room. They and the moonlight made Mick's face into a play of shifting shadows. Winnie stared, doubting herself for a moment, as she watched his lips curve in a barely discernable smile.

His head turned toward her, and he opened one eye. He gave her a one-eyed, inquiring look, then he let his head rock back. He closed his eyes again, while she thought she saw a smug smile spread.

With his eyes still closed, he said, "What'll you give me, if I grow my mustache back?"

"Pardon?"

"I have an idea."

"What?"

"You go over to the wall, Win, and lift your nightgown up. All the way up over your bum. Then turn around and put your head like you did that time against the wall. I get to kiss my way up your legs. You can't stop me, no matter what I do, for ten minutes. If you can do that, I'll grow the mustache back. Just for you."

"No," she said, laughing, a little bit nervous. "We're married now. We're not doing—um, that. We don't do *that* anymore."

His head turned toward her again, one sleepy eye slitting enough to look at her. "Winnie, I think in this area you better let me decide what we do and don't do. For a while yet." In the purple-gray of the room, she watched his head roll back again, his expression relax.

What she could see of his smile was faint, fond—and wistful in a way that could only be called wicked.

From the shadows, he said, "You be the student. I'll be the teacher now."

When she said nothing, he rolled his head toward her again and gave her another slitted look, this time with both eyes. "What are you waiting for, loovey? Come on. To the wall with you."

She didn't move.

He nudged her, then he came up onto one elbow, over her, and said, "Do you want the mustache back or not?"

"Um—" It seemed like a trick question. "Um, yes."

"All right, then. You can have it, but up with you now." He gave her rump a push. He was serious. "To the wall, Win. And I'm putting you on notice." He bent his lips down her ear. The heat and humidity of his breath tickled as he whispered, "I'm kissing the backs of your legs all the way up to your bum, and anyplace else I want. For ten minutes."

Winnie lay there on the pillows, speechless. For a full two seconds. Then she laughed and said, "Fifteen." She changed her mind. "No, twenty!"

Ah, what a good bargainer she'd become.

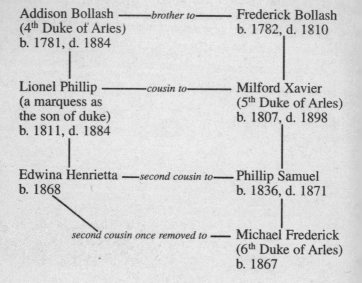

Addison Bollash ——*brother to*—— Frederick Bollash
(4th Duke of Arles)   b. 1782, d. 1810
b. 1781, d. 1884

Lionel Phillip ——*cousin to*—— Milford Xavier
(a marquess as   (5th Duke of Arles)
the son of duke)   b. 1807, d. 1898
b. 1811, d. 1884

Edwina Henrietta ——*second cousin to*—— Phillip Samuel
b. 1868   b. 1836, d. 1871

        second cousin once removed to —— Michael Frederick
                              (6th Duke of Arles)
                              b. 1867

Have you ever wondered why opposites attract?

Why is it so easy to fall in love when your friends, your family . . . even your own good sense tells you to run the other way? Perhaps it's because a long, slow kiss from a sensuous rake is much more irresistible than a chaste embrace from a gentleman with a steady income. After all, falling in love means taking a risk . . . and isn't it oh, so much more enjoyable to take a risk on someone just a little dangerous?

Christina Dodd, Cathy Maxwell, Samantha James, Christina Skye, Constance O'Day-Flannery and Judith Ivory . . . these are the authors of the Avon Romance Superleaders, and each has created a man and a woman who seemed completely unsuitable in all ways but one . . . the love they discover in the other.

Christina Dodd certainly knows how to cause a scandal—in her books, that is! Her dashing heroes, like the one in her latest Superleader, SOMEDAY MY PRINCE, simply can't resist putting her heroines in compromising positions of all sorts . . .

Beautiful Princess Laurentia has promised to fulfill her royal duty and marry, but as she looks over her stuttering, swaggering, timid sea of potential suitors she thinks to herself that she's never seen such an unsuitable group in her life. Then she's swept off her feet by a handsome prince of dubious reputation. Laurentia had always dreamed her prince would come, but never one quite like this . . .

SOMEDAY MY PRINCE
by Christina Dodd

*A*stonished, indignant and in pain, the princess stammered, "Who . . . what . . . how dare you?"

"Was he a suitor scorned?"

"I never saw him before!"

"Then next time a stranger grabs you and slams you over his shoulder, you squeal like a stuck pig."

Clutching her elbow, she staggered to her feet. "I yelled!"

"I barely heard you." He stood directly in front of her, taller than he had at first appeared, beetle-browed, his eyes dark hollows, his face marked with a deep-shadowed scar that ran from chin to temple. Yet despite all that, he was handsome. Stunningly so. "And I was just behind those pots."

Tall and luxuriant, the potted plants clustered against the wall, and she looked at them, then looked back at him. He spoke with an accent. He walked with a limp. He was a stranger. Suspicion stirred in her. "What were you doing there?"

"Smoking."

She smelled it on him, that faint scent of tobacco so like that which clung to her father. Although she knew it foolish, the odor lessened her misgivings. "I'll call the guard and send them after that scoundrel."

"Scoundrel." The stranger laughed softly. "You *are* a lady. But don't bother sending anyone after him. He's long gone."

She knew it was true. The scoundrel—and what was wrong with that word, anyway?—had leaped into the wildest part of the garden, just where the cultured plants gave way to natural scrub. The guard would do her no good.

So rather than doing what she knew very well she should, she let the stranger place his hand on the small of her back and turn her toward the light.

He clasped her wrist and slowly stretched out her injured arm. "It's not broken."

"I don't suppose so."

He grinned, a slash of white teeth against a half-glimpsed face. "You'd recognize if it was. A broken elbow lets you know it's there." Efficiently, he unfastened the buttons on her elbow-length glove and stripped it away, then ran his bare fingers firmly over the bones in her lower arm, then lightly over the pit of her elbow.

Goose bumps rose on her skin at the touch. He didn't wear gloves, she noted absently. His naked skin touched hers. "What kind of injury are you looking for?"

"Not an injury. I just thought I would enjoy caressing that silk-soft skin."

She jerked her wrist away.

What could be more exciting than making your debut . . . wearing a gorgeous gown, sparkling jewels, and enticing all the ton's most eligible bachelors?

In Cathy Maxwell's MARRIED IN HASTE, Tess Hamlin is used to having the handsomest of London's eligible men vie for her attention. But Tess is in no hurry to make her choice—until the meets the virile war hero Brenn Owen, the new Earl of Merton. But Tess must marry a man of wealth, and although the earl has a title and land, he's in need of funds. But she can't resist this compelling nobleman . . .

MARRIED IN HASTE
by Cathy Maxwell

"*I* envy you. I will never be free. Someday I will have a husband and my freedom will be curtailed even more," Tess said.

"I had the impression that you set the rules."

Tess shot him a sharp glance. "No, I play the game well, but—" She broke off.

"But it's not really me."

"What is you?"

A wary look came into her eyes. "You don't really want to know."

"Yes, I do." Brenn leaned forward. "After all, moments ago you were begging me to make a declaration."

"I never beg!" she declared with mock seriousness and they both laughed. Then she said, "Sometimes I wonder if there isn't something more to life. Or why am I here."

The statement caught his attention. There wasn't one man who had ever faced battle without asking that question.

"I want to feel a sense of purpose," she continued, "of being, here deep inside. Instead I feel . . ." She shrugged, her voice trailing off.

"As if you are only going through the motions?" he suggested quietly.

The light came on in her vivid eyes. "Yes! That's it." She dropped her arms to her side. "Do you feel that way too?"

"At one time I have. Especially after a battle when men were dying all around me and yet I had escaped harm. I wanted to have a reason. To know why."

She came closer to him until they stood practically toe to toe. "And have you found out?"

"I think so," he replied honestly. "It has to do with having a sense of purpose, of peace. I believe I have found that purpose at Erwynn Keep. It's the first place I've been where I feel I really belong."

"Yes," she agreed in understanding. "Feeling like you belong. That's what I sense is missing even when I'm surrounded by people who do nothing more than toady up to me and hang on my every word." She smiled. "But you haven't done that. You wouldn't, would you? Even if I asked you to."

"Toadying has never been my strong suit . . . although I would do many things for a beautiful woman." He touched her then, drawing a line down the velvet curve of her cheek.

Miss Hamlin caught his hand before it could stray further, her gaze holding his. "Most men don't go beyond the shell of the woman . . . or look past the fortune. Are you a fortune hunter, Lord Merton?"

Her direct question almost bowled him off over the

stone rail. He recovered quickly. "If I was, would I admit it?"

"No."

"Then you shall have to form your own opinion."

Her lips curved into a smile. She did not move away.

"I think I'm going to kiss you."

She blushed, the sudden high color charming.

"Don't tell me," he said. "Gentlemen rarely ask before they kiss."

"Oh, they always ask, but I've never let them."

"Then I won't ask." He lowered his lips to hers. Her eyelashes swept down as she closed her eyes. She was so beautiful in the moonlight. So innocently beautiful.

Across the Scottish Highlands strides Cameron
MacKay. Cameron is a man of honor, a man who
would do anything to protect his clan . . . and he
wouldn't hesitate to seek revenge against those
who have wronged him.

Meredith is one of the clan Monroe, sworn enemies
of Cameron and his men. So Cameron takes this
woman as his wife, never dreaming that what began as an act of vengeance becomes instead a
quest for love in Samantha James's HIS WICKED
WAYS.

HIS WICKED WAYS
by Samantha James

*C*ameron faced her, his head propped on an elbow.
His smile was gone, his expression unreadable. He
stared at her as if he would pluck her very thoughts
from her mind.

"It occurs to me that you have been sheltered," he
said slowly, "that mayhap you know naught of men
. . . and life." He seemed to hesitate. "What happens
between a man and a woman is not something to be
feared, Meredith. It's where children come from—"

"I know how children are made!" Meredith's face
burned with shame.

"Then why are you so afraid?" he asked quietly.

It was in her mind to pretend she misunderstood—
but it would have been a lie. Clutching the sheet to her
chin, she gave a tiny shake of her head. "Please," she

said, her voice very low. "I cannot tell you."

Reaching out, he picked up a strand of hair that lay on her breast. Meredith froze. Her heart surely stopped in that instant. Now it comes, she thought despairingly. He claimed he would give her time to accept him, to accept what would happen, but it was naught but a lie! Her heart twisted. Ah, but she should have known!

"Your hair is beautiful—like living flame."

His murmur washed over her, soft as finely spun silk. She searched his features, stunned when she detected no hint of either mockery or derision.

She stared at the wispy strands that lay across his palm, the way he tested the texture between thumb and forefinger, the way he wound the lock of hair around and around his hand.

Meredith froze. But he stopped before the pressure tugged hurtfully on her scalp . . . and trespassed no further. Instead he turned his back.

His eyes closed.

They touched nowhere. Indeed, the width of two hands separated them; those silken red strands were the only link between them. Meredith dared not move. She listened and waited, her heart pounding in her breast . . .

. . . Slumber overtook him. He slept, her lock of hair still clutched tight in his fist.

Only then did she move. Her hand lifted. She touched her lips, there at the very spot he'd possessed so thoroughly. Her pulse quickened as the memory of his kiss flamed all through her . . . She'd thought it was disdain. Distaste.

But she was wrong. In the depths of her being, Meredith was well aware it was something far different.

Her breath came fast, then slow. Something was happening. Something far beyond her experience . . .

What could be more beautiful than a holiday trip to the English countryside? Snow falling on the gentle hills and thatched roofs . . . villagers singing carols, then dropping by the pub for hot cider with rum.

In Christina Skye's THE PERFECT GIFT, Maggie Kincaid earns a chance to exhibit her beautiful jewelry designs at sumptuous Draycott Abbey, where she dreams of peacefully spending Christmas. But when she arrives, she learns she is in danger and discovers that her every step will be followed by disturbingly sensuous Jared Mac-Inness. He will protect her from those who would harm her, but who'll protect Maggie from Jared?

THE PERFECT GIFT
by Christina Skye

*J*ared had worked his way over the ridge and down through the trees where he found Maggie Kincaid sitting on the edge of the stone bridge.

Just sitting, her legs dangling as she traced invisible patterns over the old stone.

Jared stared in amazement. She looked for all the world like a child waiting for a long lost friend to appear.

Jared shook off his sense of strangeness and plunged down the hillside, cursing her for the ache in his ribs and the exhaustion eating at his muscles.

He scowled as he drew close enough to see her face.

Young. Excited. Not beautiful in the classic sense. Her mouth was too wide and her nose too thin. But the eyes lit up her whole face and made a man want to know all her secrets.

Her mouth swept into a quick smile as he approached. Her head tilted as laughter rippled like morning sunlight.

The sound chilled him. It was too quick, too innocent. She ought to be frightened. Defensive. Running.

He stared, feeling the ground turn to foam beneath him.

Moonlight touched the long sleeves of her simple white dress with silver as she rose to her feet.

He spoke first, compelled to break the spell of her presence, furious that she should touch him so. "You know I could have you arrested for this." His jaw clenched.

Her head cocked. Poised at the top of the bridge, she was a study in innocent concentration.

"Don't even bother to think about running. I want to know who you are and why in hell you're here."

A frown marred the pale beauty of her face. She might have been a child—except that the full curves of her body spoke a richly developed maturity at complete odds with her voice and manner.

"Answer me. You're on private property and in ten seconds I'm going to call the police." Exhaustion made his voice harsh. "Don't try it," Jared hissed, realizing she meant to fall and let him catch her. But it was too late. She stepped off the stone bridge, her body angling down toward him.

He caught her with an oath and a jolt of pain, and then they toppled as one onto the damp earth beyond the moat. Cursing, Jared rolled sideways and pinned her beneath him.

It was no child's face that stared up at him and no child's body that cushioned him. She was strong for a woman, her muscles trim but defined. The softness at hip and breast tightened his throat and left his body all

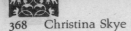

too aware of their intimate contact. He did not move, fighting an urge to open his hands and measure her softness.

What was wrong with him?

Imagine for a moment that you're a modern woman; one minute, you're living a fast-paced, hectic lifestyle . . . the next minute, you've somehow been transported to another time and you're living a life of a very different sort.

No one does time-travel like Constance O'Day-Flannery. In ONCE AND FOREVER Maggie enters a maze while at an Elizabethan fair, and when she comes out she magically finds she's truly in Elizabethan times! And to make matters more confusing, the sweep-her-off-her-feet hero she's been searching for all her life turns out to be the handsomest man in 1600's England!

ONCE AND FOREVER
by Constance O'Day-Flannery

*M*aggie looked up to the sky and wished a breeze would find its way into the thick hedges; she couldn't believe she was in this maze, sweating her life away in a gorgeous costume and starving. Thinking of all the calories she was burning she wondered, who needs a gym work out? Maggie stopped to listen for anyone, but only an eerie silence hovered.

Suddenly, she felt terribly alone.

Spinning around, she vainly searched for anyone, but saw and heard nothing. "Hello? Hello?" Her calls went unanswered. She stopped abruptly in the path. She felt weak. Her heart was pounding and her head felt light. Grabbing at the starched collar, she released the top few buttons and gasped in confusion. Okay, maybe she could use that shining knight right about now. She didn't care how or where he appeared, as long as he led her out, for the air was heavy and still, and Maggie found it hard to breathe.

"Help me . . . please."

Silence.

Her heart pounded harder, her stomach clenched in fear, her breath shortened, her limbs trembled and the weight of the costume felt like it was pulling her down to the ground.

Spinning around and around, Maggie experienced a sudden lightness, as if she no longer had to struggle against gravity and push herself away from the earth. Whatever was happening was controlling her, and she was so weary of struggling . . . flashes of her ex-husband and the alimony, her failed job interviews, the bills, the aloneness swirled together. It was bigger, more powerful than she, and she felt herself weakening, surrendering to it. The hedges appeared to fade away and Maggie instinctively knew she had to get out. Gathering her last essence of strength, she started running.

Miraculously, she was out. She was gasping for breath, inhaling the dust and dirt from under her mouth when she heard the angry yell that reverberated through the ground and rattled her already scrambled brain.

She dare not move, not even breathe. If this were a nightmare, and surely it couldn't be anything else, she wasn't about to add to the terror. She would wake up any moment, her mind screamed. She *had to!*

Drawing upon more courage than she thought she had left, Maggie slowly lifted her head. She was staring into the big brown eyes of a horse.

A horse!

She heard moans and looked beyond the animal to see a body. A man, rolled on the side of a dirt path, was clutching his knee as colorful curses flowed back to her.

"Spleeny, lousey-cockered jolt head! Aww...
heavens above deliver me from this vile, impertinent,
ill-natured lout!"

Pushing herself to her feet, Maggie brushed dirt,
twigs and leaves from her hands and backside, then
made her way to the man. "How badly are you hurt?"
she called out over her shoulder.

The man didn't answer and she glanced in his direction. He was still staring at her, as though he'd lost
his senses.

Shoulder-length streaked blond hair framed a finely
chiseled face. Eyes, large and of the lightest blue Maggie had ever seen stared back at her, as though the man
had seen a ghost. He was definitely an attractive, more
than average, handsome man... okay, he was down-
right gorgeous and she'd have to be dead not to acknowledge it.

Wow... that was her first thought.

Everyone knows that ladies of quality can only marry gentlemen, and that suitable gentlemen are born—not made. Because being a gentleman has nothing to do with money, and everything to do with upbringing.

But in Judith Ivory's THE PROPOSITION Edwina vows that she can turn anyone into a gentleman . . . even the infuriating Mr. Mick Tremore. Not only that, she'd be able to pass him off as the heir to a dukedom, and no one in society would be any wiser. And since Edwina is every inch a lady, there isn't a chance that she'd find the exasperating Mick Tremore irresistible. Is there?

THE PROPOSITION
by Judith Ivory

"*S*peak for yourself," she said. "I couldn't do any-thing"—she paused, then used his word for it—"chancy."

"Yes, you could."

"Well, I could, but I won't."

He laughed. "Well, you might surprise yourself one day."

His sureness of himself irked her. Like the mustache that he twitched slightly. He knew she didn't like it; he used it to tease her.

Fine. What a pointless conversation. She picked up her pen, going back to the task of writing out his progress for the morning. Out of the corner of her eye, though, she could see him.

He'd leaned back on the rear legs of his chair, lifting the front ones off the floor. He rocked there beside her as he bent his head sideways, tilting it, looking under the table. He'd been doing this all week, making her nervous with it. As if there were a mouse—or worse— something under there that she should be aware of.

"What *are* you doing?"

Illogically, he came back with, "I bet you have the longest, prettiest legs."

"*Limbs*," she corrected. "A gentleman refers to that part of a lady as her limbs, her lower limbs, though it is rather poor form to speak of them at all. You shouldn't."

He laughed. "Limbs? Like a bloody tree?" His pencil continued to tap lightly, an annoying tattoo of ticks. "No, you got legs under there. Long ones. And I'd give just about anything to see 'em."

Goodness. He knew that was impertinent. He was tormenting her. He liked to torture her for amusement.

Then she caught the word: *anything?*

To see her legs? Her legs were nothing. Two sticks that bent so she could walk on them. He wanted to see these?

For anything?

She wouldn't let him see them, of course. But she wasn't past provoking him in return. "Well, there is a solution here then, Mr. Tremore. You can see my legs, when you shave your mustache."

She meant it as a kind of joke. A taunt to get back at him.

Joke or not, though, his pencil not only stopped, it dropped. There was a tiny clatter on the floor, a faint sound of rolling, then silence—as, along with the pencil, Mr. Tremore's entire body came to a motionless standstill.

"Pardon?" he said finally. He spoke it perfectly, exactly as she'd asked him to. Only now it unsettled her.

"You heard me," she said. A little thrill shot through her as she pushed her way into the dare that—fascinatingly, genuinely—rattled him.

She spoke now in earnest what seemed suddenly a wonderful exchange: "If you shave off your mustache, I'll hike my skirt and you can watch—how far? To my knees?" The hair on the back of her neck stood up.

"Above your knees," he said immediately. His amazed face scowled in a way that said they weren't even talking unless they got well past her knees in the debate.

"How far?"

"All the way up."

*Celebrate the Millennium
with another irresistible
romance from the pen of
Susan Elizabeth Phillips!*

The beautiful young widow of the President
of the United States is on the run, crossing
America on a journey to find herself. She
plans to travel alone, and she's chosen the
perfect disguise. Well, almost perfect...and
not exactly alone...

FIRST LADY
by Susan Elizabeth Phillips

Coming from Avon Books February 2000